For Darryl
from a re
bigga

Phil Booth

LATE SWIM

the first Sam Rigby novel

set in Constantia

copyright © Phil Booth 2018

first published 2018

cover design: Jamie Davidson

ISBN 978 1 5272 1754 6

www.philboothwriter.com

a note on Southaven

The events and characters of Sam Rigby's world are fiction. Southaven doesn't exist, but it shares a grid reference with a similar town which does. I've sometimes taken liberties with the geography and history of Southaven's original. I hope no one will find cause to be offended.

acknowledgements

Many people supported me in writing this book, but particular thanks are due to the wonderful staff of Sefton public libraries, especially at the Atkinson in Southport, and to Harold Somers of UMIST (Manchester) for general Manchester guidance and pointers on Artificial Intelligence. Thanks also to Anete Smith and David Richards, who read each chapter upon completion as if it were a Dickens serialization, and helped me to keep my nerve; and finally, to Francesca Baker, for assistance in bringing the book to publication. Any anachronisms and other mistakes which have slipped through the net are entirely my own work.

in memory of my father

Monday evening

On the stool next to mine in the public bar of the Railway Tavern, a square-built young man with a handsome, honest face was shifting awkwardly from buttock to buttock. There's a knack to sitting on bar stools, and he didn't have it. I would have pegged him as more of a lounge bar drinker, or perhaps no drinker at all – he'd taken just two sips from the pint in front of him, which now stood forgotten while other things played darkly on his mind. He wore the sharp blue suit with style. Most days he cared about such things, but not today. The left elbow rested in a patch of spilled beer, and even if he'd noticed he would have let it lie.

I reached my pack of No 6 towards him and said, 'Cigarette?' He took his hand from the glass and waved the packet away. Given that his fingers were unstained, this didn't surprise me, but I'd expected at least some word of acknowledgement. He had Please and Thank You running right through him, like Southaven rock.

Some people would have backed off at this point, but the man in the blue suit had piqued my interest. 'No offence, my friend, but this doesn't seem right.'

'I'm sorry?' Although he turned towards me a little when he spoke, you couldn't say he was looking at me, not yet. Those dark thoughts were all he saw.

'A man like you – young, good job, not long married – ' I shook my head. 'It's against nature. You should be lying half-naked by a pool somewhere unpronounceable, with a bright pink cocktail in one hand and your wife smoothing sun-tan lotion on those out-of-the-way places. Instead of which you're sat here in front of an untasted pint with a face like a Welsh Sunday.'

I had his attention now. 'How do you know those things? Who are you?' The words came edged with anger.

'Just guessing. Fancy new briefcase, and your finger's tucked in like you're not used to that ring yet.'

'A regular Sherlock Holmes, aren't you.'

'Yes, I am, since you mention it.' And I went through my usual charade of trying three other pockets before locating the one with the business cards in it. Round here, no-one trusts you if you seem too organized.

The young man took the card from my hand and read it, then looked up at me briefly and back to the card again. Whatever image of a private detective he carried in his head, it seemed I didn't square with it. He made to return the card but I said, 'Keep it. You never know when it might come in.' To my surprise, he removed his wallet from his inside pocket and carefully slotted the business card in place. But then he turned away from me and took a more generous swig of the beer. Perhaps he felt he couldn't just toy with it any longer, now he had an audience.

Minutes went by. I offered myself a cigarette and accepted. The young man had resumed his examination of the contents of his own head and clearly believed that our chat was now over. I knew better. It looked to me like he was in trouble, and if that made him hard to resist, why fight it? Besides, trouble is money in the bank to me. It was no accident that the young man had tucked my card so neatly away, he clearly had some need for my services. But hiring an investigator would be a big step, consciously or otherwise he had to work it through. From time to time I glanced sideways to see how far he'd got.

It was a few minutes past six on a Monday evening. Wilf, the landlord, was busy slaking the thirst of workers from the station redevelopment across the street. The old Victorian station had been declared structurally unsound and demolished, and in its place we were being treated to a concrete bunker studded with mosaic tiles. Since Beeching, half the platforms had lain unused, and now these would be replaced by shops, with others folded around the shrunken remnant of the concourse. All this was being trumpeted in the local press as a significant step in the town's renewal. It was twenty-five years now since the war, Southaven had struggled to regain the old vigour, the old pride. Visitor numbers kept falling year on year as people began to find better things to do with their free time than trek along the pier in the pouring rain. Shopping was to be our salvation. Moneyed folk had always come here for the upmarket emporia along the Boulevard, the jewellers, the furriers, the high-class men's outfitters with their panelled walls and dusty window displays. Now we were going to turn ourselves into a shopping Mecca for the entire north-west, and soon we'd all be dancing once more to the merry music of the cash tills, just like in the good old days.

If I was sceptical about this, it didn't stop me appreciating the incidental benefits of a large building project in the middle of town during a hot July. I'd always liked the public bar of the Railway, there was no nonsense about it and Wilf had a gift for not prying into other people's affairs. But now, crowded every evening with builders in vests and t-shirts, the place had acquired a whole new attraction. Once I'd even got lucky, though you had to be careful. It was legal now, this past three years, but that didn't mean you wouldn't risk a thumping if you made a mistake.

'Mr Rigby?'

I'd been eyeing up one of the builders, a chunky youth, brown as a nut, wearing a filthy white t-shirt with one shoulder ripped out. The voice took me by surprise, but now I turned to the young man in the blue suit, said, 'Sam – call me Sam,' and extended my hand.

The Please and Thank You side of his nature came uppermost as he politely shook the hand and said, 'Martin Berry.' He tried to smile, and I had a glimpse of how he must look when he really turned it on. He was probably ten years younger than me, but what's ten years between friends?

'So – is there something I can do for you, Martin?'

The hesitant smile was replaced by a frown. He lifted his glass and took another deepish drink. In the few minutes since our previous exchange he'd been drinking much faster, as if he needed alcohol to help him make his decision. Then he put the glass down again and gave me a long appraising look which began with my face, hair and clothes and didn't stop until it had peered through the misted window at my inmost soul. He said, 'I'm not sure. You're not exactly – ' But whatever it was that I wasn't exactly, he couldn't bring himself to say.

I stubbed out my cigarette alongside the butts of the three or four I'd smoked already. I thought I was trying to cut down but the ashtray thought different. I said, 'Come on, Martin! You've been issuing tragic sighs at the rate of two a minute ever since you sat down.'

'Honestly, it's nothing.'

'But have you considered your health? Bottling things up is really bad for you. It can give you ulcers, Martin, and spots. Spots! – too terrible to contemplate, and all because you refused help when it was sitting right next to you.'

He gave me a quick look, less penetrating than before. 'How do I know you're any good?'

'If you'd care to step up to my office I can show you testimonials by the yard. But in any case, sometimes you just have to bite it and see. Tell me what's on your mind and I'll suggest a plan. If you don't like it, all you have to do is walk away.'

Martin stared down at the bar in front of him and thought this over. He looked young and friendless and very much alone. Then he turned towards me and said, 'Could we go somewhere quieter? It's not the sort of thing I want to shout about.'

It was true that we were having to raise our voices to be heard. Most of our companions in the public bar had spent the day yelling at each other in the open air, and a couple of pints had done nothing to persuade them that now they were indoors it wasn't strictly necessary to bay across the open spaces like wounded moose. Martin was right, we would have to move on. I took a regretful glance at the boy with the ripped t-shirt. 'OK then. Drink up.'

Martin glowered uncertainly at what remained of his pint, as though it might poison him. Then he drank it anyway. 'Where to?'

'Hotel bar – the Feathers. Quiet, anonymous. The muzak cloaks your conversation.'

'I see you've done this before.'

'Once or twice. You're in safe hands.'

Out in the street, the day's heat had barely abated. I wore an old brown leather jacket over my shirt and jeans. It was too warm for this weather but somehow in recent years we'd become inseparable. Martin and I set off down Station Road towards the Boulevard. Weary trippers passed us going in the opposite direction, weighed down with all the plastic tat they'd accumulated during the day. The older kids picked on the younger ones, the younger ones cried. It would be worse in the confinement of the trains.

At the Boulevard we cut through between the columns of the war memorial and walked on in silence along the garden side, where the pavement was less crowded. Across the wide street the shops were closed, but holidaymakers foraged beneath the wrought iron verandas in search of a cheap fish supper.

I noticed now that the Empire cinema, set back behind the gardens on our side of the road, had been boarded up. Martin spoke for the first time since we'd left the Railway. 'Been in there a fair bit lately.'

'What, staring at a blank screen? It closed last month.'

'I work for the council, borough surveyor's office.'

'What's the borough surveyor got to do with it? I thought those Save Our Empire people were taking the place over. It said in the Gazette they hoped to re-open in a few weeks, start doing live shows again.'

Martin shook his head. 'Something's come up.'

'What kind of something?'

Instead of answering, Martin said, 'Isn't that the Feathers over there? Shall we cross?' He'd clearly changed the subject on purpose. My mother worked at the Empire as an usherette during the war, and I'd always been fond of the place. If Martin was privy to the inside story on its future, I thought the least he could do was share it with an old friend like me. I'd have to try again later, when he'd had another drink or two.

Over at the Feathers, we pushed our way in through the revolving door and took a table in the lounge bar. Recklessly anticipating a cash boost within the next couple of hours, I volunteered to buy the drinks. As it happened, I'd been at primary school with the bar manager, Sandra Snelgrove. A dozen years ago she'd married a garage mechanic called Paul and strictly speaking she was now Sandra Sidebottom, but she kept quiet about that and you couldn't blame her. I chatted with her for a minute or two while my Guinness settled.

Back at the table, Martin looked anxious. 'Do you know that woman? Did she ask who I am?'

I put his pint of Tartan down in front of him and sat next to him with my back to the wall, so I could keep an eye on the room. 'No offence, Martin, but present company excepted there isn't a soul in here who gives a toss whether you live or die. You see that fat bloke sitting up at the bar? That's Jack Spalding – Alderman Spalding these days. Owns this hotel, and Southaven Football Club too. And his ginger mate there, with the eyebrows like two roosters in a fight? Alan Baybridge.'

'Baybridge Construction?'

I nodded. 'Built most of anything that's gone up in this town in the last ten years. So unless you're in the Masons, or you've got a membership up at Royal Welldale, they won't even see you, never mind care who you are. Everyone else in here is just having a quiet drink before dinner.' The Feathers catered more to business customers than the bucket-and-spade crew. Most of our fellow-drinkers were men smartly dressed like Martin, though none of them looked quite so good in a suit.

'But her behind the bar?'

'You don't need to worry about Sandra. Sees no evil, hears no evil. I went to the secondary modern with Sandra's brother Dick. Well, his name's Malcolm but we called him Dick, owing to a certain anatomical – Am I boring you, Martin? I don't seem to have your full attention.'

'I'm sorry, Mr Rigby, I think I've made a mistake.'

My prospective client was rising to his feet. I rose faster, clamped a hand over his shoulder and shoved him down again. It wasn't difficult, he was shorter than me and I needed the money. 'Martin, you're going nowhere. What's the matter? Is it the muzak? Gnaws at the soul, doesn't it.'

His face blazed with shame. 'She'll never forgive me!'

'Ah – progress.' I patted him on the shoulder with the hand responsible for the recent shoving. 'Well done, Martin, well done. *She*. The wife, I take it?' He nodded miserably. 'And she would never forgive you for revealing your affairs to a gumshoe?'

'Not my affairs, Mr Rigby.'

'Sam. The name's Sam.'

'*Her* affairs.'

'She's having an affair?'

He raised one dark eyebrow expressively. I don't know where he'd learned the trick, but you could read that eyebrow as plain as typescript.

'She's having affairs, plural?'

Now Martin leaned towards me and whispered hotly in my ear. 'I think Monica's a nympho.' Then he turned away, picked up the pint and drank off at least half of it in a single draught.

I dried my ear and said, 'Martin, have you never heard of women's lib?' He didn't answer. 'It's this new thing we're importing from the States, and it says that if a lady – beg pardon, start again – if a woman has a healthy sexual appetite, that does not make her some sort of freak.'

Martin looked sideways at me. 'Are you making fun of me?'

'Why would I do that? I'm hoping you're going to pay me large amounts of money.'

He drank some more, reflectively this time. 'Only, people do make fun of me. All the time. They think I'm naïve.'

'Surely not. Who are they, these people? Let me at them.'

'They said I was naïve to marry Monica.' He turned and looked straight at me with little-boy-lost eyes. 'She's a cut above me, Mr Rigby, I do realize that. Her people have got money. My sister said it would *amuse* someone like that to marry a – a proletarian, I think she said. I'm nobody. My dad's got a novelty shop in Jubilee Avenue. But I thought Monica loved me.' He took solace in the beer again. He'd really picked up speed since his previous effort in the Railway. And luckily for me, the second pint was loosening his tongue.

'When were you married?'

'Last September, over in Manchester. Big wedding. Her dad paid. He pays for everything.'

I thought I detected the sound of a young man's testicles being painfully crushed. 'I'm guessing he bought her a house?'

Martin nodded. 'Cash down. One of those Barratt homes by the new coast road out at Otterdale. Monica complains sometimes, it's not very big, not what she's used to.'

'Does your wife work?'

He gave a hollow laugh.

'So you're the breadwinner. How long have you worked for the borough surveyor?'

'Six months. After I got my degree, I had this dead-end desk job in Liverpool, I was going nowhere.' He looked shifty. 'But then, Monica's dad knew someone at the town hall.'

I was beginning to wonder what price Monica's sainted father exacted for all this beneficence. 'Who is he, this paragon?' Martin looked blank. 'Monica's father, I mean.'

'Oh – Walter Wetherley. Wetherley Associates. They're Manchester people, he has lots of property there.'

The name meant nothing. I liked to think I knew all there was to know about Southaven, how it worked, who pulled the strings. But beyond the borough boundary, darkness reigned.

Martin tossed back the last of the beer. I picked up the glass. 'Another one?'

He nodded and I made to get up from the table, but for a moment he held me back, one hand on my arm. He said, 'Thanks for listening,' then fixed me with those eyes again. There was a lot going on in them. I tried to work up a smart retort, but nothing happened. Then Martin dropped the restraining hand and I went to the bar.

'Same again?' said Sandra.

'Just the Tartan, thanks. My friend seems to be outpacing me. How's your Malcolm these days?'

'Bringing shame on the family, as usual. Gone and got some girl pregnant.' Sandra seemed oddly cheerful about this. 'What beats me is, what on earth do they see in him?'

If she didn't know, I wasn't about to tell her.

Sandra deposited the fresh pint on the mat in front of me. 'That's two and six, love.' Steep, of course, but it was meant to deter the common people. I paid, and glanced along the bar towards Jack Spalding. He and Baybridge seemed more than usually pleased with themselves. For a second I wondered idly how it must feel to be one of life's winners, on the inside, looking out at losers like me. Then I turned, with the glass in my hand. Martin had disappeared. For a moment I thought he'd walked out on me, but then I saw the briefcase on the floor. A second later, the man himself emerged from the door to the toilets.

We took our seats again at the same time, and Martin warily examined the full glass in front of him. 'Turning into a bit of a session, isn't it?' He loosened his tie and unfastened the top button of his shirt, allowing a few dark chest hairs to curl into view. Then he raised the glass, said 'Cheers!' and sank about a third of the contents with no apparent difficulty. He said, 'I could get the hang of this, with practice,' and wiped the Tartan moustache off his top lip with the back of his hand.

'Do you not get out much?'

'I've always been more of a home bird. Monica grumbles. I can't see the point of parties, a lot of boring people stood around talking about nothing, but she's always off to some do or other. She's out with the girls tonight, staying over at her friend's in Manchester. At least, that's what she said she was doing.'

'You think she might be seeing someone?' Martin didn't reply. 'Do you have any real evidence for this, Martin? Because I'll tell you how it looks to me. Decent bloke meets fast lady, opposites attract, big chemistry, boom! – they get married. Then they're in trouble, they can't find enough common ground. On top of that, decent bloke, not realizing that he is in fact one in a million and any woman ought to thank her lucky stars that she's got him – decent bloke has an inferiority complex that would dwarf Blackpool tower, so can't imagine why fast lady would want to stick with him when she could be running around after every other man in the county. That's it, isn't it, Martin? That's what this is about.'

Martin's ears had turned a dangerous red. He took another slug of beer to calm himself. When he spoke, he avoided my eyes. 'Monica's got this girlfriend called Leah – the one she's meant to be staying with tonight. Leah's got a thing for me. A few weeks ago she told me Monica's still sleeping with her ex back in Manchester. Rupert, Rupert Heysham, used to be her tutor at the Uni. At first I thought Leah might just have been trying to come between me and Monica, but then it all clicked, the way Monica talks about him, the presents she brings home sometimes.' He smiled bitterly. 'She has to have it all, does Monica. Why should she give Heysham up if she can get away with it?'

'And you said there was someone else.'

'Danny. Danny Craven.' The thought didn't please him. 'Local builder, put up a little extension for us in the spring, a sun room. Last week I came home early one day. Danny and Monica were standing right there in the hallway, really close. He said he'd come back to check there were no problems, but they'd had sex, I'm sure of it.' Now he turned to look at me, hostile, sneering. 'One in a million. What do you know about anything?' Then he turned away, and washed down his contempt with the beer.

A distinct *froideur* interposed itself between detective and client. I tried to warm up my side of it by lighting another cigarette. I'd have to start cutting down again tomorrow.

After a while I said, 'Sorry, Martin. Shouldn't have doubted you.' Though to be honest, I still wasn't convinced.

There was another pause. Then Martin said, 'You're not drinking. Can't drink on my own.' And I thought his tone had softened.

I conceded the point and applied myself to the Guinness again, wondering how I could regain Martin's trust. I was still wondering a minute later when with a decisive motion he drained his glass. I said, 'One for the road?'

He said, 'Is there somewhere quieter – ?'

'What, quieter than this?' Most of the other customers had gone in to dinner now. At the bar, Jack Spalding and Alan Baybridge were talking in hushed tones. 'If it gets quieter than this, Martin, you've died.' He gave me a quick look. That eyebrow was involved in it again, and I tried to read what it was saying. Then my get-lucky angel put words into my mouth. 'We could go to my flat if you like. I'm just round the corner on Preston Road.' My professional angel now tried to claw back lost credibility. 'We can talk business.' I wished the two of them would make their minds up. Martin clearly represented some kind of prospect, but what?

'Got anything to drink?'

'There's coffee.'

He screwed up his face. 'I mean, drink.'

'There's an old bottle of Blue Nun I was saving for my

retirement.' This line was wasted on him. 'Yes, Martin, there's stuff to drink. You won't go thirsty.'

'Let's go.' And he was on his feet, making for the door. I stubbed out the cigarette and grabbed my jacket, but then I noticed that Martin had left the briefcase beside his chair. I picked it up and went after him, and as I pushed my way out through the revolving doors he was pushing his way back in. Seeing that I had the briefcase, he followed me onto the forecourt.

Outside, the light had begun to fade but the air was still thick with heat. Martin had removed his tie now and when I gave him the briefcase he opened it and dropped the tie inside. The shiny brown leather had been monogrammed with the initials MOB. I said, 'What's the O stand for?'

'Oliver. They called me Ollie at school, after Stan and Ollie. I went through a plump phase. Kids, eh?'

I said, 'It could have been worse.' I didn't feel like telling him the things they'd called me.

Martin's dark brows met in a frown. 'I'm ravenous. Do you fancy chips?' So we bought a large portion at the chip shop a few doors down, and sauntered slowly across towards Preston Road. 'These are good. Only one chippy in the village at Otterdale and it's streets away. By the time you walk them home they've gone cold.'

'I hadn't got your Monica down as a huge fan of the British chip.'

'Her people go in for all that foreign crap – spaghetti Bolognese, chicken something-or-other.'

'Chasseur?'

'Don't tell me you eat that stuff too? Even my mum's getting into it lately.'

'I did night classes. Continental cookery.'

Martin looked stunned. 'You're pulling my leg.'

'I've done every possible night class at the Tech: accountancy, life drawing, local history – '

'Strewth.'

'Though mostly I'm an autodidact.'

'Come again?'

'I teach myself. I don't like being ignorant.'

'I thought you said you went to the secondary modern.'

'Are you deliberately trying to be offensive, Martin, or does it just come naturally? I take it you were at King Edward's?' He looked sheepish. 'The secondary mod was a perfectly good school, every bit as good as the grammar. Now have a chip and shut up.'

He took one. We were just coming round onto Preston Road.

'This is the place. I hope you're feeling fit, I'm on the top floor.'

*

Leigh Terrace is a row of eight five-storey houses in late-Victorian Gothic, with one flat to each floor. I'd been there ten years now, longer than anyone else in my building. The location was fantastic, right in the middle of town. But on the other hand the stairs were filthy, the roof leaked, some of the tenants were psychos and the landlord made Rachman look like Florence Nightingale.

As we climbed up in the dingy half-light from unshaded bulbs, Martin took the stairs by twos. It was like coming home with a puppy. From time to time he would stop and wait for me to catch up, his tail wagging with eager delight. He was less than sober. I followed at a steady pace, finishing off the last few chips. When we got inside the door of the flat he put down the briefcase and said, 'Toilet? Small bladder, always been the same.' I pointed out the bathroom, and went into the kitchen to squash the chip paper into the rubbish bin. The flat would stink of vinegar for a couple of days but at least that would mask the background aroma of stale cigarettes.

I hung my leather jacket on a hook in the cramped hallway and went through into the living room to wait for Martin. The building faces north-east, but although I'd left the windows open all day the heat was still oppressive. I switched on a couple of lamps and squatted to look through my record collection, which was gathering dust under the long window-seat. What might Martin like – the Stones, Janis Joplin?

'Wow! Fab!' He stood in the doorway. I was viewing exactly the same scene and to my eyes there was nothing remotely wow-fab about it. 'Great place to live!'

'Are you blind? It's a dump.'

His jacket slung over one shoulder now, Martin crossed to look out of the window. 'This is cosy, isn't it?' The double-windowed gable formed a recess where it projected from the front wall. I suppose the general effect had character; it was just a shame about the squalor.

I rose to my feet. 'Hang up your jacket?'

He said, 'You still offering that drink?'

'Cold beer, Scotch – ?'

'Scotch. Too full for beer.' He patted his stomach. It looked trim and flat and I suspected he was proud of it. He handed me the jacket.

On my way out of the door I said, 'Find us something to listen to.' I hung the jacket next to my own in the hallway, then turned into the kitchen in search of whiskey. Leftovers from last night's casserole were fermenting in a dish on the gas stove, so I took a moment to scrape it all into the waste bin and soak the dish. I found the Scotch and one clean glass, and rinsed another for myself. The glasses didn't match, but then neither did we. As I added ice cubes, the stereo blared out. I took the bottle and glasses and walked through.

He said, 'You've got enough books.' Privately, I felt that not even Southaven Central Library had enough books. Or rather, it had plenty, but invariably the wrong ones. Some of my own collection had found their way onto shelves, but far more festered in boxes or were piled precariously in odd corners of the room. The window-seat too was stacked high with books and magazines. I had a plan to organize them by subject some day but it's no good rushing into these things. I put down the bottle and glasses on the coffee table by the old two-seater settee. There was nowhere else to sit except a brown corduroy bean bag I kept meaning to throw out. I didn't get a lot of visitors.

Still reading book spines, Martin said, 'Is this too loud? You don't want the neighbours complaining.'

'They won't. Florrie downstairs is deaf, and the hippies through the wall play Hendrix at three in the morning.'

'Monica can't stand the Beatles, I have to listen when she's out.' Martin had chosen the *Help!* album, but I still wasn't sure if it was help he wanted, or something else.

I poured the Scotch and sat down on the settee. While I'd been out of the room, Martin had rolled up his shirt sleeves and unfastened a second button. Now he looked at the vacant seat beside me, then across at the bean bag. He said, 'Is that thing safe?'

'I don't think it's eaten anyone yet.'

He picked his glass up from the table, then settled himself down onto the bean bag. It wasn't a huge success, but he stayed put. He was a sticker, was Martin. 'Cheers.'

I raised my glass, and we drank. Then I said, 'So – what's it to be? Do you want me to work for you, or not?' His face fell. This sudden striking of the business note brought back the reality of his situation. 'If you want to fix the marriage, having your wife followed may not be such a great idea. These things can leave a nasty taste.'

'Not if she doesn't find out. Even after what I said before, about Heysham, about Danny Craven, there's part of me still doesn't believe it. I need to be sure of my ground.'

'What if I dig stuff up that you really don't want to know?'

He tilted his head back and finished off the Scotch. The ice cubes rattled in the glass. 'Just get proof, one way or the other. I'll handle the consequences.'

The almond eyes were resolute. He wouldn't go back on this decision. I said, 'I charge ten pounds a day plus expenses, minimum payment thirty quid, and I need that up front.'

He thought for a moment, but only a moment. 'Cheque all right?' I nodded, hoping my disappointment didn't show. I would need to withdraw some cash in the morning. Martin struggled up out of the bean bag and left the room. I filled his empty glass. Then he was back, with the briefcase. He opened it, rummaged, took out a cheque book and pen, kneeled at the table, wrote the cheque, completed the stub. 'I'll put my address on the back so you'll know where to find me.'

I said, 'Obviously it's best if I don't call you at home. My office number's on the card, but I'll give you the one for the flat as well.' I wrote the number on the cover of his cheque book. Then I returned it and took the cheque from him, and we shook on the deal. Martin kept his eyes fixed on mine. Suddenly he looked very grown up. I said, 'If you've not rung by Thursday, we'll meet in the Railway at six.'

Martin stood up, slipped the cheque book into his back trouser pocket, then hovered indecisively. He checked his watch. Our evening together was probably over. A large moth had flown in and was fluttering noisily round one of the lampshades.

I said, 'Do you need to catch your train?' Otterdale was three stops up the line, towards Liverpool. 'If you want to stay a while, that's fine by me.' Then I realized he was listening to the music. Paul McCartney was singing *Yesterday*, and every word was hitting its target. Actual tears stood in Martin's eyes. Appalled, I heaved myself out of the seat, crossed to the stereo and lifted the playing arm off the record.

'What did you do that for?'

I was pleased to see sentimentality giving way to indignation.

'The thing is, Martin, your Monica's right. The Beatles are shit.'

'They're great! I saw them at the Empire in '65. And at least I don't listen to Alma Cogan.'

He had me there. 'It was a youthful indiscretion.' I slotted the album back in place and searched for some civilised replacement. 'Do you like Miles Davis?'

'Don't know. Try me.' He looked me in the eye. 'I love trying new things.' But then he turned away. Perhaps he'd lost confidence. Then again, perhaps I was just misreading those eyebrows.

I left Martin adjusting his ears to the change of style while I went out to use the toilet. When I returned, he'd made himself at home on the settee and was knocking back the Scotch. For an imbecile moment I considered trying the bean bag, which sat in mid-floor like some huge corduroy dog-turd. Then common sense prevailed and I squeezed in next to Martin instead. The settee had seen better days and tended to swallow your behind, leaving your knees wide apart in front of you. I said, 'How's the music?'

'Mellow.'

I struggled forward to refill my glass, then sank back again. I could feel the heat from Martin's shoulder.

He said, 'So your office is in Crowburn House?'

I was briefly surprised that Martin knew this, but of course the address was on my business card. I said, 'First floor front. My aunt and uncle have the flat out the back, they're the caretakers.'

'I was in the office downstairs the other day, Crowburn Estates.'

'What for?'

'Trying to find some deeds in the strong room. Crowburn owned most of Southaven in the old days, but the council have bought bits and pieces over the years.'

'This wouldn't have anything to do with a certain cinema, by any chance?'

He studied the whiskey glass. Then he said, 'How did you come to be a private dick?'

There it was again, the brush-off, unmistakeable. He must be sitting on some really hot information about the Empire. As a rule, something in my face compels people to tell all, and Martin's slipperiness irked me. But I answered his question anyway. 'I was a cop. There was an incident. They asked me to take extremely early retirement. Then I couldn't think what else to do.'

'What sort of incident?'

'Just a personal matter.' If he could be tight-lipped, so could I.

'Did you like it – the police?'

'Sometimes. You could learn stuff, they sent you on courses.'

'But what about all that beating people up and planting drugs on them?'

I smiled. 'Do I detect cynicism? I hadn't expected this from you.'

'You shouldn't judge a book by its cover, Mr Rigby.'

I sniffed. 'Do you have to keep calling me Mr Rigby? You're drinking my Scotch, Martin, we've crossed a line.' But he didn't speak, and pretended to be listening to the music. The moth was still beating its wings against the lampshade. Somewhere amongst my books there was a guide to British moths and butterflies, but I'd never got round to studying it.

To break the silence I said, 'So, what do you get up to in your free time?'

'You're the detective, you tell me.'

'OK, well – I'd say you do something to keep fit, some kind of sport. And – you have gardener's hands. In fact – ' I took a risk and picked up his right hand. With one finger I traced the faint lines of earth around his finger-nails. 'Before you went to work this morning, you were out in the garden, weeding.'

'Not weeding, no. Lifting early carrots. They're just perfect now, really sweet. As soon as we moved in I dug over a patch for vegetables. Monica says I'm mad.'

'You can't have had much of a garden at Jubilee Avenue. Didn't you live over the shop?'

'Dad's got an allotment. Hand.'

'I'm sorry?'

'My hand.'

'Oh – yes.' I replaced Martin's hand on his knee, and gave it a quick pat for good measure. 'What about the sport?'

'Football. Otterdale B team, local league. Danny Craven plays for them too, that's why I gave him the building work. It was his dad's firm, but the old man died last autumn. His mother's been dead years, Danny was on his own, I felt sorry for him.' Martin shook his head. 'That'll teach me, won't it? Danny sodding Craven. I could kill him.'

Martin's mood was taking a definite nose-dive. I tried to steer him off the subject of Danny Craven. 'You train much – the footie, I mean?'

'We have a kickabout Tuesday evenings, and a few of us go swimming sometimes, but that's about it. The A team have a proper coach, it's not fair.'

Our knees were touching now. The settee didn't leave them much choice.

I said, 'Are you a fish or a rock?' Martin looked blank again. I seemed to have that effect on him. 'You know, put someone in water and they're either a fish or a rock.'

'Oh, fish every time.' His eyes widened. 'You don't think we should have had a piece of fish to go with those chips? I wouldn't want to get squiffy.'

I thought it was a bit too late to shut the stable door now, but I kept my counsel. He was sipping at the Scotch again, his shoulder resting companionably against my own, and with a sudden tremor of anticipation I knew from the quality of his silence that he wasn't just thinking, but thinking about me. Martin had been giving me confusing signals all evening, but now I had a hunch he was about to make his move.

Martin said, 'You're one of *them*, aren't you?'

This wasn't the move I'd expected. I felt a powerful urge to break the contact with his knee, but that would have been a mistake. I said, 'One of what?' though I knew perfectly well.

He flipped one limp wrist and said, 'Them.'

Annoyingly, I felt the blood rush into my face. I said, 'Such a colourful turn of phrase. How good to learn that your time at King Edward's wasn't wasted. We used to watch your lot playing rugby, over the fence, but you never seemed to return the favour.'

He said, 'It's not my fault I passed the 11-plus! I suppose you think I've had it easy? Took me *four years* to do that degree, I had to sit the Finals twice! And now there's all the surveyors' exams, it never seems to end.'

'But you've got your foot in the door, you've got connections, nothing's going to stop you now. Look at you – ' And I took the fabric of his shirt between my fingers. 'All crisp and smart.' I let go of the shirt and turned away from him, as much as that was possible on the narrow settee. For our knees and shoulders this spelled the end of a beautiful romance, but sometimes only the dramatic gesture will do. 'And yes, I am one of *them*, as you so charmingly express it. I trust this won't affect our business arrangement.'

There was another hiatus in the conversation. Miles was wrapping himself round musical lines like velvet round your finger. Eventually Martin said, 'I won't tell anyone, honest.'

I turned on him. 'What on earth makes you think it's a secret? Grow up, Martin, for God's sake.'

This time the silence lasted even longer. I was damned if I was going to break it myself. After what seemed like a fortnight, Martin said, 'Do you normally talk to your clients like that?'

I looked at him out of the corner of my eye. His ears had gone red again. I said, 'Only when I'm vexed.'

More silence, thick and treacly. But Martin was a sticker, like I mentioned. He gave it another try. 'If I'd known you were going to be so touchy – '

'Touchy? Who's touchy?'

'I'm sorry, OK?'

Well, there's only so long I can hold a grudge, especially when the other party has a face like Martin's. I shifted in the seat, allowing our knees to renew their acquaintance. 'Apology accepted. But can you blame me? "One of *them*," indeed.'

'I could have said worse.'

I shook my head. 'I blame your education. Still, what can you expect from a school that's named after a potato.' He sort of laughed. He'd probably heard it a thousand times so it was good of him to make the effort. I said, 'What time's your train?'

'Last one's at three minutes past eleven. Eusebio'll be complaining. I should probably make a move.'

I looked at my watch. Ten thirty. 'Eusebio?'

'The cat. Little ginger number, hoovers up food like it's going out of fashion then shits on the living room carpet.' He looked at his watch. 'Not really that far to the station, is it?'

I shrugged my shoulders. 'Ten minutes. Eight to a fit man like you.'

'One more glass?'

So we drank one more glass of the Scotch, then Martin got his things together. I said I'd come along, just for the walk. It was pleasant down on the Boulevard, under the tall trees threaded with coloured lights. There weren't many people about and we had the garden side of the road more or less to ourselves. We passed my office building, we passed the church. When we came to the cinema, I said, 'You were going to tell me about this change of plan at the Empire.'

Martin was drunk by now, no question, and I was optimistic this would produce results. But he smiled and said, 'No I wasn't. You're just trying to take advantage. Pouring drinks down a boy's throat all evening – it's disgraceful. My mother warned me about men like you.'

'Oh, go on, Martin. I'm the soul of discretion, I swear I am.'

But he simply lifted up the briefcase, gave it a little shake and said, 'See no evil, hear no evil,' then set off again at a cracking pace which left me standing.

At the station we wound our way through the temporary lights of the building site and onto the grim new concourse. The old station clock had been a famous local landmark. Beneath its black and gold splendour, soldiers en route to two world wars had kissed goodbye to wives and girlfriends who would never see them again. But the old clock had been swept away with the rest of the station, and in its place hung a bland excuse for a timepiece with hands so slender you could barely make out that eleven had just passed.

Martin stopped for a moment where the old clock used to be, and put his briefcase down on the concrete floor. He said, 'I'll phone you on Wednesday. If I don't get you – ' He pointed across in the direction of the Railway, out of sight beyond the scaffolding. 'Thursday, six.'

I said, 'I'll do a good job for you, Martin, I promise.'

He nodded, those exaggerated nods people do when they've had a skinful. His chin showed dark with stubble. Once more, he fixed his eyes on mine. 'Good to know you, Mr Rigby.' I shook the hand which he held out to me. His grip was firm. Then he let go, lifted his hand to my face, and ran one finger down the ridge of my nose. 'Sam.' The ghost of a smile came and went on his lips. He lowered his eyes and turned away from me, picked up the briefcase, and crossed to the barrier, where a short bloke with a battered uniform stood on duty, yawning. Martin showed his contract and was waved through. I watched his back as he walked on down the platform, the briefcase held close at his side. At the second carriage of the electric train he stepped in. The guard blew his whistle. The doors slid shut. The train pulled out of the station.

As I headed back, a few drops of warm rain fell on my cheek. The vinegar smell met me as soon as I opened the door of the flat. In the living room I poured more Scotch, lit a cigarette. From the coffee table I picked up Martin's cheque, then sank deep into the settee and traced the meandering lines of his handwriting. I was searching for something, but I didn't know what.

Thursday at six – three days. I ran one finger down the ridge of my nose.

Tuesday

1

I woke up drenched in sweat, the sheet thrown off me. A shaft of sunlight was trying to set fire to my leg, but that was my own fault. Weeks ago I'd taken down the curtains with the pious intention of washing them, and they were still heaped in the corner. My body ached, my head throbbed. Two possibilities: either I'd been involved in a bedtime brawl, or I'd finished off the bottle of Scotch. There was a particularly sharp, stabbing pain in my side, but it turned out that I was lying on a hardback library copy of *The Interpretation Of Dreams*, which I must have brought to bed with me. I rolled over to look at the alarm clock on the bedside table. I'd forgotten to wind it, and it had stopped at five past three.

I heaved myself upright, leaned back against the headboard and lit a cigarette. As a gesture towards cutting down, I'd been trying to push back smoking my first cigarette by five minutes each day, but with my mouth tasting like yak dung this was no time for futile experiments in self-discipline.

Then I remembered Martin, the touch of his finger, the cheque. Jobs had been hard to come by lately but today I was a working man again, I was working for Martin Berry. I needed to straighten myself out. Fag in mouth still, I swung out of bed, went into the bathroom, and turned on the taps for a cool bath. In the kitchen I thumped the old Ascot heater with my fist. As ever, it fired up immediately. I'd once done a plumbing course and could see no logical explanation for this, but boilers make the rules, we are merely their servants.

My watch lay on the kitchen table. Nine thirty.

Soaking in the bath, I considered my options. There'd be no point in haring over to Manchester. If Monica Berry had been with Rupert Heysham last night, it would be too late to catch them now. Presumably she would come home this morning, especially if she was expecting another lunchtime visit from her bit of rough, Danny Craven. The obvious thing to do was stake out the house. My heart sank. This would require patience, which I don't have. What use is a detective without patience? The old sense of failure nagged at me, a devil on my shoulder. I felt a moment's envy for those established investigators who could afford to delegate the leg-work to assistants, but that would never happen to me. Sam Rigby would always be a one-man band.

I dressed, ate toast, drank black tea (I'd run out of milk), threw some things in a canvas bag, then went downstairs to greet the world. My head still felt as if it had enjoyed the recent attentions of a taxidermist, but at least my brain was no longer trying to jackhammer an exit through my skull. I'd been lucky finding a space, the Cortina was parked right outside my building in all its vomit-yellow glory. It was five years old and probably the least reliable car I'd ever owned, but unless my fairy godmother decided to pull her finger out there was little prospect of a replacement. Fortunately, I'd left the police force with a handy idea of what goes on beneath the bonnet, and Paul Sidebottom, Sandra Snelgrove's husband, was always happy to help when I ran out of ideas.

I drove the few hundred yards to Crowburn House and parked round the back. The Leightons' Rover was there, in its usual spot. William Leighton, known as the Old Man, was chief agent to the Crowburn Estate, but his son Charles did most of the work these days, since his father was now eighty-two not out. I went in at the back door. If I could spare the time I generally knocked on the door of the caretaker's flat and stopped for a word with Aunt Winnie and Uncle Fred, but this morning I had work to do. Besides, I wasn't in the mood for Aunt Winnie. She is my mother's older sister and she's always been very good to me, but from a great height. So I slipped quietly past their door and up the back stairs, then along the corridor with its brown lino and reassuring smell of leathery antiquity. A door on the right announced SAMUEL RIGBY – INVESTIGATOR. I turned the key and let myself into my office.

The room was large, too large for my needs, but I loved it. The windows looked out onto a neat lawn, a winding driveway and the humming Boulevard beyond the trees. I had a desk, two chairs, a typewriter, a filing cabinet, a telephone and a waste basket. I kept everything in perfect order, exactly the way I didn't keep my flat, my car, or anything else.

Though it galled me to acknowledge the fact, I owed all this to Aunt Winnie. Two years before, the lease had expired on my old office in Bury Street, which was grim, cramped, dirty and miles from the action. At the same time, Uncle Fred was due to retire. He and Winnie had been looking after the Estate Office for thirty years, and now they had their eye on a bungalow at Mere Cross, with a garden and a view of open country. But the Old Man abhorred change. He begged them to stay, and that's when Winnie played her card. All the upstairs rooms had been vacant for years, and Winnie now indicated that she and Fred would be prepared to stay on if the Old Man would let one of those rooms to me at a knock-down rate. He refused, she insisted, he conceded defeat. Faced with my Aunt Winnie, I don't know why he didn't just concede defeat straight off and save himself some time.

At the desk I took out paper and typed up the main points of my meeting with Martin Berry. Then I typed the contract, logged the cheque in my accounts, filed everything and locked the cabinet again.

Perhaps because of the cigarettes I'd been smoking while I worked, I then heard nature calling. This was unfortunate. Aunt Winnie stocked the little toilet on the half landing, reserved for myself and my visitors, with the harshest toilet paper ever made. I've seen better in prisons. This was personal – I knew, I'd looked in on the downstairs facilities belonging to the Estate Office, and they had soft paper, cheap but civilised. Clearly this was another of the little punishments which my aunt liked to inflict on me when she wasn't being dutifully kind. The real target, of course, was my mother, but Winnie rarely saw her these days and it was easiest to get at her through me. I'd tried bringing in soft paper of my own, but Winnie took this as a personal affront and I was forced to back down.

After a quick glance round the office to confirm that here at least my life showed some evidence of a controlling hand, I locked up, paused at the half-landing for as long as it took, then left the building by the front entrance. Three minutes later, I presented myself at the bank, a smug block of classical sandstone on a corner by the war memorial. The teller, a sour woman in her fifties, knew me to some extent, and probably also knew that the cheque I was depositing would double the balance in my account. When I asked to withdraw ten pounds in cash, she paid it out one grudging note at a time, as if convinced that I would only waste it all on gambling and loose women. Losing sight of the fact that what she'd given me was my own money, I expressed deep gratitude, backed reverentially away from the counter, and fled.

Last night's threat of rain had come to nothing, and the day was warm again. Walking along in the cool shade of the trees, it would have been easy to thank the town fathers for laying out the Boulevard with such foresight – long, straight and very broad, with ample space for public gardens on the south side. But in fact the Boulevard had been a happy accident. Travel back a couple of centuries and you would find two long rows of sandhills separated by a wide expanse of muddy swamp, the whole bleak landscape owned by Crowburn's predecessors. You couldn't build on the swamp, so the sandhills dictated your building lines. But although the planners were not responsible for the success of the Boulevard, in recent years they'd begun to make notable efforts to improve it, if improve is the word I want. As I came level with the Empire cinema, I wondered if that might be next on their list. What exactly had come up, as Martin put it, and why had he felt the need to keep me so annoyingly in the dark?

I picked up the Cortina and drove out to Otterdale along the new coast road. It followed the track-bed of an old railway, a Victorian folly which had been so unprofitable that it had jumped twenty years ago without waiting for Dr Beeching to push it. Speeding along at fifty-five with the windows down and Mungo Jerry on the radio, I couldn't bring myself to mourn the passing of the railway age. True, there was a disquieting rattle somewhere under the bonnet on the near side, but then the Cortina had disquieting rattles like cats have fleas. I ignored this latest example and turned off at the roundabout, towards Otterdale village. Two police cars were parked on the verge by the Lake View Hotel. Perhaps the manager had been caught with his hand in the till again.

There must have been otters here once – nearby there was an Otter Mere Farm, and a stream called Otterpool – but I doubt whether they've shown their furry faces to anyone now living. Years ago, someone envious of Southaven's success had thought of replicating it here, four or five miles along the coast, and a short stretch of promenade had been built. But nothing had come of it, and these days Otterdale's raison d'etre was as a dormitory settlement for middle-class types who worked in Southaven or up the line in Liverpool. Demand persisted, and Otterdale still grew. The development of which Martin's street formed part was curled tightly within the line of the coast road. Beyond the new houses, open fields remained, the last before the Southaven borough boundary.

I soon found Vaughan Close, and peeled my eyes for number five. It was the house with the police car parked in front.

When it comes to intuition, I'm deeply sceptical about everyone's except my own. I braked the car. Of course, it was possible that the police had just dropped round to tell Monica Berry she'd won first prize in their charity raffle, but I doubted it.

Every house in Vaughan Close had its driveway, so the only vehicle out on the street was the police car. I couldn't park without drawing attention to myself, but I had to find out what was happening. The road was short, a cul-de-sac of no more than fourteen houses. Those at the far end, around the turning circle, stood incomplete, without doors or windows. There was no sign of any builders. I would have to park in the next street and climb over into the empty properties from the fields at the back.

Slowly I drove past the Berrys' house, turned, and drove back again. I could see no-one in the front room. A white Vitesse convertible stood in the driveway, in front of the closed garage doors. If this was Monica's car, I doubted whether Martin's salary could have paid for it. Another example of her father's largesse, perhaps.

I turned the Cortina right onto Beach Road, then right again into the parallel cul-de-sac, Marvell Close. I parked, grabbed my bag from among the detritus on the floor and got out of the car. Work in Marvell Close had finished now, and a handy passageway out to the fields ran between the two furthest houses. In a couple of minutes I'd climbed over the fence and set myself up in the shell of a house at the end of Vaughan Close, with an unobstructed view of the front of number five.

Half an hour passed. Nothing happened. I took out my camera and fired off a couple of shots of Martin's house through the brick window frame. A cement mixer graced the sandy plot in front of me, which would some day have to be layered with imported topsoil to make the obligatory suburban garden. Half of Southaven had been built on sand like this, and there were hoary tales of whole buildings being swallowed by the shifting dunes on stormy nights, with the occupants trapped inside. But here in Vaughan Close, not a grain of sand was stirring. The street held its breath. I waited.

After what felt like a vacant century but may have been five minutes, a figure appeared at the far end of the street. It was a window cleaner, quite elderly to judge by his gait, pushing a bike adapted with braces to carry his ladder and bucket. He rang the doorbell at number eight. A woman came to the door, left him standing there, then returned with his filled bucket and a tall glass of something, which the man drank off thirstily as soon as the door was closed. There was no shade in my roofless hideout and the sun was at its highest. I'd forgotten to bring anything to drink. I smoked another cigarette instead.

More time passed, more nothing happened. The old man finished number eight's windows and moved on to number ten. He was quite close to me now and I could see him more clearly, a very short, bow-legged character in his late sixties or thereabouts, baby-faced, and wearing an unbuttoned blue shirt over a dirty singlet. I found myself wondering what he'd done in the war. Then he went round the back of the house and I was alone again with my boredom. If this was a typical day in Vaughan Close, Monica Berry must be going slowly insane. So far I'd been taking a pretty negative view of Monica. Whatever game she'd been playing it had clearly hurt Martin badly, but this past hour of numbing tedium felt like the first evidence in her defence. Perhaps you couldn't blame her if she at least had thoughts about someone like Danny Craven. After a few weeks of this, even the window cleaner might begin to seem like an option.

Finally, just as I was beginning to fantasize about calling in at the labour exchange in the morning to look for a job where things actually occurred from time to time, a van turned in at the top of the Close. It was an old Bedford and had perhaps been bottle green when new, though the years had gifted it with a blotched and faded look. Slowly it cruised along the road. Could this be the builders putting in a late appearance? I might have to pack up and leg it over the back fence. The van drove the whole length of the Close, then slowly made a three-point turn just yards from my den, and as it turned I was able to read the lettering on the side: *H Craven and Son, Building Contractor*. Then the battered Bedford drove back the way it had come, still slowly, and disappeared onto the main road. As it went, it passed the old man, his work at number ten complete now. In another minute he'd pushed the bike out of sight around the corner, and I was left alone in the silence of the Close.

So, Danny Craven had come calling. Interesting. Though the driver's window had been wound right down, Danny's face had been in shadow, and all I'd really seen of him was the slim, tawny arm which rested on the door as he drove off. I'd managed to take a couple of shots when the van turned, so there was half a chance his face might show up in those. Why had he not stopped? Had he been put off by the police car, the same as me?

But I had no time to consider this before another vehicle appeared. Things were really hotting up in Vaughan Close. The newcomer was a long black Jaguar, clean, smart, expensive. Unlike the Bedford, the Jag moved decisively, smoothly passing the police car, then reversing neatly up to it, tail to nose. The engine cut out, the driver's door opened, and a tall young man got out, wearing full chauffeur's uniform complete with cap and gloves. I set to work with the camera. The man then opened the rear offside door, and a slight, pale, middle-aged woman stepped out onto the pavement. The cream trouser suit looked too big for her, and its colour washed out what little tone she had in her face. Not looking at the driver and with head bowed, she now drifted up the path and rang the door bell. Very soon the door opened and she went inside. The driver leaned indolently against the Jag, peeled off his gloves and began to roll a cigarette.

What the hell was going on? Neither of these people had paid the least attention to the police car, so they must have expected to see it. Had the house been burgled this morning? I was making the assumption that the cream woman must be Monica's mother, Mrs Wetherley. Martin hadn't mentioned her, but the car, and the chauffeur too, fitted neatly with what he'd said about her husband Walter. When I was a kid you often saw chauffeurs in Southaven, but now they were a rare sighting. Like a twitcher with his first clear view of a Dartford warbler, I took a couple more shots of the chauffeur for good measure.

The driver had barely put a match to his roll-up when there was a fresh development. The front door of number five opened, then closed again behind WPC Cilla Donnelly. She had joined the force since I'd left, part of a drive to recruit more women, and I only knew her to chat to. But if I didn't know her particularly well, I knew a man who did – Mark Howell. We'd been on the beat together, and he'd now gone over to CID. It suited Mark and Cilla for people to think they were an item, though their interests lay in other directions. This constituted a breakthrough, my first bit of luck all day. I would be able to lean on Mark for information. He owed me, though like most people who owe you it often slipped his mind.

Cilla was a redhead, and as she came down the path towards the street the sun caught a lock of hair which had escaped from beneath her cap. She had a pretty face but to be honest she was a bit stumpy, and I doubt if people would have found it plausible that a looker such as Mark would fancy her if they hadn't been so desperate to believe that he'd outgrown the indiscretion which had almost scuppered his early career. Now she acknowledged the chauffeur, who returned the compliment with a barely perceptible motion of his head, and then climbed into the panda car, backed it up a little, and pulled out into the road. As the car approached the turning circle I ducked further into the shadows. Cilla wasn't the type to miss anything and I had no desire to be quizzed over my presence in Vaughan Close. I heard the car turn and drive back up the road and out of earshot.

What to do? Of course, I could wait until I was able to get hold of Mark, but that might take hours. Whatever was happening, it must involve Martin somehow, and I needed to know what it was.

Then I had an idea. The deity in charge of manufacturing such things has always shown me a liberal hand, though admittedly there can be issues with quality control. Stifling any doubts, I put my camera and cigarettes back in the bag, lifted it onto my shoulder and set off over the fence to hunt for the ancient window cleaner.

I found him almost immediately, just leaving a house on the turning circle in Marvell Close, the ladder and bucket neatly fixed in place. Sometimes it's best not to give these things too much thought. I marched straight up to him and said, 'Ten bob to borrow your bike, mate?'

If he was surprised, he recovered quickly. The little piggy eyes in his baby face wrinkled suspiciously. He said, 'Think I'm an idiot, do you? Fuck off.' He was a Scouser – we don't hear much Scouse spoken in Southaven – and I thought his response was encouraging. A lot of people would have cut straight to 'Fuck off' and left it at that.

'You'll get it back, I promise. Look, that's my car there.'

The old man glanced at the Cortina, then back at me. 'Could be anyone's frigging car.'

I took the keys out of my pocket and dangled them.

He said, 'Prove it.'

I sighed, quickly walked the thirty yards to the car, unlocked it and opened the door. 'Satisfied?'

He wheeled the bike towards me, then stopped and said, 'What do you want it for?'

I said, 'I'm working under cover. I'm going to pretend to be you.'

Now the old man laughed, a disgusting, wheezy laugh which terminated in a hacking cough. There was a whiff of dental caries. When he'd recovered he said, 'A long streak of piss like you, pretend to be me?'

'I won't be more than half an hour with it, honest. You could take a break, treat yourself to a pint in the Lancaster.'

I could tell this suggestion had hit home. His eye was on the note now. 'Half an hour?'

'Not a second longer. Tell you what, I'll wheel it over to the pub when I'm done.'

'Well – '

He was on the point of saying yes when I realized that I looked much too clean and tidy for the part. I said, 'Oh – and, borrow your vest?'

The eyes narrowed again, the little wrinkles clustered round. He said, 'Sod off, you pervert.'

I said, 'Come on, help me out. Dressed like this, who's going to believe I've been up a ladder all day?'

Now the old man checked me up and down with close attention. I wasn't sure, but I began to think an artist's eye had come into play. He said, 'CID, are you?'

I shook my head. 'Special Branch.'

He said, 'Is that right? Well, good on you. Can't have them Russian bastards walking all over us.' He tut-tutted. 'You look like shite, you know that? Get that poncey shirt off.' I laid my shirt on the bonnet of the car, while he removed his own shirt and vest and slipped the shirt on again. Then as he was reaching the vest towards me, he suddenly drew it back. 'Make it a quid, eh? Nice round number. I'm sure Her Maj won't object.'

I nodded, reluctantly, took the vest and dived into it. There was a sharp stench of old sweat blended with cycle oil. Meanwhile my new assistant had picked the filthy cloth out of his bucket. He signed for me to bend towards him, and when I did so he grabbed my head and smeared my face with the cloth. Then he let go, and while I spluttered and wiped God knows what out of my eyes he tucked the end of the cloth inside my trouser waistband so that it hung down at one side. Now he stepped back to review his handiwork, but apparently it fell short of his aspirations. He said, 'Jesus Christ,' shook his head and raised his eyes to heaven.

Personally I think he was milking it a bit, but that's the artistic temperament for you.

Now it was the turn of my white canvas deck shoes to come in for withering scrutiny. 'Those the only shoes you got?' I had to admit that they were. The old man frowned, then stamped hard on each one, giving the sole of his boot a twist as he did so.

I said, 'Ow.'

'Taking some right poofters in the Service nowadays. And what in God's name have you been doing to your hair? You look like Jayne frigging Mansfield. Ah!' A light bulb flashed on over the old chap's head. He reached behind him and pulled a brown peaked cap, torn and stained, out of his back pocket. Standing on tiptoe, he rammed the cap down hard over my brow. From choice I think he would have covered my entire face if he could, but even Leonardo had to work with what he was given.

He took a couple of steps back now, sized me up one last time, then shook his head in bitter disappointment. 'I'll tell you what it is, right? You look exactly the same as you did before. For a role like this, it's not costume you want, it's research. You want to take a tip from them Method actors – you know, Marlon Brando and them lot. If you're going to impersonate a window cleaner, you've got to clean some windows. Six months, maybe a year, you'd start to get the feel of it.'

I said, 'Thanks, you've been a great help. I'll inform my superior officers. What's your name?'

'You're not catching me out like that. I know too much, you could have me silenced. Knock on the door, gunshots, me and the missus stone dead in front of the telly. Anyway, best of luck. See you at the Lanky in half an hour. And don't leave drips or smears.' He took the note I gave him, held it up to the light to check the watermark, then ambled off along the street, buttoning the blue shirt as he went and whistling *Love is a Many-Splendoured Thing*.

Locking my own shirt in the Cortina with my bag, I pushed the bike onto the main road and around the corner into Vaughan Close. It was a bugger to manage and I wouldn't have fancied riding it.

Ten minutes must have passed since I'd quit my post at the far end of the Close. Presumably it was a fresh roll-up which the young chauffeur was now smoking, but otherwise nothing at all had changed. Things were going my way. I began to whistle *Lola*, in my best window cleaner whistle.

The young man gave no sign of interest as I approached along the pavement. Just as I drew near, he yawned.

I said, 'Late night, was it?'

He turned sharply, as if he'd been lost in his own thoughts. The cap had been tilted forward to shade his eyes, and he pushed the peak up now with his left hand, to get a better look at me. It gave me a better look at him, too. He can't have been much more than twenty-two or twenty-three, but the uniform lent him a certain maturity. He said, 'Late night? Yeah, something like that.'

I said, 'Feds gone now, have they?'

He arched one eyebrow, clearly sceptical as to what business the police could be of mine.

I said, 'I was along earlier. She's one of my regulars, Mrs Berry. But there was a cop car here, I didn't like to intrude. Thought I'd come back later. So I've come back.' This wasn't going well. My patter sounded forced, and I was distracted by the driver's pale, downy moustache, the hair so blond and delicate that from a distance I hadn't seen it at all.

The young man seemed distracted too. His sharp blue eyes kept wandering southwards towards my waist. The grubby singlet had fitted its rightful owner perfectly, but on me it strained at the armpits, pulled tight across the chest, and dismally failed to come even within hailing distance of my trousers. Eyes still flickering, he said, 'Cops went a while ago. But I'd leave it for another time if I were you.'

I was worrying now about the state of my belly. Some years had passed since it could have gone into competition as my best feature. I said, 'Not a good moment?'

He shook his head. His hair brushed against his collar.

I said, 'Family crisis?'

Again he said, 'Something like that.'

This was getting me nowhere. Perhaps I should stop asking questions. I said, 'Nice woman, Mrs Berry. Always gives me a bit over the odds. Not short of a few quid, are they?' I indicated the Vitesse. 'Smart car, doesn't come cheap. Don't expect her husband cleans windows for a living.'

There was something I didn't like about the silence which followed. I rested the bike against the wall and said, 'This her dad's car?' The driver nodded. I said, 'We were talking cars one day, she told me he had a Jag. Must take some cleaning. Not a mark on it. That down to you, is it?' He nodded again. 'Well, I'm impressed. See those windows – no drips, no smears – ' Then I turned towards the house and frowned. 'It's been six weeks now, she's probably thinking I've let her down. Is her dad here, then?'

He said, 'Mother,' then dropped the stub of his cigarette and ground it beneath his heel.

'Her mother? And the windows so black with dirt she can hardly see out. Thanks for the advice, and all that, but I think I will just go and knock at the door.'

I turned a little, ready to move off towards the house, but as soon as I did so the driver placed a warm hand on my bare arm. He said, 'No. You're not going to be welcome.'

I said, 'You've got me really bothered now. I like Mrs Berry, she's a good sort, you can have a laugh with her. What is it, has there been some sort of accident?'

The man removed his hand, though I'd quite liked it where it was. He said, 'Something like that.'

'She's not hurt?'

'No, no, she's fine. Well, maybe not fine exactly – '

'You're not making any sense. What's happened?'

The chauffeur looked away from me, along the street. His face was in shadow now.

He said, 'Martin Berry drowned last night.'

2

From our feet came the sound of insistent miaowing. A small ginger tom had appeared from nowhere – it must have been hiding under the Jag. The driver's face lit up, and he bent down to scratch the cat on the top of its head. Mewing gave way to purring. The driver said, 'Hello, puss puss puss. You're a nice little thing, aren't you?' The cat rubbed itself against his legs.

This must be Eusebio, the small cat with the big appetite. I was grateful to him for buying me some time and keeping the driver occupied while I tried to regain control of the muscles in my face.

After a while I said, 'Drowned? How? They're not long married, poor Mrs Berry'll be doing her nut. What happened?'

Without looking up, the driver said, 'I only know what my boss told me. I drove him to work this morning, he'd no sooner arrived than Mrs Wetherley was on the phone. He'd have come himself, but he had meetings. That's right, isn't it, puss puss?'

'But I don't understand, people don't just drown. Where was it?'

'Mr Wetherley said something about a lake. He must have gone swimming.'

'The boating lake? Over at the Lake View?'

Still cat-scratching, the driver shrugged his shoulders. 'Couldn't tell you, mate. And I never had a word out of Mrs Wetherley the whole way over.'

I was stumped. If Martin had drowned at the boating lake behind the hotel, that would at least explain the presence of the police cars I'd seen earlier. But what on earth could he have been doing there? The lake wasn't deep, and Martin had claimed to be a strong swimmer. It's true that he'd had a bit too much to drink, but – what if this hadn't been an accident?

Apart from the regular wage, I don't often find myself wishing that I was back on the force. But this was one of those times. As a cop you can barge right in, ask questions, tread on toes. As a private sector snoop, on the other hand, you always need some excuse for your enquiries, otherwise you find yourself dressing up as a window cleaner and smearing your face with filth. It wasn't dignified, and it wasn't even effective. I needed to talk to Monica Berry, I needed to talk to the officer in charge of the investigation, instead of which I was out here doing amateur dramatics on the most boring street in the whole of Southaven.

Now Eusebio decided that you can, after all, have too much of a good thing. He ducked out from beneath the driver's hand and strolled off up the street with tail erect. The driver rose to his feet and said, 'Great, aren't they?'

I'm a cat agnostic, but I said, 'Yeah, great. That's Eusebio, Mrs Berry's cat.'

The driver said, 'As window cleaners go, you're quite a friend of the family, aren't you?' Then he took his tobacco tin from his pocket and removed the lid. 'Roll one of these for you?'

Now that he was no longer leaning against the Jag, our eyes were on a level, and he seemed friendlier somehow. Perhaps the contact with feline society had refreshed his spirit. I said, 'Go on then. Bit of a shock, what you're telling me. Could do with a fag to brace me up. Left mine at home today, I'm trying to cut down.'

He smiled, as his practised hands set to work. 'You don't want to do that. It's a slippery slope, isn't it? First the fags go, then the beer, next thing you know you're eating Special K for breakfast and buying bathroom scales.'

I said, 'What, are you saying I'm fat?'

Again his eyes flickered involuntarily as he tried not to look at my belly. 'You're just at a difficult age, that's all.' He handed me the roll-up and lit it for me with the lighter he kept in the tin. It tasted good. Then he began work on one for himself.

I said, 'Were you acquainted with the deceased?' Somehow I found the old interrogation habits hard to shake.

'Was I what with the what?'

'Did you know Mr Berry at all?'

'Oh – yes, a little. We had a chat at the wedding, and he's been over to Didsbury a few times, family do's and that.' He moistened the paper with his tongue, neatly rolled the cigarette, then lit it and blew out smoke. 'Lovely chap, actually, Mr Berry. Serious-minded. You could see why Monica would go for someone like that. I suppose you'd met him?'

'What, me? No, never set eyes on him.'

'Good-looking bloke. Popular with the ladies, I should imagine.'

I said, 'You come over here much?'

'This is my first time. The bother I've had, finding Vaughan Close. Not on any map, just been built. Stopped and asked people, they'd never heard of it. Still, got here eventually.'

'Work for the family long?'

'Three years or so. Did odd jobs at first, then they let their old chauffeur go and I stepped in.'

'Just driving, is it, or – ?'

He shook his head. 'Do whatever I'm asked. I've got my own little flat above the garage, if they need me they don't have far to look.' He made eye contact and said, 'Married, are you?'

I said, 'Not as such, no.' The conversation had taken an interesting turn.

Just then the front door opened and Mrs Wetherley appeared. I could sense the driver bristling beside me, and he hid the cigarette behind his back. 'Gerald – what have I told you about gossiping with strangers?' The voice was quiet, but this was a woman unused to being contradicted. 'Now get inside and make yourself useful. Monica needs your help. And bring my overnight case from the boot.'

'Yes, Mrs Wetherley. Sorry, Mrs Wetherley.' But he was speaking to her back already, and she soon disappeared, leaving the door open behind her. Now the driver ground this latest cigarette beneath his heel, then opened the car door and dived inside. He took something from the glove compartment and seemed to be writing. Then he emerged, shut the door, locked it, and handed me a scrap of paper torn from some kind of work schedule. There was a phone number written on it in a small, neat hand. He said, 'Gerry Gibbs. Call me. Worse places than Manchester on a Saturday night.'

I said, 'Might take you up on that. I'm Sam.'

We heard a cry of 'Gerald!'

'Coming, Mrs Wetherley!' Gerry winked at me, took the suitcase from the car boot, then walked off towards the house with no great show of urgency.

Eusebio was watching me from the front wall of the house next door. If he was waiting for Martin to come home, he was in for a very long wait.

*

Half an hour later, I'd parked on the beach among scores of other vehicles. If there was still a police presence at the boating lake, which seemed probable, I was afraid that one of my old comrades might recognize the Cortina, but here there would be safety in numbers. And I doubted if anyone would spot me walking around amongst the holidaymakers with a camera on my shoulder.

I'd returned the bike to the anonymous window cleaner, who was greatly enjoying his second pint in the Lancaster and seemed to have lost whatever interest he might previously have had in window cleaning, the Special Branch, or me. I took a moment to clean myself up in the toilets, but my forehead had acquired some sort of permanent stain. I might have to get the Ajax on it back at home.

I could see no point in hanging around Vaughan Close any longer. Clearly Mrs Wetherley intended to stay the night and there was little chance of getting a private word with Monica. I needed to find some new angle of approach. For something to do, I drove over to Danny Craven's yard, which lay amongst small industrial units by the railway line, but the place was deserted. I didn't really want to speak with Danny yet, I had nothing to say, but it would have been good to get some physical impression of the man who Martin thought was sleeping with his wife. If I didn't catch him at the yard some time, his home address was just a few streets away. I left

Danny for another day.

So now I was climbing the sandhills which stood between the boating lake and the beach. And when I reached the top, I saw the last thing which I'd expected to see, namely that it was business as usual on the boating lake this hot July afternoon. If the police had initially closed the lake then they must now have changed their minds. About a dozen rowing boats were out on the water, where I was supposing that Martin had lost his life. The air carried squeals of pleasure from the small children who paddled in the shallows, watched by anxious mums. It was another glorious day in holiday paradise.

I moved further along the ridge of the hills, my white pumps filling with sand as I went. In the middle of the lake there stood an island, grown over with scrubby bushes. As I passed this I could now see that one section of the further bank was still cordoned off, and half a dozen uniformed officers, some on their hands and knees, were searching the ground amongst the sand and rocks and marram grass. There isn't exactly a glut of manpower on the Southaven force. If you see two cops, there's been a burglary. If you see six –

I raised the camera and took several shots of the men at work, but though my vantage point left me with a clear view I also felt exposed. It could only be a matter of time before one of the men glanced up and saw me across the lake. I took the prudent course and retreated.

Again I felt stumped, starved of facts. I could see no better option than to look for Mark Howell and remind him that he stood forever in my debt.

Retrieving the Cortina from the beach, I drove back into town along the coast road, showing even less regard for the speed limit than I had done on the way out. When you bank your client's cheque at eleven in the morning, then learn at half past one that he's dead, it starts a train of thought. I was on that train now. Why had Martin gone to the boating lake so late at night? More than anything, I wanted his death to have been an accident, terrible enough but a normal part of life in an unpredictable world. Somehow I couldn't bear the thought that someone had wanted Martin dead – wide-eyed, honest Martin with his weekend football and his carrots. But you don't get six cops for an accident.

The parking goddess looked kindly on me again. I left the Cortina right in front of the flats and took my bag inside. Another quick attempt to clean my face brought only limited success. Then I went out, bought a meat and potato pie from the chippy near the Feathers, and began eating it as I walked the three hundred yards to the police station. One reason I'd chosen the flat was its convenience for work. It stood opposite the fire station, with the police station side on to it just out of sight around the corner. The whole block had been occupied at one time by a huge private house and its grounds. When central Southaven became an unfashionable address for wealthy individuals, Martin's old school, King Edward's, had moved in for a short time, but between the wars that too headed out to the leafy suburbs, the old house was demolished, and the emergency services took its place.

There was a petrol station opposite the cop shop, so I called in and picked up a copy of the Southaven Gazette for something to read while I waited for Mark to show up. The Gazette comes out three times a week and is compulsory reading for all bona fide citizens of the town. It's considered extremely bad form not to know what Alderman Franks said about the proposed foreshore redevelopment, or who left floral tributes at whose funeral. Connoisseurs also relish the paper's tradition of typographical errors and other howlers. If a photograph of two small boys with a model railway is not captioned, 'Members of the Women's Gas Federation enjoy their annual dinner and dance at the Imperial Hotel,' you feel cheated. I ran a regular ad with the Gazette, despite the fact that they had once referred to me as a Private Instigator.

When the pie had become all pie and no meat and potato, I shoved the remains in a bin and positioned myself behind a mature beech tree from which I had a good view of the side door of the police station, which Mark was most likely to use as he came or went. I checked the sports pages of the newspaper for any mention of Otterdale FC, but notwithstanding the recent World Cup fever it seemed that local football had graciously made way for cricket. Then I ran my eye over the news pages, but if the Gazette knew anything of the change of plan at the Empire cinema, they were following Martin's tight-lipped example.

Buying the Gazette turned out to be a mistake, because inevitably when Mark did emerge from the side door into the car park I was so enthralled by the saga of a Saturday night punch-up outside the Temperance Institute that at first I missed him. Luckily he wasn't heading for a vehicle, and when I glanced up it was his back that I caught sight of as he walked rapidly towards the corner of Preston Road. I tried to fold the newspaper but it fought back, so I carried it with me as a misshapen lump at my side while I hurried after Mark.

Once round the corner I saw Mark cross the road towards Leigh Terrace. My intuition mumbled something, and I slowed down. Sure enough, when he reached my building he climbed the steps to the front door and rang the top bell, the one for my flat.

What did he want? It was one thing for me to seek Mark out and grill him for information, but Mark coming in search of me was something else entirely. I didn't like the look of it, and I hung back, undecided. But as he waited for a response to the bell, or buzzer to be more accurate, Mark happened to turn and look around him, and he could hardly miss me standing fifty yards away across the street. He yelled 'Sam!' and with a couple of characteristic leaps he was back at street level and speeding towards me.

Mark Howell was not the tallest cop on the Southaven force. If he hadn't worn thick socks to the medical, he'd have failed the height requirement. He was also not the sturdiest, having been built for speed rather than strength. This gave him a lithe physique which unfortunately had captured my attention from his very first day in Southaven as a cadet. Having furnished him with a bright, sharp, intelligent face, Nature had struggled to know how to complete the picture, and had eventually decided, some would say cruelly, to add the smallest, roundest pair of ears She had in stock at the time, like little pink confections from the pick-and-mix counter at Woolworths. They were cute, and I happened to like them, but they were not serious, and I'd often caught Mark examining his reflection to see if they'd matured.

I stood my ground while Mark caught up with me. You could see from his whole demeanour that he felt himself to be on an errand of importance, and this had even added an inch to his height. Stepping up onto the pavement in front of me, he was about to announce his business when his eye was caught by the papery mass in my hand. He said, 'What on earth's that?'

I said, 'The Gazette. They got bored with printing it flat.'

He let that go and said, 'Harry Hargreaves wants to see you.'

This news brought a mixed reception from its audience. Presumably DI Hargreaves had been put in charge of the Martin Berry investigation, in which case I should really have been eager to speak with the man. On the other hand, we had history. I said, 'Why?'

'Why do you think? Yesterday a man wrote you a cheque. Today he's dead.'

So they'd found Martin's cheque book. I said, 'What else do you know? Are you on the team?'

'You know I can't tell you anything.'

'Don't give me that shit, Mark. It's me, Sam – remember? The one you owe your job to.'

I felt his mood darken. He said, 'Why do you keep doing this? It was seven years ago. Just drop it.'

I said, 'Actually, Mark, the last time you called round for a little entertainment was more like seven months ago. In fact, I'm about due for another visit.'

'If Hargreaves finds out I've been passing you information – '

'How's he going to know? I won't tell if you won't.' Mark made no response. 'So – how about meeting me in the Railway at six and giving me what you've got? I can be very grateful if you play me right. Well?'

Mark muttered a reluctant 'OK,' and we made our way in silence towards the police station.

Soon I was alone in an interview room with my crumpled newspaper. Having nothing better to do, I lit a cigarette and refolded the newspaper so that it made some kind of sense. Minutes passed. I began trying to solve the quick crossword in my head, and I was just racking my brains for a six-letter word for tremble, second letter U, when the door opened and Harry Hargreaves strolled in. From force of habit I began to rise from my seat. This was the sort of mistake I always made when I found myself in the Presence. He didn't speak, so it was left to me to give myself permission to sit again.

Now Hargreaves sat down opposite me, still silent. I detected the subtle odour of warm Harris tweed. He removed his pipe and tobacco tin from his pocket, patiently filled the bowl, tamped it down gently and lit it with a match. After three or four good puffs it had drawn to his satisfaction. He pushed the tin and matchbox a little away from him and lowered the pipe, smoke curling upward from the bowl. For the first time he looked at me. He smiled. It was a very broad smile, and the teeth were sharp and crooked. He said, 'Samuel – good of you to come in like this. How's business?'

DI Hargreaves was a large, well-built man nearing sixty, with a massive head thatched by wayward hair. He was the only man in CID to sport a waistcoat beneath his jacket, probably because as a committed pipe-smoker he needed all the pockets he could get. He wore a permanent mask of unruffled serenity which became no less unsettling after years of familiarity. Some had tipped him for superintendent at one time, but there had been no real likelihood of that, because Hargreaves was not clubbable and preferred to keep the hem of his trouser-leg around his ankle, not rolled above his knee. As a rookie cop I idolized him. I could never understand why he hated my guts.

I answered the question. 'Business is good, thanks, Henry.' Since I'd left the force, Hargreaves had insisted on our being on first-name terms. Though universally spoken of as Harry, he preferred the formal Henry, and I stuck to it.

'I'm very glad to hear it. I like to think of our jobs as complementary, yours and mine. Much as I wish it otherwise, we in the police lack the manpower necessary to lie in wait for adulterous husbands outside seedy hotels. You perform a vital service.' He took another puff on the pipe. The smoke hung purple round his head. 'It follows that from time to time we may need to co-operate on particular cases, where the public interest demands it. How is your mother, by the way?'

I said, 'She's extremely well. It's thoughtful of you to remember her.'

'Not at all. How could I forget? Highly unfortunate when a woman of such obvious integrity becomes embroiled in a misunderstanding like that. Perhaps you would give her my regards?' The misunderstanding concerned two shoplifting incidents about ten years before. Without the intervention of Hargreaves, she might not have got off with a fine.

I said, 'I will do, Henry, thank you. I'm sure she would want me to pass on her very best wishes. Mrs Hargreaves in tip-top form, I take it?'

Hargreaves nodded complacently. 'Naturally, yes. Edna is a marvel in that respect. Never a day's illness since we married. I believe it's all down to her deep-rooted sense of duty.' The couple were childless. Edna Hargreaves appeared only rarely at official police functions, and when she did she was not always sober. 'But – Samuel – to return now to this matter of co-operation. As you know, I would do anything in my power to help you if you were to request it, provided, of course, your request fell within the regulations. Some things, alas, I cannot do. I'm a public servant, Samuel, I'm answerable to others. You, on the other hand – '

But now Hargreaves discovered that the pipe had gone out. Calmly, he removed a suitable tool from his waistcoat pocket and redistributed the tobacco in the bowl. He took a match from the Swan Vestas box, struck it, and once more took several good puffs, until again smoke billowed from the bowl and from the side of his mouth and swirled out into the room.

'What was I saying?'

I said, 'Co-operation. Answerable to others. I, on the other hand.'

'Yes, of course. You, on the other hand, labour under no such constraint. So I ask myself, what possible reason could you have for failing to report your involvement in the matter of this man Berry, who turned up dead in the lake at Otterdale this morning?'

I didn't answer. I was trying to think, but Hargreaves had the knack of sucking up all the available intelligence in the room. Perhaps this explained why he so often outmanoeuvred me long before I'd even discovered what game we were playing.

Hargreaves hadn't finished. 'I believe you drive a yellow Cortina, is that right?' I said it was. 'Then perhaps someone borrowed it this morning. Because if it was you yourself who parked it in Marvell Close, I feel sure that out of courtesy you would have made your presence known to WPC Donnelly, who was visiting the wife of the deceased in the next street.'

It was just as I'd thought, you couldn't get much past Cilla Donnelly. I said, 'Was he – was he murdered? I need to know what's happened. I've been watching things from a distance all day, I'm sick of it.'

But Hargreaves merely chewed the stem of his pipe. Then he said, 'Berry was employing you. Why?'

I said the first thing that came into my head. 'He thought he was being followed.' Now it was out, it didn't sound too implausible.

'Followed? By whom?'

'If he'd known that, Henry – '

'Of course, stupid of me, I do beg your pardon. And in your – ' He hesitated, and his lip curled slightly. 'In your – *professional* judgement, is there likely to have been substance behind this?'

'Do you mean, do I think he actually was being followed?' With a gracious nod, Hargreaves acknowledged that I'd interpreted him correctly. 'No. No I don't.'

'Why not?'

'Because Martin Berry wasn't exactly James Bond. He was a suburban Mr Average with a dull job at the town hall, whose chief excitement in life was growing carrots.'

Hargreaves looked perplexed. 'Then surely, Samuel, the obvious course of action for you to take would have been to try and allay Mr Berry's fears, thus saving him unnecessary expenditure.'

I considered this argument. 'You know you asked me how the business was doing?'

'Yes.'

'And then I said it was good?'

'Yes.'

'I lied.'

A very slight shake of the head expressed Hargreaves' disappointment in my behaviour. 'How many years were you on the force, Samuel?'

'Nine. Nine happy years. Just nineteen years old when I had the privilege of making your acquaintance. But I doubt if you would remember me back then, Henry. Just another faceless cadet to you, I expect.'

'Oh no, Samuel, you're quite wrong, quite wrong. I remember you vividly in those days. Young, fresh, confident, willing – I recall my impression of you like it was yesterday. I watched you hob-nobbing with the lads in the canteen, telling stories, making jokes, asking questions, always endless questions, never satisfied with the answers, and I thought to myself, 'That cadet's a liability.' A liability, Samuel. Amazing how often first impressions turn out to be correct.'

A silence followed, while Hargreaves messed with his pipe again. There was nothing sensible I could say, so I just sat there, feeling like I was made of glass. After a time, Hargreaves seemed to grow weary of his efforts and laid the pipe aside. He said, 'As usual, Samuel, you have been no help to me at all. I turn to you for facts and I learn nothing. Tell me at least when Berry approached you?'

I hesitated for a second, no more than that, but it was quite enough for Hargreaves. He said, 'Berry didn't approach you?'

'We happened to get talking.'

'Just like that?'

'Yes. In a pub. I told him what I did, he seemed interested, I gave him my card.'

'When was this?'

'Yesterday. Yesterday evening.'

'I'm told he was a nice-looking boy.' Hargreaves gave me a level look which I didn't like. 'Did you – confine your activities to the pub?'

'Yes. We had a couple of drinks, then I walked him to the station.' Apparently I'd decided that the interlude at my flat was none of Hargreaves's business.

'Specifics at last. Hallelujah. What time was this?'

'Eleven. He caught the last train.'

Hargreaves took out his pad and made a note. 'Now – Samuel – think carefully before you answer this. You didn't catch the train with him?'

'No!'

'Berry knew that his wife would not be home last night.'

'No, it wasn't like that. Ask the guard at the barrier, he must have seen us.'

For a moment, Hargreaves maintained a sceptical silence. Then he said, 'Anything else?' I said there wasn't. 'Are you sure? Because if I learn that you've been withholding information or obstructing us in the course of our enquiries – ' He let the threat hang in the air. Then he pushed back his chair and stood up slowly, collecting his smoking kit from the table top as he did so. He said, 'It shouldn't be necessary for me to say this, Samuel, but one learns from bitter experience. If by any chance it should occur to you to make enquiries of your own into Mr Berry's unfortunate death – don't. Because, if I discover that you've been tramping your size elevens all over my investigation, you'll never work in this town again. Do you hear me?'

Actually I took size tens, but I thought the point still held. 'Loud and clear, Henry, loud and clear.'

'Good. I'm glad we understand each other.' He allowed himself a half smile, enough to give me a partial view of the nicotine-stained teeth. 'Nice to see you again, Samuel. You can give your statement on the way out.' He glanced momentarily at my forehead. 'Incidentally, you'll find we have soap and water in the toilets here. I can see no excuse for a dirty face.' He turned and left the room.

3

Six o'clock found me at my post in the Railway Tavern, waiting for Mark Howell. Half past six found me there as well. It looked as if Mark intended to stand me up.

Twenty-four hours had passed since I had sat there at the bar with the young man in the blue suit beside me. Now he was dead. Hargreaves could threaten me as much as he liked, it would make no difference. I was going to find out what had happened to Martin Berry, and if that meant getting under Hargreaves' feet from time to time then so be it. I remembered Martin's troubled face, his elbow in the spilled beer. Had it just been Monica on his mind, or was there something else, something he wasn't telling me? I needed facts, I needed to know everything that the police knew. I needed Mark Howell. But Mark apparently felt that his attendance at this meeting was purely optional. Anger rose inside me. If things had gone differently, it could have been me still on the force and Mark out here struggling to keep his life together. Yet really it was all my own fault.

Like I said, Mark caught my eye from the very beginning. It was a case of something-or-other at first sight, though I never quite knew what. He was smart, he had those cute little ears, and the way he looked at me I could tell exactly what he was thinking. I took him under my wing. We were assigned duties together, we hung around together after work though Mark was never so keen on a drink as I was. He was a country boy really, from up Rossendale way, and I began to teach him the facts of Southaven life. There were other things I wanted to teach him too, but I held back, because of the job, because he was younger than me. It was Mark who made the running, inviting himself round to my flat, making himself comfortable on the old two-seater settee. He'd never been with a man before, though he'd always known that's what he wanted. We began an affair, snatching time together as best we could without drawing suspicion. Mark was still in police accommodation so he could never stay the night, the other cadets would have started asking questions. I wanted him there with me, wanted to wake up beside him in the mornings, and I pressed him to get his own place, but he said be patient, all in good time. Of course we had to be careful at work now. We were cool with each other, I remember one of the lads even asking me if we'd had a falling out. All this should have been easy for Mark, who'd been a fully paid-up conformist since birth and was already getting a reputation as the station swot and all-round Infant Phenomenon. But in the end it was Mark who slipped up, not me.

We were alone in the locker room one evening, just coming off shift. I was minding my own business and buttoning up my shirt when Mark, suddenly overcome by my irresistible allure, spun me round and stuck his tongue down my throat, not to mention his hand down the front of my underpants. The locker room door normally had a really useful squeak to it, but Maintenance must have come in to oil the hinges because when we were joined in the room by Cal Shaunessy we knew nothing about it until he coughed.

Unfortunately, Cal was not the type to keep something like that to himself. He was the sort of middle-aged plod who regarded the force as a job for life, kept a low profile and did the minimum amount of work necessary to keep his nose in the trough. I rather liked him. He had no particular animus against me, against Mark, or even against men who fancied men, but his weakness was that he recognized a good story when he saw one, and he was seeing one now. Consequently it came as no great surprise when late the following afternoon we were called in to the Superintendent's office to give an account of ourselves.

Things looked bad for us. This was back in '63, seven years ago, when sex between men was illegal in any circumstances. Even after the law changed in '67 it only applied to men over twenty-one, so at barely twenty Mark would still have been under age. Of course, we weren't actually seen having sex, but there was a grey area around indecency and I wouldn't have cared to argue that we'd fallen on the right side of the line. But that was only half the problem. The fact was, the police force had no place in it for homosexual men, or women either. If they discovered you were queer, you were out. Thirty seconds of poor impulse control in the locker room would almost certainly spell the end for our careers.

But I saw a chance, and I took it. I thought I might be able to draw the whole blame down on myself and let Mark come through with nothing worse than a reprimand. After all, as I've said, Mark was already quite the blue-eyed boy, while there were people at Southaven – Hargreaves prominent among them – who would shed few tears if Sam Rigby left under a cloud. So I told the Super that I'd had my eye on Mark for some time, that I'd never touched him before the incident the previous day, that he'd only responded because I was older and senior to him and he thought his career would suffer if he didn't. Mark sat in heavy silence beside me, accepting these lies without a murmur. Admittedly the story clashed with what Shaunessy had been saying, that Mark had had me pinned back against the lockers and was showing enthusiasm far beyond the call of duty. But everyone knew Cal Shaunessy for an embroiderer of tales, and besides, as usual in such matters, they believed what they wanted to believe. The Super told me to resign with immediate effect, gave Mark a half-hearted ticking-off, and dismissed us both with obvious relief.

I've often wondered why I did it, why I torpedoed my own career, my life in the force, just to save Mark's skin. It galled me afterwards to watch his progress, his smooth passage from uniform to CID. Now everyone said he'd make Sergeant in a year or two, though he was still only twenty-seven. At first some faint miasma of suspicion had lingered, but once Cilla came along people seemed only too willing to forget, and he must have grown weary of being asked exactly when he intended to make her an honest woman. He hadn't changed, naturally. Most of the time he went out of town for sex, where no-one knew him. But though our affair had died that afternoon in the Super's office, just occasionally, maybe once or twice a year, he still came to me. And despite everything, each time I welcomed him with open arms.

Afterwards, of course, I always cursed myself and vowed that it would never happen again. Mark Howell was nothing but a slick, ungrateful little shit and I wasn't going to let him pick me up and put me down whenever he felt like it. So ran the theory, and it was good. A shame I always failed the practical.

Still the minutes ticked on, still no sign of Mark. Thinking was doing me no good, I tried to distract myself. The chunky builder from yesterday, the one with the ripped t-shirt, was playing darts with his mates. He'd managed to find an intact shirt, which covered his smooth brown shoulder and hid it from my view. They were playing three hundred up, and when he needed forty to win he threw a perfect double top. A little smirk of pride settled on his lips, and as he walked away from the board I caught his eye and smiled. He let himself smile back for a moment, white teeth in a brown face, before turning to rejoin his comrades. I went back to my beer and my sour thoughts.

It was a few minutes shy of seven and I was sitting in front of a fresh pint with my mind still churning uselessly when Mark finally came in and perched lightly on the stool next to mine, the one which Martin had occupied so awkwardly the day before. He said, 'All right?'

I said, 'Not really. What time do you call this?'

'I'm on a murder investigation, I've got things to do. The world doesn't revolve around Sam Rigby.'

'I know it doesn't, it's too busy revolving around you. So it is murder, then?'

Mark regarded me with something close to pity. 'I realize you're old school, but does it never occur to you to switch on a radio or watch TV? The Super went on Look North just now appealing for witnesses.' He glanced at my pint and said, 'I'll have a tomato juice, if you're offering. Easy on the Worcester Sauce.'

I called Wilf over and ordered Mark's drink. Mark straightened his tie, a knitted thing in mustard no doubt intended to bring a flash of colour to the sober shit-brown terylene suit. He was apt to pride himself on his dress sense, so I said, 'Clothing allowance been cut again, has it?'

He looked down his nose at my outfit, the usual leather jacket, the lilac shirt. He said, 'Why on earth are you wearing that heavy jacket? It's boiling today.'

'I always wear it. If it's any consolation, I'm too hot.' Then it was my turn. I looked down my nose at his outfit and said, 'I sense you're dressing down for some reason.' The juice arrived and I paid for it.

Mark took a sip, then said, 'I wore a new jacket to work last week, really smart, big lapels. But – '

'Let me guess. There were remarks.'

He nodded. 'Liberace was mentioned. End of jacket.'

'Do you never think of getting out? It's ludicrous, your life's not your own.'

'What else would I do? I'm a cop. So I have to wear brown to fit in, so what.'

I looked at him hard. 'Not just about the jacket though, is it? Think of the other things you've had to let go.'

He turned a little, saw my expression, turned back again, looked down at the damp beer mat in front of him. He said nothing for a while, and he wasn't the silent type. I lit myself another cigarette. Finally he said, 'I can give you twenty minutes. What do you want to know?'

'Twenty minutes? That's really big of you, I'm touched.'

'I shouldn't be here at all, and you know it. Hargreaves thinks I'm at the railway station talking to the staff.'

'Look – I'm grateful, Mark, honestly. I've just had a bad day, that's all. Give me some facts. When did Martin die? Who found him?'

'"Martin"? I thought you only met him yesterday.'

'Never mind that. Just spill.'

Mark took a moment to clear his head. He was different from me, he was a systematic thinker, he liked things to come out in the proper order. 'You're the last person we know of who saw Martin Berry alive. Some time either side of midnight, if the doc's got it right, he went up to the boating lake, stripped off, left his clothes in a neat little pile on top of his shoes, allowed himself to be whacked violently on the back of the head with a rock, and got rolled into the lake.'

'Was it the blow that killed him? Someone told me he'd drowned.'

'That was the official line this morning, but the post mortem report came through just before I left the station. No water in the lungs, he was dead before he went into the lake. There was a clear mark at the edge where the body had been rolled in, but nothing else useful on the ground. You know what it's like there, sand and more sand, hopeless for shoe prints in such dry weather. An ideal spot if you're wanting to do someone in.'

'Did you find the rock?'

'Yes. You'd think the murderer might have slung it in the water, but it was just lying there near Berry's clothes, blood on it, hair. The interesting thing is – no, I'll come to that in a minute. So the body was in the lake all night, face down. They have a live-in cook at the hotel with a room up in the attic, she noticed the body around six o'clock when she opened her curtains.'

'And the interesting thing?'

'It seems Berry had been in a fist fight. Bruised knuckles, fresh cuts to his face – '

'There was nothing like that when I saw him off at the station. And it doesn't make sense. Why get in a dust-up with someone then obligingly turn your back so they can pop you one with a lump of granite?'

'Limestone, as it happens, but yes, you're right. Unless, of course, you and your opponent have just kissed and made up.'

I turned this over for a moment. 'Could they tell if it was much of a fight? Might just have been a pre-season friendly.'

'Pathologist didn't want to commit himself.'

I'd arranged to see Mark in the hope of getting answers, but all I had was more questions. 'What does Hargreaves make of all this? And I should warn you, if you try to tell me it's a robbery gone tragically wrong I may be forced to strangle you with that vile excuse for a tie.'

'You know what Hargreaves is like. With so little evidence, he's just keeping an open mind.' This sounded very much in character. Hargreaves probably hadn't jumped to a conclusion since he was in nappies. 'And Berry's wallet and cheque book were in his pockets, so there's no question of theft.'

Something was bothering me, but I would have to be careful how I approached it. I said, 'Presumably you brought the divers in?'

Mark turned to me with a greater show of interest than I would have liked. 'No. Should we have done?'

I shrugged. 'Body in lake, not much to go on, seems like the obvious thing to do.'

'But we already have his clothes, we have the murder weapon. What would we tell them to look for?'

I pretended to think about this. 'You're right, of course. Waste of resources.' I wasn't going to take the risk of telling Mark about the briefcase. I didn't want Hargreaves tramping his size elevens all over my investigation. Clearly the briefcase hadn't turned up at the lakeside or Mark would have mentioned it – unlike me, he wasn't the sort to leave things out – and I was guessing the police had no idea it even existed. Perhaps Martin had dropped it off at home before walking the half mile to the lake. Perhaps he'd changed his clothes, picked out something more suitable for a late swim. I said, 'What was he wearing? When he caught the train he was in his work clothes, blue suit with all the trimmings.'

'All the trimmings – you mean that? What about a tie?'

'Yes.' Or rather, no. Martin had put his tie in the briefcase as we were leaving the Feathers, but I saw no reason to share that morsel with the police.

'Are you sure? We found his shoes with the socks tucked inside, blue jacket neatly folded on top of them, trousers on top of the jacket, white shirt on top of those. But no tie, so that's missing as well.'

'As well as what?'

'His underpants.'

'You're kidding.'

'No sign of them anywhere. Unless of course he wasn't wearing any in the first place.' Now it was Mark's turn to give me a level look. 'I don't suppose you'd be in a position to shed light on that?'

'For heaven's sake, Mark! I had the same crap this afternoon from Hargreaves. Martin Berry was a client, that's all. It's true we had a few drinks together, but it took at least two pints to get him to tell me what was bothering him. You know the way people open up to me as a rule, well it was different with Martin. But I kept trying because he was in such a state.'

Suddenly I was aware of having said too much. Not that I'd given away anything specific, but I'd begun to sound like a man with something to hide. Perhaps Mark picked this up. After a moment's thought, he said, 'You told Hargreaves that Berry had no idea who was following him. Is that true?'

I didn't like the way things were going. Now Mark was interrogating me. I said, 'Yes, of course. He was Mr Dull of Dullchester. Who would want to follow a man like that? Convenient that he died, really, I hadn't a clue where to start.'

It was a good enough line, but it came out false and brittle. Mark took a swig of the tomato juice, then quietly he said, 'You'd taken a shine to him, hadn't you.'

'What?'

'I won't tell Hargreaves, I promise.'

'There's nothing to tell, what are you talking about?'

Mark looked me in the eye then, but only for a couple of seconds. I don't know what he saw, but the questions stopped coming. He glanced at the clock behind the bar. 'I ought to be going.'

I said, 'Stay a bit – have another drink.'

'No can do. Got to get back to work. There'll be officers on the last train tonight, by the way, in case there's anyone who noticed Berry yesterday. And there's two lads at Otterdale questioning everyone who comes off the trains there. Best hope we've got, really. We've been door to door up Beach Road, but nothing so far.' He slipped down from the stool. 'Thanks for the drink.'

'Have they got you working through the night on this?'

He shook his head. 'We'll take a break, most likely. No use knocking people up to talk to them at one in the morning.'

'How's Monica taking it – Mrs Berry?'

'You'd need to ask Cilla. She's got her mother staying so she won't be alone. OK, I'm off. See you when I see you.'

I touched his arm. 'Mark – when you get off tonight – I don't suppose you'd want to – ?'

It was the sort of thing you hear yourself saying, then immediately wish you were dead.

Mark just said, 'Best not, eh?' Then he tapped me lightly on the shoulder and walked away.

*

If some aspects of the meeting with Mark had not quite gone according to plan, at least I had facts now. After hours of feeling blocked and confused, it should be possible to see a way forward. I needed to think. The Railway had lost its savour, perhaps a brisk stroll on the Promenade would focus my ideas.

I said cheerio to Wilf and went out the back to the Gents, and I was just standing there doing the business when who should come breezing in but my young friend the darts champion. As etiquette required, he picked a spot some distance away along the urinal, and when his piss hit the porcelain he let out a rather theatrical groan of relief. In the past half hour my agenda had moved on somewhat, but still, this was as good an opener as I was likely to get. So I said, 'Bit of a session this evening?'

The chunky boy said, 'Celebrating.'

'I see. Celebrating what?'

'Tuesday.'

'Tuesday?'

'Tuesday. There's sod all else to celebrate, and you've got to have a drink, haven't you?' I couldn't argue with that. Then he said, 'You staying for another?'

I glanced sideways. He was staring straight ahead, minding his manners. I don't know why, but it wasn't the right moment. I said, 'Do you celebrate Wednesdays too?'

'Might do.'

I finished off. 'Perhaps tomorrow then.' I ran cold water over my hands, then went out through the busy bar into the street.

It was pushing on towards eight o'clock now, but the air still hung warm and heavy. At the Boulevard I headed left then walked along to turn up Jubilee Avenue in search of the novelty shop where Martin's parents lived. The Avenue was a narrow lane, pedestrianized for as long as I'd known it and much used as a cut-

49

through to the Promenade. It was lined on either side by holiday businesses of all descriptions, souvenir shops, amusement arcades, cheap cafés which were best avoided. Nevertheless, the Berrys' shop was easy enough to find, one of the biggest and best-kept on the Avenue, occupying a commanding position on the corner where the lane was crossed by Wright St. It was closed, of course. I looked up at the blank windows above me and wondered what scenes of sorrow and disbelief might be playing in the unseen rooms. This time yesterday the Berrys had been an ordinary couple marked out for no greater troubles than the town's steady decline in trade. Now their son lay in the police mortuary with a crater in his skull, and no one had the least idea why. Perhaps I would need to talk to them at some point, but it wasn't something I looked forward to. I left them to their grief and walked on up the Avenue.

As I reached the Promenade the air seemed suddenly to cool by five degrees, and I mean proper Fahrenheit degrees and not those weird centigrade ones which I can never get the hang of. Now I could breathe, now I could think.

One of the things which distinguishes Southaven from other seaside resorts is the near-total absence of the sea, which has been in retreat for more than a century. At first this seemed like abandonment, a betrayal by Nature. The town boasted one of the longest piers in the country, but soon after it was built the ebbing tide began to leave it standing in a wilderness of furrowed sand. Alarm and panic spread amongst the town fathers and the Victorian predecessors of Martin's parents, all those who made money from the swarms of visitors who every year abandoned their smoky hells in the county's mill and mining towns for just one glorious week beside the sea. There was an up-and-coming resort across the estuary, a place named Blackpool, as blessed with surging tides as Southaven seemed cursed. If the sea couldn't be tempted back, everyone knew where the miners and the millworkers would go.

But there was no help for it. Out went the sea, further and further, until the white tops were barely visible from upper windows of the Promenade's hotels. And at last it occurred to people that less sea meant more beach, or foreshore as I should properly term it, and hence more space for visitors. Gardens were planted, a fairground sprang up, a Marine Lake was dug and then extended and further extended. Instead of tempting the sea back, efforts were diverted to keeping it out, and a great sea wall was built with a coastal drive running along the top of it.

So it was not beside the sea but beside the Marine Lake that I now strolled along, mulling over what Mark had told me. There were a few families about, taking the evening air. A mother pushed a pram whose tiny occupant wore an old sun hat which proclaimed I'M BACKING BRITAIN, with evidence of chewing round the rim. On the calm surface of the lake, two grey cygnets followed in the wake of their unhurried parent. Life seemed straightforward here, benign. On an evening such as this, what possible motive could make you want to kill another human being?

If it had been Danny Craven who'd fetched up dead in the water, the answer would have been easy and the culprit not hard to find. Jealousy can make even the mildest of us lose all reason. But it was not Danny, it was Martin. Apart from his troubles with Monica, what else had been on Martin's mind? I could picture him now lifting the briefcase in the air as we passed the Empire cinema, giving it that little shake. He'd said, 'See no evil, hear no evil.' Unlike Hargreaves, if I saw a likely conclusion I didn't hesitate to jump to it. Martin knew something dodgy about what was happening at the Empire. The evidence was in his briefcase. He intended to blow the whistle, and now the briefcase was missing and Martin was dead.

For a moment I was so excited by the logic of this that my heart began to race and my vision blurred. I sat on a bench in one of the oriental-style shelters overlooking the water and tried to concentrate. I reminded myself that Hargreaves had a point. It was far too soon to conclude that I understood the motive for Martin's death. His wife had allegedly been playing away from home with the local builder. It could easily have been Danny who'd killed him. Come to that, it could have been Monica herself, since so far we only had her word for it that she'd been out of town.

And was the briefcase even missing? What if it was sitting quietly at home in Vaughan Close all this time, with nothing more sinister inside it than Martin's tie?

I decided to call Monica the next morning and invite myself over to see her. I could tell her exactly what I'd told the police, that Martin had suspected he was being followed and had hired me to look into it. It wasn't a great story but on the other hand it was hard to disprove. No doubt I would then be able to think of some equally plausible reason to enquire after the briefcase. And I would be one step further forward.

Buoyed up by the fact that at last I had a rational plan of campaign, I walked rapidly back to the flat. With the kitchen blacked out, I developed the roll of monochrome film which I'd shot during the day and took a hard look at the negatives. There didn't seem to be much worth printing. All the pictures from the boating lake were redundant now that I'd heard Mark's account of what had happened. But I did decide to print the shot of Danny Craven's wiry forearm emerging from the window of his van, even though his face was no more visible in the photo than it had been at the time. I also chose one of Monica's mother walking up the path to the house, her head bent forward. And to make up a trio, there was a nice close-up of Gerry Gibbs leaning back against the Jag with a roll-up hanging from his mouth, cap tilted low over his eyes, like something out of Joe Orton. In my trouser pocket I still had the scrap of paper he'd given me with his phone number written on it. Why had he done that? Was he just being friendly, or did he perhaps have more to tell me?

I pegged up the wet prints over the sink, took a can of beer from the fridge and went through into the living room. There was a Soft Machine album I'd been failing to make sense of, and I thought I'd try it again. I settled down on the old settee with the beer, the music and a copy of Bradley's *History of Southaven*, which I'd read twice before. I'd reached the part about Crowburn buying up the whole district from two of his impecunious relatives in the 1860s. Apparently he'd left the country a few years earlier no more than mildly affluent, but he'd returned a wealthy man. No one could discover then, or now, how he'd acquired the money, though presumably it had something to do with grinding the faces of the poor. Just as Bradley and I were mulling this over, the phone rang.

It was midnight. I dug the phone out from under some old copies of the Gazette on the floor, and lifted the receiver. 'Hello, Sam Rigby.' Nothing. 'Hello?' Then whoever it was rang off. Perhaps they'd caught an earful of Soft Machine and decided to do a runner, in which case I sympathised. I thought I ought to like it, but I wasn't on the right drugs.

I put the receiver down and went back to Bradley. Whether it was him or the drink or the music I don't know, but at something like one o'clock I woke up on the settee with pins and needles in my arm and a trickle of beer running down my right leg onto my foot. I took the hint and went to bed.

Martin Berry and I were sitting in the front row of the circle at the Empire cinema, smoking cigarettes and chatting our way through the film, some kind of sword and sandals epic which occasionally spilled off the screen into the stalls. Martin wore his football kit, and I was resting my hand on his leg in a comradely manner. We couldn't hear the dialogue properly because of a loud ringing noise in the auditorium. Martin said, 'Is that the phone?' Then I woke up, and it was. Daylight streamed in. I'd remembered to wind the bedside clock the previous night, and a glance now told me it was five past seven. Though I kept meaning to run a phone extension to the bedroom, somehow it never happened. I hauled myself out of bed, walked through, and once more picked up the receiver.

'Sam? Is that you?'

'Aunt Winnie – yes, of course it's me, why do you ask?'

'Well it didn't sound like you.'

'But I hadn't said anything yet.'

'That sounds more like you now.'

'Because it is me. I keep telling you.'

'You can't be too careful, I might have been talking to anybody.'

'But you're not. Who else would recognize your voice instantly like that? What do you want, anyway? It's seven o'clock.'

'If you went to bed at a decent time instead of drinking till all hours, you might be able to shift yourself in the mornings. Some of us have been up since half past five.' Her tone switched to heavy irony. 'Perhaps sir would like me to call back later, when he's had a chance to sleep it off?'

Something occurred to me, and I said, 'I don't suppose it was you that rang last night? Midnight or thereabouts?'

'Certainly not, your uncle and I would have been asleep long since.' Then she fell silent for a moment, and when she resumed her tone had changed again. 'Listen – there's been an incident. I think you should get down here now.' There was no mistaking her unease. I began to worry.

'What is it? Is Uncle Fred all right?'

'Thirty-two years we've been here, but never anything like this! What on earth am I going to say to the Old Man?'

'Aunt Winnie, please – just tell me what's happened.'

'I am doing! Can you not wait two seconds while I get the words out?'

Then she made me wait two more before she finally said, 'It's your office, that's what. Someone's paid you a visit in the night.'

Wednesday

1

Ten minutes later I parked up behind Crowburn House and walked in through the door which separated the outer from the inner yard. I could see that the back door to the flat stood open, so I climbed the few steps into the scullery and called out, 'It's only me!'

My uncle's voice answered from the kitchen, 'Sam! Come in. Cup of tea?' I found him sitting at the old drop-leaf table amongst the remains of what must have been a substantial breakfast. It was not difficult to see why Uncle Fred tended to put on weight, though in fairness this was as much the result of enforced lack of mobility as of over-indulgence. A motorbike accident before the war had left him with damaged knees, and as time passed both legs had become increasingly arthritic.

'Morning, Uncle Fred. Yeah, I'd love one. I didn't bother with breakfast, came straight here.'

The third cup and saucer already stood in place, and Uncle Fred now poured the tea. It had always been left to my uncle to provide a welcome in the household. He was heaping a second spoon with sugar when I said, 'No thanks, just the one. I'm trying to cut down.'

'Whatever for? You're built like a whippet, always have been.' I took a little fold of belly in my hand to show him, but he frowned dismissively. 'That's nothing, just puppy fat. If you ask me there's a lot of nonsense talked about health nowadays. A little of what you fancy does you good. How about a couple of eggs? It won't take me a minute.' And he began to push back his chair.

'No thanks, Uncle Fred, I'd best get on and see Aunt Winnie. What's this all about?'

He shook his head. 'A rum affair. She can tell you herself, I think she's in the reception office. Come and see me when you're done.'

Pleasingly, a literal green baize door separated the private space of the flat from the office hallway beyond. I can remember stroking the soft material when I was a child and wondering why on earth anyone would want to cover a door in cloth. Now I walked on down the hallway and turned into the front office, pursuing a powerful smell of beeswax and lavender.

Aunt Winnie, resplendent in a floral housecoat, stood on the far side of the mahogany counter, rubbing it impatiently with a yellow duster. She stopped and looked up as soon as she saw me, and I knew at once that she was not in her sunniest frame of mind. She said, 'Oh – it's you.'

'Yes. You said I should come.'

She turned on me a look of such withering disapproval that for a moment I was a mud-stained schoolboy again. She said, 'You realize we're not used to this sort of thing round here? The Old Man's going to have a fit.'

'Then don't tell him.'

Aunt Winnie regarded me with plain distaste. 'Every inch your mother's son. A fib here, a little white lie there – '

'We can talk about this later. What exactly has happened?'

Disappointment fleetingly crossed Aunt Winnie's pale, pinched face as she realized that her lecture had been cut short. It was replaced by an expression of frigid formality. She lifted the flap to come out from behind the counter, leaving the cloth and polish where they stood. Not saying anything, she brushed past me and went out into the corridor. I followed meekly. We began to mount the stairs, but to my surprise Aunt Winnie stopped at the half landing, outside the toilet door. She said, 'They got in through there.' I went in to take a look while Winnie remained outside.

The lower half of the sash window had been raised to its fullest extent. Beneath it, the rim of the hand basin was faintly marked with black dust, and there was more on the lino beneath that. Winnie said, 'That'll be coal dust. You can see what's happened. He's got in over the yard wall and dropped onto the roof of the coal shed, then as he's come down he's trodden on a few bits of slack.' What we called the coal shed was simply a lean-to with a sloping roof which kept off the worst of the rain.

I said, 'Have you touched anything?'

Aunt Winnie bridled at that. 'Most definitely not. I knew straight away there was something wrong when I saw the window. I always do my rounds at bedtime and I'm positive it was shut last night. I checked downstairs first and all the office doors were locked, so I realized it had to be you they were after. You'd better come and see.' She led the way now up the remaining stairs and along the corridor to my office door. It was open.

'And you found it like this?'

Winnie nodded. 'I'm afraid I did just step in and have a little walk round. It was all so neat and tidy that I couldn't believe anyone had been in here at all. But then I saw the message.' Her eyes went to the typewriter. I'd left it clear, but now a sheet of paper lay against the backrest.

In two seconds I'd crossed the room to go behind the desk. Someone had taken a piece of paper from the drawer, rolled it onto the machine and typed

it might be an idea to keep your mouth shut

about a third of the way down the page.

I took my fingerprinting kit from the file drawer of the desk. Well, I say it was mine, but actually I'd nicked it from work when I was on the force. Thefts from the station were a terrible problem at the time, you could hardly put your tea down but someone had walked off with it, and of course that provided good cover if you happened to take a fancy to some paper-clips yourself. On one occasion, half a dozen office chairs disappeared overnight. I didn't know who'd done it, or how, but they made me proud to be a policeman.

Carefully I brushed powder onto all the likely surfaces, the doorknob, my desk drawers, the typewriter, the filing cabinet. There were no fresh prints, and my own recent prints had been smudged here and there, presumably by someone wearing gloves. It was the same story when I dusted the window-ledge and doorknob in the toilet. Aunt Winnie, silent and watchful, followed me round as I worked. We returned to the office, and I began to check whether anything was missing. I'd left the desk drawers tidy enough by my standards, but it seemed to me that now they were tidier still. Someone had patiently searched through every one. Likewise in the filing cabinet I felt, though I could hardly be certain, that every single document had been examined and then neatly returned to its place. That is, every single document except Martin Berry's file.

Aunt Winnie must have noticed the change in my attitude. 'Well? Is there something missing?'

'One of my case files.' Later I would have to try and think what I might have written that could be so important. 'Have you any idea how they got out?'

'Let themselves out of the front door, calm as you like. The bolts had been thrown back, I didn't spot it at first.'

'So the only locks they had to pick were my office door and the filing cabinet.' Neither of which was in any way sophisticated. I'd bought the filing cabinet from a second-hand shop in Mission St, more for the price than anything else. I could have picked the lock myself.

'I take it you'll call in the police?' Aunt Winnie gave me an odd sideways look as she said this. She'd always known there was some awkwardness between myself and my former employers, but never worked out why.

I said, 'No need for that, Aunt Winnie. They've got what they came for, I'm sure that'll be the end of it.'

Aunt Winnie stiffened. 'The Old Man would want a thorough investigation. There's priceless documents downstairs, we can't have people tramping through the building without so much as a by-your-leave.'

'Everything that matters is shut away in the strongroom, safe as a bank vault. We'll leave the police out of this, if you don't mind.'

The thin line of Aunt Winnie's mouth now thinned still further. 'You're forgetting that this is my home. It gave me a nasty turn when I realized someone had got in.'

'I'm sure they're not remotely interested in you and Uncle Fred.' This had come out less sympathetically than I might have wished, but I carried on. 'Besides, like I say, it's over now. They won't be back.'

I could see Aunt Winnie didn't quite believe this, but she said no more. Not for the first time, I reflected how soundly she always behaved when the chips were down. Less satisfactory aunts would have nagged to know whose file was missing and what the cryptic message was all about, but not Aunt Winnie. True, I've known her to look more fondly at a cockroach in the cutlery drawer than she usually does at me, but fond looks aren't everything.

Back in the kitchen we rejoined Uncle Fred. The newspaper had just been delivered and he laid it aside as we came in. I told him about the missing case file, neglecting to mention that its subject was M. Berry, recently deceased. Then I said, 'I can see how they got up the drainpipe and in through the bathroom window, but how did they manage the yard wall without a ladder? It must be eight or nine feet high.'

Uncle Fred said, 'Perhaps they did have a ladder. Perhaps they came in a van.'

Aunt Winnie said, 'We'd have heard a van pulling up out there, you know what a light sleeper you are.' She turned to me. 'He can never get comfortable in the night. Your uncle's a martyr to his joints.'

'What about a bike, then?'

'Don't be daft, Fred. You can't get a ladder on a bicycle.'

I thought of my little friend the window cleaner, but Uncle Fred said, 'Not a push-bike, Winnie, a motorbike. He could have pushed it up the drive, then left it against the wall and climbed on the seat.'

I said, 'Back in a tick,' and went out to check the theory. Against the yard wall, time had covered the asphalt in a wide layer of blown dirt in which a few parched weeds now failed to thrive. There were no clear wheel prints, the weather was much too dry for that, but the ground had been freshly disturbed. Uncle Fred could possibly be right.

Having finally accepted Uncle Fred's offer of breakfast, it was a quarter to nine by the time I got back to the flat. I washed and shaved, then picked up the phone and rang the house in Vaughan Close. A voice said, 'Angela Wetherley.'

This threw me slightly as I'd been expecting Monica to answer. I said, 'Yes, hello, my name's Rigby, Sam Rigby. Could I speak to Monica Berry, please?'

'No, you may not. You people are nothing better than ghouls.' She was clearly about to put the phone down.

I said, 'I'm not a journalist, Mrs Wetherley. I knew Martin. I was with him the evening he died.'

Monica's mother was silent for a moment. Then she said, 'And why do you want to speak to Monica? Can't it wait for another time?'

I said, 'I'm a private investigator. Martin Berry was employing me in a – in a particular matter. I should like to tell Mrs Berry about it in person. I'm sure it's what her husband would have wanted.'

'I don't know.' Angela Wetherley considered this in silence again. 'I'm not prepared to have you talk privately with her on the telephone. But if you could come to the house – '

'This morning? Let's say in half an hour?'

'You seem to be in a great hurry. Ten o'clock would be quite early enough. Monica's just trying to eat some breakfast.'

'I'm sorry, yes, of course. Ten it is, then.'

'You have the address?'

'Yes.'

'Then we'll see you in an hour's time.' She rang off.

Before leaving the flat I tried to smarten myself up a bit. While it seemed unlikely that Angela Wetherley and I would ever become bosom pals, I thought it could do no harm to present a respectable exterior. I even considered donning my all-purpose suit and got as far as laying it out on the bed. But then I remembered how alien and self-conscious it always makes me feel, not to mention the fact that I could hardly breathe in it because the waist needed letting out. Shoving it back into the chaos of the wardrobe, I changed into a white shirt and brown cord trousers, combed my hair, grabbed the leather jacket and headed down to the street.

The speed limit on the coast road is fifty miles an hour, and when I noticed the needle touching seventy I realized that my haste demon must be driving the car instead of me. At this rate I'd be half an hour early reaching Vaughan Close. I tut-tutted at this latest display of Rigby neurosis and lightened my touch on the pedal. It was all anxiety, of course. I was anxious about talking to Monica, and when I get anxious I rush in with guns blazing and speech set to automatic. I needed to get a grip on myself, so when I came to the boating lake I pulled over onto the verge, switched off the engine, took a few deep breaths and thought back over the morning's events.

What puzzled me most was that my office intruder had removed Martin's file. Overnight I'd been clear in my mind that Martin's death had something to do with this business at the Empire cinema, and at first the break-in seemed to confirm that. Martin was in possession of damning evidence of some kind. The murderer had expected to find it on Monday night, but failed. Going through Martin's things, he or she had discovered my business card in the wallet, as well as the stub of a cheque in my name, and concluded that Martin had given the evidence to me for safe keeping. Hence the unwelcome visit to my office, preceded by a quick silent phone call to the flat to make sure that I was out of the way.

But then, why take Martin's file? When I'd written my account of our meeting, I'd made no mention of the Empire. Instead, it was all about Martin's suspicions, all about Danny Craven and Rupert Heysham. Then the message: *it might be an idea to keep your mouth shut.* Perhaps it wasn't about the Empire after all, perhaps Martin had been right all along: Monica was having an affair, and her lover had killed him.

I looked at my watch. It was still too soon to be moving on. I wanted to get the interview over and done with, because my history with women like Monica was not good. From Martin's story I'd concluded that she was just the sort of high-maintenance female who presses my buttons, shallow, materialistic, cold. If you once get ensnared with a Monica you're well and truly up shit creek, since the only act more recklessly expensive than marrying such a woman is divorcing her. But I needed answers from Monica Berry, so I would have to suppress my personal feelings and concentrate on the job.

The minutes passed. I drove the few hundred yards to Vaughan Close, parked outside number five and rang the doorbell. I could see a figure approaching on the other side of the glass, and Monica's mother opened the door.

I said, 'Sam Rigby,' and held out my hand. Mrs Wetherley took it for a moment in her own cold, limp hand and then let it go.

'Come through, please, Mr Rigby. I've told Monica what this is about.' It was the same voice of quiet authority she'd used with the chauffeur the day before. I followed her down the narrow hallway. The pale trouser suit of yesterday had been replaced by a blouse and calf-length skirt. The kitchen lay ahead of us, but now we turned right into the back room, from which an extension with large windows jutted out into the garden. This must be the famous sun room which had brought Danny Craven into the house, and the sun's rays were just beginning to penetrate its southerly aspect. A door stood open, letting in fresh garden air. The whole room was cheerful and modern, with a light patterned wallpaper and Scandinavian-style furniture. On the cream-upholstered settee a small, slim woman with blonde hair fringing her face sat hunched against cushions, her bare feet drawn up beneath her.

Angela Wetherley said, 'Monica, here's Mr Rigby come to see you.'

Monica's eyes rose very briefly to mine, then she looked down at her hands again. The eyes were red from crying. So was her nose. One end of a handkerchief protruded slightly from her clenched fist.

My intuition kicked in again. This picture of abject grief was not the Monica I'd been expecting. And if I'd got Monica wrong, perhaps I'd got everything else wrong too.

Mrs Wetherley said, 'Can I get you a cup of tea, Mr Rigby?'

What I really wanted was a cigarette, but there were no ashtrays visible. I said, 'Thanks, that would be good.'

She was studying my face with interest. She said, 'Have we met somewhere before?'

I'd been afraid of this. It was less than twenty-four hours since she'd seen me in the street talking to Gerry Gibbs. But I was pretty sure she hadn't looked at me very closely then, and besides, I'd been wearing an oily vest, a greasy cap squashed down over my forehead and half a hundredweight of unspecified facial muck. I opted for stout denial. 'I don't think so, Mrs Wetherley, no. Unless you were at the Holy Trinity Bring and Buy last weekend?' She expressed her contempt for this suggestion by walking off into the kitchen without a word. When the sun room was added, a new kitchen doorway had been cut through, and with the door left open she would be able to hear anything that was said while she worked.

Left alone with Monica I couldn't think what to say. After an awkward couple of moments she said, 'Do sit down if you want.'

I lowered myself into an easy chair more smart than it was comfortable. There was another brief silence, then I said, 'I'm very sorry about your husband.'

Monica began to cry. This was no major outburst of grief, just a slow leaking of tears, but even so she seemed uncomfortable to show her feelings like this in front of a stranger. She dabbed at her eyes with the linen handkerchief and fought to regain control. After a while she said, 'Just like Martin to get himself killed.'

'Why do you say that?'

'He was never the world's luckiest person. Problems right from the beginning. Then look who he goes and chooses for a wife.'

I risked saying, 'I think you made Martin very happy.'

Her eyes went to mine again, but held the gaze now. 'Did I?' She looked away and shook her head. 'Perhaps you think you're being kind, but I know what I know.'

Now Monica's mother returned and set the tray of tea things down on a side table. She said, 'So, Mr Rigby, you say Martin was employing you?'

'That's right. Somehow he'd got it into his head that he was being followed.'

'Followed? How very bizarre.'

'To be honest, I was sceptical. It seemed out of kilter with what he told me of his life.'

Mrs Wetherley said, 'I do believe you're right. The idea seems ridiculous. Martin wasn't exactly one of life's players, was he, Monica? In a room full of people he'd be the last you'd pick out.'

I wondered how that speech had gone down with Monica, but she remained silent. I said, 'Still, perhaps events have borne him out. Perhaps there was someone on his tail after all.'

'And you've spoken to the police about this?'

'Yes, of course. I went in as soon as I heard what had happened.'

'How was he?' Monica had looked up again, her large grey eyes still bright with tears. 'Mother said you were with him on Monday evening. How did he seem?'

This wasn't the easiest of questions to answer in the circumstances. I said, 'He was – well, he was concerned. Concerned for your safety, more than anything. He wanted to be sure you were in no danger.'

'Were you with him for long?'

'Well – yes, quite a long time. We went over most aspects of his life trying to work out who might want to have him followed.'

'Then I suppose you were the last person – ' The voice cracked and broke off.

Uncomfortable with her daughter's grief, Mrs Wetherley poured tea. 'Sugar, Mr Rigby?'

'Just one, please.' I took the cup from her then and sipped the hot tea while Monica calmed herself. Then I said, 'Martin was fine that evening. It was a business meeting, that's all. I'm sorry if that brings you no comfort, but that's just how it was. You'd have heard about it from the police eventually but I wanted to tell you myself, it seemed the right thing to do.'

Monica said, 'If only I hadn't gone to Manchester.'

Mrs Wetherley now handed tea to her. 'You mustn't blame yourself.'

I said, 'Martin told me you were staying with a friend.' Monica nodded, without looking up. I went on, 'Leah, isn't it?'

Hearing the name, Monica now looked at me, and I thought she was searching for something in my expression. She said, 'Yes, Leah.' I found that I didn't believe her.

I decided to push a little. 'How did you learn what had happened?'

Angela Wetherley put down the cup which had been on its way towards her mouth and said, 'Must you ask questions, Mr Rigby? We've had enough of that from the police.'

I smiled. 'Habit, I'm sorry. I used to be on the force myself.'

Monica said, 'I couldn't sleep. Leah has this truckle bed that she puts up when I stay – it's a tiny flat, a bedsit really, she hasn't got much money.'

Mrs Wetherley turned to me. 'Leah Armstrong would do anything for Monica. They've been close since they were girls, university together and everything.'

'So at – I don't know – about five or six in the morning I decided to get up and drive home. There was no traffic, I was back here long before eight o'clock. And Martin wasn't here. Normally he doesn't set off for the station until twenty past. And his bed hadn't been slept in, I didn't know what to think. I even started to wonder – but then the police came. At first they said Martin had had an accident. Then a different man came along, more senior, Harper I think his name is – '

I said, 'That would be DI Hargreaves. One of our best people. I consider him a personal friend.'

'And he said it wasn't an accident at all, it was – it was murder.'

Out in the hallway the telephone rang, and Angela Wetherley stood up immediately. 'I expect that's the police now. That nice DC Howell told us he'd call this morning and let us know what's happening.' She left the room.

I looked towards the open garden door and said, 'I believe Martin had dug a vegetable patch out there?'

For the first time, a tentative smile lit Monica's tired face. 'He told you about that? It was one of his enthusiasms. To see him out there hoeing or weeding, it was like he was a boy again.'

'Mind if I take a look?'

'Of course not. I'll come out with you, I could do with the air.' She slipped her slender feet into a pair of white sandals and led the way into the garden.

There was still a great deal to be done. A few young shrubs stood at intervals around the perimeter, and a central area had been turfed, though the dry summer had burned off much of the grass. But just as Martin had said, there were vegetables. I'd expected neat rows of carrot tops, but instead a bewildering confusion of interplanted vegetables occupied three raised beds on the north side of the garden. Monica must have seen my expression because she said, 'Martin was never very systematic. He just stuck things in any old how.'

'They seem to like it just the same.'

'He had the gift, Mr Rigby. He loved his plants.'

'Call me Sam, won't you.' Just then I noticed Eusebio curled up amongst the cabbages. I said, 'Your cat?'

Monica nodded. 'He won't eat anything since it happened. Just looks at his dish and walks away.'

I glanced towards the house. Mrs Wetherley must still be on the telephone. I said, 'Monica – I'm sorry, is it all right to call you Monica? I feel like I know you already.'

'Just don't try calling my mother Angela, that's all.' And again she smiled.

'The thing is – I want to try and help the police find whoever did this terrible thing to Martin. I was with him in the last hours of his life, I can't help feeling involved. But I don't want to do this without your backing.'

Monica was thoughtful. She took a few steps away from me and stood in silence. Then she turned. 'Do you need money? I don't suppose you make a fortune doing what you do.'

'Is it that obvious? I'll have you know these are my best trousers.'

Monica smiled again. Her cheeks dimpled slightly when she smiled. I was catching glimpses now of the normal, everyday Monica, the Monica whose husband hadn't just been murdered. She said, 'We've got money – the Wetherleys, I mean. Whatever the bill, we'll pay it. Just find the person – ' She turned away.

After a few moments I crossed the dry lawn and stood close to her. I said, 'There's something I haven't told the police. I don't want them to get the idea that Martin was involved in anything dubious.'

She turned sharply. 'You think he was?'

'No, no, of course not. The point is, his briefcase has disappeared, and that could be crucial. I'm hoping that before going to the boating lake he called in and left it here.'

Monica frowned. 'I'm sure I would have seen it. Let me check upstairs.' And she as good as ran indoors. It looked as if she was glad to have something constructive to do after the hours spent sitting around.

It was not Monica but her mother who came out into the garden next. I said, 'We've been studying Martin's vegetable patch.'

'Apparently his father has an allotment. Not the sort of thing I know very much about.'

'Have you spoken to his parents?'

'I rang Mrs Berry yesterday. They're rather odd people, Mr

Rigby. To be honest I don't think she'd quite understood what had happened, she kept speaking of Martin as if he was still alive. But then, they're religious. Methodists, or something like that.' She was silent for a few seconds, looking with faint distaste at the results of Martin's labours in the vegetable bed. Then she said, 'Did you know that Martin and his sister were adopted? Chalk and cheese, as it happens, you'd know straight off that they weren't related by blood. Grace was at Manchester University with Monica, they were both reading Psychology. That's how she came to meet Martin.'

'I'd wondered about that.'

'You know – we were never quite sure he was right for her, Walter and I. Monica had had a more suitable offer but to our disappointment she turned him down.'

'From whom?' Evidently in Mrs Wetherley's presence my grammar was on its best behaviour.

'A lovely man named Rupert Heysham. He'd been her tutor at Manchester, still quite young really and very ambitious. Oh, don't get me wrong, Martin was pleasant enough, but he didn't have much about him.' I made no comment, but perhaps I made it pointedly because she said, 'You must think I'm heartless to be talking this way, with Martin lying dead, but we just wanted the best for Monica. Do you have children yourself, Mr Rigby?' I said I didn't. 'Well if you had you would understand. And with Monica being an only child – '

Monica herself now appeared in the doorway. 'There's no sign of it anywhere, I'm afraid. Mother, you've not seen Martin's briefcase lying around, have you?'

'I'm sorry, dear, no.'

I said, 'Not to worry, I'm sure it'll turn up. The other thing is, would you happen to have a photograph of Martin which you could spare?'

Mrs Wetherley said, 'But we've already given a photograph to the police.'

'Mother, Sam's going to help the police with the investigation.'

I said, 'That's right. And you know how a photograph can jog people's memories.'

'Come in here again and I'll see if I can find you one.' Monica disappeared, and I followed Mrs Wetherley back indoors. Monica had opened the drawer of the console table and was rummaging. 'I think there's a spare set of the wedding photos. Yes, here we are. I don't see any of Martin on his own, though.'

Mrs Wetherley said, 'Nobody wants to see the groom at a wedding.'

'Mother!'

'Well, it's true. Men get in the way so. Imagine if your father was at home all the time, I'd never get anything done.'

Monica said, 'You don't do much as it is.'

'Really, Monica, what a thing to say.' Mrs Wetherley turned to me. 'I'm afraid we've rather spoiled our daughter, Mr Rigby. Far too much letting her have her own way.'

'Oh, Mother, don't be so frosty, you know I don't mean anything by it. And I don't know what I'd have done without you this last twenty-four hours.' She planted a girlish kiss on her mother's powdered cheek, which bent towards her to receive it. Then she handed me one of the photographs. 'How about this one? I look like I'm about to be sick, but it's really good of Martin.'

And it was. The happy couple posed conventionally enough in front of the church lych gate. Monica's smile seemed strained, but the man at her side had been captured for all time in a moment of unmixed joy, his broad, handsome face cut across with a smile so vital and immediate that with a sudden stab I found it impossible to believe that he was dead. I still felt the heat from his shoulder as we sat hip against hip on the old settee in my flat. I still felt the touch of his finger on my nose.

Mrs Wetherley said, 'Are you all right, Mr Rigby?'

'Yes – yes, of course. Thank you, this will do very well. Was that the police on the phone just now? Any developments?'

'Apparently Martin was seen speaking with someone on the train that night. They're trying to put together one of those pictures – oh, what do you call them, now?'

'Identikit?'

'That's right. They'll bring it to show us later.'

I dug in my jacket for the business cards, going straight to the correct pocket on this occasion, and gave one to Monica. 'Let me know if you think of anything, or if that briefcase turns up.'

She nodded, and Mrs Wetherley said, 'It was very good of you to call round.'

Monica said, 'I'll go crazy if I sit here any longer. Mother, can we take a walk up to the beach, like we did yesterday?'

'Of course, dear. I'll just see Mr Rigby out.'

I was surprised when Monica's mother followed me out to the Cortina. As I unlocked the door she said, her voice even lower than usual, 'If I were you, Mr Rigby, I'd make a start with Martin's family. I wouldn't want Monica to know it, but there's something I really dislike about those people.'

Like I said, Angela Wetherley was by no means a high-decibel individual, but you don't need a foghorn voice to make your opinions clear. If Monica hadn't realized long ago that her mother looked askance at the Berrys, she was a simpler soul than I took her for. I said, 'Surely you're not suggesting they had something to do with Martin's death?'

Mrs Wetherley pursed her lips. She wanted to say yes, I could see it. 'Not directly, of course. But if there are no secrets boiling away in that family then my name's Zsa Zsa Gabor.' She turned and went back into the house.

In the car I slipped the wedding photograph into the glove compartment, though to make room for it I had to empty various items of junk into the footwell. Then I lit a cigarette and fired up the engine. My mind was turning over too. How could I square the young woman I'd just met with the portrait Martin had painted? And more to the point, if Monica hadn't been with her friend Leah on Monday night – where was she?

2

I drove inland on Beach Road, crossed the railway line by the station and managed to find a parking space on Station Parade, in the heart of Otterdale village. The eight or ten shops in the parade served most of the community's needs, and there was even one of those apparently deserted dress shops, essential to all such parades throughout Southaven's suburbs, selling idiosyncratic clothing for the fuller figure. In the newsagents I bought a packet of cigarettes and a new lighter, since my old one was playing up. Then I crossed to the telephone box which stood at the kerb outside the butcher's. Armed with a supply of loose change, I stepped into the box and lit a cigarette.

If you are a smoker yourself you will already know that it's physically impossible to enter a call box without lighting up. The evidence lay on the filthy floor all around my feet, and someone had even left a neat line of roll-up butts on the chest-high metal shelf kindly provided by the GPO. I stood my fags and lighter on the shelf next to them, and put through a call to Mark Howell. Before connecting me, the girl on reception asked for my name. I said, 'Bunbury – Ernest Bunbury.' It was the name I always used if I needed to speak to Mark at work.

While I waited for an answer from Mark's extension in CID, my nose detected evidence of another obligatory call box activity. There was a public toilet fifty yards away across the street, but perhaps only the most rigidly conventional locals used it while the free spirits all pissed in here.

There was a click and, amazingly, the man himself came on the line. He said, 'What do you want?' If he was pleased to hear from me, he disguised it well.

I said, 'Can you talk, or has this got to be a Bunbury call?'

'There's no-one around, I can talk. I'm just not particularly sure that I want to.'

'Because you're busy?'

'No, because I'm employed, and I'd like to keep it that way.'

'Ah, the old paranoia. Anyway, Mark, I'd love to stand here making idle chit-chat but I've got things to do. Why haven't you got an officer keeping an eye on the Berrys' house?'

He said, 'Should we have?'

I said, 'How can you be sure Monica Berry isn't in danger?'

He thought about that for a moment. Through the narrow glass panes I watched as a train from Southaven pulled into the station. Then Mark said, 'Do you know something we don't?'

Was this the time to come clean about the briefcase? I knew now that it wasn't at Vaughan Close, but the murderer didn't, and he or she had already come looking for it at my office, or else for the documents it had contained. Vaughan Close could be next on the list, and if they'd killed once to get what they were after why should they not kill again? I said, 'I just don't understand why you're not concerned for Monica's safety.'

Again there was a brief silence. A very fat woman in a blue work coat was now loitering outside, waiting to use the phone. Mark said, 'You've been out and talked to her, haven't you?'

'Possibly.'

'For God's sake, Sam, Hargreaves'll do his nut if he finds out!'

'Were you thinking of telling him or shall I? Which reminds me, how's he getting on? Any leads? I hear Martin was seen talking to someone that night.' The woman in blue rapped impatiently on the glass with her knuckles. She wore very thick glasses, and I found myself wondering whether she was diabetic. I turned my back on her in time to see the last carriage of the train just disappearing as it pulled away from the platform. A few passengers were filing out onto Beach Road.

Mark said, 'If you're so well-informed, why are you pestering me? Apparently Martin was with someone on the train, they got off together. Witness is coming in this afternoon to do an Identikit, if we're lucky we'll get it on TV tonight.'

'Fast work.'

'Trouble is, it's all we've got. The station staff at Otterdale didn't notice anything – they said they look at the ticket, not the person.'

'Still nothing from house to house?' Another rap on the glass.

'Not really. But a woman in Vaughan Close did say she saw – '

At that point the pips went, and I had to shove in another coin. 'Hello? Mark? You've not sneaked off, have you?'

'Now why would I do that?'

'Because when it comes to sneaking off you hold the UK and Commonwealth record. Especially at four o'clock in the morning. What did she see, this woman?'

'Well, she wasn't sure if it was Monday night or not, but she thinks there was an unfamiliar car parked in the street, a red Mini. No registration, of course.'

Rap rap rap. I said, 'Not much to go on. Oh, and did you check out Monica's alibi?'

'Alibi? You think she's a suspect?'

'Since you ask, I don't think she'd hurt a fly. But sentiment doesn't exactly weigh heavy in the Hargreaves Method, so did you check it or not?' Rap rap rap again. Honestly, some people.

'Yes, we rang that friend of hers in Manchester, Leah Armstrong. She said Monica was with her all night, left about six in the morning. Come on now, Sam, level with me. You wouldn't be asking if you weren't onto something.'

'Sorry, Mark, got to go now.' And I stubbed my cigarette out amongst the butts on the metal shelf. I'd disturbed their neat arrangement, but then that's the sort of thing I do.

'This isn't fair! You grill me for information but you give me absolutely nothing back.'

I said, 'Shocking, isn't it. But then, how can I? Hargreaves has forbidden me from coming anywhere near this case, so naturally I have no information to share.'

Mark said, 'You know what you are, don't you?'

I said, 'Love you too,' but he'd already rung off.

Picking up the cigarettes and lighter, I swung open the call box door and stepped out. To my astonishment the large blue woman indignantly exclaimed, 'You again! I might have known.'

As best I could with the cigarettes in one hand, I held up open palms and said, 'Not guilty, I'm afraid,' then left the woman staring after me as I strolled off. Danny Craven's yard was only a few minutes' walk away so there was no point in taking the Cortina. As I walked, I thought about Leah Armstrong. Perhaps I should ask Monica for the number and call her myself. On the other hand I knew from personal experience that people are much more comfortable telling porkies on the telephone than when you're fixing them with a steely gaze. A little trip to Manchester might be required. If necessary I could try and talk to Rupert Heysham at the same time.

The Otterdale Industrial Estate was a modest development of no more than half a dozen businesses, with the result that the site map at the entrance made less than essential reading. At the second lot I came to, a flaking board on the tall wire fence announced this as the home of H Craven and Son, Building Contractor. I stepped through the wide gateway into the yard. A rough wooden workshop-cum-office backed onto the fence opposite, with the railway running on a high embankment at the rear. The tired old van I'd seen in Vaughan Close was parked in front of the open workshop doors, rusting where it stood. I assumed that it was Danny Craven who, stripped to the waist in the midday heat and with his back to me, was now shovelling sand into sacks from a large pile in the corner of the yard. He was a slim, athletic-looking man in his mid-twenties, his skin bronzed by the sun, his dark brown hair much shorter than the current fashion. Silent, I watched him working for a couple of minutes, until he turned, leaned on the shovel and said, 'Enjoying yourself, are you?'

I said, 'You know you can get that stuff pre-bagged.'

He said, 'Buy it in bulk, bag it yourself, half the price.' His eyes narrowed. 'If you've come from Braithwaite, you can tell him he'll have his money soon.' The eyes narrowed further. 'Or are you a cop?'

I crossed the yard towards him, playing the old game of trying each pocket in turn until I found the business cards, right where I'd

left them. I handed one to him and he studied it. Sweat gleamed on
his torso. He smelled of hard work. Then he made to hand the card
back to me, but I said, 'Keep it. Fold them twice, they stop sash
windows rattling. Works every time.'

'Is there something you wanted? I don't recall sending for a
private detective and I've got work to do.' If this was his attitude
with customers too, no wonder business was bad.

I said, 'Do you always wear gloves to shovel sand?'

'I get blisters.'

'Unpleasant for you, given that you're a builder.'

'You'll find the way out is right behind you.'

I was beginning to sense that Danny Craven and I might be
getting off on the wrong foot. Admittedly he hadn't given me much
encouragement, but what on earth had become of the famous
Rigby charm? Then I found myself trying really hard not to look
down at Danny's chest, smooth, brown, trickling with streams of
sweat. It wasn't just work he smelled of, he smelled of sex, but I
suspected that if I made some move to touch him, even the first
hint of a move, a gloved fist would land right in my face. I said, 'I
believe you knew Martin Berry.' He didn't speak, so I went on. 'I
understand you're also friendly with his wife.'

Perhaps it was my tone of voice, but even the deep tan could
not hide the fact that Danny Craven now flushed right to his ears. I
felt a moment's anxiety about the gloved fist. I was taller than
Danny, and heavier, and I knew I could take him if necessary. In
fact, a nice little scrap in the sunshine might be just what was
needed to ease the tension between us. But still, provoked or not,
Danny said nothing.

I said, 'You do realize that Martin Berry has been murdered?'

Immediately he looked away from me. When he looked back he
said, 'Have you seen Monica? Is she all right?'

'Why don't you go round and ask her yourself?'

Again he looked away, right down at the ground this time. His
expression had softened a little. 'Might not be welcome.'

'But you have been round, haven't you, or tried to? You were in
Vaughan Close on Tuesday morning.'

Danny looked up. 'How do you know that?'

'I know a lot of things, Danny. For starters, I know Braithwaite
won't be getting his money next week, or next month, either. And
he doesn't like waiting, does he?' Naturally I hadn't the faintest idea
who Braithwaite was, but I can make educated guesses just as well

as the next man. I needed some sort of leverage with Danny Craven if he was going to open up to me.

He said, 'Have you been nosing around in my business?'

'So what exactly were you doing in Vaughan Close?' But Danny made no attempt to reply. His jaw had tightened, and his pectoral muscles kept tensing and relaxing beneath his skin. I moved a little away from him and began to look around, making myself at home. 'Had this yard for long?'

'My dad took it ten years ago, when the estate first opened.'

'Be a shame if you had to give it up for any reason.' I looked in through the workshop doors. 'That's a nice-looking bike. Enfield?'

'BSA. Was my dad's.'

'You'd get a few quid for that, I should think.'

'It's not for sale.'

'Using it yourself now?' Again he didn't answer. Resting the shovel against his leg, he removed the left glove and scratched his chest just above the right nipple, leaving a livid streak amongst the golden brown. He replaced the glove, and I moved closer to him. His eyes had followed me at every step, alert, watchful. I said, 'What you have to realize, Danny, is that it will all come out eventually. A man turns up dead, skull bashed in, your name is linked to his wife's. Believe me, the cops will be paying you a little visit any time now, and they will push until they get answers. You could think of this as a rehearsal, a chance to get your story straight.'

'I haven't done anything wrong.'

'There you go, you see – perfect example. You're going to need much better lines than that if you don't want to find yourself spending time with the Queen. Tell me about you and Martin Berry. When did you last see him?'

'I don't have to answer your questions.'

'Danny, Danny – ' I felt my arm wanting to move, to give his shoulder a reassuring caress, perhaps, or just to circle around the slender waist. 'You're still not getting it, are you? I'm your friend, Danny. Use me as a dummy run for the real thing. I should warn you, there's a cop in charge of this investigation who eats people like you as a snack between meals. So let's try again – when did you last see Martin Berry?'

Thought now took place in Danny Craven's brain. He was used to working his body at full stretch, and it had grown strong and supple in response. The same could not be said of his brain. Effort contorted his brow. Finally he said, 'Two or three weeks ago. A few of the lads from the footie club had a kickabout.'

I nodded thoughtfully, as if I might be prepared to accept this. Then I said, 'So you didn't see him one lunchtime last week when you were round visiting Monica?'

More thought. Despite the bags of sand, I was willing to bet this was the hardest Danny had worked all day, and for the first time I felt something like sympathy towards him. He said, 'You're right, I'd forgotten.'

'Now – Danny – I don't like to carp or cavil, but I'm afraid I've shot one past you there without you even noticing.' He looked blank, so I continued. 'What you should have said was, that you weren't actually visiting Monica, you simply wanted to check that the foundations of the new extension hadn't subsided in the exceptionally dry weather we've been having. If you say you were visiting another man's wife, what are people going to think?'

Again, Danny coloured a little at that, but he didn't speak.

I said, 'Are you having an affair with Monica Berry?'

'No!' The word exploded from him, and his eyes flamed.

'Why should I believe you?'

'Ask her! Ask Monica! We're just – '

I said, 'Good friends?' And I may have injected poison as I said it.

'You don't know anything about it.'

My hand went to my chin as an aid to concentration. I was getting frustrated, though whether it was the straight bat Danny was playing or the fact that he had 'don't touch' tattooed on his forehead I couldn't be sure. It seemed as if Monica had brought out in him some unaccustomed mode of behaviour. He was suffering, for her sake. Yes, that was it: chivalry. Monica was his lady, Danny Craven her parfait gentil knight. I glanced around me for a moment, but this really was Otterdale Industrial Estate in 1970. I'd stumbled on a latter-day Lancelot and Guinevere, so Martin must have the role of –

I said, 'Were you and Arthur good friends?'

'Who the hell's Arthur?'

'Martin, I mean, you and Martin. Did you like him?'

Danny's eyes wandered as he struggled to reply. 'He was all right, I suppose.'

'Just "all right"? But didn't he make sure you got that building work when you needed it? I'm surprised you're not more grateful.'

The word made him look straight at me again. 'Grateful?'

'Yes. When someone shows you a kindness – '

'They've got you right where they want you. That's how it works, isn't it? They think they can ask for something back.'

I didn't understand. I said, 'Did Martin ask for something back?'

He hesitated, just for a moment. My intuition stirred in its cave, I heard that hum of the uncanny which presages a breakthrough. But then Danny Craven turned, lifted the shovel, and plunged it hard into the soft sand. He tipped the load into the sack which he'd been filling when I arrived, then dug the shovel in again. I said, 'Danny?'

Without turning he said, 'Fuck off.' The interview was over.

I couldn't see much point in standing there watching Danny's back as he worked, so I said 'Call me if you want to talk.' A waste of breath, obviously. I've known chattier breeze blocks than Danny Craven. I left him to his shovelling and quit the scene.

By now it was past one o'clock, and civilised people throughout the town were sitting down to a spot of lunch. I opted for a cheese and pickle roll in the Lancaster, washed down by a pint of the gassy substance which the Lanky passes off as beer. The juke box, like every juke box everywhere, was playing Mungo Jerry, but you couldn't really complain; after all, last summer it had been *My Way*. While drinking I also smoked about a hundred cigarettes, convinced that they would trigger a light-bulb moment. I knew Danny Craven fitted somewhere in the picture of Martin's death but where, how, why? Fag followed fag, my chest tightened, my lungs screamed, and still I had no answers.

I drove back to Crowburn House and parked around the back. I could hear Uncle Fred mowing the lawn on the far side of the building. Bypassing the flat, I ran up to my office and set myself to work retyping my notes of the evening I'd spent with Martin Berry. But this time it was different, this time I knew that he was dead. Instead of giving a rough outline with a few names, I put down just about everything I could remember, what Martin said, what he drank, how he looked, the visit to my flat, everything. With my words I tried to make Martin live again, and it took time. When I'd done I looked over every line searching for something new, something I'd been missing. But it was the familiar problem of the mind against itself. The tracks are laid down already, you see only what you've seen before. Or worse, you see what you want to see. Disgusted with myself, I locked up and went home.

As I drove up to Leigh Terrace, a car was just pulling away from the kerb, leaving a generous space right outside my building. Thus the gods mock us with favours we don't need. I'd happily have walked any distance in exchange for a lead in the case, but no help came, and I fancied I heard the merry tinkle of divine laughter as they looked down on my cack-handed efforts.

But then, as I was hauling myself up the stairs and wondering if someone hadn't added an extra storey to the building while I was out, an idea of sorts did occur to me. I'd been obsessing about Danny Craven's gloves. The fist which had left Martin Berry with cuts to his face would probably be marked itself – bruised, scuffed, even cut right open. Because of the gloves I'd been unable to see Danny's hands, except briefly when he'd removed the left glove to scratch his chest. But now I realized that the one photograph I'd taken of Danny in Vaughan Close, and which had disappointed because it didn't show his face, had caught something far more important – his right arm and hand.

Taking the remaining stairs by twos, I let myself into the flat and turned into the kitchen, where the three prints I'd pegged up the night before still hung above the sink. Pulling down the photograph of Danny's van, I took it to the gable window in the living room where late afternoon sunlight poured in. As photographs go, it wasn't exactly a competition-winner. The judges would have marked it down for sloppy composition and poor focus. But still there was focus enough to make out some line, some bump, which disturbed the smoothness of Danny's knuckles and showed pale against the darker skin. There was a sticking-plaster on Danny Craven's hand, right where a swinging fist would meet a stubbled chin.

Suddenly I remembered the witness, the Identikit picture. Mark had said they would try to get it on the TV news this evening, but it was now five past six, I'd already missed the first few minutes of the local bulletin. With luck, something major would have happened to knock mere murder down the running order. I crossed to switch on the TV. The set was meant to be portable – I'd had fantasies of watching TV in bed – but in fact it weighed a ton, so I rarely shifted it from its perch on top of two carefully equalized piles of books. The drawback was that this effectively placed all those books beyond use, it being far too much hassle to move the TV, dig them out, then put them back again afterwards. Unfortunately I'd included a half-read copy of *Ulysses*, so now I might never find out who'd done it.

After a few seconds the set warmed up and some kind of picture graced the screen. As usual, every single one of the six hundred and twenty-five lines appeared to be suffering its own unique malfunction. I grabbed the aerial from on top of the set and carried it to the window, hoping for a clearer signal from the Winter Hill transmitter. Matters improved, but not enough. I opened the window and held the aerial outside. Bingo – a serviceable picture, marred only by the consideration that I was now watching it side on. Jamming the cable beneath the lowered window, I moved back into the room just in time to see a woman with big hair reminding us of the need to conserve water. It looked as if I must have missed the update on the police investigation, but I waited for the next story just in case. When it came, it featured two schoolgirls from Blackburn who'd decided to raise money for the RSPCA by doing a sponsored knit. Clearly it was a heavy evening for local news. Weariness overcame me, my eyelids drooped. It had been a long time since my early morning call from Aunt Winnie, and I seemed to have done a lot of running around for nothing. I needed rest. Sleep stole over me, sweet, soothing sleep.

'Police have issued this Identikit picture of a man seen talking with the victim on Monday night, shortly before he was killed. He is described as in his twenties, above average height, and slim with dark brown hair...' By now I was wide awake, eyes fixed on the screen. Up came the Identikit. It was a head Dr Frankenstein himself might have balked at. No human in the entire history of the species had ever sported such ill-stitched features. Yet somehow it did the job. Though what we saw was a travesty, it was surely a travesty of the face of Danny Craven.

I tried to heave myself off the settee but it sucked me back. At the second attempt I broke free, switched off the television, picked up the car keys and the leather jacket, and made for the door.

Eight minutes later I was out on the coast road again, flooring the throttle. The disquieting rattle had switched to the offside now but I tried to ignore it. If I could see that Danny Craven was the subject of the Identikit, then so could anyone else. I wanted to get to him before the police did. He'd lied to me. He'd travelled with Martin Berry on the train from Southaven, got off at Otterdale with him, and then somehow got into a fight which had led to Martin's death. That had to be the story. I knew that Martin was angry with Danny and could easily have started the fight himself. What I didn't understand was, why the boating lake? Why would Martin have stripped off for a swim? And what on earth had become of the briefcase? I needed answers, and this time I wasn't going to be fobbed off.

Danny's home address was in one of the older residential streets in Otterdale, off Beach Road and inland of the railway station. It formed one end of a modest terrace, and even without the number I could have picked it out from among the rest because like all builders' homes it stood sadly in need of loving care. There was no sign of any police presence outside, and I strode quickly up the short pathway and hammered on the door. A doorbell at the side had been taped over, some time ago by the look of it, since the tape itself now needed replacing. There was no answer. Again I thumped hard on the door, then leaned down and called 'Danny!' through the rusting letter box. When this brought no result, I tried peering in through the small bay window to my right, and was heartened to discover that Danny's approach to housekeeping closely resembled my own. He was clearly not the sort to waste energy by putting things away after he'd used them, and quite right too. There's always the chance that you might want to use them again some time in the next few years.

A woman's voice behind me said, 'You've just missed him, I'm afraid.'

I straightened up. Danny's neighbour had come out onto her front step, a few feet away from me. She was in her mid-forties and of a type which passes for glamorous in Southaven. She looked familiar. I said, 'He's gone out, then?'

She said, 'He didn't so much go as get taken.' She was wearing an extraordinary amount of make-up, given that this was Otterdale village at seven on a Wednesday evening.

'Taken?'

She nodded. 'Police took him ten minutes ago. I expect it was about that kerfuffle on Monday night.' She shook her head. 'I do hope he's not in any trouble. Such a good boy as a rule. Are you a friend of his?'

As usual, I said the first thing that came to mind. 'Football. Otterdale FC. I'm Sam.'

I extended my hand, which the woman shook gently and rather doubtfully. 'Faye, nice to meet you. You look a bit old for football, if you don't mind my saying.'

I did mind, but I said, 'Someone has to make the younger ones look good. What kerfuffle?'

'I beg your pardon?'

'You said there was a kerfuffle on Monday night.'

'Yes, there was. Not like Danny at all, he's normally so quiet, especially since he lost Bert. You knew his father, I expect?' I nodded, and she went on. 'They'd never been right since Vera passed away. Such a lovely woman, they were lost without her. Cancer. And Danny barely in his teens.'

'What time was this?'

'Was what?'

'This kerfuffle.'

'I was just going to bed, so towards midnight I should think. I might not have heard anything from the sitting room but I was on the stairs. It was rather alarming, I'm here on my own, my husband's away at sea and we don't have children. A woman on your own, you feel vulnerable.' Faye patted her hair unconsciously. It was back-combed and sprayed, and when she touched it the whole mass moved at once.

'Did it go on for long?'

'Did what go on for long?'

This was like pulling teeth. Faye had an Olympic capacity for drifting off the point. 'We were talking about the kerfuffle.' It was possible I'd never used the word kerfuffle in my life before, yet now it dominated my vocabulary.

'Not very long, no. There were raised voices, Danny and another man, I couldn't hear what they were saying. Then a lot of noise, like furniture moving, and I think something got broken, there was a crash. Next thing I heard the front door slam and that was that.'

'Do you think they both went out, or just Danny's visitor?'

Faye now gave me a rather wary look and said, 'You're asking an awful lot of questions.'

'Well I'm worried about Danny. Fact is, he owes money to some not very nice people. I was at the yard today, we were talking it through.'

Faye tut-tutted. 'Poor Bert wasn't very industrious but he did at least have a head for business. I'm amazed Danny keeps going at all.'

Suddenly I realized where I'd seen Faye before. I said, 'Just a minute – don't you work on the cosmetics counter at Butterworths?'

Faye beamed with pleasure at this unexpected recognition.

'That's right. Been there longer than I like to think.'

'You were very helpful the Christmas before last when I was trying to choose perfume for my mother.'

'A tricky thing, scent, very personal. I always think it's best if a woman can choose for herself, really.'

That had been exactly the contingency I was trying to avoid, but I didn't say so. My mother's taste in perfume matches her taste in clothes. I said, 'So – Monday night – do you think this visitor left by himself or did Danny leave too?'

Faye frowned. 'It's hard to say. I didn't hear anything after that, but then I rarely hear a squeak out of Danny when he's in. I just went up to bed and forgot about it.'

'The police didn't talk to you when they came for Danny?'

'No. I saw it all out of the window. You do think he's going to be all right?'

'Yes, yes, I'm sure it's just something and nothing.'

Faye pulled her blouse together across her chest. She had a lot of chest and not much blouse, and the more she pulled the more it sprang open when she let it go. She said, 'Danny's always been very good to me. I get lonely when Olaf's away.'

'Olaf?'

'My husband. He's Norwegian. Sea's in his blood, I can never keep him five minutes on terra firma, things will crop up when he's not here. Danny's always very obliging.' She patted her hair again and gave me a quick look up and down. 'I don't suppose you'd fancy a cup of tea?'

I liked Faye, but I doubted whether she would find me quite as obliging as Danny, so I looked at my watch and said, 'Another time, perhaps, I'm afraid I'm meeting someone in town. Thanks for your help!' And I left her watching me from the step as I walked back to the Cortina.

Though my exit line had been mere improvisation, I was just opening the car door when it suddenly occurred to me that I was indeed supposed to be meeting someone, though the arrangement was not of the firmest: I'd told the young builder with the ripped t-shirt that I would help him celebrate Wednesday. He and his mates had generally left the Railway by eight, and it was now almost seven thirty. I executed a hasty three-point turn and was about to join Beach Road when a panda car entered Danny's street from the opposite direction. I didn't recognize either of the officers inside, but I could take a shrewd guess that they were the bearers of a

warrant to search Danny Craven's house. Martin had obviously
been there on Monday night and left in something of a hurry, with
or without Danny. What if in his haste he'd forgotten the briefcase?
Now there was a chance the police would get their hands on it
without even realizing its potential importance. On the coast road
again I gnashed my teeth at the thought of this. Hargreaves was
getting ahead of me and there was absolutely nothing I could do
about it.

3

There was never anywhere to park near the Railway Tavern, so I
drove straight home and left the car outside Leigh Terrace in what
had now begun to feel like my own private space, then legged it up
to the pub by the quicker, back street route which avoided the
Boulevard. Though cooler than recent evenings, it was plenty warm
enough to bring a glow to the cheek of anyone taking vigorous
exercise, and I was forced to remove the leather jacket and carry it.
A familiar tightness gripped my chest. For a moment I wondered
whether to confound such doubters as Danny Craven's neighbour
by taking up some kind of sport, but luckily the madness passed.

To avoid the risk of bursting in like an armed robber, I
slackened my pace a few feet shy of the door to the public bar.
Once inside, I lit a cigarette and looked around me while Wilf
poured my pint. The place seemed quieter than it had been earlier
in the week, and although a few of the builders were sitting in a
noisy group in one corner I didn't at first notice my chunky friend
among them. I paid for the pint and took a welcome draught of it,
then glanced at the builders again. And he was there after all,
sitting with his back to me, wearing, or rather half wearing, an
unbuilderly short-sleeved checked shirt. The left side of it seemed
to be draped over his shoulder, and an odd knot in some pale
material jutted above the collar at the back, half hidden by his
curling auburn hair.

I was unsure how to play the situation. The chat we'd had the
previous day could hardly justify my joining the group. Perhaps I
would have to wait for him to make the first move, and there was

no guarantee that it would come. I settled on a bar stool and told myself to be patient. After all, what did it matter? Still, I wished that I'd had time to change; I was wearing the white shirt and brown cords in which I'd visited Monica and her mother, and I felt over-dressed. For what it was worth, I rolled the sleeves a little higher, and as I did so I seemed to catch sight of myself from somewhere up near the ceiling and realized that I was wholly in my element and could even temporarily be described as happy. Here I was, preparing to flirt with a total stranger, having not the least notion what cards might be on the table or where it all might lead. I was soaking in a warm bath of possibility, just the way I liked it. It reminded me of the way I'd felt on Monday night with Martin, that same delicious uncertainty.

Now my friend the builder pushed back his chair and rose a little awkwardly to his feet. His left forearm and hand were encased in plaster, the arm was supported in a sling, and his shirt sat open over a sleeveless white vest. Perhaps that made two of us whose day hadn't gone according to plan. Someone in the group now made a joke about him, they all laughed, and he laughed too, flashing white teeth. Then he left them, and walked across to me.

I smiled, he smiled back. I said, 'At least it's not your right arm.'

He said, 'I'm ambidextrous.'

I said, 'Why am I not surprised?'

He thought for a moment and said, 'You could come over and join us, but you'd be bored.' The thick hair tumbled forward over his brow.

I said, 'How do you know?'

'Because I'm bored myself. Do you want to meet me later? Say, the Albion? Half an hour?'

I nodded and said, 'It's a date.'

He said, 'You wish,' and started off towards the toilet, but I called after him.

'What happened?' He looked puzzled, and I had to add, 'Your arm.'

'Oh, that. I fell off a very tall man.' He continued on his way.

So, when I'd finished my pint and the three or four cigarettes which it had seemed imperative to smoke while drinking it, I left my new friend with his mates in the Railway and strolled up to the Albion, which stood in one of the back streets on the landward side of the Boulevard. It was the town centre's oldest pub and attracted some of its oldest inhabitants, and it was considered terrible form among the regulars to admit to possessing any of your own teeth. Despite the addition of horse-brasses in recent years, the decorative scheme remained unsophisticated, and the floor, walls, ceiling, furniture and drinking glasses were as dirty as they could possibly be without actually getting the place closed down. During the last hundred and fifty years the building had settled somewhat, with the result that you now stepped down into it off the street. This gave the Albion a distinctive underworld character, as if you were leaving mundane existence behind and descending into the Pit of Doom. Contributory to this, the smoke in the single small bar was thicker than at any other pub in town, largely because it issued as much from pipes as cigarettes. I'd always loved the Albion and would have drunk there more often if I'd been a more committed gerontophile.

I bought a pint and took a seat at an empty table. The two ancient blokes at the table next to mine courteously acknowledged me as I did so and then resumed their conversation. I leaned a little closer in order to eavesdrop. Though neither of them would see eighty again, they were discussing a question of burning contemporary significance, namely whether Pete Best or George Best had more right to be referred to as the Fifth Beatle. After all, with the new government only a few weeks old it was too soon to start laying into them, an activity which could safely be held in reserve for the long winter evenings.

About five minutes later, with Pete now edging ahead of George in the deliberations beside me, the checked shirt and its injured owner materialized out of the smoke. I began to rise to my feet and gestured, 'What do you want to drink?' but the boy shook his head and went to the bar to deal with it himself, handicap notwithstanding. He returned with a pint of draught bitter – at the Albion they kept the barrels behind the bar, since effectively the whole pub was a cellar – and my neighbours now acknowledged him too as he sat down opposite me. He said, 'Cheers,' and we both drank. Then he said, 'Remind me again why we're meeting like this.'

I said, 'Because you suggested it. And you seemed like a nice boy, so I said yes.'

'Appearances can be deceptive.'

'What, so you're not nice after all?'

'I'm not sure. I might be, and then again I might not be.'

'Well! – this is most unexpected.'

'I'm not saying I'm definitely *not* nice. But it isn't my place to judge, is it?'

'I see. So basically you're saying *Caveat emptor.*'

'*Emptor*? You think I'm for sale?'

'No – no, of course not.'

'I thought we were just meeting for a chat.'

'We are.'

'Well then.'

'Right.'

In something of a huff now, the boy looked away to the side, did a double-take, then fixed his eye on the two old-timers at the next table. I realized only then that they'd abandoned their discussion and were staring at us, open-mouthed. Perhaps they found our conversation more interesting than their own, and you couldn't blame them. I said, 'You're both wrong. The real Fifth Beatle is George Martin. Think about it – where would they have been without George Martin?'

The slightly less ancient of our neighbours now said, 'I believe you've got a point there. Then again, there's that Brian Epstein.' His dentures clicked as he said it.

The older one said, 'Is he talking to us?' Then they turned to one another and the Fifth Beatle controversy resumed.

I looked cautiously across at my companion. 'Did we just have a real misunderstanding or were you winding me up?'

'Depends whether you really thought I was rent.'

'No, never. Why would I?'

'It was in the back of your mind, though. *Caveat emptor.* Let the buyer beware.'

'Just an expression.'

'People don't say things by accident. The front of your mind was thinking, oh, we're having a nice little chat here, but the back of your mind was all about, I wonder how much? So you said, *Caveat emptor.*'

I examined the stocky young man sitting opposite me with new interest. I said, 'Have you heard of Sigmund Freud?'

'Is he that German mid-fielder? I'm not up to speed on football, to be honest.'

'Not to worry, you can't know everything. Got to leave room up there for all those Latin tags.'

'They were big on Latin at Our Lady.'

'Quite right too.' I extended my hand. 'I'm Sam.'

He gripped it firmly and shook it. 'Matt.'

'So who was the tall man you fell off?'

'Big Barry. About six five and built with it. I wanted to get up on this low roof, someone had borrowed the ladder, he offered to stand in. I was just stepping up from his hands onto his shoulder when this girl walks past, breaks his concentration. Straight off to Casualty. End of job.'

'I'm guessing you don't get severance pay.'

'I'll be down the dole office tomorrow.'

'So afterwards you came back to the Railway to tell your mates all about it.'

'Yeah, and to show off the cast, like you do.' Matt's forearm had been signed by at least ten people already. 'Broken ulna, two broken metacarpals. Besides – ' He now chewed his lip. It was a very nice lip, as indeed was his other lip. 'Besides, I thought you and I might have a date.'

'Ah! – you said date.'

'Damn it! I did, didn't I. I meant to say, casual arrangement to meet.'

'See, I'm not the only one with a back-of-the-mind.'

But Matt looked thoughtful now, even uncomfortable. The lip came in for further mistreatment. Then he said, 'I've got a girlfriend.'

Well, it wasn't what I wanted to hear but I said, 'OK.'

'Just so you know. I wouldn't like you to be getting ideas.'

I said, 'A bit late for that. I've been getting nothing else all evening.'

He said, 'Sorry. I think you're nice.'

'What, nice as in, harmless?' And it's just possible a trace of bitterness may have crept into my tone.

He arched a very sexy eyebrow. 'Nice as in, nice. But I've sort of settled with Eileen the last three or four months. I always liked girls too but she's the first, you know, big one.'

'You've got feelings?'

'Yeah, those. Ironic really, I met her on my twenty-first birthday. The minute I turned legal I stopped – you know.'

I offered Matt a cigarette but he said he didn't smoke. I said, 'Are you living with her?'

'No, no, her mum would go ballistic. They're heavy Catholics, her brother's a priest. I'm still at home, out at Marshfield, Causeway Road.'

Marshfield was one of Southaven's northern suburbs, once home to most of the town's fishermen and shrimpers. I said, 'My mother lives round the corner from you on Duck Lane. At least, that's where she was last week.'

'I don't follow you.'

'She gets restless. Also, broke. Has a habit of needing to find new accommodation at very short notice.'

'And your dad?'

I took another good look at Matt now. The problem was, I found myself seductively comfortable in his presence. I knew next to nothing about him and we'd barely talked for ten minutes, yet if he'd asked me where the treasure was buried I would have told him without demur. My guard was down. What's more, I didn't give a damn.

Which is why I said, 'My dad? You're assuming I have one.'

'What, he died?'

'I've no idea.'

Matt now did some thinking, but unlike Danny Craven it came easily to him. He said, 'Do you know who he is?'

I shook my head. 'The old girl's never said.'

Matt took a pensive mouthful of beer, put the glass down, scratched the cast on the back of his hand and for about half a second registered surprise at the lack of relief. He said, 'I'll bet they gave you a hard time at school.'

'Depends what you mean by a hard time. I got called the b-word quite a lot at first, but you get used to it, and that stopped after a while. But then they put all their energies into finding new epithets for my mother.'

'Kids can be very cruel.'

'Not just kids, either.'

'You got it from the teachers as well?'

It's generally a mistake to look back along the stagnant ditch of time, and if it had been someone else asking the questions I'd have changed the subject. As it was, I said, 'A couple of times my mother came to parents' meetings. I still have nightmares. After that the teachers just couldn't help themselves.' I stubbed out the cigarette I'd been smoking and lit another.

Matt didn't speak for a while. Come to that, neither did I. When he did speak again he must have diagnosed my mood because he went off on a new tack entirely. 'Saw you talking to that bloke who got killed.'

That shocked me. I'd imagined that my conversation with Martin had taken place in some kind of bubble which shut out the world.

Matt said, 'Nice-looking bloke, too. You gave him your card, I was trying to work out what it must have said, business card obviously but what business? He seemed a bit preoccupied but you weren't taking no for an answer. Then you left together. I couldn't make head nor tail of it. Next thing, he's dead, his photograph's on the local news.'

'And quite naturally you wondered if I'd had something to do with it.'

'Not really. It was on the late bulletin last night, by then I'd also seen you with that cop in the terrible brown suit, I assumed you must be on the side of the angels.'

This wasn't a view of myself I'd ever entertained before, but I let it pass. 'How did you know he was a cop?'

Matt shrugged his shoulders. 'Keep your eyes open, you notice stuff, don't you? Such as, I could see you've got a bit of a thing for him but he wouldn't play ball. He looked a complete tosser if you ask me, you're better off without him.'

'Kind of you to take an interest. We were on the beat together, as a matter of fact.'

'You were a cop yourself?' This seemed to surprise him.

I nodded. The ghost of an idea was forming in my brain. Slowly – if I'm honest, teasingly – I drew one of the business cards from my pocket and handed it across the table. Matt read it, and his face at once lit up with a thousand bulbs. 'Wow! Fab! Brilliant!'

The effect was pleasing but showed a certain lack of restraint, and I became aware that once again we had the full attention of our neighbours. To them I said, 'Young people today – always so excitable.'

The older man nodded rapidly, as if his head was coming adrift on his neck. He said, 'I was just the same myself. Remember it all like it was yesterday, every minute crystal clear.' Then to my surprise he loosened his tie, reached down behind his collar and hauled out a long piece of string with a label attached. 'Trouble is, short-term memory's shot to pieces. Isn't it, Horace?' He turned to his friend for support. 'He'll tell you, will Horace. Have to go out with my address round my neck, like a dog. Where's the dignity in that?' A hint of colour had risen to his yellow cheeks.

His companion said, 'Now then, Nev, don't start. You know

what you're like, it'll be your haemorrhoids next. Leave these boys in peace.'

'Well, I'm only saying.'

The two men now turned away from us again, and Matt leaned closer to me over the table, waving the business card in his uninjured hand. 'You're a private detective!'

'I know.'

'That's brilliant!'

'You said.' I hesitated for a moment, the brain performing elaborate calculations to no purpose. Sometimes you just have to go with your gut. 'So – Matt – would you be interested in doing a little casual work for me?'

He sat back again. 'I'm not doing smutty photographs, if that's what you're thinking.'

I rolled my eyes. 'For goodness' sake – '

'Oh! You mean, private detecting?'

'Yes, private detecting.'

'How much?'

'That was quick.'

'A boy's got to live.'

'Well, I was thinking in terms of giving you absolutely nothing whatsoever.'

'Nothing whatsoever?'

'Sod all, if you prefer. You should consider it a privilege to have this opportunity of working with a dedicated professional who's a leader in the field.'

'Cheapskate.'

'Correct.'

'Skinflint.'

'Also true.'

'When do I start?'

'How about, as soon as I get back from the bar?'

So we shook hands on it, and I got the round in. Then I talked him through everything that had happened since Monday evening. He proved to be an exemplary listener, interrupting only to ask for clarification when I chose my words with insufficient care. When I'd done, he said, 'Now what?'

'What do you mean, now what?'

'Well, what do you want me to do?'

'I've no idea. I don't even know what to do next myself, never mind you.'

'Then why rope me in?'

'Two heads are better than one.'

'Not if they're both idiots. You realize I failed O level metalwork?'

'You took O levels? This gets better all the time.'

There was a silence now and I felt the mood darken. Matt finished the pint, glanced around him in the bar, stared at the table top. Then he looked up, thoughtful. He said, 'This isn't a game, is it? There's a good man dead.'

I sat back a little and examined my new assistant from a fresh perspective. He was an adult, of course. And like I said, he was solidly built, and looked as if he could handle himself if things turned nasty, though I'd have been happier if he'd been blessed with a full set of working arms. I said, 'I imagine murderers can get quite upset if you come after them. Now you know what this is about, you might want to reconsider.' He didn't reply, and I was trying to read his expression. I said, 'I'd not think the worse of you if you backed out.'

'Never!' The eyes flashed indignation. 'We're going to get this bastard!' And I must have winced, though you'd think I'd have got used to it by now. 'I'm sorry, I didn't mean – ' His good hand crossed the table and rested on my own.

I'd been here before and there was nothing much to be done. 'Forget it. Everyone says bastard. I say it myself.' I patted his hand with my spare. 'Just as long as you know this could be dangerous. I don't want you taking risks. Please suppress the side of your nature which sees Big Barry as a viable ladder.'

Matt looked sheepish and withdrew his hand. 'We're all a bit reckless in the Standish family. The admissions nurse in A&E knew my name without asking.' While I tut-tutted, Matt turned to look at the clock behind the bar. 'I should go really, if that's all right. My dad's been decorating, I said I'd give him a hand putting the stuff back before we go to bed.'

'Won't you be excused in the circumstances?'

'I like to show willing.'

'So is it just you and your parents at home?'

'I'm one of six, but there's three of us left home now.'

'Must get crowded.' For want of company, when I was young I used to people my world with imaginary characters, but I also liked it when they went home for their tea and you could have the place to yourself.

Matt shrugged. 'All I've ever known.'

'Do you need a lift?'

'No, it's all right, I'm in good time for the number 4.' I could see that Matt liked to be independent, and I wasn't about to complain.

We got up now, said goodnight to Nev and Horace, and stepped up again from the bar into the world outside. The air blew cool on my face. We walked along together as far as the bus stop but Matt wouldn't hear of me waiting with him. I said, 'Call me at home in the morning. Here – ' And I wrote the number on the back of the business card. 'Perhaps you'll have worked it all out in the night.'

'You don't really believe this Danny character did it, do you?'

I frowned. 'I don't know. Something's not right. There's something I've missed but I can't put my finger on it.'

'The back of your mind.'

'Yeah, that's right. I know something, but I don't know I know it. Anyway – perhaps see you tomorrow. Hope the arm doesn't bother you too much.'

He said, 'Sweet dreams,' and there was a smile on his face which made me want to kiss him goodnight. I wondered whether to try it, I wondered whether he'd mind, I wondered why I could never just do things without having to wonder about them all the time.

I said, 'Your Eileen's a lucky cow.'

The smile faltered a little. 'Why?'

I said, 'You know why.' Then I left him at the stop and carried on along the Boulevard.

The evening had turned everything around. True, I was no nearer to discovering why Martin Berry had died or who'd killed him, but now at least I felt there was hope. Southaven glittered in the July night, light blazed cheerfully from the window displays. I stopped off once again at the chip shop, and walked round onto Preston Road eating from the open bag. Leigh Terrace seemed oddly gloomy after the brightness of the Boulevard. Then I realized that the street lamp directly in front of my building wasn't working, the steps were in almost total darkness. For years I'd boasted that I could find my way home with my eyes shut, and now, pulling the keys from my pocket, I set about proving it.

But as I reached the top step I felt rather than heard movement behind me, my legs were buckling, suddenly I was down on my knees, my arms pinned to my side. Something soft and damp slid down over my nose and mouth.

The really important thing on these occasions is not to breathe in. If you breathe in, you take the fumes right down into your lungs, the active agent passes rapidly into the bloodstream and in a couple of seconds reaches your brain. If you don't breathe in, you buy precious time, during which you can struggle and throw off your assailant.

But you know how it is. In the heat of the moment these things can slip your mind. I breathed in and went down, down, down.

Thursday

1

It can be hard to find the time for a visit to the laundrette, especially if you're not really trying. Consequently my bed-linen may not get changed as often as it might, but even so I couldn't understand why, when I woke up in the middle of the night, it smelled so strongly of rotting fish. The bed also seemed more cramped than usual, so that apparently I'd chosen to sleep sitting up, with my left leg folded awkwardly beneath my backside. Nor could I explain why I was fully clothed, or why, after an evening of such moderate consumption, my brain was swelling in its cavity like a rising loaf in a tin, threatening to ooze out of my eye sockets at any moment. But all became clear when I opened my eyes and discovered that I'd been folded up and rammed in between two dustbins beneath the steps leading to my front door.

I was pleased to have solved the mystery of the rotting fish, because that left head-space for tackling another: why was I gripping a large ball of paper between my teeth?

When I tried to move, the bins moved with me, and somewhere nearby the dog which always barks on these occasions duly barked. Something had severed the connection between my legs and my brain. Normally I say unto my leg go, and it goeth, but its current response to commands was a weary 'Ask me again in the morning.' I was damned if I was going to spend the night in the rubbish bay waiting for my legs to come back on side, so I poked them, prodded them, stretched them, shook them, and generally harassed them in every possible way until they reluctantly resumed normal service and allowed me to struggle to my feet.

Without the street lamp it was too dark to examine the ball of paper, so I slipped it into my jacket pocket, where I was pleased to find my door keys. They'd been in my hand when I lost consciousness, so presumably my assailant had borrowed them and then thoughtfully returned them after use.

Of course, I should have seen this coming: first my office, then the flat. Anyone could find my address, I was listed under Samuel

Rigby in the phone book. As I forced my legs up the four flights of
stairs and unlocked the door, I thought I knew pretty much what I
would find. And I wasn't disappointed.

From time to time – perhaps once every six months or so – I
take leave of my senses and try to tidy the old place up. This
exposes a great acreage of dusty carpet, which I then run over with
a Ewbank sweeper which I found on a rubbish dump when I was on
the beat. It makes no obvious difference to the dust, but you feel
good about yourself afterwards. My intruder had perhaps spared
himself this activity, but otherwise the flat looked much as it
usually does after one of my blitzes. Everything which could
possibly be neatly stacked had been neatly stacked. Clear paths
crossed the living room floor. My bed had been stripped and then
carefully remade. In the kitchen, the drawers had been re-
organized, although, sadly, a mountain of washing up still stood in
the sink.

With a sudden chill I was reminded of the neat pile of clothes at
the boating lake where Martin had died. It couldn't be Martin
who'd folded them like that, easy-going Martin of the chaotic
vegetable beds, tipsy that night in any case. No – with Martin dead,
already floating face down in the water, his murderer had calmly
tidied up, brought order to the scene of violence and sudden death.
Surely that must rule Danny Craven out of the picture, at least if his
slapdash housekeeping was any guide.

I took a quick look round to see if anything was missing, but all
seemed present and correct. The intruder had left empty-handed
for a second time.

Then I remembered the ball of paper. I removed it from my
pocket and unfolded it. It was a sheet torn from a large memo pad
which I kept hanging on the kitchen wall in a bid to bring some
kind of system to my domestic life, a plan which might have
succeeded if I'd ever remembered to use it. Printed in block
capitals, using a black felt-tip pen from the kitchen table, were the
words I REALLY WOULD BACK OFF IF I WERE YOU.

Well, it was a threat, just like *it might be an idea to keep your
mouth shut* was a threat, but as threats go it felt oddly restrained,
even fastidious. So too with the violence I'd experienced out on the
steps, no strong-arm stuff had been required, just a moderate and
unexpected blow behind the knees to bring me down, then the
ether over the nose and mouth, after which I'd simply been tidied
away with the rest of the household rubbish. Perhaps it had been

the same with Martin, the same element of surprise, one simple well-aimed blow to the skull, perhaps while Martin crouched or bent forward, no mess, no drama, just clean and effective and deadly. I had been thinking of Martin's killer as almost certainly a man, but now I began to wonder. There had been no use of brute force, everything was about timing, intelligence, agility. Even moving my unconscious body from the steps to the rubbish bay would have been easy enough for a lightly-built person, since gravity could have done nearly all the work. The killer's sex was yet another unknown in a dense thicket of unknowns, and at the full realization of my ignorance something beyond tiredness coursed through me, as if the drug was taking effect all over again. I could do nothing more tonight, I needed sleep.

But as I lay in the newly-made bed sleep would not come. Despite the cooler air of the past evening my bedroom remained stickily warm. Recently I'd replaced my old blankets with a fancy continental quilt bought on a rare outing to Manchester, but its synthetic filling made sweat break out wherever it rested over my skin. And all the time I was thinking about Martin, naïve, transparent Martin, but also almond-eyed, sexy Martin, his hand warm in my own, his shoulder pressing against mine on the narrow settee. With men like Martin in the world, why had I always ended up with hard-faced pieces of work like Mark Howell? Only, Martin wasn't in the world any longer.

But I did have his photograph. In the madness of the day it had remained forgotten in the glove compartment of the Cortina, but perhaps with Martin's photo beside me I'd be able to sleep. I switched on the bedside lamp, swung out my legs, and looked around me for the old dressing gown which usually lay on the bedroom floor amongst whatever else had settled there. But apparently that too had been tidied up. I couldn't be bothered to search for it, and at nearly three o'clock in the morning I doubted if there'd be any problem with just streaking out to the car and back again. So I collected the car keys, left my flat door open, padded down the stairs, left the front door on the latch, looked up and down the street in the near darkness, then ventured down the steps to the pavement. And just as I reached the bottom I heard a squeak, bang and click behind me as the door swung shut in the draught and the jolted latch descended.

I climbed the steps again and pushed the door, but it was just as I'd expected. First, the charmed parking space right outside the building, time after time, day after day. Next, payback. Naked outside my own front door at 3 a.m. with only my car keys for company.

Except for my downstairs neighbour Florrie, who was too deaf to hear her own doorbell, I didn't get on well enough with anyone in the building to warrant getting them out of bed in the middle of the night. The obvious course of action would be to drive over to some sympathetic person's home and throw myself on their mercy. But who? Not Aunt Winnie, I would never hear the last of it. Not Mark Howell, it would look like the worst kind of desperation. And so I ran through my mental address book, but at each entry, though the reason possibly differed, the answer remained the same. I had nowhere to go.

In fact, that wasn't strictly true. My mother would have been delighted to see me, not least because she could entertain her drinking buddies with the tale for weeks to come. If locking yourself naked out of your flat in the middle of the night is a heritable trait, I have it from my mother, but that didn't mean I was prepared to give her the satisfaction of knowing that I'd done it.

I would have to try and sleep on the back seat of the Cortina. A couple of years before, I'd left an old raincoat in there for emergencies, and somehow, like most things I put in the car, it had stayed there ever since. So I opened the car door and felt around amongst the selection of car junk until I found the coat. It smelled musty, but it would have to do. Sweeping everything else onto the floor, I curled up on the seat with the coat draped over me and my head resting against the offside window. The upholstery stuck damply to my skin, and when I tried to get more comfortable it let go reluctantly with a report like a burst balloon. I hadn't had so much fun since my nights under canvas doing National Service. But as I felt myself beginning to sink down into welcome oblivion, with a start I remembered why I'd come out here in the first place, and after that I couldn't rest until I'd unstuck myself again, leaned over the front passenger seat, opened the glove compartment and removed the photograph of Martin and Monica on their wedding day. In the half dark I couldn't actually see the picture, but nevertheless when I once more contorted my body to fit the narrow seat I held the photo against my heart and imagined myself somewhere else, where I was not alone.

But all of that must have passed because now I was in the phone box at Otterdale, just stubbing out my cigarette on the metal shelf while behind me the woman in blue rapped repeatedly on the window. Rage boiled in me. If she didn't shut up soon I would turn and shove the door right into her fat face. Rap rap rap. Enough! But then I was awake, my eyes were open. The new sun had risen, bringing the new day, and its light through the steamed-up windows told me that I'd slept in my car. Every nerve ending from my compressed head to my crumpled feet shrieked with pain.

Oddly, the rap rap rap behind me still went on.

At the cost of further pain, I twisted round enough to gain the distorted view of a human form beyond the screen of glass and water droplets. Checking first that the coat covered sensitive areas, I wound down the offside window, and the freckled face of WPC Cilla Donnelly leaned in.

She said, 'Morning, Sam.' Her tone was matter-of-fact, and I found this wounding. Astonishment, concern, sarcasm – almost anything would have been better. Clearly, Sam Rigby sleeping naked on the back seat of his car was no more than she'd come to expect.

I said, 'Hi, Cilla. How's tricks?' which was all I could think of at the time.

She said, 'I expect your ears were burning yesterday evening.'

I tried to make sense of this, but what with one thing and another my brain hadn't turned up for work yet. I said, 'Sorry, Cilla, you're going to have to translate.'

'Danny Craven.'

'Ah.' Cilla was good that way, a woman of few words, all of them worth hearing. 'So, he happened to mention our chat?'

'You might be best avoiding Hargreaves for the next few lifetimes.'

Perhaps it was the acute pain in my back, I can't be sure, but Cilla's guiltless attitude grated. I said, 'When have I ever dumped you in it?'

For a moment her round, wholesome face withdrew a little from the window frame. Then she leaned forward once more and said, 'I'm sensing hostility.'

'Too right you're sensing hostility. You told Hargreaves I was parked in Marvell Close on Tuesday. He hauled me in for a kicking.'

'Sorry, Sam, it was nothing personal. We'd found your business card on the victim, I couldn't just ignore the fact that I'd seen the Cortina. What is it with you and Hargreaves, anyway?'

I shook my head, and instantly regretted it. Waiting first for the sensation of falling rocks to subside, I said, 'Too early in the day for questions like that. Actually, what is the time? I seem to have left my alarm clock on the bedside table.'

'Ten to six.'

The civilian clothes announced that Cilla was not on duty. 'You're coming in early. Or are you going home?'

'Just been home to grab a few hours. It's all hands on deck until we find this killer. Anyway, I hope I haven't disturbed your beauty sleep. I saw the condensation on the windows, thought I should investigate.'

'Public-spirited of you.' An idea was doing its best to occur to me. 'Did you say ten to six?'

'Yes, why?'

'Keep an eye on my front door, would you?'

While Cilla obliged, I fought my way into the sleeves of the raincoat. Daylight showed patches of mould growing on it, but this was no time to be particular. The wedding photograph had dropped to the floor, so I rescued it and stuck it in the coat pocket. Somehow the car keys had remained in my hand. I got out of the car on the nearside, opposite Cilla, and just as I was locking it the house door opened and Florrie, my downstairs neighbour, came out onto the steps, wearing, as always, a paisley pattern headscarf. She'd supposedly retired, but still put in a couple of hours' cleaning every morning at the town hall, where I knew she clocked on at six. I called out 'Florrie! Florrie!' but she didn't hear. She now closed the door firmly behind her and continued down the steps, eyes intent on the ground. Perhaps incautiously I hurried up to her, met her at the bottom of the steps, and said 'Florrie!' again, too abruptly it seems, because she gave a yelp of surprise and fell backwards, her bottom settling down squarely round about the third step. Instinctively I lunged forward to help her, the raincoat flapped open, and she screamed.

'Help! Help! Get away from me!'

'Florrie, it's me, Sam.'

At this point Cilla joined us. 'It's all right, Madam, I'm a police officer. Do you wish to make a complaint against this man?' There was enough trouble already without Cilla Donnelly piling in, but just then Florrie recognized me and some sort of normality was restored. I borrowed her key to let myself in, thanked her, and watched as she set off unsteadily for work. Cilla indicated the car and said, 'I presume there's some perfectly rational explanation?'

There was, but I didn't care to disclose it, so I said, 'Are you still holding Danny Craven?'

She shook her head. 'He admits he travelled out to Otterdale with Martin Berry but says they parted at the station. We searched his house, got nothing. So we let him go, about ten o'clock.' It seemed that Danny Craven was a tougher nut to crack than I'd imagined. Lying to Hargreaves is never easy, but somehow he'd got away with it. From what Faye had told me, it was almost certain that Martin had been at Danny's house that night. I knew, Hargreaves didn't. I felt a thrill of triumph. I would have to talk to Danny Craven again. Something must have happened between him and Martin, something which now prevented him from telling the truth.

Cilla said, 'By the way, I think he likes you.'

'What, Danny Craven? Officer speak with forked tongue.'

'No, not Craven, you idiot. Harry Hargreaves.'

I stared at her. She didn't appear to be running a fever, and the usual pedestrian good sense sat square on her freckled brow. But before I could launch a counter-argument, with illustrations, she said, 'Anyway, must dash. See you in court,' which was her accustomed sign-off and her idea of a joke. With that she turned and stumped away in the direction of the police station.

*

About five minutes after I got back into bed, or so it seemed, the phone rang. If this was Aunt Winnie again, there might have to be reprisals. My head, still thick from its recent adventures, begged me to ignore the summons, and my aching back took a similar line, but if I was going to catch Martin's killer sleep would have to wait. Besides, according to the bedside clock it was actually eight fifteen, so I must have been dead to the world for two whole luxurious hours.

When I picked up the receiver, a voice I hadn't expected said, 'Sam? Is that you?'

I said, 'Uh,' only then discovering that my own voice hadn't wakened with the rest of me.

Matt said, 'You sound like you've just got out of bed. I thought you were supposed to be a dedicated professional and a leader in the field.'

I said, 'Uh' again, though when I'd opened my mouth I'd hoped for better.

'So I take it you haven't seen today's Gazette? Sam? Hello, is there anybody there?'

'Do you have to be so loud? I've passed a rather difficult night.'

Matt said, 'Pah!' I'd imagined that Pah! had dropped out of the language not long after Zounds! but apparently not. 'You want to try sleeping with your arm in plaster. The itching drives you nuts, and you can't even toss and turn. I've been awake since six o'clock.'

I considered mentioning that six o'clock was roughly when I'd finally got to bed, but decided against. I said, 'Poor you.'

'Anyway, I can't bring the paper with me, it's my mum's, she gets it delivered. You'll have to get your own.'

Sluggishly, a few of the brain cells in charge of Inference now fired up. I said, 'Bring with you? You're coming over?'

'Of course! We need to talk about this. It must be what Martin Berry meant when he said something had come up about the Empire.'

'You're not making sense.'

'Just buy the paper and you'll see. I'll be with you in half an hour, maximum. What's the address?'

Since launching my new career seven years earlier, I'd somehow managed to scrape by without an assistant, and my life had been pretty much my own to organize. Now, less than twelve hours after appointing Matt my honorary side-kick, I was already beginning to regret it. Show me a fresh-faced man with nice teeth and I seem to lose all natural caution, especially if he has nice deltoids too. The whole thing was rather shaming, and I felt rather shamed. Why did Matt have to sound so bloody enthusiastic at eight fifteen in the morning?

But I recognized an unstoppable force when I saw one, so I gave Matt my address and said, 'Save me a trip, would you? Pick up a Gazette on your way in and I'll pay you back.'

He said, 'You're going back to bed, aren't you?'

I said, 'Certainly not!' though it was such a good idea that I wished I'd thought of it myself. Nevertheless, when Matt had rung off I made for the bathroom instead, turned on the bath taps, went through into the kitchen, fed the meter, thumped the boiler, looked around without success for something edible, then climbed into the bath and let it soak away something of the past night's trauma. I'd bathed and dried myself and shaved, and was just dabbing Old Spice here and there, when the door buzzer buzzed.

Keys in hand, I raised the front window and leaned out. Below, Matt looked up. His face was indeed fresh, lips parted, eyes bright and eager. He said, 'You're not even dressed yet.'

I said, 'Shut up and let yourself in,' and dropped down the keys. With two hands he might have caught them, but as it was, and with his single useful hand busy holding a copy of the Southaven Gazette's Thursday edition, the keys fell past him, and he was forced to go back down the steps to look for them. I said, 'Sorry,' but really I thought it served him right for being young and positive and generally annoying. Leaving the flat door open, I searched my newly-tidied underwear drawer for the least old pants, and stepped into the brown cord trousers again. Then I caught sight of the photograph of Martin and Monica, propped up on the bedside table where I'd put it when I came in. I didn't propose to give Matt a house tour, but just in case he did happen to poke his head round the bedroom door I didn't want him to get the wrong impression. I slipped the photograph onto the shelf beneath, face down.

'Anybody home?'

Shirt in hand, I walked out into the hallway. Briefly, reflexively, Matt looked my torso up and down. I probably wasn't meant to notice, but I did. He said, 'You smell nice.'

I said, 'It's ambrosia.'

He said, 'You eat creamed rice for breakfast?'

Despite the bath and shave, I wasn't yet fit to unravel misunderstandings, so I simply took the keys from Matt, put them in my trouser pocket, and went through into the living room, drawing on my shirt as I went. This brought relief, because I could now stop holding in my stomach. Matt followed me. Buttoning the shirt, I said, 'Take a seat. Do you want tea? There's no milk, obviously.' Following the widespread failure of tenants to pay their bills, milk was no longer delivered to Leigh Terrace, so if you wanted it you had to get it yourself. Strictly speaking there was no tea either, but I could always fish a couple of old teabags out of the bin and send them round for another go.

Matt said, 'I'm fine, I've had about ten cups already. Come and look at this.' Sitting to the left on the settee, where he could keep the broken arm out of harm's way, he unfolded the front page of the newspaper. I sat down on his right. He said, 'Cosy, this, isn't it? Could you not get a bigger one up the stairs?'

I said, 'A friend was throwing it out.' I never seemed to choose furniture for myself but just waited for friends to get rid of theirs.

Matt said, 'I bet it's seen some action.'

'Do you think you could possibly focus your mind on the work in hand?'

'Oh, right. See for yourself.'

The Gazette normally ran two main stories on its front page. Today, the less prominent of these was Martin Berry's murder. Murders were rare in Southaven, in fact the last one I could recall had been just after I left the force seven years earlier, so you might have supposed that the Gazette would milk them for all they were worth. Instead, the policy was to play them down. Not surprisingly, Morgan Williams, the editor, though too much of a loner to belong to the inner circle, was nevertheless quite chummy with the likes of Jack Spalding and Alan Baybridge, all the local movers and shakers whose finances ultimately depended on the town's good image. Murder was bad for business. The strange consequence was that you could expect to be written up less sensationally if you were hacked to death than if your chip pan caught fire.

So it proved with Martin. A small, rather fuzzy head-and-shoulders picture of the victim accompanied a brief, straightforward account of the few known facts, followed by an appeal for witnesses. The headline, not overlarge, read simply *LOCAL MAN FOUND DEAD*.

By contrast, the main front page story ran beneath a vast banner headline: *THE EMPIRE: FINAL CURTAIN? – Addison's in shock talks with council,* and there was a large photograph of the exterior of the building in its present forlorn condition. I couldn't understand what Addison's had got to do with anything, but that's what the text is for, so I read it:

> The Southaven Gazette has learned that plans to re-open the Empire Cinema as a cooperatively run entertainment venue have been shelved.
>
> In a shock move, the borough surveyor this week condemned the building, which will now be demolished.
>
> The supermarket chain Addison's is understood to be in talks with council leaders over development of the site.
>
> Sandy Smythe of pressure group Save Our Empire, which was to have leased the building from the council, said, 'This situation is wholly unacceptable.
>
> 'Only last month we were given assurances that the project would go ahead. We intend to fight this decision

at the highest level.'

There was a small inset photograph of Sandy Smythe looking extremely cross, but that was nothing new. In recent months he'd often figured in the Gazette, and he never looked less than furious. Perhaps this was merely the inevitable result of trying to get anything done in Southaven.

I read on to the end of the story, but it simply rehashed old material. I said, 'What do you make of all this?'

Matt blew out his cheeks while he thought. 'Hard to say. You'd expect there to be some kind of response from the council, but there isn't. It's like we've only got half the story.'

'And why do you suppose that is?'

'Because – ' He went into thinking mode again. It suited him, but then so did a wide range of other modes. 'Because they've got the whole thing from this Smythe person.'

'Correct! We need to talk to him.' Pleasant as it had been to hobnob with Matt's deltoids, one of us would now have to move. I said, 'Make yourself useful, look his number up in the book.' And I indicated its whereabouts on the window sill.

For a moment Matt didn't reply. Then, avoiding my eye, he said, 'I'm a bit slow.'

In any discussion of Matt's characteristics, slow was not the first word which would have sprung to mind. But presumably the man knew what he was talking about, so I just said, 'Well then, be slow,' and watched as he crossed to the window, opened the directory, and flipped forward to the S's. It was then that he seemed to hesitate. As he turned individual pages, more slowly now, he blinked repeatedly as if struggling to focus. Finally he said, 'There's two S. Smythes.'

'Addresses?'

'Erm – Crompton Street – '

'It won't be Crompton Street, that's council. I get the impression he's got money behind him.'

'The other one's Traherne Close.'

'Traherne? Does it say what part of town that is?' Matt shook his head. 'Were they big on the metaphysical poets at Our Lady as well?'

'Who the hell are the metaphysical poets? We seemed to do a lot of Hopkins, that's all I remember. Anyway, why are we talking about poetry all of a sudden?'

I crossed to the telephone and picked up the receiver. 'Because I'll lay odds that Traherne has to be somewhere near Vaughan and Marvell. What's the number?' Matt told me and I dialled, but got the engaged tone. Slamming down the receiver, I grabbed the car keys. 'We're going out there.' I felt dynamic and strangely virtuous. I couldn't tell whether I would have been like this anyway or whether acquiring an apprentice had messed with my style.

'What's wrong with the phone?'

'Engaged. Anyway, I hate the phone, people lie through their teeth. Chop chop, you'll have it dark.'

Matt picked up the newspaper, I picked up my jacket, and we thudded down the too-many stairs to the street. While Matt waited for me to unlock the car, he said, 'That's odd – come and look at this,' so I joined him on the pavement. 'Don't they keep these things locked?' In his functioning hand, the door to the metal housing at the base of the lamp post swung on its hinges. I peered inside. I hadn't the remotest idea how it should look in there, but I felt sure now that the broken street lamp had been no coincidence. With the police station just yards away round the corner, the murderer had coolly tampered with the light and then waited for me in the shadows, calm, confident.

I said, 'I've got a story to tell you,' and as we drove out to Otterdale by the inland route I filled Matt in on some of the night's activities, ruthlessly suppressing any mention of photographs or sleeping in cars. This was despite the fact that we were having to drive with all the windows down in the hope of expelling the damp. I tried claiming that the Cortina always dripped wet like this because the windows leaked, which they did. But I don't think Matt believed me.

The fuel gauge was hovering close to zero, so just short of Otterdale village I stopped to bung in a quid's worth. At this rate the ten pounds which I'd withdrawn from the bank on Tuesday wasn't going to last very long. Then I climbed into the driver's seat again, having first hurled a fresh sheet of Green Shield stamps into the back to join their fellows. I still cherished the fanciful notion that I might some day get round to sticking them into books.

Matt, the newspaper open on his knee again, said, 'Shouldn't it be an E?'

He was wearing that irritating expression younger people always wear when they know better than you do. I said, 'All right, go on. Shouldn't what be an E?' And I drove off the garage forecourt.

'"Enquiries and observations." You've put "inquiries".'

He'd obviously been reading my ad under Personal Services. I found myself suddenly questioning everything I'd ever learned about the use of English. If Matt always had this effect on me I would be in a loony bin within days. I said, 'If you look it up, I think you'll find the spelling is optional.'

'No it isn't. You make enquiries but you hold an inquiry. Simple.'

I said, 'Everything's simple when you're twenty-one.'

He said, 'Doesn't mean I'm not right,' and it didn't. I'd been running that ad for years: *Private investigator: confidential inquiries and observations*, followed by the phone number. Now I would have to consult the dictionary, always assuming it wasn't stuck in one of the piles supporting the TV. And this was just Matt's first day at work. I said, 'You know what they're like at the Gazette. Never knowingly accurate.'

Appalled, he said, 'You're blaming the Gazette?'

We were still about a quarter of a mile from our destination, but I resorted to saying, 'What number was it in Traherne Close?' and to my relief Matt now took his claws out of me and replied that it was number one. We drove the rest of the way in silence. I felt righteously irked with him for nosing out my imperfections like that, and I couldn't help wondering whether he subjected the lovely Eileen to similar indignities.

In the village, we had to wait at the level crossing while trains passed in both directions. It seemed a long wait, but neither of us spoke. Further up Beach Road I pulled in so that Matt could ask passers-by for directions to Traherne Close. The first pleaded ignorance, but the second, a young mother with a pram, seemed distinctly taken with Matt and took about five hours to tell him that it was the third road up on the left. I seemed to see flashing white teeth reflected in her adoring gaze. More than likely, that was just the way Eileen gazed at him. With nothing better to do, I drummed my fingers on the steering wheel. When finally the tryst drew to a close and we were able to drive on, I said, 'She seemed like a nice girl,' but Matt didn't respond.

It turned out that Traherne Close backed onto Marvell Close, with number one standing at the corner on the seaward side. From the house there would be a clear view back along Beach Road towards the station. I parked up and said, 'Do you want to come in with me?'

'And see how the expert conducts an interview?'

Had Matt leaned slightly on the word 'expert'? Perhaps I was being over-sensitive, but it seemed to me that I had enough to deal with already without the additional burden of an assistant who questioned my spelling and cast doubt on my interview technique. Aunt Winnie had always said I was a poor judge of character, and that if ever I made a new friend at school it would only be a matter of time before they found themselves expelled for some egregious crime. But Matt's sun-bronzed face was turned to me now with the recent question still hanging on his generous lips, and the expression was all innocence, I could detect not the least evidence of side or malice. In fact, studying that face I could have sworn that he liked me, perhaps even quite a lot. So I might have been reading him wrong but you have to go with your gut and I said, 'You can ask him questions too, if you like. I've got a feeling you're going to be good at this.'

My reward was a smile and a glimpse of the white teeth. I wasn't at all sure what had been going on between us for the last ten minutes, but I tried to leave it behind now. We got out of the car and walked up the short pathway to Sandy Smythe's front door.

Inside, a piano played *Let's Do It*.

2

Number one Traherne Close looked identical in form to the Berrys' house a couple of streets away, but the exterior had been painted in a rather powerful red and Sandy Smythe had not yet begun to civilise his small front garden. I tried pressing the doorbell, without success. Clearly it had been drowned out by the noise of Siamese twins doing it, which seemed to be emanating from the front room to our left. I rapped on the window. Immediately Cole Porter fell silent, and a large man soon appeared at the window wearing dark-rimmed glasses and a ferocious glare. When he saw us, the ferocity intensified, and he disappeared. I leaned towards Matt and said, 'Brace yourself.'

A moment later the front door was flung open and we had a view of the proprietor full-length. There was a lot of him. Still glaring ferociously, he said, 'For goodness' sake! Will you people never give it a rest? Once and for all, *there is no God.* Do you hear me? Nothing, *nichts, nada, rien du tout!* We're just animals, that's all, spinning round on a ball of rock ninety million miles from the sun, and our life is utterly meaningless! There are no miracles, there's no heaven, there's no hell, there's no life after death, Jesus didn't die to save your sins, and God doesn't give a damn what you do with yourselves because he *doesn't exist!* The only reason you think there's a God is because someone somewhere has told you there's something the matter with you and you need saving. Well you don't, you're fine as you are, or at least you would be if you could just desist from polluting my doorstep and hammering on my windows when I'm trying to work. Face your fear! Strike out into the unknown! Take risks for a change! There may be no God but we still have each other, we still have music, art, science. Throw off this childish nonsense, embrace your humanity! And if you can't do that then for crying out loud will you stop trying to shove your insane delusions down other people's throats!'

This speech, or rant to be more accurate, proceeded from the beard-fringed mouth in the very large head which topped the very large body of its owner. Surrounding the bald dome, a circle of vigorous whitish-grey hair stuck out wildly. Sandy Smythe in full flow was certainly an impressive sight, but I'd been hoping to slip in the odd word here and there so when he came to the bit about miracles I dipped a hand into my jacket pocket expecting to find the business cards. But apparently there was a God after all, albeit a cruel one, because the business cards weren't there. I searched through pocket after pocket with the same result. Obviously this was intended as my punishment for years of pretending that I couldn't just lay hands on them straight off. I began to wonder if I'd left them on the table in the Albion the night before, but just when I'd given up all hope, there they were after all, in the seat pocket of my trousers. I transferred them to the jacket where they belonged, but kept one in my hand and held it up a few inches in front of Sandy Smythe's purplish face. We'd reached the section on art and science now. He ducked sideways to avoid the card but it pursued him, so he snatched it out of my hand without reading it and continued his tirade.

I didn't have a plan B, and I began to resign myself to the possibility that when the monologue drew to a close Sandy Smythe might simply slam the door in our faces and rejoin the Dutch in Old Amsterdam, or wherever it was he'd got to, leaving me with the choice of trying the bell again or giving up and going home. Luckily, Matt was made of sterner stuff, and I now noticed that he was holding out his good hand while giving S. Smythe the benefit of one of his broadest and white-toothiest smiles. It was this, rather than any want of material, that caused the man to break off and take a proper look at us for the first time. What he saw gave him pause, and he decided at last to read the business card. That done, a slight mellowing of his mood could be detected. He extended a powerful hand, and Matt shook it. 'Matthew Standish – Mr Rigby's assistant. We've been looking forward to meeting you, Mr Smythe. Haven't we?'

Recognizing my cue, I said, 'Absolutely.'

'We're both keen admirers of your work with Save Our Empire. Would be a black day for Southaven if this Addison's thing goes through.'

Sandy Smythe must have taken a fancy to Matt's hand, because he still hadn't let go of it. And perhaps it wasn't just the hand. The lenses of the dark-framed glasses were thick, and he didn't so much look through them as peer, with the consequence that he seemed to be building up a full picture of Matt one slow piece at a time. Some young men would have found this sort of attention alarming, but Matt wasn't some young men. Then Smythe drew himself up another inch or two and said, 'They'll have me to deal with first.' And still he gripped Matt's hand.

There was only one thing for it, so I proffered my own hand and said, 'Sam Rigby,' though he already knew that from the card. Reluctantly, Smythe detached himself from Matt, and his big, hot hand closed over mine. It must have lacked the charm of Matt's, though, because after a brief squeeze which almost broke my knuckles he let it go. I said, 'We're looking into the murder of Martin Berry.'

This took Smythe by surprise. 'Really? I don't see how I – '

Matt interrupted. 'If we could just ask you a few questions.'

The big man considered this for a moment. 'Well – I suppose you'd better come in. But I can't give you much time, I've got a pupil coming at ten.' We followed him down the narrow hallway, past the door to what I took to be the music room. Framed posters for various musical productions lined the walls, some dating from long before the war. We turned right into the back sitting room, disappointingly small and dark in comparison with its equivalent at 5 Vaughan Close. What Sandy Smythe needed was a smart new sun room. Perhaps I should give him Danny Craven's number.

'So – take a seat, if you want. What were you thinking I could tell you?'

Matt and I both settled ourselves on a wonderfully comfortable old three-seater settee which appeared to belong to a more relaxed and spacious age than the modern house it stood in. I looked around. The rest of the furniture gave a similar feeling of having been transplanted here from some more traditional setting. An old typewriter rested on a table in the corner, surrounded by books and documents. The walls, though papered with contemporary swirls, were hung with art, and I don't mean cheap reproductions. There was no television, but an up-to-the-minute hi-fi took pride of place on the Art Deco sideboard, its sizeable speakers some feet away to either side. The whole effect suggested that our host was a man who kept up with the times but chose quality over modernity where possible. I should like to be able to say that he was also a man who offered tea when you were gagging for it, but this was not the case. He sat impatiently now on an upright chair, and his habitual air of simmering rage could not quite conceal that our presence made him nervous.

I said, 'You teach piano, then?'

'No, no – singing. One time or another I've taught most of the better voices around these parts. Not so much the classical types, they're away to Manchester mostly, but the ones who do musical theatre, with perhaps a bit of oratorio in the season. Semi-professional, that's the level.'

'I noticed all those posters in the hallway – your pupils?'

'In some cases, yes. I collect posters from local productions.'

'Do you perform yourself?'

He smiled at that, as if recalling happier times. It was a warm enough smile, unexpected, and I realized I'd been pigeon-holing him as Angry Fanatic without waiting to see what else might have been thrown in the mix. He said, 'Not any more. I was a useful baritone in my day, though never one of the best. But I'll say this for my younger self: there was no problem hearing me at the back of the upper circle.'

This I could well imagine. While his recent philosophical

lecture may have lacked variety of tone, you couldn't fault it on projection.

Matt now said, 'Have you been living here long?'

'It'll be a year next month. I was across the other side of town before, but this suits me better.'

'I suppose you find it more – *convenient?*'

This time I was in no doubt. Matt had unquestionably leaned on the word 'convenient', but I couldn't for the life of me understand why. Perhaps this was what happened when you took on staff without references: confronted with a possible source of vital information, they cracked up and started talking tripe.

Nevertheless, it now appeared that Sandy Smythe found more sense in the question than I had done myself, because he seemed faintly uneasy as he responded. 'Convenient? Well, yes. Many of my students don't drive, and I'm only a few minutes' walk from the railway station.'

Matt wasn't done with the topic. He nodded and said, 'Yes, but – convenient for *other things* too?'

There was a brief silence during which I was unable to decipher Sandy Smythe's thoughts. By way of contrast, my own were clear as day. It was obvious now that becoming the unpaid hanger-on of a struggling provincial private investigator had broken Matt's sanity, and I would have to return him to the shop first chance I got. Hoping to quash the subject of whether 1 Traherne Close was convenient or not, I said, 'To come to the nub of it now, Mr Smythe, were you already aware of the connection between these goings-on at the Empire and Martin Berry?'

'If you mean, did I know he worked for the borough surveyor's office, then yes. I take it you're familiar with the history of Save Our Empire?'

Matt opened his mouth to say that we were, but I broke in. 'There might be something we've missed. Why not assume we're ignoramuses and take it from the top.'

There was a grinding of cerebral gears as Sandy Smythe marshalled his facts. Then he said, 'Well – the Empire's owned by Associated English Cinemas, or at least the building itself is. The council own the freehold. AEC have run the Empire nigh on twenty years, but what started out as a cash cow for them has become a liability. This past five years they just can't get punters through the doors. You'll remember they used to run a mix of film and music, and all the big names used to come: The Beatles, Cliff Richard,

Helen Shapiro, The Bachelors, pretty much anyone who was anyone. Drew sell-out crowds, of course. Then a few years ago AEC got new management, word from the top was it had to be films and nothing but, live entertainment had to stop. So the big acts all went out of town, and the audiences went with them. Management must have been insane because this was just at the point where cinema attendance was crashing because everyone had television, we lost three cinemas in the town centre in as many years. Truth was, AEC wanted rid of the place, it didn't fit the company profile any longer, too old-fashioned and out-of-the-way.

'So that's when we got involved – Save Our Empire, that is. I wasn't a member myself in the early days, it was mainly film enthusiasts, and the idea was to put pressure on AEC to show a wider range of films, preserve all the traditional trappings of the old cinema and bring some life to the place in the daytime.'

I said, 'My mother worked there when I was a boy. The café would be open all day, everybody went there.'

Sandy Smythe nodded. 'Brought people in, generated trade. Absolutely key to the life of the building, so naturally AEC closed it down. Madness. All they wanted to do was show films and take your money, they never understood that a night out's a night out, it's an occasion, an experience. You don't just want to goggle at the screen and then go home again, you want a bit of atmosphere, don't you?'

I said, 'So did SOE make any sort of impact?'

'Yes and no.' He frowned. 'More no than yes, if I'm honest. AEC wanted to scrap the old Compton organ, been in the cinema since the last big rebuild of 1929, and we talked them into keeping it. But that's about all. Then some of us had an idea – I'd joined the group myself by then, someone had tipped me off about what was happening. The plan was to persuade the council to buy the Empire off AEC, then lease it back to us.'

Matt said, 'But how could you expect to make a go of it when a big company like AEC had failed?'

Sandy Smythe now redeployed some fifty per cent of his trademark glare. 'That's exactly the sort of hostile criticism we faced at the time. People said we were romantic, soft in the head. But we had a good, hard business plan. First of all, we organized ourselves as a cooperative, and where AEC had shareholders to worry about, we intended to plough our profits back into the business. And we still do, don't imagine we're going to take this latest nonsense from the council lying down, because we're not. Secondly, we're going to use an element of volunteer labour to help with things like running the café, leafleting and so on. Thirdly, where AEC put all their eggs into the one auditorium, we're going to use every part of the building to generate cash. There's space for rehearsal rooms, group meetings, dance classes and so on. And finally, we intend to go back to a mix of film and live entertainment, just like it was when the place first opened in 1914. We think Variety's going to make a big come-back in the next few years, this pop music mania's just a fad, it'll fizzle out sooner or later like everything else. The Amateur Operatic are keen to stage all their big productions with us. I've directed them a few times myself – you may have seen my *Seven Brides For Seven Brothers* last year.'

I confessed that owing to pressure of engagements I'd missed it.

Sandy Smythe continued. 'Anyway, you get the picture. It'll be mix and match, mix and match. We have brilliant ideas on the film side of things as well, but you'd be better talking to one of my colleagues about that.'

Matt said, 'So what went wrong? From what they've said in the Gazette, I thought AEC had agreed to sell and you and the council were ready to take over.'

'This is where it gets interesting. Until about a month ago, that's what I thought too. There was just one remaining hurdle. For some reason, the borough surveyor hadn't managed to find the time in his busy diary to cast an eye over the Empire and declare it seaworthy. Council obviously couldn't proceed if they were going to be faced with a massive bill for structural repairs the minute the building changed hands, and though we've got a contingency fund in SOE we certainly couldn't afford to pay for anything like that ourselves. But everyone thought it was just a formality. The Empire isn't that old really, and it was built to last, top quality materials right through. There's a spot of damage to the stonework from exposure to the sea air, but nothing serious, and that's the worst thing anyone could point to. I couldn't understand why Colin Cudleigh didn't just get on with it, conduct his survey, make his report, and let us all move on to the next step.

'Anyway, I started to smell a rat, so last week I phoned up the borough engineer, Norman Breeze, and asked him what the hell was going on. Ultimately, new council acquisitions all go through him, you see, so it's him we've mostly dealt with. A bit of a cold fish is Norman, you wouldn't want to go on a walking holiday with him, but he knows his job backwards. And he said there was absolutely nothing to worry about, we should just sit tight. So I sat tight for another five days or thereabouts, and then on Monday afternoon, just gone, the man calls me up and says the deal's off. I said, why, are AEC not selling? And at first he wouldn't tell me, so I threatened to camp out in his office until I had the whole story, and he came clean, said Colin Cudleigh had found a great list of problems, from rust in the roof girders to subsidence round the foundations, and the whole place would have to come down. I said, you can't do that, it's a listed building, and he just said that was unlikely to be an obstacle. I don't know if you ever get hunches – '

I said, 'I do, as it happens. Occasionally correct.'

'Well I suddenly had a hunch that there was another buyer waiting in the wings whose only plan for the Empire was to see it reduced to rubble in double-quick time. So I asked Norman if anyone else had expressed an interest in the site, but he wasn't for saying. I must admit that by now I was seeing red, and I really launched into him, went on and on at him until finally he caved in and said there'd been discussions with Addison's about a new Boulevard supermarket. Discussions, my backside! If you ask me, they're a damn site further down the road than discussions.'

At the recollection of all this, Sandy Smythe had turned a deeper purple, but I risked cutting in. 'Wait a minute – are you suggesting that the borough surveyor's report is a piece of fiction, that the building is actually quite sound?'

He shifted in his seat. 'In my position, what would it look like to you?'

'But surely, for that to work other people would have to be in on it too. We're talking about significant corruption.'

'Not necessarily. There might be one or two others at most. Everyone trusts the borough surveyor, and there's nothing odd or implausible about this report of his, it'll just be nodded through.'

Matt said, 'Couldn't you commission your own independent survey?'

Sandy Smythe regarded him admiringly. 'I can see you've eaten your porridge this morning. Yes, that's exactly what I told Norman Breeze that I intended to do. And you know what he said? He said AEC saw no reason to grant access to the building to anyone except bona fide buyers, and everyone knows we haven't got that kind of money. It's all been stitched up!'

I said, 'So that's when you decided to give the story to the

Gazette.'

'Oh, no, we don't work like that in SOE. We talk everything through before we make a move, everyone has to agree, so I called a meeting for the Monday night. We meet at a member's house in Welldale, I haven't got the space here.'

'And did you drive over there?' I had my reasons for asking.

'I took the train, as a matter of fact.' A rare defensive note crept into Smythe's useful baritone. 'I don't drive any more, not since last year. Had a bit of a bump, actually, nothing major but they took away my licence. It's my eyesight, you understand. Never been good, but it's slipped even further this past couple of years. Anyway, it was a rowdy meeting as you can imagine, and the upshot was that I was delegated to have a word with the editor at the Gazette and see if he'd run the story. I thought he might be anxious about treading on council toes, but he's always backed our scheme and he said the people of Southaven had a right to know what was happening. Of course, he couldn't suggest any kind of wrong-doing because we've got no proof, but we did hope that a bit of exposure might at least stir things up. Now we'll find out.' So greatly did Sandy Smythe relish this prospect that it caused him to rub his hands gleefully together.

I said, 'And it was when you were travelling back from that meeting on Monday night that you happened to see Martin Berry on the train.'

The result was highly satisfying. The hand-rubbing ceased, and two very startled heads were turned in my direction. Sandy Smythe hesitated for a good five seconds before he responded, and five seconds can be a very long time.

'Well – yes, since you mention it. But how did you know?'

I shrugged. 'Just call it a hunch.' Which was fair enough, because a hunch is exactly what it was. 'Did you speak to him at all?'

'No, no. I happened to sit in the seats across the aisle from him and his friend. I'm not sure that he even noticed me. Of course, I did wonder if he might know something, with working in Colin Cudleigh's office. I'd seen him there a couple of weeks ago when I dropped in to ask Colin how much longer we'd have to wait for the survey. Perhaps I'm wrong, but the impression I got then was that Martin Berry was just the office gofer really, the sort who holds the end of the tape measure when they're on site. I recognized him from Beach Road, going to and fro in that smart suit of his, I knew he must live further up that way, in the next street or two. So if he'd been on his own I'd have introduced myself, but as it was I didn't like to interrupt their chat. Besides, I did think that when he got off the train at Otterdale he'd be walking up my way, so I could speak to him then, but it turned out he and his chum set off in the opposite direction.'

'You say, "chum". Did the two of them seem to be on friendly terms?' I found the concept strange. An hour or so earlier, Martin had been sitting on my settee taking a very different line about Danny Craven.

'Oh, yes, no question about it. The other fellow was telling Martin Berry about some kind of racy film he'd just been to see, they were having a laugh. Then Berry invited him to come back for a drink, but the other chap said he'd got plenty of beer in the fridge and his place was nearer. If you ask me, I think Martin Berry had had a few already.'

I smiled. 'I don't know about your eyes, Mr Smythe, but there's nothing much wrong with your ears.'

He didn't take this well. 'I never meant to eavesdrop, the carriage was half empty, I couldn't help overhearing them.'

'So then did you just give up the idea of questioning Martin Berry, or what?'

Another lengthy hesitation now followed. I'd have given a week's wages to know what Smythe was thinking, if I'd only had a job. Eventually he said, 'The fact is, I'm a bit of a late bird. Five or six hours' sleep normally does me, and in any case my head was still buzzing from the meeting, there was no point in trying to go to bed. I thought perhaps it wouldn't be long before the lad came past on his way home. So I settled down in the front room with a hot drink, where I could see back along Beach Road, and I waited. That time of night there was next to no-one about, if anyone came along there was a fair chance it would be him. My sight may not be brilliant but you learn to recognize people by other things, the way they walk perhaps, or even what you might call their aura. I was sure I'd know him if he made an appearance.'

'And did he?'

One, two, three, four, five. 'No.'

'How long did you wait?'

'I'm not sure. I think it was getting on for one o'clock when I went to bed.'

I scratched my head. Sandy Smythe was certainly proving good value, this was almost too much to take in. Of course, he was lying, or possibly just leaving out the juicy bits, but why? I wondered if he realized how much depended on his testimony. I said, 'When did you find out that Martin Berry had been murdered?'

'My neighbour said they'd found a body up at the lake. Police came door to door, apparently, but I've been out a lot. I didn't know who it was until I read it in the Gazette this morning. You could have knocked me down with a feather.'

'So naturally you called the police and told them what you've just told me?'

The idea seemed to alarm him. 'Do you think I should?'

I did my best to look stern and disapproving, though I have all the wrong facial muscles. 'Mr Smythe – I think you're missing something here. You were one of the last few people to see Martin Berry alive. And since that story was written, there's been an interesting development. The police have questioned the other man you saw on suspicion of murder.'

'Good Lord!'

'Good Lord indeed. So you understand how significant it would be if you'd seen Martin again later on.'

'But they seemed to be getting on so well. Have they charged the man?'

I shook my head. 'He claims to have said his farewells to Martin at the station and gone home alone.'

'That isn't true. They wandered off down Beach Road, all pals together.'

'So you are quite certain that Martin Berry didn't pass by here later that night?'

I'd counted to four this time when Sandy Smythe suddenly hit on a new approach. Consulting his wrist watch, he said, 'I wonder where Hazel's got to? Not like her to be late.' And immediately the door chimes ding-donged, and our tonsured friend leaped up from his chair and left the room.

I turned to Matt, Matt turned to me. He said, 'Well then.'

I said, 'How about that?'

He said, 'You're actually quite good at this, aren't you?' and I may possibly have nodded agreement.

We heard Sandy Smythe, out in the hallway, welcome his pupil and usher her into the music room. Then he came back for us. There was a new energy and confidence about him now that the interview was over. He said, 'I'm sorry, gentlemen, we're going to have to leave it there.' We rose to our feet and went ahead of him into the hallway, but I found myself coming to a halt in front of a framed sepia photograph of what I took to be a stunningly handsome soldier from the Great War. Noticing this, Smythe said, 'Striking, isn't she? That's Rosie Walmsley, Southaven's answer to Ella Shields.'

Matt said, 'Who's Ella Shields?'

'One of our great male impersonators. Used to sing *Burlington Bertie from Bow*, died onstage at Butlins, tragic. They all appeared at the Empire back in the glory days, the cream of the British music hall: George Formby Senior, Marie Lloyd, Little Tich – '

Feeling that I'd heard enough of this sort of thing for one morning, I said, 'You certainly seem to know the history of the Empire.'

He said, 'Should do, I'm writing a book about it. Out next year, with a bit of luck.' And on that optimistic note he propelled us from the building and shut the door. Clearly he was not a teacher who wasted much time on small talk, because in a matter of seconds we heard him strike a couple of establishing chords and the unseen Hazel began to winch herself slowly up through her tessitura, to the syllable *moo*.

Beside me, Matt too seemed to be bursting with an unsung song, but when he opened his mouth to give voice to it I felt obliged to cut him short. I said, 'Please, not a word. I can't take any more. Unless I eat a substantial breakfast in the next twenty minutes, I may well die.' And I drove us to the workers' caff on Station Parade.

3

Few things glad the bruised soul more than a full English breakfast, even when cooked by Italians. I'd never visited Frankie's Café on Station Parade before, so it was only now that the proprietor stood revealed as one Francesca, from Milan, who ran the joint with the help of an uneconomically large contingent of her fellow-countrymen. This discovery pleased me, because I'd always felt that an injection of cosmopolitanism might help to revive Southaven's failing pulse. I'd been at school with Terry Wong, whose parents owned what was said to be the first Chinese restaurant in the north outside Liverpool's Chinatown. But in those days the Wongs would have opened and closed your list of exotic Southaven residents, unless you counted a handful of Armenians whose ancestors had fled here from the Ottoman persecution around the turn of the century. Although recently things had begun to change, Southaven still viewed outsiders with suspicion, so it was encouraging to find this splash of Latin colour in torpid Otterdale.

And they could cook; the full English breakfast satisfied on all points. My one-armed assistant, meanwhile, had opted for the spaghetti. He was not a slow eater and had cleaned the plate before I'd even started on my second rasher. I suppose he'd made a good choice for a man with only one working hand. I said, 'I'm guessing Smythe was wrong about the porridge?'

Wiping his mouth, Matt said, 'All I've had is toast, and tea by the bucketful. I had toast with my dad when he got up around half six, I had toast again with my sister at seven, and I had toast with my mother and my brother Ryan some time after that.'

I said, 'I interrupted you.'

'What?'

'Back at Traherne Close. You attempted speech, I interrupted you.'

'Right, yes, I remember.' Aware that he already overflowed with tea, I'd suggested Matt try a small espresso, and he took a sip of it now and winced. 'Serious coffee. You'll have me on the ceiling.'

I'd have been content with any surface really, but I let that go.

He said, 'I was going to say, I think I know why Sandy Smythe moved across town when he lost his driving licence. What I don't know is, whether that's got anything to do with Martin Berry.'

'Yes – why on earth did you keep banging on about convenience? I thought you must be having some kind of psychotic episode.'

Matt leaned towards me and lowered his voice. He said, 'The dunes.' Then he backed away again.

I said, 'The dunes?'

He nodded and said, 'The dunes.'

It was becoming apparent that the answer had something to do with the dunes. I said, 'Explain.'

He said, still rather quietly, 'You know – the dunes. Blokes looking for a bit of action. Can't be much more than ten minutes' walk from Traherne Close.' And he gave me a half-pitiful and half-reproachful look as if uncertain where to place me in the line-up of historic sad-sacks and losers. 'Surely you must have been up the dunes one time or another?'

I said, 'Oh – you mean the dunes!' Perhaps because of the unexpectedly hot tomato which I'd just bitten into, I spoke more loudly than I'd intended, and several customers looked over in our direction. The place was busy, but then there was absolutely nowhere else to go in Otterdale. I lowered my voice to Matt's more confidential level. 'If you meant the dunes, why didn't you say so?'

'Smythe's up there all the time. Stands on top of a sandhill bollock naked except for his glasses and waves his willie around.'

'Please, I'm eating.'

'I don't know whether it's his age, but his balls hang somewhere round his knees.'

'You're doing it on purpose. And how's his success rate?'

'Poor. He scares people. But you get the odd one there who does it for money, and I think he takes advantage of their services.' Matt shook his head. 'The wrong attitude, isn't it? But I've only ever seen that once or twice.'

This started me thinking. I said, 'You don't suppose he recognized you just now?'

'No, positive. He's half blind, and I've always kept my distance.'

I chewed a last reflective mouthful of sausage and laid down the knife and fork, well pleased. Then I said, 'You know what I'm going to say next, don't you?'

He looked at me all innocence, head tilted a little, soft brown eyes very wide. 'No – what?'

I said, 'Your in-depth knowledge of Smythe's sexual habits suggests many happy hours of observation.' Matt's expression hadn't changed, so I tried again. 'The reason you know he's always up the dunes is because you're always up the dunes yourself.'

This did the trick. 'Not since Eileen, I don't go any more. It was just – functional. I mean, where else can you go around here?'

'There's always the Velvet Bar.'

'The Velvet Bar! Hah! All those mincing queens in mauve hipsters – '

I wasn't standing for this. 'Excuse me, I happen to quite like the Velvet Bar.' And I did. It had been the cocktail bar of the George

Hotel on the Promenade, but since acquiring a barman of style and character, known locally as Leslie Lush, its clientele had become more specialized.

Matt said, 'You're joking. I've only been in there once, but it was like a throw-back to the nineteen-thirties. Everyone just stopped talking and looked me straight in the crotch. And they all call each other girls' names and say "she" this and "she" that.' He shivered at the recollection. 'I'm surprised at you, to be honest.'

Annoyingly, I could feel the heat rising to my face. 'Well, perhaps I'm surprised at you for making yourself so much at home on the dunes, a good Catholic boy like you. Besides, I'm a throwback to the nineteen-thirties myself, I thought you realized.'

It cheered me now to see a reddish tinge in Matt's brown cheeks. 'What's being Catholic got to do with anything? That's a really cheap shot.' Which it was, but it had hit home, and that's the main thing.

I said, 'I bet your family don't know, do they? About you liking men.'

But he didn't pick that up. Instead, he gulped down the rest of the coffee and said, 'I've just noticed – you're not smoking.'

And I said, 'I've given up.'

You know how sometimes you just say things, and then they're out and you can't take them back and you have to live with the consequences. In rushing Matt out of the flat I'd accidentally left my fags on the table. After the interview in Traherne Close, my chief concern had been to appease my rumbling stomach, so I'd not wasted time stopping off at the newsagent's. It was only when I set down the knife and fork that I first thought seriously of having a cigarette, but that would now be entirely out of the question.

He said, 'Oh – good for you. What brought that on?'

I tapped my chest. 'I get short-winded on the stairs. No good at thirty-four, is it?' I was amazed how plausible this sounded.

He nodded assent. 'Mind you, you'll have to be careful not to get fat.'

'I'm not fat. What is this? Everybody keeps saying I'm fat.'

'I didn't say you were fat, I just said you'll have to be careful not to *get* fat. No more full English breakfasts.'

The cruelty of this defied belief: only a few seconds since the fatal utterance and already my full English breakfasts had been axed. I recalled what the Wetherleys' chauffeur had said about a slippery slope. Anxious to change the subject, I said, 'Anything else strike you about Sandy Smythe?'

'Oh, yes. I expect you thought I'd missed it, but I hadn't.'

'Missed what?'

'He's left-handed. That always turns out to be important, doesn't it?'

Other investigators would probably have fired their side-kicks immediately in response to such a fatuous remark, but he made it so charmingly, and his lips hung open so appealingly afterwards, that I chose to stay my hand. I noticed now that a patch of tomato sauce still clung to Matt's lower lip, so I reached out and gently removed it with my finger. I suppose some people would have flinched away, but Matt moved a little towards me as I moved towards him. Life is so much easier when people don't fight you all the time, and something in me opened gratefully in response. I sucked the sauce from my fingertip.

I said, 'All right, let me ask you this: what new questions do you have since the interview?'

Matt chewed his lip, the way I'd seen him do before. He said, 'OK. Number one: why were Martin Berry and Danny Craven all lovey-dovey when Martin was supposed to have hated Danny's guts? Number two: why did Sandy Smythe claim that he'd not seen Martin again later that night? He was obviously lying, you could tell. And number three: was Smythe right about the surveyor's report on the Empire being dodgy, and how much did Martin know about it?'

Although in some ways it vexed me that this was turning out to be National Gaze Admiringly At Matthew Standish Day, there seemed little choice now but to gaze admiringly across the formica at my mop-haired friend. All the key questions had featured in his list, pithily framed. I said, 'Not bad, for a beginner. A few more years of training and I might feel obliged to pay you pocket money of some kind. So what do you think would be the quickest way to get answers?'

The lip came in for more attention. 'Well – you could go back and talk to Danny Craven again – ' He sounded unconvinced.

'But?'

'But, you have to prioritize. You've been neglecting the whole Empire cinema angle for the last couple of days, you need to make up for lost time. I'd go and see the borough surveyor if I were you.'

I hesitated before speaking again. It wouldn't do to build up Matt's ego too much. 'Why have you been working on a building site? You're obviously not without abilities. If pushed, I'd go so far as to say you show promise.'

Matt wrinkled his nose. 'You sound like my mother. Things don't always work out, do they? I hate office jobs, I keep wanting to be outside. I did a couple of months on the post but they sacked me, I was crap at sorting.' He seemed embarrassed about this. 'The words jump about when I look at them. So I did gardening jobs for a while, then someone said I could make more money building. I worked for a local builder in Marshfield but the boss turned hippy and dropped out. Now I'm mostly with Baybridge Construction. Anyway, it won't matter soon.'

'Why not?'

'We've got our first gig coming up next month.'

'You're in a group?' And if I sounded horrified, it was no more than the situation demanded. It seemed as if two out of every three young people in Southaven had formed a group in the past ten years, and my personal view was that this had to stop. There was enough suffering in the world already.

'Why shouldn't I be?'

'You're not the drummer, are you?'

He looked hurt. 'I'm the lead singer. And I write all the lyrics.'

'What's the name of this ensemble?'

Matt looked faintly abashed. 'The Sand Lizards.'

'I'm beginning to think you're obsessed with those dunes.'

'We're really good, honest. We practise every Sunday afternoon.'

I didn't trust myself to pursue this without my tact slipping, so I looked at my watch and said, 'You're right – I need to see the borough surveyor. I've been wasting effort on the bit part players, it's time I set my sights a little higher.' As we'd come in I'd noticed a payphone on the wall beyond the counter. I checked my pockets. 'I don't suppose you've got change for the phone?'

Matt frowned. 'You already owe me sixpence for the Gazette.'

It was my mother's proud boast that she'd never once paid for a drink provided there happened to be a man in the bar at the time, and I didn't want Matt to think I was cut from the same cloth. I said, 'Didn't I say? The spaghetti's on me.' Which was foolish, because now he'd expect free spaghetti every day.

I went up to the till, paid for the food and got change while I was about it. As a rule I'm useless at remembering numbers, but the council's main switchboard was on 78787 and formed an exception.

I was transferred to the office of Colin Cudleigh, but it turned out that in response to an earlier call he'd left the building. I asked that he ring me, gave both my phone numbers, and was then put through to the borough engineer's office. Norman Breeze was unavailable too, and his secretary tried to persuade me that he was likely to remain that way until hell froze over or I stopped bothering him, whichever came sooner.

I said, 'I'm investigating the murder of Martin Berry. I feel sure Mr Breeze will want to cooperate.'

Presumably she'd registered that I wasn't from the police, but choosing the right vocabulary counts for everything on these occasions. She said, 'I suppose Mr Breeze might be able to squeeze you in at two fifteen this afternoon. But he does have another appointment at half past.' This was better than nothing, so I thanked her and rang off.

At the table, I brought Matt up to date. He said, 'Danny Craven?' I nodded, and we went outside.

The major world religions are united in recommending that we forgive and forget, and it's heart-warming to live at a period when humankind gives currency to such fine ideas. On the other hand, it was less than twenty-four hours since Danny Craven had told me to fuck off, and if I meant to give it back to him with knobs on then he only had himself to blame. Once again, it was beautiful weather for a stroll, but I wasn't in strolling mood, so I drove us round the corner to the industrial estate. Danny's gates were closed and padlocked, the Bedford was nowhere in sight. If he'd gone out on a job we stood little chance of finding him. The only hope was that he might still be at the house, and a couple of minutes later, seeing the van minding its own business outside, I parked opposite, crossed the street with Matt in tow, and knocked on Danny's door. Nothing happened, so I knocked harder, and when that also failed I reprised the thumps and hammerings which I'd tried the previous evening. Attacking the door like this was entertaining, but I was just warming up for the main bout.

After a couple of minutes, the door swung open. Danny looked me in the eye, said, 'Sod off,' and attempted to shut the door again. It always amuses me to see the astonishment on the faces of lightweights and amateurs like Danny Craven when that old door-in-the-face routine unaccountably lets them down. Of course, my foot hurt and the shoe would never be the same again, but it was worth it.

I said, 'Sorry, Danny, can't do that,' and with a firm hand in his chest I pushed him back into the house and stepped inside, with Matt following. Ahead, to the left, ran the narrow staircase. On the right there were two doors, of which the nearer must lead into the chaotic parlour I'd seen through the window the previous day. I chose none of these options and instead pushed Danny further along the hallway and down a single step into the back kitchen.

This was bigger than I'd expected, and much less untidy. At some stage, perhaps in a first rush of enthusiasm after moving into the house, Danny's father must have enlarged the rear extension. There was certainly plenty of room for the small round table and two chairs against the near wall. Beyond the kitchen, an arch opened onto a lobby area stacked with boxes, from which a door led out to the garden. Further still came the open bathroom door, hung about with wraiths of steam from the bath which Danny Craven had recently vacated because some annoying individual was trying to pummel his way into the house. We were just in time to hear a throaty gurgle as the last of the bathwater swilled down the plughole.

I should have mentioned that Danny himself, who had now come to an angry halt in the middle of the kitchen floor, wore nothing but a towel, which clung tightly to his wet skin. As bath towels go, it would have made an excellent face flannel, and if it had been any smaller or his waist less slender the two ends could hardly have met. Already disposed to be irritated with Danny, this only irritated me the more. When last I'd interviewed him, my efforts to ignore his all-too-present body had undermined my tenacity and allowed him to get away with lies and evasions, but at least on that occasion he'd been wearing trousers. I now ran the particular risk of becoming fascinated by a line of short brown hairs which spilled down from his tight little navel and disappeared beneath the towel. Perhaps I should have told him to get dressed, but where's the fun in that?

Danny said, 'You've got no right barging in here like this!'

I said, 'Sit down.' He checked my face for evidence of weakness. With a tilt of my head I indicated which chair it would be wise for him to sit in. He complied. The lower edges of the towel now settled down to either side of one long brown leg. On the table, a half-finished mug of tea stood next to a copy of the Gazette, front page uppermost. Matt had chosen to lean against the stove, but Danny took no notice of him and I decided to leave him unexplained.

Pacing a little on the lino floor, I said, 'You know what, Danny? I don't like you. Yesterday I went out of my way to be reasonable. I warned you to expect a little visit from the constabulary, I encouraged you to get your story straight, I advised complete honesty because you're obviously far too stupid to play smart with the rozzers or anyone else. And how do you repay this kindness? Lies. All I've heard from you is lies. So while yesterday I gave you the benefit of the doubt, I'm done with that now. You're a worthless piece of shit, aren't you? No wonder Monica won't let you fuck her.'

The chair scraped back, he was on his feet in a second, right arm raised to strike. But this was exactly what I'd wanted, my left hand blocked the fist, my right came down hard on his wet shoulder and shoved him down into the seat. With my knee rammed into his chest, I pinned him back while I grabbed his chin and pushed his head against the wall, which it smacked into with a satisfying crack. I felt him yield to me. He smelled of fear and coal tar soap.

I stood down, let go of the chin, picked up his right hand and examined it. The sticking plaster had gone, and I could see where the cut had begun to heal. 'Is that how it was with Martin? He said something you just couldn't take and – bam! – out came the fist.'

'I don't have to tell you anything.' He pulled the hand away, then rubbed the back of his head. I hoped it hurt.

'But he was here, wasn't he – Monday night? When you met him on the train you invited him back. You were seeing a different Martin, one of the lads, you thought perhaps you'd misjudged him. And you were glad of the company. It gets lonely, living by yourself.'

I could hear Danny's brain attempting thought again. He must have decided on a new tack, because then he said, 'It started on the train. He got into my carriage just before the doors closed. I thought he was going to spoil the journey, usually he makes me feel awkward, but there was something different about him, more confident. We started to have a laugh about something – '

'You're slipping again, Danny. Not just "something". You'd been to see *Do You Want To Remain A Virgin For Ever?* The whole truth, if you don't mind.'

He looked dumbstruck. Of course, it was a guess, but a pretty safe guess all the same. With the Empire out of action, there were only two cinemas open in the town centre, and while *The Lion In*

Winter has been called many things, 'racy' isn't one of them.

It was clear from Danny's expression that he now regarded me as a sort of Southaven Nostradamus. He said, 'Have you seen it? That wasn't you sitting along the row from me in a brown mac?'

'Never mind about the film. Did Martin tell you why he was in this improved frame of mind?'

Danny's eyes darted sideways. If what came next wasn't an outright lie, I doubted if it would be the whole truth either. He said, 'He reckoned he'd got one over on his boss. It seemed to have made his day.' He scratched the inside of his thigh. I wished he wouldn't.

'So what happened when you came back here?'

Danny pointed through the wall. 'We had a couple of cans in the lounge, on the settee. There isn't really anywhere else to sit. My dad hoarded stuff, I don't like to get rid of it.'

'Must have been hard for you, losing him like that.'

Danny was quiet for a few moments. Then he said, 'Martin was making a big deal of that. He said if I was lonely I should phone him, he'd always be happy to come round.' Danny seemed uncomfortable now. I didn't know why, but it had to be progress. He was opening up, perhaps he needed me to be more open in my turn.

I said, 'The thing is, Danny, none of this makes sense. The Martin I spent that evening with was in a jealous rage. He was convinced you were having sex with his wife. He talked about killing you, and I wouldn't have put it past him.'

Danny nodded, thoughtfully. He said, 'There's more. He told me that if I was really broke he'd find something else for me to do at the house, maybe a loft conversion. He said, "Stick with me and you'll be fine," or words to that effect.'

'And what did you make of all this?'

The eyes moved sideways again. Reflexively he picked up one side of the towel and tried to pull it across his exposed leg, but it fell back as soon as he let go. Then he shrugged his shoulders and said, 'Nothing. I thought it was just talk, I thought he was showing off. He'd had a couple of drinks.' And he took another sip of the cold tea.

Well, what with the half-truths and the towel I'd had about enough of Danny Craven, so I dragged out the second chair and sat down in it, knee to knee with Danny, my right foot resting on his left. I took the mug from his hand and passed it back to Matt, who placed it on the draining board out of harm's way. There was fear in

Danny's eyes, and he shrank back from me. I said, 'OK, Danny. I'm trying to be patient with you because I can see you're way out of your depth, but you've got to realize you're the world's worst liar. The fact is, you had a theory, didn't you? Martin's behaviour had always puzzled you, but on Monday night your little bird-brain finally came up with an explanation. Why don't you tell me what that was?'

Danny tried to speak, but he couldn't. His jaw worked, his mouth opened, nothing came out.

I said, 'Is that one too hard for you? We can leave it for a moment, if you like, and try another. What happened next?' He looked me straight in the eye, and now I understood that it wasn't so much me that scared him as something else, something that scared him all the time. He was trying to find a way to talk about it, but it lay beyond his powers.

I hadn't got all day, so I said, 'Is this what happened, Danny?' Gently I lowered my right hand onto his leg. He seemed mesmerized, kept his eyes fixed on my face, while the hand made itself at home. Then slowly, inch by inch, the hand ran up along the taut flesh of his thigh.

And finally Danny made his move, which was just as well because I was running out of leg. With new strength he was on his feet, pushing me back off the chair and onto the floor. It was time to let Danny score some points, so I didn't put up much resistance. In a second he was on top of me, kneeling on me, pinning down my shoulders with his hands. Matt made no effort to intervene, beyond bending to pick up the towel, which had settled at his feet after parting company with Danny's waist in mid-lunge. Red-faced, raging, Danny spat out the words he'd been holding back before. 'I'm not a poof, all right? I'm not a fucking poof!'

Trying for a tone of sweet reason, I said, 'Did Martin think you were a poof, Danny?' It came out squeakier than I'd intended, but then I had a naked builder kneeling on my abdomen.

'No!' He thought for a second, and his ferocity slipped back a notch or two. 'I don't know. He made me feel like he'd done me a good turn, now he wanted something back. He put his hand on my leg.'

I said, 'I hate to complain, Danny, but you're grinding my car keys into my groin and it's really uncomfortable.'

Danny said, 'Oh,' and stood up. With a helpful smile, Matt held the towel out for him, and I think it was only then that Danny realized he was exhibiting what the Gazette would no doubt have called his genials. Though this didn't appear to bother him, he still turned his back for a second while fixing the towel in place again, and I could see that he was in the habit of sunbathing without the pointless constraint of clothes. My second-in-command took the opportunity to throw me a look which involved a lot of eyebrow work, and which I interpreted to mean that should Danny ever change horses and become a regular up the dunes, he wouldn't be short of company.

Getting up now, I gave myself a perfunctory dusting down, surprised to have found that the floor was actually quite clean. I began to wonder whether Faye came in and did, and if so, what. I said, 'And that's when you hit him?'

Facing me again, Danny nodded. 'It took him a second or two to react, but then he had a swing at me himself, only I'd ducked out of the way and he caught the edge of the sideboard. Must have hurt. Then he accused me of getting it on with Monica. I told him he was wrong, I've never laid a finger on her. He called me a lying bastard and came at me again, we wrestled a bit, the coffee table went over and the lamp smashed. He was too drunk to fight properly, I got on top of him and told him what I thought of him, told him he was a jumped-up little snob and Monica was too good for him. Then he got out from under, and he went.'

'Leaving his briefcase behind.'

'Briefcase? What briefcase?' And I could see that Danny had no clue what I was talking about. He sat down again now and glanced up at the wall clock.

I said, 'Not keeping you, are we?'

'I'm meeting a customer.'

'That why you're not at the yard?'

'I went down there and came back again. But I'd managed to get filthy in about ten minutes, some customers don't like it, I thought I'd take a quick bath.' He scratched his thigh again, but now we'd enjoyed the full floor-show that didn't bother me any more.

'A well-paid job, is it?'

I thought he hesitated. He said, 'With a bit of luck.'

'Well then, we'll let you get on. But just one more thing. Why did you lie to the police? They know you're not playing straight, until you tell them exactly what happened you're going to stay right up there at number one, chief suspect.'

Danny shifted in his seat, lowered his eyes. 'What if they decide there's no smoke without fire? I mean, suppose I say Martin was a bit – you know – they might start wondering about me too.'

I took a moment to study the man. Though Danny's face couldn't be called handsome, there were times, especially if his subject was Monica, when some strain of nobility briefly possessed him, lending him an almost military dignity. This was not one of those times. I said, 'Let me get this clear – are you saying you'd rather they suspected you of murder than of batting for the other team?'

And he said, 'Well, yes. Wouldn't you?' He looked at the clock again. 'Are we done? I have to get moving.'

I said, 'Listen, Danny – no more lies, all right? Think of Monica. Martin may not have been your favourite person, but she needs to know how he died, and so far you've done nothing but waste everybody's time.' This idea had stung him, I could see, but he didn't speak. I said, 'Do you understand me, Danny? Don't give us any more shit.'

But there was still conflict in Danny's face, and I knew that I hadn't done with him after all, he was still trying to play me for a fool. There would be no point in leaning on him again now, I'd had as much out of him today as I was likely to get. It might be best to let him think we were on good terms, so I offered my hand and said, 'No hard feelings, eh?' His expression neutral, he took the hand, gripped it briefly, then slipped right out of it again. He rose to his feet.

'I'll see you out.' Danny walked ahead of me, up the step and along the narrow hallway. There are few perks when you're investigating a murder and it's wise to seize them with both hands, so naturally as we went I took a good look at the small, round buttocks where they strained against the towel. Again I found myself wondering about Faye. Just how useful did Danny make himself while her Olaf was at sea?

I'd taken no more than half a dozen steps towards the front door when I could have sworn I heard the sound of tearing paper behind me. But it must have been my imagination.

4

By the time Matt spoke, we were half way back to town on the coast road and I'd almost forgotten he was in the passenger seat. In the meantime, frustration had dominated my thoughts. Half a story can be so much worse than none, and the further we travelled from Otterdale the angrier I was becoming at Danny's persistent refusal to give me all he'd got. There must, after all, be some level of intelligence behind his stupid obstinacy, and I was as much angry with myself as with him, because I'd been too busy amusing myself at his expense to read him right.

Then Matt said, 'I hope I never get the wrong side of you.'

'What?' My consciousness now made the two-mile flight from Danny's back kitchen to rejoin my body in the Cortina.

'Was it really necessary to whack him around like that?'

I said, 'Of course it was,' though of course it wasn't. 'You have to play rough with some people, it's the only language they understand.'

'He still isn't telling the whole truth though, is he? You've let him slip through your fingers.'

'Are you questioning my methods? Perhaps you'd like to have a crack at him yourself next time.'

'Yes, I would, as a matter of fact.' His tone was huffy.

'Well then, be my guest.' So was mine.

'I'll do that.'

'Pleased to hear it.'

We drove the next half mile in silence.

Then Matt said, 'There was a frying pan in the sink, and two greasy plates.'

'Ah – good work.' And I explained how Faye and Danny had something going between them, though I wasn't sure what.

Coming off the coast road then, I turned onto Floral Parade. As always, the displays showed fussy, over-planted, municipal, as if each bloom had been stamped *County Borough of Southaven* in the top left-hand corner. There were trippers here, and on the Promenade too, the old and the very young predominating, and for a moment I indulged the delusion that Southaven could yet rise to become a fashionable resort again.

Matt said, 'I need to go to the site office for my P45, so I can sign on.'

There were things I wanted to sort out before my meeting with Norman Breeze. I said, 'Let's get together this afternoon, when I've seen the borough engineer.'

'I'll be hanging around with nothing to do.'

'You can have the keys to my flat. And if you're at a loose end, I've got a little job for you.'

'Yes?' I could feel how Matt's spirits rose. He was nothing if not keen, and on top of that he was observant and he thought things through. Who could tell? Perhaps my spur-of-the-moment suggestion in the Albion might furnish me eventually with a genuinely useful assistant, in the long run even a partner. Perhaps we could expand the business, start looking beyond Southaven for customers.

But just now, there was donkey work to be done. 'Yes. I need a couple of Manchester phone numbers. First off, Monica's friend – '

'Leah Armstrong.'

'And her unsuccessful suitor, whose name your irritatingly efficient memory has also stored.'

He nodded. 'Rupert Heysham.' But the boost to Matt's spirits had proved short-lived. 'Haven't you got anything more interesting?'

'If you think that's dull, wait till you try surveillance work. But it's important, I've got to have those numbers. I could ask Monica but I'm not sure I want her to know what I'm up to, where Rupert and Leah are concerned. Anyway, it's a challenge for you, I don't have an address for either of them.'

Matt considered this. 'I suppose I could go to the reference library.'

'Good scheme. They love to be of service.'

I gave Matt the keys for Leigh Terrace and dropped him off opposite the end of Station Road. In the rear-view mirror I watched as he crossed the Boulevard, all youth and energy and optimism. Of course, I was sorry that he'd broken his arm, but as the man said, it's an ill wind that blows nobody any good. If Matt played his cards right, he might have done his last day's work on a building site.

I parked behind Crowburn House and hurried through to the front office to have a word with Derek Lethbridge, the office manager. Martin Berry had visited Crowburn House recently, or so he'd told me, and it would be Derek who had dealt with him. But annoyingly, the sole occupant of the room was the ancient secretary, Miss Forshaw, who was bashing away at an Imperial of similar vintage as if it had wronged her in some bitter dispute. I stood at the counter for a minute, hoping that she would notice me. She didn't, so I said, 'Miss Forshaw?' The vicious assault on her typewriter continued. 'Miss Forshaw?'

Miss Forshaw stopped typing and glared at me over her left shoulder, hands still poised above the keys. She was not a woman much given to speech, and she didn't speak now.

I said, 'Is Derek about?'

She shook her head.

I said, 'Will he be long?'

She shrugged her shoulders.

'Where's he gone?'

Miss Forshaw removed her left hand from the keyboard, tilted back her head, and pointed with her forefinger into her open mouth.

'He's at the dentist?'

She straightened up again and nodded.

'Do you think he'll be in at all this morning?'

Miss Forshaw shook her head, then clutched her jaw with an expression of deepest agony.

'Oh – as bad as that?'

She resumed her usual, rather bleak demeanour, which I took to mean that it was indeed as bad as that.

I said, 'What if I tried again at two o'clock?'

She sucked her tongue now, as if chewing over the proposition, then shrugged not so much her shoulders as her face. I understood from this that in her view a reasonable person might not be going astray in concluding that the hour of two o'clock would produce the man Lethbridge referred to previously, but that in the event of disappointment she herself could not be held responsible. Miss Forshaw had a very expressive face, but then she needed one.

I thanked her for her help and quit the room. It was my private belief that Miss Forshaw had been nursing a violent passion for Derek Lethbridge for the last forty years, during which time she'd watched him marry, raise a family and begin the gentle slide into old age, without ever once telling her love, or anything else for that matter. But I could have been wrong.

Upstairs, I let myself into my office. The recent intruder had demonstrated that this was something any Tom, Dick or Harry could do if they put their mind to it. At some point I would have to take security more seriously, but I decided that could wait for some future slack period in the business. There were enough of those, heaven knew.

I began typing up a rough account of what had happened since the previous morning. It was my habit to smoke while engaged in composition, and by now the nicotine craving had built up a fine head of steam. Perhaps I should take a break and run out for a packet of cigarettes. After all, Matt would never know that I'd been smoking in the office, and if he began to use the office himself I could simply remove the tell-tale ashtray.

And that's when I noticed that somebody had removed the tell-tale ashtray already.

The hairs stood up on the back of my neck, and although there was absolutely nowhere to hide in the under-furnished room, still I looked around me, half expecting Martin's killer to have materialized from thin air.

Of course, I'd checked the previous morning to see if anything was missing, but I'd been thinking about documents, not anything so crass as a simple ashtray. I felt sure now that if I looked again, some trivial object would be missing from the flat too. Missing, like Martin's underpants from the pile of clothes at the lakeside. A little souvenir.

The telephone rang, and as usual I leapt about six inches in the air. What especially puzzles me is, that if I'm actually expecting the call the effect is even worse, and I've heard other people say the same. Perhaps at some point a dedicated team of rats and psychologists can be persuaded to look into the matter. Pulling myself together, I lifted the receiver. The voice said, 'Mr Rigby? Sam?'

It was Monica Berry. 'Monica – good to hear from you. How are you?' In the circumstances perhaps this was a stupid question, but on the other hand I wanted to know.

'Oh – all right, I suppose. I just try to keep going.'

'Is your mother still with you?'

'I sent her home. She means well, but – In any case, I've got to get used to being on my own.' I could think of nothing worth saying, so I didn't say it. Eventually Monica said, 'How's the investigation?'

Relieved to be on less delicate ground, I said, 'There've been developments, but nothing conclusive. You know the police took Danny Craven in yesterday evening?'

'Danny, of all people! This morning they asked me all sorts of embarrassing questions about our "relationship", as they called it. That man Hargreaves was here. He was so friendly to me on Tuesday, but this time he made me feel like a common criminal.'

I could well imagine it. 'You mustn't take any notice of Harry Hargreaves. He squeezes everybody, just to see what comes out.'

Monica said, 'Are you still all right for money?'

'For now, yes.'

'Don't go short for want of asking. The police are getting it wrong, Sam. I'm pinning all my hopes on you.'

It crossed my mind that Monica could have done better than pin her hopes on someone who took twenty-four hours to notice that his ashtray was missing, but I kept that to myself.

Monica said, 'Anyway, I've got something to tell you. I was really angry when the Inspector left the house this morning, I wanted to do something constructive. I started to think again about Martin's briefcase, and I realized I'd never looked in the garden shed.'

My heart sang. This was the breakthrough I'd been waiting for. 'You've found the briefcase?'

'No – no, I'm sorry. But – '

'Don't tell me, let me guess. The shed's been tidied up.'

'That's what I wanted to tell you. How did you know?'

'Was anything missing?'

'You'd have to ask Martin that.'

If only, if only. The list of things I would have liked to ask Martin Berry grew longer by the hour. I said, 'And do you think anyone's been in the house?'

'Not as far as I can see.'

Promising Monica that I'd call her in a day or two, I rang off. I doubted whether Mark Howell would have acted on my advice to keep the house in Vaughan Close under observation, but it had clearly been justified. If he'd done so, we might now have the killer behind bars. But then of course, I'd never actually mentioned the briefcase, so perhaps really it was all my fault. Things so often are.

I finished typing up my notes, then took a few moments to write my home phone number on the back of some of my cards. If you're tracking missing persons or pursuing an errant wife, you have a limited need for telephone communication. Knowing that I'm not in the office for more than an hour or two each day, clients generally keep in touch by post. But this week I'd discovered that investigating murder required a different approach. I'd have preferred it now if people could reach me wherever I was, at any time of day or night, but the closest I could come to that was to give both my numbers and hope for the best. Even so, I didn't amend all the cards. There are some people whose voices you just don't want to hear in the sanctuary of your own home.

It was now nearly one o'clock. I locked up, left Crowburn House by the front door, and jay-walked across to the retail side of the Boulevard. The good weather had brought out the crowds, and it was too busy to walk in the shade beneath the verandas, with all the window-shoppers. There'd been talk lately of demolishing the old verandas, on the grounds that in the modern age they were too expensive for shopkeepers to maintain. Here and there, paint was peeling from the columns to expose rusting iron, while coarse weeds sprouted from the rainwater hopper-heads below the sloping glass. Appalled by this neglect, the local Civic Trust types fired off dyspeptic letters to the Gazette at every opportunity. And it was true enough that the covered walk, which ran with only short breaks for almost a mile, was one of the town's most distinctive attractions, marking Southaven off from less caring resorts which allowed their visitors to get wet when it rained. But everything goes in the end. It could only be a matter of time before the verandas joined the old railway station buildings in the great landfill site of history. The question now was, would they or the Empire cinema get there first?

My destination was Butterworths department store, which stood just short of the Feathers Hotel. Threading my way as best I could amongst the shoppers, trippers and office workers on their lunch break, I tried not to reflect on what was causing this rare foray into the town's retail sector. I don't have the volume to hand, but it was probably Sartre who said that if you're anxious not to know something about yourself, you have to not know it with exquisite accuracy, or you might stumble upon it by mistake. I may have misquoted, but you get the gist. The thing I didn't want to know just at the moment was this: I'd seen the way Matt looked at Danny Craven; if he could look at a man like that then the lovely Eileen was going to have a job keeping him; if she couldn't keep him, perhaps I could; and finally, one glance from Matt at even the least old occupants of my underpant drawer might scupper the whole affair before it had even started. *Ergo*, new pants must be bought without delay. Unfortunately, my backroom team took the view that any attempt to pursue Matthew Standish must end in failure. As a self-styled realist I pretended to agree with them, so it was vital to my self-image that I not know my underlying motive for this visit to Butterworths. I was hard at work not knowing it as I swung open the door and stepped inside.

The would-be shopper's progress was now thwarted by five or six strategically placed cosmetics counters, forming a sort of purgatory which you had to pass through in order to gain the rest of the store. As always, I was instantly laid low by a wild sneezing fit, brought on by the miasma of unnatural odours which afflicted the place. Finding no handkerchief in my pocket, I wiped my nose with the back of one hand and my eyes with the knuckles of the other, then pressed on for the interior. But I'd not gone far when a woman's voice, whose penetrating quality would surely have drawn the admiration of Sandy Smythe, could be heard angrily screaming, 'Sam! Sam, or whatever your name is!'

Caught up as I was in trying not to know what I was really doing there, it had completely slipped my mind that Butterworths, and more especially the cosmetics department, formed the domain of Danny Craven's neighbour Faye. I turned in time to see her wriggle out from behind her own counter and set a course for my location, leaving a startled customer gawping after her, an unfinished sentence still hanging on her lips. As the gap between us narrowed, I tried the defence of looking harmless and saying 'Hello,' but she bore down on me with hostility undimmed and came to an abrupt halt about six inches away.

She said, 'You *lied* to me,' emphasizing the point by jabbing one finger into my ribs.

She was right, I had. I said, 'No I didn't.'

'You *lied*!' The finger again. 'You told me you played for the football club, you don't. You told me you were Danny's friend, you're not. You're a sneaking, snivelling, private investigator, snooping into other people's business like a – ' She groped for the *mot juste*.

'A snake?'

'Yes! Like a snake! Trying to make out you were worried about him – '

'But I am worried about him.' And it's the strangest thing, but it was only when I said it that I realized it was true. In particular, my intuition didn't like the sound of this Braithwaite character, in whose debt Danny apparently stood.

'I don't believe you.'

'Well you should.' I could sense my backroom team redeploying staff previously engaged on the underpant fiasco. They were usually quick off the mark in a crisis, and Faye turned up to maximum certainly constituted one. 'You worry about Danny yourself, don't you?'

'Well – yes, I do.'

'And why's that?'

'Because – because he doesn't take care of himself properly.'

'Exactly. And just at present he ought to be taking particularly good care of himself, because if I'm right he's got the police on one side of him and an unpleasant bunch of Southaven low-lifes on the other, and he's not very popular with either. If he had any sense he'd be throwing himself on my protection.'

Piqued by this, Faye lodged an objection. 'He does have sense, he's quite a bright boy when you get to know him.'

I shook my head. 'The problem is, he's clever enough to get into trouble but not to get out of it again. I'm doing my best to help but he won't let me.'

I wasn't sure that the picture I'd just painted was an accurate one, but at least it had the merit of calming Faye down. She patted her hair, which crackled in response. After a brief silence she said, 'He's been like a lost boy since his mother died. Bert did what he could, but a father's not the same, is he? I tried to step in, help out a bit. You know the sort of thing, cooking for them sometimes, bringing a woman's touch to the place. Bert hardly noticed really, he'd got so turned in on himself after he was widowed, but it was different with Danny, there was a spark.' She turned away from me and lowered her eyes. 'I couldn't bear it if anything happened to him.'

I said, 'Nothing's going to happen to him, I promise. Anyway, he's got you looking out for him. He's a lucky man.'

Faye smiled weakly. 'Do you think so?'

I dug one of the freshly-doctored cards out of my pocket and held it out to her. I said, 'Call me any time if you think I can help.'

It seemed that Faye was still uncertain of my bona fides, because for a second she hesitated. When finally she did take the card between her scarlet-nailed fingers, her eyes narrowed, and she said, 'You'd better not mean Danny any harm, or I promise you your life won't be worth living.' Then she turned and walked back to the counter, and I heard her say to her customer, 'So sorry to have kept you waiting,' in that strained, inhuman tone unique to shop assistants.

Feeling that, by and large, the skirmish with Faye hadn't gone too badly, I now padded across the carpeted floor towards the menswear department at the rear of the store. In an advert somewhere, I'd noticed some purple Y-fronts which seemed to me to compromise between fashion and tradition. With luck I should be able to find them, pay for them, and be out in the living, breathing world again within no more than a couple of minutes. It was only during the last year or two that Butterworths had abandoned the ancient practice of keeping all the stock in drawers, so that your every purchase had to be mediated by an assistant. These days, thank heaven, it was possible to choose, settle up, and flee, without exchanging more than half a dozen words with the sinister creatures commonly employed there.

Approaching the display of underwear, I caught the back view of a brown terylene suit topped by a neat head with very small ears. Mark Howell was ruefully fingering a pair of multi-coloured socks. I advanced silently, unseen, and began to pick my way through the piles of plastic-wrapped pants, a few feet to Mark's left. Pleased to discover the purple Y-fronts among them, I lifted out a pack of two pairs and held them up to get a better look. Then I said, 'Better not risk those socks, Mark, you don't want people talking.'

Like a young animal sensing danger, Mark turned sharply to look at me, then dropped the socks and strode rapidly away. Actually, he didn't have the legs for striding, but by whatever means he certainly covered some ground in double-quick time. I wasn't sure what he was playing at, but I didn't like it. Laying down the underpants, I gave chase. 'Mark!' He was making for the stairs to the first floor, and he must have taken them by twos in his usual fashion because by the time I got up there myself he was nowhere to be seen. In no very positive frame of mind, I quartered the floor with a determination rarely seen in Butterworths, even during the January sales. At last, I ran Mark to earth in the kitchen department, where he was feigning interest in a whisk. He'd foolishly taken up a corner position, and if he wanted to pass me now he would need to fight me first.

I closed with the man, took the utensil out of his hand, and said, 'Don't you *ever* do that to me again.'

Building on Faye's example I'd lent weight to the key word by unleashing the whisk on Mark's solar plexus, but if this bothered him he gave no sign. Anxiously trying to peer over my shoulder, for which he lacked the necessary height, he said, 'I can't be seen with you.'

There was real paranoia in those bright little eyes. I'd never known him like this before. I said, 'What the hell's got into you? Have you eaten one of Cal Shaunessy's hash cakes?'

The absurdity of this suggestion – he was, after all, Mark Squeaky-Clean Howell – seemed to ground him a little. He said, 'Don't be ridiculous. But if anyone from work saw us choosing underwear together – '

'Oh, so that's what this is about. Correct me if I'm wrong, Mark, but I hardly think that Butterworths is the resort of choice for Southaven's off-duty plods.' He didn't appear convinced. 'Why this sudden anxiety? You were perfectly happy to have a drink with me the other day, in plain sight.' This brought no reply, only a deepening of the gloom which underlay his fear. I began to feel anxious in my turn. 'Has something happened, Mark?'

He tried peering around my shoulder this time. 'Sort of. It's Cilla.'

'Cilla? She's not in trouble?'

'No, no, it's not that. But – ' He shrank from the thought he was about to share with me. 'She was in the locker room with a couple of the other girls this morning. They were taking the mickey, you know, saying it was obvious I was never going to lead her to the altar and she'd be better off looking elsewhere. And one of them said something like, "In any case, Cilla, you're not really the type to get married, are you?" That was the line – *not the type*. Cilla couldn't tell if the girl meant anything by it or not, but she wasn't going to take the chance. So she said, "If you must know, me and Mark are engaged. I don't wear the ring to work because I don't want you all making a fuss."'

'Jesus Christ, Mark.'

'Jesus Christ is correct. And you can probably guess what the other girl said next.' I couldn't, so Mark continued. 'She said, "When's the big day?" Well, Cilla couldn't just say "some time, never" because we'd have been back at square one.'

'Don't tell me she's named the day on your behalf?'

'Not exactly. But she hinted at next spring.'

Ever since Mark and Cilla had started playing their dangerous game, I'd been afraid that it would end badly, and I'd warned Mark about it time and again. Still, as Mark's friend I realized it would be an insensitive moment to say I told you so. I said, 'I told you this would happen.' Well, it just slipped out. 'You're too pig-headed to listen, that's your trouble.' To my surprise, Mark seemed to accept this criticism, which was in any case no less than the truth. 'So what are you going to do now?'

If possible, Mark's face took on an even deeper hue of desperation, but he made no reply.

I said, 'For God's sake, Mark. You're not actually thinking of marrying the woman?'

'May I be of assistance to you gentlemen?'

This speech had come from somewhere behind me, and I spun round now to see a fine-boned, silver-haired man standing just inches away from us, his slender hands clasped in front of him. Where he'd sprung from and how neither of us had noticed his approach it was impossible to say, but I knew from experience that the staff at Butterworths were trained to move soundlessly about the building like the undead. Admiration for this skill compelled you to take your hat off to them, even as your free hand reached for the garlic and the sharpened stake.

I said, 'No thanks, we're fine, just browsing.'

The assistant's eyes flickered down towards the item which I was holding, then back up to my face. 'One of our most popular lines, that whisk. As a matter of fact, I possess one myself. Extremely hard-wearing, and it never fails to give satisfaction.' Then he looked from me to Mark and back again, before gliding silently away without any perceptible motion of the feet.

Somewhat shaken, and with a sensation as of ants swarming up and down my back, I returned the whisk to the rack and wiped my hand on my trousers. Then I said to Mark, 'Well – are you going to marry her, or what?'

He said, 'I don't seem to have much choice.'

I should stress here that if things had been different Mark and Cilla would have made a pretty good match, even though to my eye, as I've said, Cilla's outward form pleased somewhat less than Mark's. She was a fine, decent and usually sensible young woman, though having apparently slipped her trolley during the recent scene in the locker room. But things were not different. In fact, I had it on intelligence from my friend Bernie (short for Bernadette), with whom I liked to pass a quiet evening at the Velvet Bar from time to time, that Cilla had been seeing a court stenographer from Preston for the last few months, and they were due to go on holiday together in August. So I meant no disrespect to Cilla when I said, 'Mark, you must not marry Cilla Donnelly. There is always a choice. Rouse yourself to action, for goodness' sake. What would your proud forefathers make of this spineless behaviour? Think of Owen Glendower!' For although it was several generations since the Howells had left their native land, Mark did occasionally express some interest in his ancestry.

But it seemed that my words had done nothing to brace the man. He shook his head, and looked into my eyes with sombre resignation. 'No, Sam, there's nothing else for it. We're trapped. If we don't marry, it'll all come out, I know it will. You can only fool people for so long.'

'Then leave the job, Mark. This has got way beyond a joke. How do you think you're going to keep this up for another thirty years?'

But rather than absorb these words of wisdom, Mark now checked his watch. 'I've got to go. I said I'd be back at the station at half one.'

I put a hand on his arm. 'Come and talk it through with me some time. I don't want to see you unhappy.'

He said, 'There's nothing to talk about.' And he pulled away.

'Then – can I just take a moment to exploit your encyclopaedic knowledge of the Southaven underworld?'

'It'll have to be quick.'

'Does the name Braithwaite mean anything to you?'

'What – Slasher Braithwaite?'

This was not exactly what I'd hoped to hear. While I'd not supposed that Braithwaite would be known to his associates as Petula, I still felt that Slasher was carrying things too far. 'Maybe. Tell me about him.'

'OK, let me see.' I watched as Mark submitted his orderly brain to the familiar process of fact-marshalling. 'Joe Braithwaite. Started out as a small-time debt-collector in Manchester, working for some of the city's less tender-hearted landlords. Got greedy, tried to reinvent himself as a loan shark, muscle in on other people's territory. Bit off more than he could chew, moved out here a couple of years ago where he wouldn't have to face such heavy competition. Making a lot of money now. He's a really nasty piece of work, Hargreaves has been trying to close him down for months but people are too scared to talk.'

None of this was cheering me up. Still, I risked asking, 'Why Slasher?'

'If you're late paying, he gets one of his thugs to cut you. If you never pay, he cuts you himself.'

'Nice man.'

'A sweetheart. Why do you ask?'

It was decision time. Much as I enjoyed holding cards which Harry Hargreaves didn't even know existed, perhaps for Danny's sake, and Faye's too, I should put this one on the table and let the police take over. What I'd just heard about Braithwaite made the decision easier. I said, 'Danny Craven owes Braithwaite money.'

'Seriously?'

'Seriously. I found out this morning.' It had been the day before, of course, but near enough. 'You'd better tell Hargreaves. Danny's trying to find work so he can get the money together, but if that doesn't come off – '

Mark mimed the slicing of a blade across his own face. He said, 'What about Martin Berry? Did Braithwaite have something to do with that?'

I'd no idea, and I said so.

Mark checked his watch again. 'I ought to be moving. Listen – were you actually thinking of buying those purple Y-fronts downstairs?' I confessed that I was, and he tut-tutted. 'You should keep to white, or grey at a push.' And he looked me up and down. 'Honestly, Sam, you really need someone to take your wardrobe in hand.'

I said, 'You can take me in hand any time you like.'

He didn't find that funny. While skimping on his ears, Nature had skimped on his sense of humour as well. Shaking his head as over some lost cause, he turned smartly on his heel and left me there among the cheese graters.

I'd come into Butterworths doing my damnedest not to think about one unattainable prize, and now I was going to leave not thinking about another. I could feel a strop coming on. At some point, without noticing it, I must have been promoted to Chief Local Sap, doomed for ever to the humiliating pursuit of inappropriate men. It wasn't dignified, and I resolved to knock it on the head. Abandoning the misconceived underpant quest, I put a tiger in my tank and headed back to Crowburn House, where with any luck Derek Lethbridge would soon be making an appearance, plus or minus teeth.

5

I waited for Derek Lethbridge in the back kitchen at Crowburn House.

Derek was a dedicated Moultoneer, having been amongst the first in Southaven to own one of the small-wheeled bicycles which have brought innocent amusement to so many of us. It was his firm belief that if the cherished machine could be glimpsed from the street, the envious multitude would steal it, so he always left it in the courtyard, protected from rainfall by the coal shed canopy. Sitting in the kitchen with the back door open, I'd be able to hear Derek grappling with the yard door as he came in, and so have as much time to speak with him as possible. Already the kitchen clock showed one forty-five, and I was due at the town hall for my micro-appointment with Norman Breeze in exactly half an hour.

Uncle Fred had persuaded me to eat a slice of apple pie with custard, despite the fact that my Anglo-Italian breakfast was still under review from the appropriate gastric juices. Aunt Winnie sat very upright at the table, studying my every mouthful as if hoping to identify the exact moment when the poison began to take effect. This occupied so much of her attention that she seemed not to realize she was holding her teacup in mid-air, half way between the saucer and her lips. After a period of cogitation during which she must have been considering various opening salvos and rejecting them one by one, she finally said, 'Have you been to see your grandad?'

The question hung unanswered for some seconds, because Winnie had timed it to coincide with the arrival in my mouth of a large spoonful of pie. With other aunts, not that I had any, you might wonder idly if this had been done on purpose, but with Aunt Winnie you knew it for a fact. When speech became possible again, I said, 'Not recently. Must be a couple of weeks.'

Aunt Winnie frowned at that. 'You'll not have him for ever, you know. All the time you've got on your hands, I would have thought the least you could do was go and cheer him up for an hour or two.'

Grandad Eli was eighty-five, and lived in a council care home by Marshfield traffic lights. He was a man of settled views. After my mother became pregnant it had been more than ten years before he could bring himself to speak to her again, but because I spent so much time with Aunt Winnie when I was little, Eli had grudgingly accepted my existence, bastard or no, and had even taken some sort of interest in me. This largely consisted of trying to toughen me up, because he was afraid that without a father I'd be sure to end up as what he termed a 'nervous Nellie'. My grandmother had died when I was still a baby, of TB I think, though personally if I'd found myself married to Grandad Eli any excuse would have done. I'd like to pretend that age had mellowed him, but he'd been born with a heart of granite and he had it still.

I said, 'If he does cheer up when I visit, he's careful not to let it show.'

'Circumstances he's in, you can't expect him to go dancing the Gay Gordons every five minutes. Promise me you'll go and see him soon.'

'I'll try. But there's a lot going on just now.'

'I dare say. A lot of drinking and staying out till all hours, if I know anything about it.'

All previous attempts to persuade Aunt Winnie that my life occasionally featured other activities had proved futile, so although for one foolish moment I did open my mouth to answer back I managed to spot the mistake in good time and eat more pie instead. Winnie then fell silent for a moment, building herself up for the day's main business. At last she said, 'And what about your mother? Any sightings?'

Across the table, Uncle Fred shifted uncomfortably. He'd heard that tone before, and it usually meant trouble.

I said, 'No, not lately. Must be five or six weeks since I saw her. I think she's got a new man.'

Winnie said, 'Your mother's always got a new man. The wonder is, there's any man left in Southaven she hasn't tried yet.'

This was too much for Uncle Fred. 'Now then, Winnie, there's no need for that.'

Just then, to my relief, I heard the rattle of the door latch out in the yard. Dropping the spoon and calling out thanks for the pie, I hurried outside to greet Derek Lethbridge. No doubt the sudden rupture in our conversation would have annoyed Aunt Winnie, but that was just an incidental bonus.

As I emerged into the yard, Derek was propping up the Moulton against the coal shed wall, and when he heard me on the steps he turned towards me. For a man of even temper, I thought he looked somewhat down in the mouth. I said, 'Derek, you're a lifesaver! Can you spare me a few minutes in the front office? I'm seeing the borough engineer at quarter past and I need briefing first.'

Derek seemed puzzled but said, 'Certainly, Mister Sam, glad to helk if I can. What's it agout?' Which is when I realized that half his face must still be frozen from the dental treatment.

Not wanting to mention Martin Berry within earshot of my aunt and uncle, I ushered Derek through the back door and along the corridor to the front office. It was only five to two, but Miss Forshaw had already concluded her lunch break and taken her seat at the Imperial, prepared to begin the afternoon's work. As Derek came in, she stole a glance at him before returning her attention to the papers on her desk. And in his way he was certainly worth looking at. Calm blue eyes rested in a squarish, handsome face beneath a crown magisterially bald. He had an air of cool intelligence about him, and I imagined that if he'd been more ambitious he could have risen to a higher station than office manager at Crowburn Estates. But his nature demanded a quiet life, and the steady, unchanging work in the estate office's museum-like conditions had duly delivered it.

There can't have been many offices in Southaven which still lacked an intercom system, but this was one of them, which is why Charles Leighton now popped his head around the door to ask Miss Forshaw if she could spare ten minutes to take dictation. Without replying, she picked up her pad and pencil, went through into the next room, and closed the door behind her.

Derek said, 'So, Mister Sam, why are you seeing Norman Greeze?' When I was about four Derek had taken to calling me Master Sam, a tradition he'd maintained until the first time I turned up in the front office wearing police uniform, at which point Master had given way to Mister.

I said, 'It's about the Empire cinema.'

Derek gave me a knowing look. 'Oh, I see, the Enkire. What a turn-uk for the gooks, eh?'

'Had you heard anything about it before this morning?'

'No, no. I read it in the Gazette. A sukermarket, of all things! Crowgurn would turn in his grave.'

'So you know about Martin Berry too?'

'Yes, I'd seen that on the news.' Derek shook his head. 'Koor goy. Seemed like a harmless enough fellow, always terrigly kolite when they sent him over here for anything. He was in only last week.'

'I know. That's what I want to talk to you about.'

Derek's mood changed. His mind had made the connection between Martin and the cinema redevelopment. 'I don't understand. What's your involvement with all this?'

'I was working for Martin on another matter, nothing to do with the Empire. He happened to tell me there was something going on, without quite saying what, and I'm hoping he was a bit more forthcoming when he spoke to you. I presume he had come about the Empire, not something else entirely?'

'Yes, he said Colin Cudleigh had sent him to check our files and conkare them with the information the council had agout the site – he'd grought some kakers with him, I kresumed they were council cokkies of the deeds and so on. Gut after a while I started to suskect he'd come on his own account, he seemed unusually keen. I left him gy himself eventually, to study the file.'

'Did he ask about anything specific?'

Derek considered this. 'Yes, as a matter of fact he did. Do you want me to get the file? It might helk me to exklain.'

I checked my watch. After two already. By the time Derek had opened the strongroom door and located the papers, I'd have to leave the building. 'Perhaps later. Can you just give me the potted version? I've only got fifteen minutes with Norman Breeze and I'm going to need every one of them.'

After a moment's thought, Derek obliged. What had particularly interested Martin, apparently, was the development restrictions which Crowburn had imposed on the Empire site from its earliest days. Crowburn's vision of this central section of the Boulevard was that the north side should be given over largely to retail, while the south, on which the Empire stood, was kept for residential use, civic buildings, churches, professional offices, public amenities such as banks, and places of entertainment. Originally, the Empire site had been occupied by a grand mansion belonging to a Manchester manufacturer, and when that was sold and demolished in 1913 the no-retail restriction had been inherited by the new leaseholder. The same had applied when AEC bought the cinema in 1952.

I said, 'So, if there's this restriction on retail use, they can't put a supermarket on the site, can they?'

Derek nodded, pleased that I'd grasped the point. 'That's right,

Mister Sam. Or at least, they couldn't have done until last year.'

'What changed?'

'The freehold was held gy Lady Tufnell, Crowgurn's great-granddaughter. Eighteen months ago, the council akkroached us to see whether she might like to sell it. Getween ourselves, Lady Tufnell's on her ukkers, and the lease was years away from laksing so this was her gest chance to turn it into cash. The deal went through in June last year.'

'Wait a minute – does that mean the council would now be free to ignore the retail exclusion clause?'

'You're quite good at this, aren't you? I thought nothing of it at the time, council has always liked to acquire land in the town centre given the chance. Gut now this gusiness agout Addison's has come uk – '

'You're starting to wonder if somebody hadn't already hatched the whole plan eighteen months ago.'

Derek nodded. 'Of course, it could just ge a coincidence, gut it certainly makes you think. Martin Gerry had me exklain all that to him, just like I've done for you now.'

Again I checked the time. Nine minutes past. 'That's fantastic, Derek, just what I need for my little chat with the borough engineer.'

Derek's expression changed, his eyes took on a far away look. 'You know, years ago Vera and I used to go dancing with Norman and his wife Getty. Gut that was gefore he climbed the greasy kole.' He shook his head sadly. 'Garely gives me the time of day now.'

'Talking of which, I'd better get my skates on. Can't keep the great man waiting.' Thanking Derek again for his help, I hurried out into the street.

I've never travelled in a hovercraft, but I imagine the sensation closely resembles what I was experiencing now. This highly suggestive new information formed a cushion of air on which I sped triumphantly along the tree-lined pavement. Five hours as a non-smoker must have brought a dramatic improvement in my fitness, and at two-fourteen I galloped up the town hall steps with an eagerness rare in its visitors.

Southaven's town hall is a modest early Victorian structure finished in clean white stucco, and is the only classical building in the borough designed to inspire affection rather than awe. It felt at once grand and domestic, as if anxious not to get above itself. Alas, the same could not be said of some of the public servants and representatives who had occupied it over the years, but whatever airs and graces a few might have allowed themselves, the many, the councillors and aldermen and the permanent officers who advised them and executed their decisions, had helped to turn the muddy swamp of 1800 into a handsome, thriving town with a unique and proud identity. If it no longer thrived to the same extent, that had more to do with the Costa del Sol than the council, though ratepayers seemed not to think so.

Presenting myself at the reception desk, I was sent up to the first floor, where the borough engineer's secretary told me to take a seat. Norman Breeze was overlord to a vast fiefdom with offices scattered throughout the municipal buildings in the town centre, presiding as he did over departments concerned with planning, housing, highways, sewerage, waste disposal, and just about everything else which hadn't found a natural home under some other roof. Although the town's administration had long since burst the banks of the original town hall building, the dignity of the borough engineer's position required that he still be stationed there, within easy reach of the town clerk, the borough treasurer, and the other senior officers. The functional quarters made no pretence at grandeur, all of which was left to the heavy-busted secretary, a woman in late middle age who, with her erect carriage and rigid expression, seemed to double as an architectural feature. The seconds of precious interview time were ticking away, but I soon grasped that the secretary had kept me waiting not because I was early but because she would sooner have danced naked on *It's Lulu* than send anyone through directly to see her lord and master. Convinced that signs of impatience would be punished by further delay, I forced myself not to wriggle in the chair, and my self-suppression was so complete that by the time the secretary buzzed through word of my arrival, I'd stopped breathing altogether.

Looking across at me, the secretary said, 'Mr Breeze will see you now, Mr Rigby.' I thanked her, and was rewarded with a grisly smile. A pane of dimpled glass in the door to my right was over-painted N. BREEZE, and on the line below, BOROUGH ENGINEER. Taking in a fresh supply of oxygen, I heaved open the door, which weighed about three times as much as I could reasonably have expected, and passed into the realm beyond.

Southaven council is often accused of being profligate with ratepayers' money, but they'd certainly wasted few resources in the appointment of the borough engineer's HQ. The room was dark, and its fading paintwork appeared to date from the era of Attlee, or perhaps even Chamberlain. As I crossed the threshold, colder air played suddenly about my face, as if the summer's reach did not extend here. A threadbare carpet muffled my steps. It took a moment for my eyes to accustom themselves to the twilight, but when they did they picked out a tall, stooped figure leaning towards me from behind a huge desk at the far side of the room, and holding out one slender, bony hand.

I crossed rapidly, with the show of confidence which on these occasions is almost as good as confidence itself, and shook the proffered hand. Either it was very cold, or mine was very hot. To avoid any possible confusion, we both declared our names, and Norman Breeze indicated a low, cushioned seat on my side of the desk, into which I now sank like a man going under for the third time.

Himself seated on a high office chair which squeaked as it accepted his weight, Norman Breeze said, 'Well, Mr Rigby, what can I do for you?'

Although I could appreciate that a certain formality was appropriate to the borough engineer's standing, it surprised me to see that Norman Breeze wore a black suit and black tie over his very white shirt. A few brylcreemed strands of whitish-grey hair traversed the uplands of his bald and skull-like head. It occurred to me that if ever he tired of working for the residents of Southaven, any local undertaker would have been glad to employ him, though given his pallid and skeletal appearance it was doubtful if they'd get much use out of him before his long form felt the underside of the company tape measure. The name had led me to expect a cheery individual, but if he resembled any sort of breeze at all it was the bitter one which blew amongst the headstones in Merechurch graveyard on a January afternoon.

Without waiting for an answer to his question, the borough engineer spoke again. Perhaps he'd been reading my thoughts, because he said, 'I apologize for the rather severe mode of dress. I was at Stanley White's funeral this morning.'

'Alderman White? I saw the death notice in the Gazette.'

'There can't be anyone since the war who's done more for this town than Stanley. Of course, he wasn't popular with everybody – couldn't abide stitch-ups or back-room deals. But he was far and away the best chair of the planning committee we've ever had.'

The encomium was clearly heart-felt. Because aldermen were

elected by councillors rather than the general public, it was unusual for any of them to have a following amongst local people, but Alderman White's reputation for probity, coupled with his down-to-earth humour, had made him an exception. Anxious to start on the right foot with Norman Breeze, I said, 'Good turn-out, I hope?'

My interest pleased him, and he smiled. 'Oh yes, we gave him a proper send-off. You can't beat a good funeral, can you? I often think it's a shame the deceased can't be present.'

'Heart attack, wasn't it?'

'That's right. History of heart trouble, apparently, keeled over in his own back garden. Let me see, now – he was a prefect when I was just starting at King Edward's, so he can only have been about sixty-six, sixty-seven. No great age, is it?'

I said, 'Martin Berry was twenty-five.'

I hadn't meant to speak so abruptly, it just came out. The subject of Stanley White's funeral had already eaten up valuable seconds, and a faint smell of alcohol from across the acreage of leather desktop suggested that with any encouragement the borough engineer might continue to talk about it for the whole of my precious quarter hour. I had to get this meeting back on track.

'Ah – yes. Miss Hunniford did brief me when I came in just now. Terrible business. Are you assisting the police in some way?'

I said, 'Did you know Mr Berry yourself?'

'Not exactly. I was aware of him, of course.' And he said this with the complacency of one who understood that for a council drone like Martin, knowing that the borough engineer was aware of you might represent no small comfort on the long winter nights.

I didn't have much time. Norman Breeze was not quite Danny Craven, and I would need to adapt my methods accordingly, but there was still much to be said for the frontal assault. I took aim, and fired. 'Martin Berry believed that the proposed redevelopment of the Empire cinema site was in some way fraudulent. Was he right, Mr Breeze? Is there some kind of stitch-up going on, some back-room deal?'

The man across from me looked stunned. If this was acting it was first-class, certainly of a standard to bring him top billing in any Southaven Players production. As a matter of fact, I'd have paid good money to see his Malvolio. He said, 'Fraud? What on earth do you mean?'

'Until last week, everyone in town thought the council intended to buy the building off AEC and lease it to these Save Our Empire people. Everything was in place except the signatures on the dotted line. Then suddenly, from nowhere, we have a fully-developed alternative sprung on us, almost as if – forgive my suspicious mind – this had been the preferred option from day one and only the excellent condition of the building stood in the way.'

'Excellent condition? The borough surveyor's report is absolutely clear. That building is a menace. If we don't knock it down it'll fall down, the possible consequences are unthinkable. Do you want to put people's lives at risk?'

'The Empire is a Grade II listed building, you'd never be allowed to demolish it if it was still in a reasonable state. Does it not strike you as extraordinarily convenient that the borough surveyor should condemn the place at exactly the moment that suits Addison's best?'

It was difficult to be sure in the room's poor light, but I fancied that some colour had begun to rise to Norman Breeze's cheeks. 'Convenient? What are you insinuating? If the borough surveyor says that it's unsafe, then it's unsafe.'

'Try telling that to Sandy Smythe.'

The colour was now joined by wrinkles of contempt. 'Sandy Smythe? Are you telling me that you would accept the word of a *musician* over that of the borough surveyor? And this chap Berry – of course I'm sorry about what's happened, but frankly, Mr Rigby, he was no more than the office dogsbody. If he had concerns about this development he should have voiced them to his superiors rather than blabbing them all around the town.'

'Perhaps it was his superiors that he was concerned about.'

It was all Norman Breeze could do to keep his seat. He must at least have shifted in it, because it squeaked again. 'Colin Cudleigh is a man of the utmost integrity. I've known him personally for ten years now, ever since he moved here from Manchester, and if there's a more conscientious council official in the whole of Lancashire then I should be astonished. What you're suggesting is ridiculous – it's beyond ridiculous, it's insane!' And taking a large handkerchief from his pocket he now mopped his head with it. From the look he was giving me, I needn't expect a card at Christmas.

I allowed Norman Breeze a little time to calm down before I spoke again. I didn't share the man's enthusiasm for funerals, and it seemed possible that if I'd kept on pushing he might have followed the precedent recently set by Alderman White. Finally I said, 'I didn't mean to cause offence, Mr Breeze. But the machinations of the council can seem very remote to the average citizen, you can't blame us if we sometimes wonder what goes on behind closed doors.'

The borough engineer huffed, then rubbed his nose vigorously with the handkerchief. 'No, well, perhaps things would go on a damn sight better if people could learn to take things on trust sometimes. It's very hurtful to have the finger of suspicion pointed at you.'

I left another brief pause before saying, 'Why did you decide to buy out the freehold of the Empire site last year?' He looked sharply across at me, clearly surprised to find me so well-informed. 'You are responsible for acquisitions, I believe?'

'Yes, that's right. But there's nothing sinister about us buying up land. The Empire is a key site in the town centre, I'd had my eye on it for years. Then a little bird happened to tell me that the owner might be prepared to sell – '

'Lady Tufnell.'

'Lady Tufnell, yes. So I made my move, with the backing of councillors, of course. It's my job to be shrewd in these matters.'

'But again – and it pains me to keep striking this same note – doesn't it look remarkably convenient that in the process of buying out the freehold you've erased that awkward little restriction on retail development? They must have been cock-a-hoop in the boardroom at Addison's.'

Well, he was angry again, of course, but the fact that I knew so much detail seemed to be spiking his guns. 'You've done your homework, Mr Rigby, I'll say that for you. First of all, I can tell you categorically that when we first approached Lady Tufnell we'd had no contact with Addison's whatsoever. They didn't start sniffing around until – oh, September, I think it was, and even then it was all very informal. I told them they stood virtually no chance of developing the site because the Empire was a listed building, but I could hardly stop them from going ahead and drawing up plans, could I? That was entirely a matter for them.'

'May I ask who their developers are? Is it a local firm?' If there was some scam being pulled, I wanted to know who else might be involved.

'Not local, no. It's a partnership of some kind, Bayley Consortium, new to me I must admit. But you are right, by the way – about the retail restriction, I mean.' He seemed calm again now, and there was a new tone in his voice, resigned, wistful. 'I'm paid to look ahead, Mr Rigby. A seaside town in decline is an ugly thing – and that's what we are, I'm afraid, there's no disguising it. You might like to think of Southaven as a graceful old dowager sinking slowly towards her final rest, but that's all wrong. The truth is, it's more like dogs scrapping over a bloody carcase. It was all very well for Crowburn to try and impose his ideals on the place back in the old days, but now we can't afford the luxury. I've given every support to the Save Our Empire campaign, and if it had worked it would have been wonderful. But nothing lasts for ever, and I always have to think what then, what then? Even though I might be long dead by the time it happened, it seemed sensible at least to create the possibility of developing the site for retail.'

'For the good of the town.'

He scanned my face, trying to decide whether the remark had been sincere. As it happens, I didn't even know myself. 'Yes, for the good of the town.'

Somehow I'd managed to convince myself that my attack on the borough engineer would lead to his instant surrender, after which he would admit that the redevelopment plan was a contemptible swindle, hand over the names and addresses of all the key players, and obligingly reveal the identity of Martin Berry's killer. But I was looking at him now, and could detect absolutely no resemblance to a man defeated. What's more, my stock of ammunition stood at zero, and I'd begun to feel surplus to requirements in the cold, unglamorous room.

Luckily, at that moment there came a buzz from the intercom. Norman Breeze selected a button and pressed it. 'What is it, Miss Hunniford?'

'Mr Cudleigh has arrived, sir.'

'I'll be through in a second. Mr Rigby was just leaving.' Breaking the connection, he turned towards me. 'I think we've said all that needs to be said.'

'It was very good of you to see me, Mr Breeze.'

'I hope I've cleared up any misconceptions you may have been entertaining.'

'Of course, yes. Mr Berry must have got hold of the wrong end of the stick.'

There was another squeak as the borough engineer rose majestically to his feet. Less gracefully, I fought my way up out of the low chair. Shadowed by the other man's gaunt figure, I crossed to the door, and we stepped into the outer office.

A short, roly-poly man in his late forties was conversing amicably with the secretary, a sheaf of papers tucked neatly under his left arm. Round, horn-rimmed glasses of a type fashionable thirty years ago rested on his plump little nose. Though I suspected it would displease my host, I stretched out my hand and said, 'Mr Cudleigh? I'm Sam Rigby. I left a message with your secretary this morning, it's about Martin Berry's death.'

Clearly unprepared for this moment, Colin Cudleigh shook my hand. His palm was sweaty, and beads of sweat gleamed on his brow and between the islands of his receding hair. 'Terrible business, lovely young chap was Martin. What is it you want, exactly?'

'Perhaps if you could call me later on? Your secretary has the number.'

Behind me, Norman Breeze cleared his throat. 'Shall we go through, Colin?'

Flustered, and with his attention divided now, Colin Cudleigh said, 'Yes, of course,' then, to me, 'Good to meet you, Mr Rigby.'

Fixing me with a look in which I fancied that distaste fought for supremacy with something more like pity, Norman Breeze said, 'Goodbye, Mr Rigby. And a word of advice – do try to take things on trust a little more, or you'll have worn yourself out before you're very much older.'

I tried to thank him for this tip, but the words stuck in my throat. The two other men disappeared into the gloom of the office. To cheer myself up, I now favoured the secretary with a broad come-and-get-it smile, before trailing down the stairs and out into the sunlit afternoon.

I'd have killed for a cigarette, or at least given someone a damn good hiding, but my plan was to go straight back to Leigh Terrace, and if Matt was there he'd be sure to smell it on my breath. Failure now burdened my once-buoyant steps. To make matters worse, my intuition was dumb on the question of whether the borough engineer's pose of honest public servant was a brilliant performance or the genuine article. Later, I might be able to try the same questions on Colin Cudleigh, who seemed less sure of himself than the borough engineer. But if Norman Breeze chose to give him the low-down on our recent conversation, as I felt certain he would, then the invaluable element of surprise would be lost. What if I'd just ruined my one chance to get at the truth? More than ever I realized that I needed proof, I needed the evidence which had first persuaded Martin there was dirty work afoot. In short, I needed the briefcase.

At Crowburn House I picked up the Cortina, then drove it the few hundred yards to Leigh Terrace. There was nowhere to park outside the flats, so I drove round the block in search of a space. Nothing. If this was the shape of things to come, I didn't much care for it. I'd heard there were plans to restrict parking on Preston Road to a couple of hours, which would be no use to me or any of the other residents. Did they not want people to live in the middle of town at all? Or perhaps they expected us to give up our cars and walk, which would hardly strike a blow for progress and modernity. When I'd made yet another tour of the neighbourhood entirely without success, I drove back to Crowburn House, slotted the car into the space I'd only just vacated, and walked home.

After my visit to the town hall I'd intended to call in at the highways department and report my street light out of action, but the dismal outcome of the meeting with Norman Breeze had driven this thought from my mind. However, turning onto Preston Road I could see a man in overalls crouching at the foot of the lamp post, his hands working away in the open belly. Drawing level, I said, 'Complicated job, is it?'

He looked up, surprised by the interruption. He was a young chap with enough hair for two, and a greasy strand of it now fell down over his eyes and had to be flicked away. He said, 'Shouldn't be, not normally. But some bastard's been in here having fun with a blade. I've had to strip it all and start from scratch.'

I tut-tutted. 'Some hooligan, I expect.'

He said, 'If I could get my hands on him he'd think twice before doing it again.'

I too would have been keen to lay hands on the culprit, who was responsible for far worse than wasting a council employee's afternoon. I muttered commiserations and left the man to his work, then climbed the steps and pressed the buzzer for my flat. Though memory isn't my strong point, I was reasonably certain that this was something I'd never done before. It felt dangerous, illicit. This wasn't how I'd chosen to arrange my life, I should have been coming home to an empty flat as usual, trudging up to the top floor with no expectation of a welcoming voice. What if I acquired a taste for this?

Then I heard, not a voice, but a whistle from high above me, and I stepped back to look towards it. Matt was leaning out of the window, smiling his easy, uncomplicated smile. He said, 'Hi there, sexy. What took you so long? Catch.' And he dropped the keys down accurately into my hands. 'Solved the case yet?'

'No. Why, have you?'

'Not quite. But I've a feeling you might want to hear what I've just turned up.'

6

My flat door stood seductively open when I reached the top of the stairs weary from the long climb, from lack of sleep, from my recent failure at the town hall, and from all the other cumulative insults of the past thirty-four years. To find that I was spared the effort of turning my key in the lock left me weak with gratitude. As I hung my leather jacket in the hallway, Matt called out from the kitchen, 'Do you want tea?'

I called back. 'Yes, but there isn't any.' Then I walked through. Matt stood near the stove, watching the kettle. He'd discarded the checked shirt, which must have been difficult to keep in place with only one arm sleeved, and his free arm showed very dark against the white vest.

He said, 'There is now.' A new box of tea bags on the table supported this statement. 'I did a little shop.'

Now I noticed other signs of activity. I said, 'You've done the washing up.'

He said, 'Well spotted.'

'But you've only got one hand.'

'I know. Fantastic, isn't it? You should see what I can do with two.'

I said, 'I can hardly wait,' then instantly regretted the too-obvious remark. After all, it was only about ninety minutes since I'd decided that in order to avoid being taken for a sap I would have to pursue a strictly professional course in my relations with M. Standish. Apparently, all it took to undermine my resolve was an open door, a smooth, brown shoulder and a box of PG Tips.

He said, 'I couldn't manage the drying, though. Anyway, your tea towel's got stuff growing on it.'

My eye returned to the table. I'd left my cigarettes there earlier, but they seemed to have disappeared. The kitchen waste bin was empty. I said, 'Thanks for taking out the rubbish.'

'I was bored. I've been here two hours.'

'I suppose you slung out those fags?'

'No point in keeping them, was there?' The kettle having boiled, he now poured water into two mugs standing on the drop-leaf of the kitchen cabinet. 'You could open the milk if you want to make yourself useful.'

Milk as well. This was luxury beyond imagining. Between us we finished making the tea, then took it through into the heat of the living room. I gave up my willing body to the settee's embrace, while Matt hovered and tried leaning in different places around the room, too restless to settle. I said, 'So, what's this you say you've turned up?'

'No, you first. I want to know why you look as if you'd lost a shilling and found sixpence.'

So I told him about my encounter with the borough engineer. But in order to do that, I first had to wind back and explain all the business about the lease and the development restrictions, which Matt seemed to grasp readily enough, and I found myself cheering up simply because we were now in possession of some solid facts. They may not have sufficed to disturb Norman Breeze's sang-froid, but I sensed that the borough surveyor's blood ran somewhat warmer, so perhaps I'd have better luck with him later on.

Matt also wanted to know more about the council's officers and how they interacted with the elected councillors, and where aldermen fitted in, and why we bothered with a mayor and mayoress if their only function was to be photographed thrice weekly for the front page of the Gazette. Clearly Our Lady had made no effort to inform its pupils how the town they lived in was actually run, perhaps in case they acquired too much interest in the machinery of power and went on to subject Mother Church to the same scrutiny. But in fact the secondary modern had done no better, and my own understanding had been sparked only because Uncle Fred had taken me to the Local Government Exhibition at the Crowburn Gallery in 1946. I still have the souvenir brochure in a box somewhere.

As a subject, local government doesn't attract much public

interest nowadays. After a few minutes it stopped attracting Matt's as well, and at that point I said, 'Did you manage to sign on?'

'All done and dusted. Might have to wait a while before the cash comes through, though.' And he gave me a look.

I said, 'What does that look mean?'

He said, 'Nothing,' and tried to stop doing it.

I said, 'Let me guess. You think it's unfair that I'm not paying you.'

He said, 'Well – yes, I suppose I do. I'm boosting your productivity but you're getting all the benefit.'

I said, 'Have you considered industrial action?'

He said, 'Now you're making a joke of it. I'm not asking for much.'

'How much is not much?'

'I don't know, say, ten quid a week?'

'Ten pounds! Are you mad?'

'All right, nine.'

'Do you want to bankrupt me? I've only got twenty-two pounds in my account and with Martin out of the picture I don't even know where the next job's coming from.' It was true that Martin's cheque would clear in a few days' time, but so far Monica's promises of cash were no more than that. I might be just days away from having to throw myself on the mercy of the state, and I wasn't sure if it had any.

Now Matt left his tea in the window, came across to sit next to me, and placed what I took to be a conciliatory hand on my knee. He said, 'Baybridge just paid me the half week that I'd worked, and anyway I'm at home, I don't need much money. But – '

'I know, I know, it's not the cash, it's the feeling taken for granted. If I could just remind you, forty-eight hours ago we'd not even met. I need to be sure I'm backing a winner before I start parting with the readies.'

Matt was absent-mindedly massaging around the knee now. I was afraid that if he went on like that there might be consequences. I could see he was still unhappy, and eventually he said, 'So – not even a fiver?'

'For God's sake, Standish, this is totally unreasonable! Why can't you just let yourself be exploited, like any normal person?'

He said, 'Is that a yes, then?'

I removed the hand from my knee while there was still time. 'Oh, all right, all right. I'll give you five quid a week, starting next

week. I presume you can manage on Baybridge's generosity for
now.'

Matt's hand was on my knee again, but only to steady himself
while he stood up. He said, 'You won't regret this, Sam, honestly,'
then rejoined his tea on the window seat, with his backside resting
on a pile of National Geographics.

I said, 'Did you manage to get me those phone numbers?'

'Yes and no. I could have tried directory enquiries but I'm slow
writing stuff down. I knew they had all the phone books at the
reference library so I went in there and told the girl I was
functionally illiterate and needed help.'

'Functionally illiterate?'

'She offered to give me private lessons, as a matter of fact.'

'I bet she did.'

'Anyway, she dug out the Manchester phone book and wrote
down the numbers of all the L. Armstrongs.' He indicated a small
piece of lined paper on the floor beside the telephone. 'There were
six. In the end I did manage to get an answer from all of them, but
none of them was Leah Armstrong.'

'So you've drawn a blank? And for this I have to pay you five
entire pounds?'

'The girl also gave me a number for Manchester University and
a separate one for the psychology department. I tried that first, I
just wanted to make sure that Rupert Heysham worked there. But
as soon as I mentioned the name, the girl on the switchboard put
me through, and I was talking to the bloke's secretary.'

I smiled an inward smile. It's almost invariably the case that
when you're conducting a routine enquiry, the parts you suppose
will be easy prove impossible, while some random question
accidentally catapults you into the heart of the investigation, but
without a script. Here was Matt, discovering all that on his first day
in the new job. I said, 'Awkward. What did you say?'

'There wasn't time to think, I just asked if I could speak to
Rupert Heysham. And – this is the interesting bit – she said, "I'm
afraid he's not here this afternoon, he's over at the Wetherley
laboratory."'

'Wetherley!'

'Wetherley, no less. So I couldn't let it go at that, could I? I'd
only have sat here for the rest of the afternoon wondering why
Wetherley has a laboratory named after him. Anyway, the secretary
sounded – I don't know, *proud* of her boss, or something like that.

She had a young voice and I could sort of picture her. So I took a punt and I said, "Oh, really? Amazing project, that lab.'" He paused to drink, and in the excitement of story-telling managed to miss his mouth and spill tea onto the white vest. Barely seeming to notice, he went on. 'And that was all it took. She was obviously just waiting for the least excuse to crow about Heysham's success. Apparently he and some lecturer from another department are joining forces to start a new department of Artificial Intelligence, whatever that is, and Walter Wetherley has stumped up the cash for this state-of-the-art laboratory, fancy computers and God knows what. It's a huge boost for Heysham's career, the psychology chair's likely to come up in a year or two and this puts our Rupert in pole position.'

National Gaze Admiringly At Matthew Standish Day wasn't over yet, and I duly gazed. In the matter of looks, the boy on the window seat could hardly be faulted. With the afternoon sun playing on one dark brown shoulder, he resembled some Italian youth on a tea-break from sitting for Caravaggio. On the other hand, he didn't at first glance appear luminously intelligent. It was Martin who'd reminded me that we shouldn't judge books by their covers, and I knew from experience that getting information out of strangers required more than oafish persistence. Some bosses would have congratulated Matt at this point, but there was always the risk that he might get cocky and demand a raise.

Meanwhile, one detail detracted from this charming portrait, namely the tea stain at Matt's solar plexus. I said, 'Just a moment,' went through into the kitchen, ransacked the cupboards for a cleanish cloth, moistened it with warm water and returned.

I offered Matt the cloth, but he said, 'Two-handed job, really,' which it was. So I held the man and the vest steady with one hand while dabbing with the other.

I said, 'How did you leave things with this awestruck young blabbermouth?'

'Heysham's going to ring you back later this afternoon.'

I wasn't having much success with the cloth, but I stuck at it, and Matt submitted like a well-behaved child with a jam-stained face. I said, 'So tell me: given this new information, what fresh questions do you have?'

He smiled. Clearly he liked it when the apprenticeship took a formal turn, even if his employer did happen to be mopping near his nipples with a damp cloth at the time. 'Well – you could understand Wetherley funding this lab if Rupert Heysham had become his son-in-law, but since that never happened, what's in it for him?'

'Exactly. What's in it for Walter Wetherley?' I stepped back to assess my handiwork. The stain was paler now, but more widely spread. I said, 'That vest's going to need washing.'

Matt said, 'I like it when you fuss.' And I thought something in his tone had changed.

I risked saying, 'If I go up to the market for supplies, do you want to eat here this evening?'

'Can't, I'm afraid. I'm seeing Eileen. We don't normally meet in the week, she wants us to take it slow for now, but she's got this work thing tomorrow so we're doing tonight instead.' Then Matt seemed to read my face, and he said, 'But I'd be free tomorrow, if you want.'

I did want, but I wasn't happy if Matt could read as much from my expression. And what on earth had happened to my plan to keep the relationship on a purely professional footing? It seemed that the spilled tea had caused yet another lapse, and now I said, 'Back in a tick,' took the cloth through to the kitchen and rinsed it out thoroughly, as if trying to wash away all trace of my own self-betrayal. It's even possible that I was muttering to myself when I found that Matt had joined me. He placed his empty mug on the draining board and said, 'I should be going, really, if you don't mind.'

'Eileen, already?'

'No, it's not that, I'm supposed to be baby-sitting for my older sister for a couple of hours.'

'Useful little chap, aren't you? Obviously I'll have to deduct it from your wages.'

'But you're not paying me yet.' He read my face again. 'Oh, you're teasing.'

'I didn't realize you were an uncle.'

'Twice over and another one on the way. Should I come round again in the morning?'

'Depends what happens later. I may decide on a trip to Manchester tomorrow, if Heysham gets back to me. Why not phone me and we'll make a plan. But – not too early, OK?'

'Who's this?' The three monochrome photographs I'd printed on Tuesday evening were still clipped up on the line, and one of them had attracted Matt's attention.

'That's the Wetherleys' chauffeur, Gerry Gibbs.'

Matt chewed his lip in the familiar way. I wondered whether he'd noticed any little mannerisms of my own, and if so, whether he liked them. I said, 'Do you recognize him?'

He frowned. 'Not really. Sort of.'

'But you can hardly see his face in the picture, just a bit of profile and a lot of cap.'

'What was that word Sandy Smythe used about recognizing people even though he's half blind?'

'Aura?'

'Yes, that's it. I'm not really sure I know this bloke, but then there's something about him – No, I'm not getting it.' I helped Matt back into his shirt and began to see him off the premises. But at the door to the flat he turned, drew a scrap of paper from his trouser pocket and handed it to me. There was a phone number written on it. 'Almost forgot. I tore this off Danny Craven's copy of the Gazette when we were leaving this morning.'

That explained the sound I'd heard behind me. I said, 'He's bound to have noticed, that's off the front page.'

'Yeah, but it was too good to miss. I'll lay odds it's the number of whoever he was going to meet.'

'Have you tried ringing it?'

'Three times, but it's always engaged. Anyway, must go. I'll call you in the morning.' For a moment I thought he meant to kiss me, nothing major, just a polite little goodbye kiss, but I'll never know because I turned away, uncertain how to react. He patted my shoulder and was gone.

Some serious thinking was in order. This new connection between Walter Wetherley and Rupert Heysham had come as a complete surprise, and such unexpected turns always deserve particular attention. But the brain refused to function. Perhaps I should try something simpler and dial the number which Matt had torn from Danny Craven's newspaper, but even a phone call seemed too difficult. I reminded myself that instead of getting my eight hours I'd been drugged and dumped in a heap beside the dustbins, then spent half the night in the Cortina. I needed a nap, right now. Stripping off, I fell back into bed, pulled the quilt over my head, and sank deep into unconsciousness.

Unusually for me, no dream disturbed my slumber. It may be that my guardian angel had arranged this. More noted for bunking off than for doing any serious guardianing, he may just this once have taken pity on me and realized that what Sam Rigby needed above all else was a few hours of absolutely nothing at all. The fact was, I'd begun to lose heart. This was the first time I'd investigated a murder, and the Rigby arrogance had imagined that I would solve the case in a matter of hours. But the third day found me more confused than ever, with too many leads, too much information, and the picture growing more unintelligible with every hour that passed. It didn't help that I'd enjoyed something like flirtation with the murder victim the night he was killed. It didn't help that the case had brought me into contact with Mark Howell again. And it didn't help that, entirely on a whim, I was now employing an attractive but maddening assistant who was clearly taking my mind off the job.

But guardian angel or no, the gods always have the final say, and this week it had been decreed that Sam Rigby's rest, however vital to his sanity, was routinely to be destroyed by the jangling of the telephone bell. Glancing at the bedside clock, I was surprised to find that I'd slept not for ten minutes but two hours. Still half asleep, I stumbled through into the sitting room, picked up the phone and uttered a vague greeting.

'Mr Rigby?' The voice was loud and abrupt.

I mumbled agreement.

'This is Colin Cudleigh speaking, the borough surveyor. Are you some kind of madman, Mr Rigby? When you introduced yourself to me this afternoon you were all smiles, all hail-fellow-well-met, but then moments later I discover from Norman Breeze, who I may say is not at all happy about it, that you're going around making vicious and quite possibly libellous accusations about my handling of the survey at the Empire cinema. I'll have you know, Mr Rigby, that I am a professional and a public servant, and I consider any such allegation to be a slight not only on my good name but on the whole council and all its officers. If you persist in making such allegations you can expect a decisive response from me, and I shall not hesitate to bear down on you with the full force of the law if necessary, do you hear me? For some perverted reason of your own which I do not pretend to understand, you obviously wish to see the reputation of this town dragged through the muck. Well I'm sorry to have to tell you that it won't happen, because the decent citizens of Southaven won't let it happen. If I were you I should think very seriously about finding yourself somewhere else to live, otherwise your life here may become intolerable. Well, I think I've said all I need to say. It's been a pleasure talking to you, Mr Rigby, and good afternoon.' He hung up.

If I hadn't quite been awake when this intemperate speech began, I was certainly awake now. And not just awake, but frankly rather pleased with myself too. I performed a brief pagan dance around the living room, as far as the stacks of books would allow. It seemed that I'd been right to view Colin Cudleigh as a more hot-blooded individual than the borough engineer, and with hot blood comes a tendency to speak out, always unwise in those who have something to hide. If he'd put up his hand and said, 'Yes! It was me! I falsified the survey!' he could hardly have made it more plain that he was up to no good. I'd touched a nerve at last.

But could I imagine Colin Cudleigh bringing a convenient rock down hard on the back of Martin's head? Just about, but it was a bit of a stretch. For one thing, he didn't seem the sort of companion Martin would be likely to choose for a late swim. And in any case, I had absolutely no evidence against him, only Sandy Smythe's suspicions and the hyperbolic rant which I'd just been subjected to.

One thing puzzled me. If the borough surveyor was indeed such a hot-head, and if Norman Breeze had informed him of my allegations at about half past two, why had he waited three and a half hours to mount this spirited defence?

I was standing in the middle of the floor stroking my chin over this conundrum, and idly scratching my balls with my free hand, when the phone rang again. I hoped it wasn't a repeat performance from Colin Cudleigh, because you can have too much of that sort of thing. Since I was now rather more alert, I managed to get my name out first this time.

'Ah, good,' said the caller. 'Just the man I'm after. Rupert Heysham here. You wanted to speak to me about the lab.'

I hadn't thought to ask Matt what reason he'd given the secretary for my needing to talk to her boss, but he'd chosen well. Probably no subject could have been better calculated to bring Rupert Heysham to the phone. But since I knew nothing whatsoever about the lab, or indeed about Artificial Intelligence, it seemed wise to come clean.

'Actually, Mr Heysham, I think your secretary and my assistant may have got their wires crossed. I'm helping the police investigate the murder of Martin Berry.'

'Oh – oh, I see.' You could hear the man deflating. 'A nasty business. But I really don't know anything about it.'

'All the same, sir, I'd appreciate it if you could spare me a little of your time. I was wondering about tomorrow.'

'Not possible, I'm afraid, I'm addressing a conference in Leeds.'

'Saturday, then.'

'Well – I'll be busy at the lab all day.'

'So much the better, you can give me a guided tour. I've always been fascinated by Artificial Intelligence.'

'Really?' And at once he came alive again. 'Amazing! Most people have never even heard of it.'

'I know, beggars belief, doesn't it? And yet it's the shape of the future.'

'How right you are, Mr Rigby, how right you are. If we get this project right, in ten years' time Britain will be the world leader in robotics and cybernetics.'

Two more subjects they'd neglected to cover at the secondary modern. I said, 'So – would it be all right if I dropped by?'

'What about lunchtime? I'll have colleagues with me all morning, we're just installing the equipment. But I should be on my own by then.'

'Around one o'clock?'

'Excellent! But – I really don't know how I can help you over Martin's death.'

'Just a few questions, Mr Heysham, nothing to worry about.' He gave me directions to the Renold building, where the lab was to be found, and after due formalities we rang off. Heysham sounded a rather jolly sort of individual, and I found myself reluctant to prick his bubble. Perhaps I should swot up on Artificial Intelligence before meeting him, but how? It was a clear measure of my ignorance that I didn't even know where to start.

But at least now my Manchester excursion was beginning to take shape. It was all too rare for me to escape Southaven's gravitational pull, and I looked forward to it. If I could get hold of Leah Armstrong's number then perhaps I would be able to see her before Rupert Heysham. And then – what about Gerry Gibbs, he of the aura and the pale moustache? He'd said there were worse places to be than Manchester on a Saturday night. If that was an invitation, why turn it down?

But still I hesitated, unsure of my welcome, and it was not Gerry Gibbs I called next. Instead, I picked up the receiver and dialled the number which Matt had smuggled out of Danny Craven's kitchen. There was no reply. It might be that I was calling some workplace, since the line had earlier been constantly engaged and now, at six o'clock, went unanswered. I would have to try again in the morning.

The next call I intended to make was to my friend Bernie, but just as I was reaching for the phone it rang, and the woman herself was on the other end of the line. We were about due for one of our nights in the Velvet Bar, and she said as much, and I agreed, and she said how about tonight, and I agreed, and the call ended.

But before seeing Bernie, there was something else I needed to do, something which I'd been putting off for two days now. I opened the directory and looked up the number for the shop in Jubilee Avenue. I dialled, and the call was picked up by Martin's father, Clive. I gave him the usual spiel. Yes, he said, I could look in this evening if I wanted to, they weren't going anywhere. No, they wouldn't mind if I had questions for them, they were used to all that now. Any time I pleased, it was all the same to them. The fragile voice faded away, rang off. Clive Berry sounded like a broken man.

It was a long time now since my breakfast at Frankie's, and I couldn't face the prospect of interviewing the Berrys on an empty stomach. I dressed with extra care, not so much for the Berrys' sake as for Bernie's, since in her theology the wearing of *casual* clothes (detested word) represented a mortal sin. Then I stepped out into the warmth of the early evening.

I'd grown so used to seeing the yellow Cortina parked directly outside that for a second I supposed it must have been stolen, but of course it was still parked behind Crowburn House, where I now intended to leave it for the night. Once again the weather had drawn out the crowds, once again the weary day-trippers made their way slowly towards the railway station, shoulders drooping, children trailing miserably behind them. Matt's chums working on the new station buildings would be pressing up to the bar in the Railway Tavern now, but I wasn't heading in that direction myself. There was a steak house I sometimes visited just down from the Prom, not exactly a distinguished local eaterie but functional, and as long as you avoided alcohol you could get the whole works for under a pound. With money so tight the meal would be an extravagance, but I saw it as my reward for knuckling down and making this awkward visit to the Berrys. I believe it's always best to reward yourself in advance for tackling unwanted jobs, just in case you chicken out at the last minute and end up with nothing.

The restaurant was pretty busy, mostly with young families

eating before they put the children to bed. I watched from an isolated table. The behaviour I witnessed, which included frequent and uninhibited corporal punishment, a great deal of chip theft, and much squalling, brawling, and general hurling to the floor of substances which the establishment had intended its customers to eat or drink, formed no great advertisement for family life, but then I wasn't in the market so that was OK. My steak was a bit on the tough side but the onion rings compensated to some degree. And all the time I tried not to think about the case, not to think about Martin Berry, not to think about the family a couple of streets away on whose private grief I was about to set my too-large feet. But inevitably the minutes passed and the food was consumed. I stumped up the required eighteen and six, then found myself outside again with no further excuses to hand.

Setting my nose towards Jubilee Avenue, I prepared myself as best I could to meet the family of my late client.

7

On closer inspection, the three-storey building which housed the Berrys and their novelty shop was one of the most handsome and well-maintained in Jubilee Avenue. Elegant courses of brickwork in a deep red broke up the façade, and at first floor level a grand oriel window projected over the pavement on the corner, giving views in all directions. Currently enjoying these views, and the strong evening sunlight, was a caged canary, which responded to its favourable circumstances with a flow of liquid song audible through the open window. If Clive Berry owned this property then there had been something misleading in the impression Martin had given me of his family's fortunes. Though they were not wealthy, like Monica's family, it looked to me as if they were in no immediate danger of insolvency.

The shop itself was closed, the shutters lowered. Meanwhile, other businesses in the narrow street were still doing a brisk evening trade. Amusement arcades and cheap cafés buzzed with life, and in the queue which snaked from the chip shop a few doors down, two teenage boys were arguing so fiercely over a lost pound note that their fellow-customers had backed away from them a little, to be out of range of any fists which might fly. With all these goings-on, and the procession of people constantly jostling me as they passed, I couldn't stand for ever looking up at the ecstatic bird in its sun-gilt cage. The Berrys' domestic quarters had a separate entrance to the side of the shop. I rang the bell.

A good half minute passed. A cigarette would have been nice, but it was too late to do anything about that now. I was just about to try the bell again when the door opened and I was puzzled to find myself looking at a young woman of about Monica's age, but different from her in nearly all other respects. She was dark and heavy-set, and her black brows met in the middle in a frown of mistrust. At first I wondered if she'd been up a ladder with a paintbrush when I'd disturbed her, but it turned out that the paint-flecked dungarees formed her usual mode of dress.

I said, 'Hello, I'm Sam Rigby.'

'And?'

This was not quite the response I'd hoped for, but I'd now realized who this young woman must be so I said, 'I spoke to your father earlier on. He's expecting me.'

Martin's sister still seemed unconvinced, but she said, 'I suppose you'd better come up.' I followed her sturdy figure up the narrow stairway. A cooking odour which I couldn't quite place began to dominate the atmosphere. When, at the top, we turned, the space opened out to an extent which surprised me, and from this large hallway we passed into the living room whose window I'd been looking up at from the Avenue. Someone had so much enjoyed furnishing it that they'd neglected to stop when it was full. There was a good deal of velveteen and onyx, and tassels hung from objects which could have managed quite well without them. If the Berrys were religious people, as Angela Wetherley had said, then it must have been entirely by accident that the general impression was of a Parisian brothel. The canary still sang in its cage, one of three cages in the room. Wimbledon played on a colour set in the corner, and as if brought low by the close, oppressive atmosphere a sparely-built man in his fifties sat unmoving in an armchair several sizes too large for him, his eyes cast down to the floor.

Grace Berry said, 'Dad? It's someone called Sam Rimmer come to see you.'

I said, 'Rigby, it's Sam Rigby.'

Clive Berry looked up now, and with a visible effort dragged his mind away from wherever it had been and applied it to the scene before him. 'Oh – oh yes, Mr Rigby, I remember now.'

He began to struggle to his feet, and I found myself saying, 'No, don't bother to get up,' as if he were an elderly invalid. Yet his face was tanned and healthy, and I guessed that only the blow he'd suffered this week had reduced him to his present condition.

Relieved to be excused from action, Martin's father sank back into the chair. He said, 'It's good of you to come round. Do you want something to drink? Grace, get a drink for Mr Rigby. And switch that television off, I don't know why your mother has to have it on if she's not watching it.'

I said, 'I won't have anything, thank you. I don't mean to keep you long.'

My arrival had caused excitement in the two larger cages, which stood surrounded by condolence cards on a chest at the far end of the room. Each cage contained a pair of brightly-coloured tenants. Previously they'd been leaving the vocal work to their associate in the oriel window, but now they fluttered from perch to perch giving loud selections from their repertoire. Perhaps they didn't get many visitors. Clive Berry said, 'I'm sorry about the birds. They think this room's theirs, really, we're just here on sufferance.'

In support of this view, one of the birds now clearly said, *'Who's a silly boy?'* twice.

'Sit down, Mr Rigby.'

I lowered myself onto the large, well-padded settee, upholstered in green and gold. 'Call me Sam, won't you.'

'Grace, tell Nessa Mr Rigby's here.' After a moment's hesitation, Grace Berry crossed to switch off the television set, then left the room. 'My wife's just cooking the tea.'

'If I've come at a bad time – '

'No, no, you stay where you are. It really doesn't matter.' And once more he gave the impression that it didn't matter because nothing mattered any more. 'You said you'd been working for Martin?'

Apart from the televion, the most up-to-date, least overwrought item of furniture in the room was a large teak hi-fi cabinet which stood near Clive Berry's armchair, and on top of this Martin's graduation photograph had pride of place. If Grace had completed her course at Manchester, her own graduation was for some reason not deemed worthy of such a position. I was looking at Martin's handsome, smiling face as I said, 'Yes, he'd got it into his head someone was following him. But before I could start my investigation – '

There was a brief silence, then Martin's father said, 'I don't know who would be following Martin. I can't understand why anyone would wish him ill, it makes no sense. He was always such a good boy, Mr Rigby, we never had to chase him up to do his homework or anything like that. It was Grace who – '

'You giving me a bad press again, Dad?' Grace had come back into the room.

'No, Grace love, no, I'm just trying to get across to Mr Rigby that if either of you was likely to get into bother then it wasn't Martin. Where's your mother?'

'She said the goulash wouldn't cook itself.' Of course, goulash; that was the quite particular aroma which had met us as we came up the stairs.

Clive Berry turned to me again. 'My wife does cookery classes, tries things out at home. Though why she can't give it a rest this week I've no idea.'

Grace said, 'If it was left to you we'd be eating out of tins. Typical man.'

'No, well, perhaps you're right. It's nice for her to have an interest. And a bit more practical than basket-weaving.'

I must have looked baffled, because Grace said, 'Last year's fad.'

Denial is a wonderful thing. I'd been so reluctant to make this visit to Martin's grieving family that I'd put all my energies into trying not to think about it, and none into considering what questions I might usefully ask them. Angela Wetherley had claimed to believe that they were hiding something, but I could see now that her dislike of the Berrys might have been based merely on the gulf of wealth and taste which separated them. Now that I was here, I would have to improvise.

To Grace I said, 'I believe you were a student at Manchester with Martin's wife?'

She didn't try to disguise the sour expression which now appeared on her face. 'The lovely Monica, yes. Rather more interested in hanging out with the beautiful people than actually studying psychology.'

'That can't have pleased her tutor.'

Grace's eyes narrowed. 'Roopie Heysham? You know about him?'

'I understand there was a relationship.'

'You understand right. Some of us had to work if we wanted decent grades, but not Monica.'

Clive Berry broke in, pained by this aspersion. 'Grace, love, you mustn't talk that way about your sister-in-law.'

'Well it's true. I'm not saying she did it on purpose, she really liked Heysham, but it happened to be convenient for her as well. She's a great one for getting people running round after her. It's her background.'

'I do wish you could learn to be more charitable, Grace. I'm sure I don't know why you're so bitter.'

If Angela Wetherley was wrong about the Berrys hiding some secret, she'd certainly scored a bull's-eye in describing Grace and Martin as chalk and cheese. Nothing could have been more different from Martin's naïve, candid manner than the crabbed and grudging attitude of his adoptive sister. Of course, the crabbed and grudging amongst us see things which others don't, and Grace's view of Monica deserved consideration. Danny Craven would no doubt have agreed that Monica could all too easily charm people into doing her bidding.

Grace now said, 'I'm not bitter, Dad, I just refuse to see good in people when it isn't there. It's because people like you and Mum can't face reality that everything's in such a mess and we've got another bloody Tory government.'

'Grace, love, you know I don't like it when you swear.'

This domestic scene, no doubt oft-repeated, wasn't getting me anywhere so I said to Grace, 'What did you decide to do after Manchester?'

'I applied to do postgraduate work, but they turned me down. Apparently my face didn't fit. But I'm still in the psychology department, I got a job as a lab assistant.'

'Must be interesting.'

Clive Berry broke in again. 'Grace is over-qualified for it, really. She's alongside people who only have A levels.'

For the first time, Grace smiled. 'Doesn't bother me, as long as I've got my rats.'

'Your rats?'

'I look after all the rats. For research. We keep dozens.'

Her father said, 'Wouldn't be to everyone's taste, but Grace seems very fond of her charges.'

She said, 'If you ask me, they're the most civilised creatures in the entire department. Would make more sense if they were experimenting on us.'

I said, 'Presumably you know all about this new lab Rupert Heysham's starting?'

The sour face was back, with a tone of voice to match. 'The Wetherley? You might think so, but I'm only a lowly technician.'

'Surely you must know something? Your brother married Wetherley's daughter.'

'Even so, I'm in the dark on this one. Old Walter's obviously decided to shower cash on Roopie like confetti, but for the life of me I don't see why.'

Which made two of us. I said, 'Have you by any chance kept in touch with Leah Armstrong?'

Grace smiled. 'Leah? What's she been up to this time?' The remark seemed affectionate.

'Nothing that I know of, but I'd like to see her and I don't have her number.'

Grace looked sideways at me from beneath her heavy brows. 'If she's done nothing, why bother her? You'll only get her in a muddle.'

I chose not to say that, as Monica's dodgy alibi in a murder inquiry, Leah Armstrong could expect muddle and worse than muddle before I'd finished with her. I said, 'Just some routine questions.'

Still clearly reluctant, Grace said, 'As long as that's all it is.' And she left the room, presumably in search of Leah's details.

Clive Berry shifted uncomfortably. 'Please don't think badly of her, Mr Rigby. She doesn't have an easy time of it. Though I have to say, some of her wounds are self-inflicted.'

Unsure how to respond, I said, 'She seems like a solid kind of person. You must be very proud of her.'

Clive Berry said, 'We try to be,' and then a new commotion arose in the cages and I saw that Martin's mother had come silently into the room. Like her husband, she was constructed on a small scale. Her small, bright eyes fixed on object after object, settling on none, and grey curls wisped uncertainly about her head. I caught just the faintest smell of sherry. Her husband said, 'Nessa, love, Mr Rigby's come to talk to us about Martin.'

I half rose to my feet and offered my hand, but Nessa Berry didn't seem to notice it and in fact barely seemed to notice the large man to whom it was attached. I said, 'I'm sorry to disturb you at a time like this.'

Genuinely perplexed, she said, 'A time like what?' Then as the chirping of the birds distracted her, she turned her head towards them and said, 'Hello, Charlie! What's for tea, Charlie?'

And a voice from the nearest cage replied, 'What's for tea, Charlie?' then added, 'Who's a silly boy?'

Martin's mother turned back to me and proudly said, 'He's a great talker, is Charlie, one of the best I've had.'

Clive Berry said, 'Mother belongs to the local Budgie Club.'

She said, 'I've told you not to call it that! It's the Southaven Budgerigar and Exotic Bird Society.'

'I can't be coming out with a mouthful like that all the time.'

'Well then, don't talk about it at all. Do you like birds, Mr Rigby?' Stuck for an answer, I was still opening and closing my mouth without results when she continued. 'I always think birds bring life to a home. They're never downcast, are they? Never gloomy.'

Before I could venture an opinion, Clive Berry said, 'Mr Rigby's been asking us questions about Martin.'

This wasn't entirely true, but would have been if I could have thought of any. I said, hoping to draw Nessa's attention away from the birds, 'It's a terrible thing that's happened. I can't imagine how it must be for you both.'

Nessa's face twitched and flickered. Angela Wetherley had wondered whether Nessa had fully comprehended that Martin was dead. They'd spoken two days ago, but even now Martin's mother seemed more bewildered than upset.

Clive said, 'The Lord giveth and the Lord taketh away. It's our faith we turn to when things go wrong. Not something Martin shared with us, I'm afraid. I'm a churchwarden, as a matter of fact, with the Congregational Methodists.'

I said, 'Then you must know my aunt and uncle, the Lathoms.' There was no answering sign of recognition. 'Winnie and Fred?' Surely no-one who'd met my Aunt Winnie would be likely to forget her.

Clive Berry now seemed to draw himself up in his chair. 'I can't say I do, Mr Rigby. Perhaps they attend services of the *Free* Congregational Methodists.' His distaste for these reckless secessionists was plain.

And now I came to think of it, it was to the so-called Free Church that Winnie and Fred took themselves every Sunday morning, preferring to drive some three or four miles out to Marshfield rather than worship with the un-Free bunch just round the corner from Crowburn House. I opened my mouth to say as much, but thought better of it.

In the meantime, Nessa Berry had drifted across to Charlie's cage, and was allowing the bird to peck at her finger through the bars. Its cage-mate, alarmed by this development, flapped around wildly, producing shrill cries. I think it was Nessa who now said, 'What's for tea, Charlie?' Well, it must have been, because Charlie had his mouth full.

Martin's father watched this behaviour with displeasure. He said, 'You can talk to the birds later, Nessa dear. We've got company just now.'

I said, 'Do you know yet when the funeral's going to be?'

'What's for tea, Charlie? Who's a silly boy?' That was Charlie, this time.

'Yes, we do. The police released Martin's body this morning, the funeral's on Wednesday next. Of course we should be pleased if you would attend.'

Clive was treating me as if I'd been Martin's friend, not some private investigator he'd hired three days before. Perhaps Martin didn't have many friends. I said, 'I was wondering whether – ' And my voice broke off. Naturally I didn't mean this to happen, but sometimes the back of the mind takes over, and then your voice is not your own.

There was an awkward silence, if silence is the right word for something so laden with squawks and shrieks. The birds in the third cage had now joined Charlie and his chum in setting up a din of apocalyptic proportions. Raising his voice in competition, Clive Berry said, 'Whether what, Mr Rigby?'

I tried again. 'Would it be possible for me to view the – to view Martin's body? I'd like to pay my respects. If it's no trouble.'

Nessa said, 'Who's a silly boy?' and poked her finger in deeper.

Martin's father said, 'Of course, Mr Rigby, of course. We're with Rothwell's in Welldale – you know where they are? They can arrange viewings any time from tomorrow morning.' To make itself heard, the canary too had now cranked up the decibels. 'We've already – I mean, Nessa and I had to go and – ' It was Clive's turn to dry. The birds kept up their din. Nessa was now provoking the occupants of the other cage with her free hand. Martin's father continued. 'They called us in to identify him.'

'*What's for tea, Charlie?*'

'He looked wretched, Mr Rigby, I can't begin to tell you. I could hardly believe it was Martin at first – no life, you see, no life. We'd spent the day with him only on Sunday.' Clive Berry's voice had begun to shake. His hands gripped the chair arms. 'You devote your whole life to looking after them, and then – No one should have to bury their child, Mr Rigby. It isn't right. Where to find him now, eh?'

As he gave voice to these disjointed thoughts, Clive Berry withdrew deep into himself, and the light dulled in his eyes. But then Nessa said, perhaps once too often, 'Who's a silly boy, then? Who's a silly boy?' and the eyes were instantly alive again, fixing themselves with sudden fury on his wife and on the cages. There was a box of tissues on the coffee table beside him. He picked it up, flung it violently across the room, and said, 'Those *damned* birds!'

If he'd meant to hit Nessa, or the cages, then he was a poor shot. Instead the tissue box hit the wall, and dropped harmless to the floor.

Nessa had frozen where she stood, her hands shielding her face against her husband's rage. The birds fell silent.

From the doorway, Grace Berry said, 'I've found that phone number you were after.'

When Grace had left the room, I'd never imagined I would be so glad to see her return. I said, 'That's fabulous, thank you. And I should be going, really.' I stood up. 'Still another appointment this evening. No rest for the wicked, is there?' Perhaps I could have found something more appropriate to say, but the important thing was to be framing speech, with one eye on the clear path to the door.

Confused after his outburst, Clive Berry made no attempt to rise, and could manage nothing more than, 'But you've hardly – ' before he seemed to lose the will to continue. Nessa lowered her hands. Her sharp eyes darted swiftly from speaker to speaker.

I said, 'You've been extremely helpful. I mustn't take up any more of your time.' Although it might seem rude, I now made for Grace, the doorway, and freedom, rather than offer my hand to Martin's grieving father.

Grace passed me a chit of paper. 'This is Leah's number. And I've given you the address in case you need it.'

'Thanks, that could be useful.'

'But mind you don't bully her, it's not her fault she's the way she is. I'll come down with you.' Leaving Martin's parents in the airless room, I followed Grace in silence down the stairs and out onto the Avenue. She said, 'Are you going far?'

'Only up to the George Hotel.'

Grace now gave me a look which suggested familiarity with the George and with the clientele of the Velvet Bar. She said, 'A regular, are you? I've never seen you there.'

'More of an intermittent, if there is such a thing.'

Grace checked her pocket for keys. 'I'll walk part way with you, if that's all right.' She called upstairs then slammed the door behind her, and we set out for the Promenade. 'Makes a change to have someone else to talk to for a few minutes.'

'When did you come over from Manchester?'

'Tuesday. I dropped everything when the call came. They'd have fallen apart without me this last couple of days, they're not very practical.'

The temperature began to dip, and we could now feel the fresher air off the sea beginning to play on our faces. After the stifling room with its pent-up occupants the relief was enormous, and if I'd been a canary I'd have let it all out in grateful song. Instead I said, 'It can't have been easy for you, either.'

Grace walked on for a while without responding. We turned onto the Promenade, continuing along the landward side in front of the Victorian hotels with their grand windows designed for viewing the long-departed sea. Then Grace said, 'I know he was my brother, but I found it difficult to be fond of Martin. Him marrying Monica was the last straw. Those Wetherleys are scum but he couldn't see it, or else he didn't want to.'

'Scum? That's a bit harsh, isn't it?'

'No-one gets to be as rich as they are without treading on people. That's probably how Monica's dad gets his kicks. But even before Monica came along, me and Martin had never been close. It felt like I was in his shadow the whole time, he could do no wrong. I suppose I regret it now but I used to take the mickey out of him for being such a goody-goody. He was a very easy person to tease, you couldn't help yourself.'

I could vouch for the truth of that.

Grace went on. 'But the odd thing was, I sometimes felt that he was just playing a part, and all the time there was a different Martin waiting in the wings.'

'What sort of Martin?'

Grace shook her head. 'Hard to say. I'm probably talking bollocks anyway. Do you think they'll catch the bastard who killed him?'

No doubt she hadn't meant to cause offence, but there was the b-word just the same. I said, 'From what I've seen, the police are just thrashing around at the moment. I'm intending to do better.'

Grace stopped walking, so I stopped too. She turned towards me and said, 'Did you like Martin, Mr Rigby? Be honest, I'll know if you're giving me flannel.'

I looked round me for support, for inspiration. Two very old women in winter overcoats walked past arm in arm, headscarves tight over their blue-rinsed hair. I said, 'Yes, I liked him. He seemed a decent sort. He seemed – harmless. In my line of work I meet a lot of people with their eye on the main chance. Martin came as a breath of fresh air.'

Grace considered this carefully. Then she said, 'Harmless? Not much of an epitaph, is it?' And without formalities she turned and walked stiffly back the way she'd come.

*

It was just after nine when I stepped from the George Hotel lobby into the Velvet Bar. Bernie was there ahead of me, sitting very tall and straight on a bar stool, and immaculate, as always, in a tweed suit and brogues. She was not a woman to let such a trivial thing as the weather over-ride her sartorial preferences.

Behind the bar, Leslie Lush gave me a cool and non-committal look and rather than greeting me said loudly to the bar in general, 'Here she comes!' The place was quiet. Three older queens I'd seen before sat primly at a corner table, but seemed to have exhausted their conversation. Sitting alone under the window, a very young man in mauve hipsters nursed a long drink shaded by a cocktail umbrella. He looked nervous, and I wondered if this might be his first visit to the Velvet Bar, and if so how disappointed he was feeling, on a scale of one to ten.

Bernie smiled an easy smile, and I kissed her cheek. She said, 'Guinness?' and when I assented Leslie deftly flicked the lid from the bottle which he'd reached for as soon as I entered the room. Little else that was sold in the Velvet Bar could be considered drinkable, and on that point Bernie agreed with me. Leslie poured out the first third of the bottle, placed bottle and glass on the mat alongside Bernie's own, took the coins she offered, and left us to ourselves. He was an excellent barman, a dedicated professional in the mode of Sandra Snelgrove, and he brought atmosphere to the place even on a dead night such as this. But on the other hand, he didn't much like me. I was too butch for him, he saw me as a freak of nature.

Settling onto the stool beside Bernie's, I said, 'Crap day at the coalface?'

'No, actually, I've got two days off. Then I'm doing an early on Saturday.' She examined my face. Bernie generally preferred to diagnose my condition from the outward symptoms rather than consulting the patient, because experience had taught her that patients were a poor judge. She was a nurse in the cardiac unit at the Infirmary. She said, 'You look terrible.'

'Thanks.' I poured out a little more of the Guinness. It still wasn't ready to drink. 'You look great, annoyingly.'

She said, 'Some of us have it. Well, what's the story? It can't be overwork, so I presume you've been burning it at both ends again.'

There is no better listener in Southaven than Bernie Foster, but I felt in urgent need of a break from my own life and couldn't yet bring myself to share the bloody details of the week so far. And there was something else I felt in need of, too. I said, 'Got a spare fag?'

She raised her rather impressive eyebrows. 'What's the meaning of this? When do you ever come out without your fags?'

'Never mind about that, just give me one.' Bernie's pack of No 6 rested on the bar next to her drink, and in a couple of seconds the cigarette was in my mouth, Bernie had lit it, and the sacred fumes were being sucked down into my waiting lungs. It was now twelve long hours since my last cigarette. How could I ever have inflicted such suffering upon myself? At last, here it came: the hit. I sighed out smoke with my relief.

Looking down her nose, Bernie said, 'You haven't given up again, have you? Where do you get this self-denying streak from? God knows it isn't your mother.' She was right about that. In the course of a long friendship, Bernie had met my mother on several memorable occasions, and knew whereof she spoke.

The mauve youth now got up and crossed to the juke box. Leslie Lush had seen to it that the piped music which defiled the air in the hotel's other public rooms was barred entry here, and instead a magnificent juke box with a suitable selection of discs stood radiant against the far wall, like a sleek ocean liner on a midnight sea. When we're in the mood, Bernie and I lay bets on people's choices, but I felt too weary for play. After a few moments, Dusty Springfield could be heard, through a great deal of hiss and crackle, declaring that it would be quite unnecessary for us to say we loved her provided we remained in the vicinity. Bernie said, 'Damn! I'd have won that one,' but anyone can be wise after the event. The boy moved away from the juke box, looked me up and down, and returned to his seat.

The stout had now settled, and what with that and the cigarette and Bernie's company I was beginning to catch glimpses of a more positive state of mind. I pressed Bernie for an update on her affairs, but most of what she had to tell me concerned arcane details of hospital shift rotas and failed to stir my interest. Bernie led a simple, almost an austere, life, alternating between duties at the hospital, where she was obliged to wear a skirt, and equally onerous but betrousered duties as mentor to half the lesbian population of West Lancashire. Tales of her adventures in this latter role generally proved more entertaining, and with that in mind I now said, 'I've just walked up the Prom with Grace Berry.'

'What – Little Red Riding-hood?'

Of course I hadn't the faintest idea what she meant. Truly the fairy folk of Southaven move in one world and the dykes in another, with the only significant overlap between them being my transgressive friendship with Bernie Foster. Catching up a little, I said, 'Is that some sort of nick-name?'

'Well yes, what else would it be? The "red" bit's from her politics of course, but I shan't explain the rest of it, you're too young.'

I am indeed some eight or nine years Bernie's junior, a fact which I'm not allowed to forget. I said, 'I've never seen her in here.'

'She doesn't come in any more since she's away to Manchester. But in any case, she only ever came to the women's nights on Mondays.' The Velvet Bar had an informal rule that on one evening of the week men should make themselves scarce, giving the women the free run of the place. Any man misguided enough to turn up on a Monday would find himself stared out of the room in double-quick time. 'A bit of a purist, is Grace. Runs a women's group in Manchester, frowns on the ones who have anything to do with men.' Then Bernie gave my face the once-over again and said, 'This is about that bloke who got murdered, isn't it?'

Once more I'd forgotten that Martin enjoyed a far higher profile in death than he ever had in life. Bernie was as devoted a student of the Gazette as anyone in town, and I watched now as her brain performed a swift calculation and made four.

She went on, 'Yes – it was somebody Berry, wasn't it? I didn't think at the time. Some relative of Grace's?'

'Martin, her brother – by adoption, anyway.'

'And how do you come to be involved? I don't recall a Martin in your long list of ex-catastrophes. Come on, Sam, I want the whole story.'

But I wasn't in the mood yet to give Bernie the whole story. In fact, before I felt able to satisfy even part of her curiosity I had to buy a double scotch to help smooth the passage of the stout. Only then did I let her have a much-edited version of the week's events. When I'd done, she said, 'You take the cake, Sam, you really do.'

'Why, what have I done now?' But keen as I was to hear the answer, I then noticed that Bernie was sitting with an empty glass, so chat had to be suspended while I bought in the next round. More customers had arrived now, and the bar was alive with talk and laughter. Only the mauve youth remained silent and alone, glancing occasionally in my direction. 'So – why do I take the cake?'

Bernie paused to give her thoughts a run-up before replying. In the meantime, she took a drink, then licked the rim of the glass with a practised tongue. 'Because, in the dozen-odd years I've known you I don't think you've ever once chased after a sensible choice of bloke. Even the best ones have only been after your body, such as it is, and the rest have either been in the closet and determined to stay there or complete head cases. But now – now, you've actually fallen in love with a man who's dead.'

'That's not true!'

'Don't argue, Sam, you know I'm always right. And to make matters worse, you've somehow managed to confuse your feelings for this Martin person by digging up the corpse of your relationship with Mark Howell.'

'Rubbish! Me and Mark – '

'Shush, I haven't finished. Then on top of that, you work yourself up over some chicken half your age – '

'Matt is not half my age.'

' – who's now batting for the other team and more likely to be made Archbishop of Canterbury than ever have sex with you.'

'He's a Catholic.'

'Well then, there you are.'

I bristled silently for a while, then ordered another scotch. But Bernie still hadn't finished.

'And there's something else: Matt – Martin – Mark – what's going on there? I suppose we should be grateful you didn't meet a Marmaduke this week as well.' Pleased with this quip at my expense, she took a complacent sip of the Guinness, which clothed her upper lip with a milky moustache. Given her dark hair and brown eyes, this rather suited her, just as the Tartan moustache had suited Martin that night in the Feathers, before he'd wiped it away. It seemed that everything reminded me of Martin now, but that didn't mean Bernie was right. There's a world of difference between having a passing fancy for someone and falling in love, and in any case, I never fall in love, it's a waste of time.

I couldn't let Bernie have it all her own way, so I then staged a counter-attack on the grounds that while she was always ready enough with the advice, her own romantic history had been every bit as much of a Hammer horror as mine. The discussion became brisk, the stout slipped down, the scotches slipped down in close pursuit, one after another. I shouldn't have been spending the money, but sometimes it seems to spend itself. The Velvet Bar closed later than regular pubs, and we stuck with it to the end, our talk pleasingly heated by abrasion. There's nothing like a good ding-dong when your soul's a-weary. We were still locked in bitter dispute when we stumbled out onto the moonlit Promenade towards midnight.

Bernie said, 'And I've been meaning to tell you, you're getting fat.'

Not that again. Why this sudden popular obsession with my waistline? 'No I'm not. Uncle Fred says it's puppy fat. Anyway, it's you that's fat.' She wasn't, of course, but still.

Bernie frowned. She'd had a good deal to drink and the frown got stuck for a while. At last she got it unstuck again and said, 'No, you're getting confused. I'm not the one who's fat. It's you – you're getting fat, I've just told you.'

I said, 'Confused, me? I'm not confused, you're confused. One minute you were telling me you were getting fat, now suddenly you say I'm fat. You drink too much, that's your problem. It'll make you fat.'

Fogged by this line of reasoning, Bernie stood silent for a moment. And while she was engaged in trying to work out exactly who was confused and who was fat, the mauve youth came out of the hotel, passed in front of us, looked back at me, risked a shy smile, then set off along the Promenade, walking very slowly. He had nice hips.

I must have been staring after him with intent, because Bernie then said, 'No, Sam, for goodness' sake, don't go after that one! Haven't you got enough trouble already?'

I shook my head and said, 'Can never have too much trouble. Makes the world go around.' Then I kissed her. 'Run along now. Samuel busy.'

She said, 'Incorrigible, that's what you are.' And I'm amazed she got the word out, considering how pissed she was. 'And fat. Fat fat fat. Fat fat fat fat fat fat fat.' Her path lay in the opposite direction, and she started out on it now with tall, unsteady dignity.

So I caught up with the mauve youth and took him back to the flat. I found a quarter of a bottle of vodka behind some bleach in the kitchen cupboard, and while we drank it and smoked his cigarettes I tried to block out the story of his young life by getting better acquainted with the mauve hipsters and with the soft skin of his belly. But in bed he had absolutely no idea what he was doing, and I quickly made the discovery that the prospect of my bed unencumbered by mauve youths held far more appeal than its opposite, so I suggested he went home. He didn't take this well. A stunned silence was soon followed by tears, and through them he wailed that it wasn't fair, and that this was the very worst day of his whole life, ever. Well, I couldn't allow that, so I told him that from the vantage point of numerous unspeakably awful days as yet undawned he would look back on this one more in the light of a carnival or riot of giddy joy. And besides, I said, he should thank his lucky stars that he wasn't at that moment being smashed over the back of the head by a large rock, with his naked body then abandoned face down in a lonely pool to be nibbled at by fishes.

He left pretty quickly after that.

Martin again, bloody Martin. I couldn't get him out of my mind, and I knew that this would go on now until I'd found his killer, that nothing else could break the spell he'd somehow woven around me on Monday night. I made myself a mug of strong tea, took it back to bed, and sat upright against the headboard determined to think through every last scrap of evidence which I'd collected. Probably the back of my mind already knew who had gone up to the lake with Martin, watched him undress, then coldly picked up the weapon which would end his life. No doubt the back of my mind was screaming, 'Hey! You there, up front! It's – ! It's – , why can't you see it?' But the front of my mind was too deaf and blind and stupid to get the message.

Nor did this fresh burst of determination bring results. Perhaps in less than a minute, I was asleep. From time to time I half emerged into a confused wakefulness, aware that I'd just been with Martin, down in the secret shadowed vault where his true self lived, laughing and playing with him in the guttering candlelight. But then I would slide back into the void.

Which is where I must have been when, in line with the regime dictated for me this week by the all-powerful gods, the phone rang. I think the back of my mind had been expecting this, because my body instantly began the journey from my bed to the living room without waiting for instructions from my still-sleeping brain.

As I picked up the receiver, I noticed at last that I was out of bed, that it was daylight, and that I was answering the phone. 'Mr Rigby?' A woman's voice I didn't immediately recognize. Anxious.

'Speaking.'

'Please will you come, Mr Rigby? It's me, Faye Christensen, Danny's neighbour.' Not just anxious – afraid. 'Oh, do say you'll come!' She'd been crying, or was trying not to start.

'What is it, what's happened?'

'I can't get in. I put the key in his door but it won't open. I've knocked and knocked, he doesn't answer. You will come, won't you? There's something wrong, I know there is!'

Friday

1

And so, for what felt like the hundredth time this week, I sped off up the coast road to Otterdale. There seemed to be some problem with the Cortina this morning, as if the clutch was reluctant to bite, but it might have been my imagination. Infected by the urgency in Faye's voice I floored the throttle at every opportunity, but as though in a nightmare we seemed to be advancing at little better than a stately *tempo moderato*, with the familiar rattle counterpointing the engine's drone.

I now understood why, after days of spoiling me, the gods had suddenly denied me a parking space outside my flat the previous afternoon. The reason they give so freely with one hand is that they get such a kick out of taking it all away again with the other, and divine laughter had almost drowned out the pumping of blood in my head as I sprinted the half mile to Crowburn House. But at last I reached the car, started it, wound down a couple of windows to let out the damp, and then was on my way.

Already as I pulled off Beach Road I could see Faye watching for me outside Danny's house. I parked up and crossed to join her. She didn't wait for me to draw level before saying, 'Where have you been? I'm at my wits' end!'

'Sorry, came as quick as I could.'

'Anything could be happening!' I looked more closely at Faye. She hadn't yet applied her war-paint, and the difference was striking. This was a face lined with age and experience, a softer, sadder and rather older Faye than I'd seen before. She wore a frilled pinafore over her work clothes, a crisp blouse and dark skirt. 'I was just going to get him his breakfast.'

'Try your key again.'

'I've tried it a thousand times!'

'Once more won't hurt.'

So she put the key in Danny's lock, and it turned, but the door held firm.

I said, 'It looks as if someone's dropped the catch on the inside.'

'But he doesn't answer – I've knocked until my knuckles are red raw. I don't understand, what's going on, what's going on?'

Faye was close to hysteria, and the long wait for the cavalry had clearly made matters worse. I placed firm hands on her shoulders. 'Now Faye, calm down, all right? There's bound to be some perfectly simple explanation. Can I get over the back from your garden?'

'No, or I'd have done it myself. The wall's very high, and we're not great gardeners, me and Olaf. It's all brambles and dog roses, you can't get anywhere near.'

'What about from the alleyway at the other side?'

'I suppose a fit person might be able to climb up.' And she gave me a sceptical look.

I said, 'Wait here,' and ran round into the alley which separated Danny's house from the next terrace. Rubbish was piled there around a couple of old dustbins. One stood conveniently beneath the high wall of Danny's back garden.

All along, intuition had been telling me that although, as I'd said to Faye, there must be some simple explanation for Danny's non-appearance this morning, it needn't also be an innocent one. Seeing the dustbin so neatly placed, intuition came close to certainty. With the sense of following in recent footsteps, I climbed onto the dustbin, drew myself up to the top of the wall, then dropped over on the other side.

I found myself standing next to a green canvas sun-bed stretched out on a small area of rough crazy paving. Though currently shadowed by the wall, this would no doubt become a perfect sun-trap by the middle of the day, with the particular advantage that it was overlooked by only two houses, Danny's and Faye's. This must be the favoured spot where Danny had acquired his all-over tan. It was evident from Faye's pale complexion that she herself preferred to avoid the sun, but I wondered whether she had watched from an upper window while her young neighbour slowly toasted those lean, half-moon buttocks. And I wondered too whether he had wanted her to watch, whether for him that was all part of the game they were playing.

I stepped down onto the dust-patch which must at one time have been a lawn. If anyone had ever loved this garden, nothing of their care remained. An outside toilet leaned against the coal-shed, which had lost its roof. Both were tumbling brick by brick into decay. Nothing grew in the dry earth but a few rank weeds, from among which rose a single proud sunflower, almost the height of a man.

Approaching the rear extension of the house, I saw without surprise that the door which gave onto the box-filled lobby between Danny's kitchen and bathroom stood wide open. There was no sign of forced entry. Though pretty sure that whoever had come this way before me would now be long gone, as I crossed the threshold I deliberately slowed my progress, eyes and ears straining. My effort was soon rewarded. Just beyond the worn doormat, the lino floor showed the clear print of a left shoe pointing towards me, marked out in some brownish substance. Beyond that again, another print, the same. Stepping in and checking behind the door, I found the key lying on the mat where it had fallen. Slowly, taking care not to disturb the prints, I followed them in reverse direction back into Danny's kitchen, where yesterday's Gazette still lay on the table, and through into the front hallway.

'Mr Rigby? Sam?' Eyes intent on the floor, I hadn't noticed that stubby fingers were forcing open the letter-box from outside, and the sound of Faye's rather carrying voice in the empty hallway did nothing to settle my nerves. 'Can you let me in?' Two brown eyes now replaced the mouth. They must have had an excellent view of my knees.

I could see nothing wrong with the Yale lock on this side of the door, but I had my reasons for thinking that it might be unwise to lift the catch and admit Faye Christensen. At the base of the uncarpeted stairway the brownish footprints turned and backed upwards. This was not what I'd wanted to find. 'Just give me a few more minutes, Faye.'

'What can you see?'

'There's nothing the matter, you just stay where you are, OK?'

'But why won't you let me in?'

'All in good time.'

Well of course that was an extremely irritating thing to say and so it was small wonder that Faye now began pounding on the door with what sounded like the flat of her hand, shouting, 'Sam! Open this door! Open this door at once!' But I didn't open the door. Instead I followed the retreating footsteps up the stairs. At the top a closed door led into the room over the extension, but the footsteps passed this by and went on to the next, the bedroom above the back sitting room where Danny and Martin had had their argument on Monday night. Here the dark green door was not fully shut, and hid the heel of a footprint whose toe peeped out as it crossed onto the landing. I pushed gently at the door with my elbow, and on silent hinges it swung open.

Covered neatly to the waist by a plain sheet which had once been white, Danny's body lay back on the bed, head lolling sideways, throat slashed from ear to ear. Blood had sprayed the wall behind, and on the bedside rug a pool had formed in which the footsteps I'd been following were finally swallowed up.

Faye had now stopped hammering on the front door, so at least I could hear myself think. I'd advanced no further than the doorway and it was obviously vital that I touch nothing and do nothing which might compromise the investigation. The sensible course would be to leave immediately and use Faye's telephone to call the police.

And yet – as long as I didn't touch anything, what harm could it possibly do just to have the teensiest peek inside the room?

Thrusting my hands into my trouser pockets to be on the safe side, and still taking care to avoid the bloody prints, I moved closer to the foot of the bed. How differently I'd felt about this body before, down in the kitchen yesterday, or when I'd first seen Danny at the yard. Now, with blood caked around the dark circles of the nipples, it was just so much meat, expertly carved by the local butcher. Suddenly I remembered what the workman had said as he fixed the street lamp outside my flat. Once more someone had been having fun with a blade.

Had Danny been sleeping like this, half covered, when death came for him? There was no evidence of struggle. Probably he'd heard nothing as his killer picked the outside lock, crept up the stairs and crossed the room to stand above him, ready to strike. There had been no intention of causing fear, in a sense no malice, just the act itself, quick and clean. And then the sheet. To me it looked as if the killer himself – herself? – had pulled the sheet up tidily to cover Danny's sprawling corpse. I was reminded of the neat pile of clothes by the boating lake. The same calm, orderly mind must be at work here too.

The body could tell me nothing more without close examination, and I would have to leave that to the police. I turned away. Only then did I see the message, written in bloody capital letters on the old mirrored wardrobe which stood behind the door:

HE SHUD HAVE PAYED.

As a by-product of my night with Bernie in the Velvet Bar, the machinery of thought was running slow this morning. Even so, this latest message from the murderer enabled me to draw two conclusions. First, Danny's death was supposed to look like the work of our old friend Slasher Braithwaite. Second, it was nothing of the kind. Someone with a poor view of Braithwaite's general intelligence was trying to set him up.

I was just congratulating myself on this insight when I thought I heard the creaking of a tread on the stairs. With a sudden chill I realized why Faye's attempts to break down the front door had stopped. She must have decided that if a shambling specimen such as myself could get over the back wall, then so could she. I moved rapidly to the doorway, but Faye was already on the landing, and when she saw the look on my face she screamed, 'No!' and hurled herself right at me, desperate to get into the room. I was stronger than Faye, but she had momentum on her side, and I suppose love also, or whatever it was that she felt for the man whose earthly remains lay stretched out on the bed behind me. I grabbed her, fought with her, eventually gained the upper hand and pushed her back to the top of the stairs. But it was too late. In the first moment she'd already glimpsed the horror in the bedroom, and the effect on her was immediate. She screamed repeatedly and wouldn't stop until I slapped her hard across the face. Then I half pulled, half pushed her down the stairs, let us both out of the front door, and carried on pushing and pulling her until we'd come to rest beside the telephone in Faye's dark hallway.

She was sobbing now, the frills on her pinafore rippling as her shoulders rose and fell. Her hands covered her face. I put through a direct call to the central police station, then a second one to the little local station at the town end of Beach Road. Then I pushed Faye along into the kitchen, smaller than Danny's, where I manoeuvred her into a chair, filled the kettle, and stood it on the gas hob. I found the teapot, the caddy with fresh leaf tea, the sugar bowl, milk jug, cups and saucers. Faye's sobbing died away. I put everything on the table, made the tea, and waited while it brewed.

Not looking at me, Faye said, 'You promised.'

She was right, of course. I'd promised her that nothing would happen to Danny, but now he was dead. Somehow I doubted whether she would have much use for an apology. Instead I poured the tea, and Faye sipped at it like the good girl she was.

*

An hour or so later I was seated at the same table but with a very different companion. Mark Howell and the technical team were busy next door, Cilla Donnelly was looking after Faye in the living room, and I myself was closeted uncomfortably with Southaven's reigning Pipe-smoker of the Year, Detective Inspector Harry Hargreaves. The usual paraphernalia of his habit were laid out on the table in front of him, and in the absence of any dedicated ashtray he'd elected to use one of Faye's saucers. He was just lighting the first pipe he'd smoked since his arrival on the scene three-quarters of an hour before. I'd been instructed to wait in Faye's kitchen until he'd finished looking around, and when he took his seat at the table opposite me I could safely assume that by now he'd be on top of his subject. The pipe having drawn to his satisfaction, he regarded me with a fond look, much as a lion stuffed to bursting from some recent feast might view the trapped animal it meant to devour later on.

But still Hargreaves didn't speak, and I found myself saying, in what emerged as a spinsterish manner, 'Are you sure you won't have tea, Henry?'

Harry Hargreaves shook his impressive head. Curling smoke dived this way and that to give it space. 'Thoughtful of you, Samuel, but no. There's an effeminacy in constant tea-drinking which I simply can't abide.' Then he was silent again, but not inactive. The stem of his pipe had to be chewed, its contents puffed at, and the pleasant kitchen filled to every extremity with its penetrating fumes. Besides all this, the unlucky private investigator sitting opposite him had to be scrutinized with clinical thoroughness until all the secrets of his guilty heart lay exposed to view. I began to wonder if Danny Craven hadn't got the better end of the deal.

At last, the great man spoke again. 'Well, Samuel – we're quite the bobby-dazzler, aren't we.'

I wasn't sure I followed this. 'We are?'

'Last Tuesday, what did I specifically tell you to do? Eh?' Receiving no reply, Hargreaves now menaced me with the loaded pipe. 'Did I or did I not instruct you categorically to keep your vile excuse for a nose right out of my investigation?'

I couldn't let this pass uncorrected. 'Feet.'

'"Feet"? What do you mean, "feet"?'

'It seemed to be more my feet that you were concerned about.'

He didn't take that well. 'Never mind which precise part of your anatomy I may have referred to at the time. The point is, you were under strict orders to keep your distance, instead of which you've pried, snooped and meddled your way through half of Southaven, interfering with my witnesses, causing unnecessary disturbance to the victim's relatives, and finally, in a stunning development of which I've no doubt you're exceptionally proud, contaminating the scene of a further appalling crime by tramping your size elevens all over the evidence.'

There were those feet again, but I didn't say anything. 'That wasn't my fault.'

'Oh, so whose fault was it then? Barbara Castle?'

'I'd left Mrs Christensen outside but she followed me up the stairs. I had to get her away from there, we smudged a few footprints, it couldn't be helped.'

'And I presume that's also when you smudged the fingerprints round the Yale lock on the front door?'

'Oh, come on, Harry, you'd never be able to lift a print off that lock. Besides, the killer wears gloves, those thin latex ones like Doctor Kildare uses.' Or at any rate, that's the conclusion I'd come to after I'd dusted my office for prints. It seemed I couldn't be bothered to be afraid of Hargreaves this morning. The body on the bed had changed things. Maybe I should have seen this murder coming, but Hargreaves was the one with the manpower. If he'd been half the cop he gave himself credit for then Danny Craven would still be alive.

Hargreaves said, 'As you know, Samuel, I prefer to be known as Henry. A small courtesy, but I'd appreciate it nonetheless. And you're talking flat bunkum, as usual. Since when did Joe Braithwaite start mincing around in Marigolds?'

I stared across at the big man I'd once venerated like a father, aware that a sneer of contempt had begun to curl my lip. 'Surely you're not buying the Slasher Braithwaite line?'

'Thanks to you, Samuel, we know Craven owed him money. And this is exactly his style.'

'Bollocks. Braithwaite cuts people. He wants to scare them, put pressure on. How do you suppose he's going to get his money out of Danny Craven now? No, this is the work of the same person who killed Martin Berry, I'd stake my life on it.'

'And why should that not have been Braithwaite too?'

'Because it wasn't, and you know it wasn't. You're so mad keen to put Braithwaite away for something that you're not thinking straight. Martin Berry had nothing to do with him. If Martin wanted money, he'd only to ask his father-in-law. Braithwaite's being set up!'

Hargreaves was shaking his head again, in slow disappointment. He knocked out the ash of his pipe in the saucer. 'You've not changed, Samuel, have you? Imagination still working overtime. You were never content with the plain facts, there always had to be some conspiracy lurking in the background. There's no place for that sort of fanciful thinking in the modern police force.' And now it was Hargreaves' turn to sneer.

But he'd sneered at me once too often. Time and again since I'd left the force we'd had these run-ins, time and again he'd bested me. Now people were dying and still he seemed more interested in playing cat and mouse with me than in hearing the truth. I said, 'It wasn't fanciful thinking that got me pushed out though, was it? It was the fact I got caught in the locker room with my tongue shoved down Mark Howell's throat. And you all fluttered around like chickens because you couldn't deal with it – pathetic! Modern police force, my arse, you're still stuck in the days of the Bow Street runners.' I pushed back the chair and stood up. 'These things happen, Harry. Here in Southaven. In your modern police force. Get used to it.' And I turned to leave.

Cilla Donnelly was standing in the doorway behind me. For a second I froze. She must have heard what I'd said about Mark, but I hoped to God she wouldn't tell him. Suddenly I remembered the insane remark she'd made the previous morning, about Hargreaves actually liking me. I turned from her to him. There was a look on his face which utterly baffled me, a look of sadness almost, of regret. Though I could make nothing of this, it forced a concession from me. I'd intended to say no more, but now I muttered, 'Good luck with the case,' before pushing past Cilla without acknowledging her and striding out into the street.

*

At the newsagents on Station Parade I bought a pack of twenty cigarettes, then set off for the telephone box thirty yards distant. To my amazement I found that the place had been cleaned up. The little line of roll-up butts which I'd disturbed on Tuesday morning had now disappeared, together with all its filtered and unfiltered cousins. But despite the smell of fresh disinfectant, the old urine stench lingered reassuringly, as if exuding from the pores of the structure itself. I lit a cigarette, placed the fags and lighter on the shelf, dialled Matt's number, and when the beeps came I thrust home the money. A woman's voice said, 'Hello?'

'Could I speak to Matt, please? It's Sam Rigby.'

There was no reply other than a loud clunk, and while waiting for my tousle-haired assistant to come on the line I took a deep and gloriously satisfying drag on the cigarette. The world seemed suddenly a fraction less intolerable. Sunshine played on two hanging baskets of petunias outside the laundrette, and in a further bonus there was no evidence of large, blue-work-coated women who might be about to rap on the window and challenge my right to use the phone. Then a sharp voice on the line said, 'I've been trying to get you for more than an hour! Have you been sleeping in?'

The injustice rankled, but I simply said, 'Danny Craven's dead.'

'Dead? How?' While I gave Matt a brief review of the morning's developments, a train pulled into the station, and soon a few brightly-dressed passengers emerged and walked away from me towards the beach. When the grim tale was done, I once more drew smoke down into my lungs. Immediately Matt said, 'Are you smoking?'

I suppose it was inevitable that this would make me cough, and I now coughed. As soon as I'd recovered, I said, 'No, of course not. I told you, I've given up.'

'You were smoking, I could hear it.'

'I am not smoking, OK? Cross my heart and hope to die. Anyway, I've got something to say, so listen. I'm going to have to let you go.'

'Let me go? I don't understand.'

'You're fired.'

'But you can't! It was all going brilliantly!'

For one deeply unwelcome moment, an image of the livid gash in Danny's throat forced its way up into my consciousness. I tried to blank it out. 'You call this going brilliantly? I'd hate to see your idea of a disaster.'

'You know that's not what I meant. I mean – us, working together. We're a team!'

'I don't care, it's too dangerous. You're off the payroll, and that's that.'

'I was never on the payroll.'

'Your services are no longer required.'

'But Sam – '

'I'm not arguing, I'm telling you. Get a proper job.' I slammed down the receiver, collected my cigarettes, and walked back to the car.

*

In Vaughan Close there was no sign of the Jag, and when I rang the bell Monica herself came to the door. I said, 'You alone?' She nodded. 'We need to talk.' And when we'd settled in chairs in the sun room I said, 'Danny Craven's been murdered. So if there's anything you've neglected to tell me, now's your chance.'

Monica's face flushed with emotion, but she didn't cry or scream or show any sign of rending her raiment. Of course the news I'd brought must have upset her, but I had a hunch that what really gave her pause was the change in my manner. There was no trace of the old Sympathetic Sam she'd met before. I'd done with Sympathetic Sam now.

After a good long while she said, 'How did it happen?' and so I told her, not sparing her the unpleasant details. Danny's death had somehow added a piece to the jigsaw of Monica's character which I'd been assembling all week in the back of my mind. I realized now that people had been shielding Monica from life's unpleasant details all her life, and picking up the tab on her behalf. I'd even started doing it myself, but that had to stop.

I said, 'The police are going to want to nail this on a loan shark called Joe Braithwaite. Danny owed him money, he's notorious for getting physical when people don't pay up. Only Joe didn't do it. The same person who killed Martin killed Danny, and for the same reason.'

'What reason?'

'I don't know. Perhaps you do.'

'Me?'

'Yes, you. This has all got something to do with you. I don't know what, but I can smell it.'

A cold, hard look came into Monica's grey eyes. 'You're mad. I loved Martin!'

'Where were you last night?'

'Here.'

'On your own?'

It didn't take her the full five beats to answer, in the style of Sandy Smythe, but something did block her speech for the briefest moment before she said, 'Yes, of course.'

I wondered how much of my hand to show her, but with two men dead it was no time to be playing the long game. 'The thing is, Monica, I'm not sure I believe you.' She didn't respond, but gave me a dismissive look as if this cynical streak in my nature, though regrettable, was no concern of hers. 'And what about Monday night? You didn't really stay with Leah Armstrong, did you?'

'Of course I did. Ask her, she'll tell you.'

'Oh, yes, I'm sure she will. Like your mother said, Leah would do anything for you, wouldn't she? Your little loyal friend.'

Much as I was enjoying playing the hard man with Martin Berry's widow, was it getting me anywhere? She sat impassive now, indifferent to my performance. Perhaps over the years she'd had practice at stonewalling her accusers like this. Perhaps I needed a different approach.

I modified my tone. 'What was it that made you think Martin wasn't happy in the marriage?' She turned her head away. This was progress. 'When I told you I thought you were wrong, you said something like "I know what I know." What did you mean?'

Monica's eyes were fixed on the carpet, avoiding mine. She said, 'Do you have a cigarette?'

'I didn't think you smoked.' She shrugged her shoulders. I took the pack and lighter from my jacket pocket, gave her a cigarette, lit it, then lit one for myself as well. There was no ashtray so I fetched a bowl from the kitchen and set it down on the floor between us. For a few companionable seconds we puffed away in silence, complicit in the pleasure of the drug. You could tell Monica was only a part-time smoker, she had that way of holding the cigarette remote from her body, as if it had nothing to do with her, and when she drew on it she blew the smoke out straight away before it could get too matey with her insides.

Monica flicked ash into the bowl. This past few days she'd been doing a lot of thinking, but not much talking. She looked pensively around the sun room. Perhaps she was thinking of the man who'd built it and who was currently helping to provide employment for Her Majesty's constabulary. But when she did speak, her subject wasn't Danny Craven. She said, 'No one had ever wanted me as

much as Martin did, in the beginning. But then – ' She fell silent
again.

I said, 'Wanted you? You mean, sexually?'

'It's very hard to talk about these things.'

'Try.'

'But I don't know the answer! At the time I thought it was
sexual, yes, but when someone's making a play for you how can you
separate sex from other things?'

This wasn't helping. 'What sort of other things?'

'Oh, you know.' She had another go at the cigarette. It didn't
please her any more, she made a face and stubbed out what was left
of it in the bowl. 'Money. Possession.'

'I don't understand. You think he was after you for your money?
I thought it was the opposite, he seemed to hate the way your
father could just write a cheque for anything you wanted.'

'Yes, he resented that. But I think I drew the wrong conclusion.
I got the idea he'd have been happier if my family had been more
like his, with no money, but perhaps it was the other way around.'

'That shop of theirs must be worth a few bob.'

She shook her head. 'They rent it. When business is good
they're very comfortable, and you could never call them
extravagant, Clive puts money away when he can. But they're
simple, working people.'

'Unlike the Wetherleys.'

Monica bridled at that. 'My father's always worked extremely
hard! He came from nothing, it takes a lot of drive to get where he
is now. But Martin wasn't like that. You heard what my mother said
about him, he really wasn't going anywhere. And I loved that in
him. High-flying men can be so boring.'

'The money comes in handy though.'

'I don't need money.' I'd have been readier to believe this if
Monica had ever had the chance to give penury a try. 'And I
thought Martin was the same. But – '

'But now you think that alongside your family Martin was
ashamed of his background.'

'I'm not sure. Possibly. He may have wanted to climb a little
higher in the world.'

'And marrying you was supposed to take him there. But I still
don't see it. What use was money to him? He showed no sign of
wanting to live the high life.'

Monica said nothing, plainly turning over some dilemma in her mind. Then she got up and left the room. I finished my cigarette and stubbed it out alongside Monica's. Looking up, I saw that Eusebio had jumped onto the window-ledge outside, and catching sight of me he began yawling through the glass. Despite the language barrier, I grasped the general tone of complaint. Apparently I was being harangued over my spectacular failure to identify Martin's killer. But when Monica re-entered the room and opened the door onto the garden, Eusebio simply came inside and walked straight past me without further comment, heading for his dish on the kitchen floor. If Martin's death had affected his appetite, it seemed he was over it now.

Monica handed me a very old envelope, on which was written in an irregular hand, *To be opened when your 16.*

I said, 'What's this?'

'Open it.'

So I took out the single folded sheet. Without address, date, or other preamble, it began:

> *Dear Martin my own dearest boy,*
>
> *If your reading this then I know your 16 now and that good folk have taken care of you and done what I asked. I wanted you to know from me that I love you with all my heart and if I could have kept you I would have but there was no money. My wage just about keeps me and Dad but thats the best you can say. You may as well know it was the boss got me in the family way but he said it was my word against his and he washed his hands of it. If he had only of been straight about it I could have kept you and you'd have had everything money can buy and lived in a big house with your own garden but it was not to be. I did wrong to go with him and I hope you will not do wrong when you grow up. There will never be a day when I dont think of you and wish you happier wherever you are than ever you could have been with me. I hope you can forgive me thats all.*
>
> *Your loving Mother*

I replaced the note in the envelope and gave it back to Monica, who held it with both hands against her breast. 'He kept it at the back of a shelf in the wardrobe. He must have known I would read it.'

I said, 'Do you think he ever tried to find his mother?'

'No. I asked him about his real parents once, he said it was best to let sleeping dogs lie. But I'd give my eye teeth now to know what he thought about this letter. I can't help wishing she'd never written it.'

'And you think this explains his attitude to money?'

She gave a wry smile. 'Explains? It doesn't explain anything.' She held up the wretched document accusingly. 'But there was a side of him that was always this woman's son. God knows how that made him feel.' The smile had faded now. 'I'm beginning to think I didn't know Martin very well.'

And in one respect she was certainly right about that. Now it was my turn to face a dilemma. If I told her the truth, I might lose her confidence completely. On the other hand, perhaps it would provoke her into a little truth-telling of her own. While I dithered Rigby-fashion over which course to take, Martin's killer was enjoying another bright summer's day of freedom. I had to take risks if I wanted that to change.

'Monica – I may possibly have bent the truth a little when I came here the other day.' She looked at me with definite curiosity. This wasn't a bad start. 'Martin never thought he was being followed. I just – I made that up. He hired me because he thought you were having an affair.' Of course that should have been affairs, plural, but sometimes it's best to keep things simple.

For the second time this morning, Monica's face flushed with colour, but once again there was no outburst of any kind. Her only action was to smooth the folds of her dress. Given that I'd hoped for instant revelations, I couldn't help wishing that Monica would practise her iron self-control some other time. Her head drew back a little, the spine stiffened. Her mother would have been proud of her. She said, 'And would you mind telling me with whom I was supposed to be carrying on this – affair?'

I could feel a fib coming on. 'Martin didn't know, I was supposed to find out. But what you need to understand is, he couldn't bear the idea of you being with someone else. You must be wrong to think he didn't want you so much any more.'

She turned to me with a sour look. 'Then why did we stop

making love?'

I hadn't expected this. There was a silence while I rejected a long succession of inadequate replies.

Monica said, 'Twice in the last six months. Twice!' Her eyes had filled with tears, but they were tears of anger. At that moment she didn't look like a woman you'd want to mess with. 'I thought there must be something wrong with me. I couldn't sleep, I stopped eating. He just didn't want me. Why?'

'But then it was the spring, and Danny was working here in the house. And he most definitely did want you.'

She spoke sharply. 'We never did anything!'

'I know. But it must have been good to feel wanted again.'

Monica allowed the letter to drop to the floor and crossed to look out of the window, her back turned towards me. After a time she said, 'Martin was the only one for me. I don't know why, perhaps I felt sorry for him.' This wasn't the moment to point out that of all possible foundations for a relationship, pity had to be the worst. 'I'm sure I could have won him round again. We'd have been fine. We'd have got through it somehow, whatever it was.' Then she heaved a deep sigh, and allowed her drooping forehead to rest against the cool glass.

An empty minute passed. Monica seemed to have lost interest in my presence, and when I mumbled something about leaving she made no response. There didn't seem to be much point in staring at the back of her head any longer, so I pocketed the cigarettes and quit the house.

Back in the Cortina, I wondered whether I'd just ruinously misplayed my hand. Coming clean with Monica about Martin's reason for employing me had gained me nothing. Should I have pushed her about Rupert Heysham? But if I'd done that, no doubt she would have talked it over with him, put him on his guard. I had an idea that in Manchester tomorrow I was going to learn far more from her old tutor than I would ever manage to squeeze out of Monica herself.

Uncertain now of my next move, I had no great desire to speed back into town along the coast road. Instead I opted for the slower, inland route, and in Welldale I stopped off at the funeral directors near the railway station to arrange a viewing of Martin's body for that afternoon. If Martin, living, had not supplied me with the answers I needed, perhaps the lifeless shell he'd left behind might inspire me to deductive brilliance. Besides, I wanted to see him again, just one more time.

As I turned onto Preston Road ten minutes later, I noticed two things. First, having enjoyed their bit of fun, the gods had now restored me to favour, and so arranged things that a Vauxhall Chevette was just pulling away from the kerb outside my building as I drove up. And second, Matt was waiting for me on the steps.

2

Luckily I'd driven onto Preston Road from Fleetwood Street, which runs parallel to the Boulevard, so when I flicked my cigarette out of the open window there was some hope that Matt wouldn't spot it. As I parked and wound up the windows (the Cortina was at last beginning to dry out now), Matt rose to his feet, and there was no mistaking the air of indignant determination on his dark features. Eager young assistants can be employed with a snap of the fingers, but it will tax your powers to the limit if you should once take it into your head to get rid of them.

Matt started before I even reached the foot of the steps. 'You're mad! You can't sack me! You need me! I'm going to carry on working anyway, and there's nothing you can do to stop me!'

I feigned indifference. 'Just go away, Matt, all right? I've had a rough morning.' And I walked past him to put my key in the door.

Matt trailed behind. 'You can't brush me off like this, it's not fair!'

'I know. Dreadful, isn't it?' I opened the door, stepped inside, and turned to block Matt's entrance as he pushed forward. There was in any case four or five inches between us in height, but the final step gave me an even greater advantage. Powerless, Matt looked up into my face, eyes blazing, lips parted in a pout of rage. It was make or break time. I knew that if I let him over the threshold now, for ever afterwards it would be his decision whether he worked for me and not mine. It was intolerable not even to be the boss of my own business.

Matt said, 'I suppose you think I'm too fragile to take care of myself.'

Again the vision of Danny Craven's body flashed on my inner eye. 'There's two men dead, Matt, young men in peak condition. They never even saw it coming. Not only are you reckless and a complete liability, with a dangerous habit of using outsize builders as a climbing frame, you also happen to be under strength to the tune of one arm.'

I thought I detected a momentary flicker of amusement in the fire of Matt's eyes. If so, I'd be sorry, because the next thing he did was to knee me viciously in the groin, push past me, rip the keys from my hand, slam the door behind him with his foot, then set off at a steady pace along the hallway and up the stairs, saying as he went, 'Didn't see that coming, did you? I'll put the kettle on.'

When you've drawn an absolutely final line in the sand, the really important thing is to keep hold of the stick so that you can draw another one later on. As I climbed slowly and painfully up towards the flat, I reflected that while it had now become clear which one of us showed the firmer resolve, and it wasn't me, at least with Matt working for me I'd be able to keep some sort of eye on his activities and perhaps even curb his wilder excesses. At the top, I hung up the leather jacket in the hallway and turned into the bathroom to empty my bladder. I'd been looking forward to this simple pleasure for at least half an hour, and wasn't prepared to let my mood be spoiled when Matt called out from the kitchen, 'You were smoking another fag as you drove up just now.'

'No I wasn't. It must have been a reflection on the windscreen.'

'You've fallen off the wagon. I'm not saying I blame you, but you'll get nowhere if you keep denying it like this.'

I finished off what I was doing. 'I'm not denying it. You can check my pockets if you like.' I'd left the cigarettes in the glove compartment of the Cortina. 'Anyway, get off my case. I've got a perfectly serviceable conscience of my own without you chipping in your three ha'p'orth all the time.' And I went through to join Matt in the kitchen, where the kettle was just coughing into action on the hob.

Wisely, Matt now chose to drop the subject of my nicotine addiction. I say wisely because I'd begun to speculate on what he would look like with both arms in plaster instead of just the one. He said, 'Did you find out whose that number was? From Danny's newspaper? It's even more important now he's been offed.'

I winced at the choice of vocabulary. 'For God's sake, Matt, show a bit of respect.'

He treated me to one of his looks. 'Yesterday morning I seem to remember you having no end of fun smashing his head against a wall.'

'Yesterday morning I thought Danny Craven was a weasel and a waste of space. Today he's dead and I'm not so sure. Apparently I'm a lousy judge of character.'

'That's not true.'

'You think so? In that case, why am I employing an assistant who thinks nothing of applying his kneecap to my bollocks whenever he's losing an argument?'

Matt's eyes fell, rather fetchingly I thought, and as he was saying 'Sorry about that' I turned to leave the room. It proved more difficult than I'd expected to find the torn-off scrap of newspaper on the living room floor, and it was only some indistinct murmur of intuition that caused me to flip through the pages of Eddington's *The Nature of the Physical World*, which was poking out from behind a cushion on the settee. The Gazette fragment had made itself at home in the section on quantum theory, and only then did I recall that the previous night, while I'd been investigating his thigh, the mauve youth had read aloud a passage which so offended all the principles of common sense which enable us to function from moment to moment that if I hadn't been drunk and distracted it would almost certainly have provoked some sort of breakdown. Grasping the rough triangle of newsprint, I once more put a call through to the number which it carried.

Matt called out, 'Tea up!'

And a woman's voice on the line said, 'You're through to the borough surveyor's office.' I froze. I'd begun to give Danny the benefit of the doubt, imagining that, after all, the number would turn out to belong to some prospective customer. Instead, it seemed he had a hotline to Martin's boss. There must be some way I could capitalise on this discovery, but how? What would Arthur Eddington have done – bearing in mind, of course, that according to him the telephone earpiece might disintegrate at any moment and reconstitute itself somewhere in the void between Aldebaran and Alpha Centauri? The voice spoke again. 'Hello? Can I help you?'

'Er – yes, thank you. Could I speak to Mr Cudleigh?'

'I'm afraid he's gone to lunch, sir. Can I take a message?'

'This is DC Howell, Southaven police. If you could just let Mr Cudleigh know that Danny Craven woke up this morning with his throat slit. I'll call again later.' And without waiting to hear what effect this might have had on the unlucky secretary, I replaced the receiver, no doubt dislodging a few loose quarks in the process.

Matt was watching from the doorway, a mug of tea in his useful hand. He said, 'Bloody hell,' then stepped forward to place the mug on the low table.

I picked it up, said, 'Aptly summarized,' took a sip, then immediately put it down again. The tea was so sweet that only some miracle can have prevented all my teeth from dropping out in unison. 'Yours, I suppose.'

Matt nodded. 'Yours is on the kitchen cabinet. I couldn't remember if you took one spoon or two.'

I fetched the tea, rejoined Matt, then brought him more fully abreast of developments since he'd left the flat to go baby-sitting the afternoon before, taking care to excise all mention of whisky chasers and mauve youths. Again he'd decided to perch on the National Geographics in the window, and as my story went on, so his tendency to fidget gradually fell away, until he became so still and pensive that the sunlit observation tower of the fire station across the road seemed to be sprouting from his right shoulder. After a silence, he said, 'This is where you get me to tell you what questions we should be asking that wouldn't have occurred to us before.'

'Go on then.'

He gave himself a few seconds. 'Well – firstly, why on earth did Danny have the borough surveyor's number, and is that who he was going to meet after we visited him?'

'Good start. When I spoke to Colin Cudleigh's secretary yesterday morning, she said he'd had a call and left the building. Perhaps it was from Danny.'

'Secondly, have we been right to discount Slasher Braithwaite? Even if Braithwaite himself isn't the killer – '

'He isn't, I'm sure of it.'

'OK, but even if he isn't, then the killer seems either to know him or to know of him.'

'There has to be some link we've not spotted. And thirdly – '

'Thirdly, why does everything keep coming back to Monica Berry and the state of her marriage?'

I took a few seconds of my own. 'I may not have handled her very well this morning. It was hard to be sure from the back of her head, but I don't think Monica likes me any more.'

'So – no fat cheque in the offing, then.'

I welcomed this reference to the commercial angle. 'Not even a slim one, I shouldn't think.'

Paralysis now gripped the fledgling partnership of Rigby and Standish. Matt at least had recourse to chewing his luscious lip, but I could think of no useful answers to his questions and no logical way forward. I couldn't just sit here like this, I needed to be doing something. I drank off the last of the tea, which had gone cold now, then went out to the hallway and searched the pockets of my coat for Leah Armstrong's telephone number. No doubt the wretched woman would be at work, but in my present mood anything was worth a try.

Not troubling to explain my intention to Matt, I picked up the phone and dialled the Manchester number. When it had rung a dozen times or so and I was on the point of losing patience, someone came on the line at the other end, but for a good while they didn't speak. Instead there were clicks and fumbles, as if a chimpanzee had got hold of the appliance and was trying to decide whether to eat it, wear it, or crap in it. At last an extremely vague female voice said, 'Hello?'

'Leah Armstrong?'

Another, thankfully shorter, silence followed. Then the voice said, 'No.'

'Could I speak to her please?'

The voice thought about this. 'She might be at work.'

I could feel an attitude coming on. 'Yes, that's fair comment. She might indeed be at work.'

This confused the voice a little. 'She goes out to work. Bookshop, lovely. She might be there now.'

'Or not.'

A silence. 'Sorry?'

I spoke more slowly. 'Or, Leah might not be at work. She might be at home.'

With a sudden access of motivation, the voice now said, 'I could try her door if you like.'

'Yes, I do like.'

Of course it was my own fault for letting my attitude get the better of me, but the voice now became doubtful again, saying, after a further silence, 'Sorry?'

I was beginning to think it might be quicker to drive over to Manchester and knock on Leah's door myself. Summoning reserves of patience, I said, in a tone of quiet authority, 'Please could you go and find out whether Leah Armstrong is at home.'

'Oh. Right.'

I had an afterthought. 'And then come back and tell me.' But she probably didn't hear this, as there was a loud clunk before I'd finished speaking.

I smiled across at Matt. He said, 'Child?'

I shook my head. 'Stoned.' Then I waited.

After about half a minute I heard the clattering of shoes on uncarpeted stairs, and the receiver was picked up again. 'Hello, Leah Armstrong.' In terms of strength and clarity, this new voice marked an improvement on its predecessor, while still not inspiring total confidence.

'Miss Armstrong – Sam Rigby speaking. I got your number from Grace Berry.'

There was a short silence. They seemed to be a house speciality. 'I suppose it's about Martin.'

'Yes. I was wondering if I could have a word with you.'

'With me? I've spoken to the police already.'

'I'm a private investigator, Miss Armstrong. I was working for Martin when he died. There are questions that need answering, I think you might be able to help.'

'I don't see how.' She didn't sound unwilling, just perplexed. I was perplexed myself, so that made two of us.

'It won't take a moment, I promise you. As it happens, I'm going to be in Manchester anyway tomorrow, perhaps we could meet up.'

'I'm not sure. I haven't been very well this week.'

'If it makes things easier, I'd be happy to come to your house.'

'No – no, I'll meet you. This place is hard to find.'

Something in her tone told me that Leah Armstrong was less than proud of her current living conditions. 'Thank you. Could you manage late morning? Say, quarter to twelve?'

'Do you like vegetarian food?'

As with coprophilia, I'd been dimly aware that such a phenomenon existed, without having felt persuaded of the need to give it a try. 'Yes, of course.'

'There's a café in New Brown Street, Eight Days A Week – bit studenty, but they do good salads.'

'Sounds perfect.'

'There's a boutique on the ground floor, then you go upstairs and the café's in the corner. How will I know you?'

I reflected that in Manchester I could usually be spotted by my general air of confusion and eagerness to get back to Southaven as soon as possible. But I said, 'Brown leather jacket. Tall. Ruggedly handsome. Yourself?'

'Oh – I'm just Leah. I expect we'll find each other.' And on this downbeat note, she rang off.

My Manchester diary was beginning to take shape now, but I was still undecided whether to contact the Wetherleys' chauffeur, Gerry Gibbs. If I dithered about it much longer, the moment would have passed. On the other hand, I could always take the number with me and see how I felt when I got there.

Matt said, 'Success?'

I nodded. Now that I'd achieved something, hunger pangs courted my attention. 'Have you eaten?'

'I've spent half the morning sitting on your front steps.'

'I could make toast.'

'Am I still invited for tea tonight?'

It was a clear sign of the shift in my priorities caused by Danny's death that I'd completely forgotten offering to cook for Matt the day before. Then somehow the event had been rolled over to this evening – ah yes, the sainted Eileen and her prior engagement. 'Your Eileen still got that work thing?'

'One of the other girls is leaving, they're having a do.' Then Matt gave me an odd look which I couldn't quite read. 'You know, for a detective you don't show an awful lot of curiosity.'

'Meaning?'

'You've never actually asked me what Eileen does.'

Annoyingly, I sensed myself digging defences. 'I had every confidence you'd tell me when the time was right.'

'That's not it. I think you don't want to hear about her.'

'Try me. What does she do?'

Now Matt looked annoyed. I'd made this too easy for him, when he'd been hoping for a drama. 'She's a nurse.'

'Excellent job. Highly suitable.'

'SRN. At the Infirmary.'

I chose not to reveal that I had an informant on the inside. Even if Eileen was not on the cardiac unit, Bernie Foster would be bound to know her. I said, 'She's done well for herself.'

'It's taken her a while. She's a year or two older than me.'

'A year or two?'

'All right, she's twenty-five.'

'And still single?'

'She's been concentrating on her career. Besides, she isn't single any more.'

There was a quiet moment, during which I dreaded discovering that I'd accidentally opened my mouth and said what I was thinking. As the wise man very nearly put it, hell is other people's relationships, especially if you happen to fancy one of the parties concerned. Now I became afraid that saying nothing might also be a mistake. Why did life have to be so complicated? What was the point of attractive young men with lips and deltoids if they were only going to turn round and have an agenda of their own?

Matt said, 'Is there anybody there?'

I tried to refocus. 'Sorry, I drifted. What about spag Bol?'

'Come again?'

'Tonight. You liked Frankie's Napoletana, I could do you my Bolognese special.'

'Mum gets that in tins.'

I prayed silently for strength. 'I promise you this will bear no resemblance whatsoever to the tinned version.'

'I like the stuff in tins. We have it Tuesdays, on toast.'

'Are you saying that since this is Friday and there's no tin involved, you'd rather I made something else?'

'Fridays we have fish.'

Somehow I hadn't expected Matt to exhibit the dead hand of conformity which curls so tightly about the hyoid bone of Southaven's average resident. Perhaps if I'd been a restaurant matters might have stood differently, but Matt seemed to be viewing me as some sort of extension of his mother's kitchen by other means. I fought to contain my feelings. 'Well then, let's have fish. I do a very edible fish pie. Unless of course your mother gets that in tins as well.'

'Fish pie would be great.'

I checked my watch. 'I'm due at the funeral directors at two thirty, we've just got time to stroll up to the market and back.'

'Why are you going to the funeral directors?'

I chivvied Matt out of the building and explained to him as we walked that I'd booked a viewing of Martin's body. He said, 'I've never seen anyone dead. I lost a few great aunts but I've always kept out of the way.'

'Do you want to come in with me?'

He thought this over. 'Not really. Is that OK?'

I don't know why but his apologetic tone touched me, and I found myself ruffling his hair. He pulled away a little. I said, 'Viewings of deceased clients are purely optional. Sandwich?' So we picked up sandwiches from the bakery on Station Road, which we were just finishing off as we approached the market. Like most of Southaven's public buildings, from the pier to the humblest public toilet, the covered market had shown a strange tendency of burning to the ground every thirty or forty years. Hardly a month ever passes without some smouldering ruin gracing the front page of the Gazette. In its newest form, the market occupied less than half the area of its antecedents, but it remained the cheapest and most cheerful outlet for supplies in the whole of the town centre, though if Addison's had their way over the Empire site this might not be true for much longer. With my reserves running low, this mattered, and I happened to know that Cotty Abram the fishmonger charged little more than pence to throw together a creative mix of shrimps and fish scraps ideally suited to the Rigby fish pie. Having also picked up eggs, cheese, spuds, mushrooms (a personal twist), peas, and half a dozen oranges for Matt who claimed he devoured them like sweets, together with two cheap bottles of Riesling from the off licence, we made our way back to the flat via the bank, where through gritted teeth I asked to withdraw another ten pounds. That would only leave about twelve pounds in my account, but I could hardly go to Manchester without money.

The provisions unpacked, we headed out to the Cortina. Matt had elected to accompany me to Welldale and mind the car while I did what I'd gone to do. Not that the car would particularly need minding. Welldale is the poshest of Southaven's posh suburbs, and the local thieves would be far too busy breaking into Daimlers to pay any attention to the rusting spew-toned heap which I was pleased to call my own.

In some ways Welldale village resembles Otterdale, but on a grander scale. Parades of shops run in all directions from the busy railway station, much used by commuters with desk jobs in Liverpool. The funeral directors found itself in one of these parades. I parked outside, left Matt chewing his lip, and stepped into the outer office at two thirty on the dot, where I renewed my acquaintance with the secretary I'd met that morning. A plain-looking woman with a well-angled Roman nose, she'd struck me earlier as a robust and fiercely practical soul, and her personality had undergone little change in the subsequent two and a half hours. She glanced up at the clock and said, 'Very punctual, Mr Rigby.'

I said, 'Time and tide wait for no man.'

She said, 'I expect you'll be keen to press on,' and rose smartly to her feet.

I said, 'It's no use beating about the bush,' and followed her through a door into an airless corridor decorated with dusty displays of paper flowers.

She said, 'You're quite right, Mr Rigby. I always say to my husband, Never put off till tomorrow what you can do today.'

I nodded sagely and said, 'After all, a watched pot never boils.'

There was a pause while both of us tried to regain our footing in the conversation. Then the secretary said, 'Mr Berry is in our Windermere Suite.' She pushed open a heavy door and held it as I walked past her. 'He was busy this morning but you've come at a good time. Give me a shout if you need anything. The toilet's just down the corridor.' Then she let go of the door, which slammed loudly on its spring, and I was alone.

A mural of Lake Windermere covered the entire far wall of the room. In the foreground, several hardy Lakeland sheep were taking a break from the monotony of their diet to regard the expansive scene beyond them, their shapes cleverly balanced by a number of fluffy clouds in the opposite corner. Centre left, a pleasure cruiser steamed away from us, perhaps making for Avalon or Bowness, and all around the lofty hills composed themselves in groups pleasing to the eye. I couldn't quite decipher the signature running out by the back legs of one of the sheep, but no doubt some local artist must have been the perpetrator. Whatever your opinion of its aesthetic merits, the painting was certainly difficult to ignore, and I was trying my damnedest.

But at last I tore myself away and brought my attention to bear on the open coffin of dark oak which stood on velvet-draped trestles to one side.

I stepped closer and looked in. The body, a poor waxwork of Martin Berry, had been dressed in a blue satin cloak with a white collar, as if Martin had met his end performing in a gospel choir. In life his cheekbones had been strong enough, but the sinking away of his flesh had left them over-prominent, and a zealous embalmer had made matters worse by applying rouge where none was needed. Worst of all, the jaw had been wired up with insufficient care, leaving a thin line of teeth just visible between the painted lips. The resultant snarl drew the eye magnetically, robbing the corpse of all sense of repose. If I imagined now that Martin was sleeping, he must have been dreaming bitter dreams.

I'd hoped that seeing Martin again might bring fresh vigour to my investigation, but the killer had destroyed all chance of that. Whatever the object in its wooden case might be, it wasn't Martin Berry. There was nothing of Martin here but his absence, an absence crudely insisted on by the corpse which teasingly made reference to him without being him in any way. If I was to find inspiration, it must come from that absence, from what was missing. I turned away, only to be sucked again into the mural, with its promise of a better world where we would no longer be bound by the irksome laws of perspective. And just as I was fixating on one of the clouds, in which I'd begun to make out the shape of a rhinoceros, I distinctly heard a voice behind me say, 'Missing.'

I spun round, half expecting to find that the secretary had sneaked silently into the room. But in truth the voice had sounded much more masculine, more like – well, if I'm to be honest, more like the voice of the late Martin Berry. I peered into the coffin again, but the man was no less dead than before. Except when very drunk, I don't believe in communication from beyond the grave, but nevertheless I'd heard what I'd heard.

Of course, the mundane explanation must be that the back of my mind had concocted this stunt in order to direct me down a particular avenue of research. I'd allowed myself to get tangled up in a bewildering thicket of seemingly random facts. Now it was time to break out and pursue what was missing. And of all the missing things in this frustrating investigation, what had gone missing most thoroughly?

When I'd already taken a couple of steps towards the door, anxious to share this question with the one-armed man in the Cortina, I found myself dragged back irresistibly towards the figure in the blue satin cloak. How could I leave poor Martin lying there with that nasty, toothy smirk? The gap between his lips was really very small indeed. It should be a simple enough matter to close them together again and so restore the honest, good-natured expression which had first drawn me to Martin as he sat with his neglected pint in the Railway Tavern. So, while the sheep obligingly kept their backs turned, I stiffened my resolve, grasped his nose with one hand and his chin with the other, and exerted gentle pressure. For a moment nothing happened. Then something did happen, but not quite the thing desired. There was a sudden, startling crack, and when in surprise I withdrew my hands, the lower jaw dropped neatly onto Martin's chest. A faint, sour aroma escaped from the open mouth.

I glanced furtively around me, but I was still alone with the sheep and the cadaver. Gingerly I moved forward again and tried to replace the lower jaw, but it preferred to stay where it was. A voice which was definitely not Martin's but my own was urging me to run away, but I steeled myself to the task and searched the room for possible solutions. A small wooden cross stood on a low table at the head of the coffin, together with a leather-bound bible and a large box of tissues. I tested all these objects in turn, except the table of course, finding with relief that the tissue box fitted perfectly in the space beneath the closed jaw, so perfectly in fact that it achieved what I'd been trying for all along. The sinister line of teeth had disappeared, and Martin looked much more like his old self, or at any rate like he might have looked with a cardboard box tucked under his chin. I now began to wonder whether his hands didn't need rearranging too, but caution prevailed, and with only a quick look back towards my late client I left the Windermere Suite at a canter, briefly exchanged conventional noises with the beaky secretary in the front office, then hurried out to the safety of the Cortina.

Naturally I wasn't taking any chances, so postponing discussion for the moment I fired up the engine, turned the car round and set a course for the town centre, nervously checking the mirror for any sign of robust secretaries. Puzzled, Matt said, 'Please tell me you haven't raided the till.'

I said, 'What's missing?'

'Missing?'

'Yes. What's missing in this investigation?'

'Well – I suppose the murderer's identity is missing.'

'Too abstract. What else?'

Matt shrugged his shoulders. 'The briefcase?'

I patted his leg approvingly. 'The briefcase. Unless I've got this whole story completely wrong, the briefcase contains solid proof of malpractice over the Empire redevelopment. I've been wasting my time blathering away to people when I should have been hunting for the damn thing high and low.'

'I still don't understand why you don't think Martin left it on the train.'

With a sharp twist of the wheel, I pulled the Cortina in to the kerb and cut the engine. There would have been no point in trying to drive. My eyes had blurred, and my heart was thumping away as if I'd just taken an entire bar of plain chocolate intravenously. 'Matt – when exactly did I tell you that Martin hadn't left it on the train?'

Matt seemed stunned by the whole trend of my behaviour since I'd escaped from the funeral directors, and was choosing his words carefully, as if I might go off at any time. 'You didn't. I just assumed. I mean, it was my very first thought but it was so obvious that I assumed you must have ruled it out for some reason. I didn't want to look stupid.'

But it wasn't Matt who was looking stupid now. If they'd been casting Doctor Watson I'd have landed the part outright. I said, 'I hadn't ruled it out. It had never occurred to me in the first place.'

Matt's eyes were very wide indeed. 'Crikey.'

'Yes. Your boss is an ass and a loon.'

There was a short silence, during which Matt failed to contradict me. Then he said, 'But if the briefcase was so important, why would Martin not have hung onto it for dear life?'

'I don't know, but there's a precedent. He almost forgot it when we were leaving the Feathers that night. I picked it up myself.'

Matt shook his head. 'Makes no sense.'

'Well, it doesn't matter now. The important thing is, he probably left the briefcase on the train, so there's every chance – ' My head had cleared, my heart stabilised. I restarted the Cortina. 'We need to find a call box. And then – how do you fancy a little trip to Liverpool?'

3

We shared the platform at Welldale station with a demolition crew. British Rail had decided that the Victorian canopies which had sheltered passengers for the past hundred years were now too expensive to maintain. No doubt this came as an affront to the citizens of Welldale, who expected their station, like their neighbourhood, to be a cut above the rest. As more debris crashed onto the platform, a wave of dust blew over us and set me coughing. This was all the excuse needed by an elderly bloke in a trilby who was standing near us. He said, 'A disgrace, isn't it? That's nationalisation for you, brings everything down to the lowest common denominator in the end. I said this would happen back in '45.' But soon afterwards the electric train arrived, and we had no further contact with our prescient friend.

The mid-afternoon train wasn't especially busy, and we sat opposite one another in window seats, with Matt insisting on facing forward. It would be fair to say that he was excited. This was the first time he'd ever travelled into Liverpool by train, and he stared out of the grimy window now with rapt concentration, absorbing every detail of the scene. On Monday evening, Martin and Danny had passed this way too. As we approached Otterdale, I pointed out the yard belonging to H Craven and Son, down at the foot of the embankment. The bags of sand which Danny had been filling stood propped up together in one corner. The landlord would need to find another tenant now.

There'd been no problem contacting the lost property office at Liverpool Exchange station. I'd given my name as Martin Berry, hoping that a murder in distant Otterdale would be unlikely to catch the attention of busy railwaymen further up the line. I described the briefcase with its monogram MOB, and the official, a man of melancholy temperament to judge by his voice, had gone to look for it, returning very quickly to report success. The only cause for concern was that the office would be closing at four o'clock, but as long as there were no delays we should arrive in plenty of time, the journey itself taking less than forty minutes.

So it would be fair to say that I was excited too. I'd begun to think that holding Martin's briefcase in my hand again might do far more to reconnect me with him than the recent abortive viewing of his body. I imagined myself opening the case, lifting out the oddly fashionable tie which it must still contain, then finding the documents, the incontestable proof of something rotten in the guts of Southaven. And if I had that proof, surely I would be a lot nearer to knowing who'd killed Martin Berry and why.

Southaven's suburbs gave way to fields and the evergreen forest of the coastal nature reserve. Eventually these in turn gave way to the first, anonymous suburbs of the city, and soon the tell-tale pink sandstone began to feature in the churches and public buildings we passed, or appeared embedded in the railway architecture itself. I knew what would happen next, the bright July sun was powerless to stop it.

Sure enough, down came my Liverpool depression. The war had knocked the life-blood out of the place, and no serious effort had been made to restore its fortunes afterwards, despite the debt we owed to the dockers and factory workers who'd somehow kept going while hell rained down on them. Here and there, instantly shabby new developments raised a tattered flag of hope, but all around their feet swirled the decaying remnants of the old city, derelict warehouses caked in soot, neglected bomb sites piled with the weed-choked rubble of workers' homes. The city centre wasn't so bad as this, a few bob had been spent to clean up its tired façade, but within yards you would leave all that behind and find yourself in another world where no amount of money could heal the wounded landscape. I wondered whether in a council building somewhere Norman Breeze had his weary Liverpool counterpart, locked in a battle with history to save the city from ruin.

With so much of the railway line elevated by its proud engineers, nothing obstructed your view of this broken world. Though the trip into Liverpool along the dock road does little for the spirits, only from the train could you see how general was the spread of desolation. From his seat by the window, Matt was taking all this in. Finally he said, 'Bit of a dump, isn't it?'

I found myself saying, 'Some people don't like Marshfield.'

There was absolutely no comparison between the home turf of the Standish clan and this wasteland, and Matt looked at me with eyebrows narrowed. He said, 'I suppose you're going to tell me that this isn't so bad when you get used to it and there's a great sense of community.' I hadn't actually thought of that but I didn't say anything, and we went on in silence until the train pulled in at its terminus.

The task which British Rail was paying a demolition team to carry out at Welldale station had been performed free of charge here at Liverpool Exchange by Hitler's bombers, so the open platform we now stepped onto baked in the unsparing sunlight. At the barrier I asked directions to the lost property office, and was given them in the local lingo, which I pretended to understand. This cost us a few minutes, since we pitched up at a couple of wrong doors and had to ask again. We were more confident about our third candidate because the wall still carried an enamel plate in the old maroon livery of British Railways, bearing the legend LOST

PROPERTY. I looked at Matt, he looked at me. If he wasn't thinking, 'At last! We've been desperate for a breakthrough all week, now here it is, just the other side of that door,' then I certainly was. My Liverpool depression forgotten now, I turned the shiny brass doorknob and we went inside.

I'd not been aware of having preconceptions about the room we were entering, but apparently I did, because it took me by surprise. I must have been expecting what cliché would describe as an Aladdin's cave, a space bursting with random objects randomly disposed. Instead, we found ourselves in a shrine dedicated to order and control. All visible objects were carefully grouped, with the larger ones – there were three prams, for example – penned in low cages. A great rank of cupboards occupied the far wall, meticulously labelled. Shelves ran along another wall, stacked with scarves, hats, shoes, toys, books, musical instruments and even a kettle, demonstrating that there's absolutely nothing which people won't leave on a train if the conditions are right. On a long rail opposite hung several yards of jumpers, cardigans, jackets, raincoats and overcoats, the men's separated strictly from the women's. Business must be conducted at the long mahogany counter, polished to a high shine, which stood forward of the cupboards and was a pretty good match for the front office counter at Crowburn House. An old black telephone stood amongst various items of stationery, flanked by three inkwells containing inks of different colours, each with its attendant steel-nibbed pen. Everything on the desk had been arranged with rigid symmetry.

The room was certainly well-stocked with human leavings, but what it didn't seem to contain was any member of staff, so I rested my palms on the counter and called out 'Hello!' My eye was directed towards a door in the corner, beyond which I imagined the punctilious overlord of this neat universe might be stealing a well-earned nap before clocking off for the day. But then the pale surface of a bald head rose from the other side of the counter a couple of feet to my right, followed by the rest of a shortish man in railway uniform, a cloth clutched in one hand.

The man's weak eyes gave us a professional once-over, then in a low voice he said, 'Sorry. You get engrossed, don't you? Polishing, that sort of thing. I was just doing the handles.' Startled by the official's unexpected appearance, I'd detached myself from the counter, and his eyes now moved to the two sweaty prints which I'd left behind. He took the cloth to them immediately, but you could tell he wasn't satisfied with the result. He said, 'Can I help you two gentlemen?'

I'd been looking over the official's shoulder trying to read the labels on the cupboard doors, but so far the only ones I'd made out were Gloves and Watches. There must be a special place for Briefcases here somewhere. Now I established eye-contact and said, 'Martin Berry, leather briefcase. I rang earlier.' I could see it all in my mind. He would say, 'Ah yes, sir,' then he would turn, open one of the cupboards, withdraw the briefcase, and place it on the counter in front of me. And after days of confusion and failure I would be back in the driving seat of the investigation, ready to press on to the chequered flag. In a matter of hours, perhaps, Martin's killer would be locked up, and Harry Hargreaves and the whole sorry bunch of Southaven police would be forced to admit that the day they kicked out Sam Rigby was the stupidest day of their stupid lives.

For a moment the lost property man said nothing. Meanwhile, the look on his face was saying a great deal, though I couldn't be sure what. Something in my innocent speech had disturbed, even horrified him. Finally he said, 'But – Martin Berry's already collected it. Twenty minutes ago. I've got a carbon copy of the receipt.' He picked up one of the pads from the counter, leafed through it, then showed me the entry. 'All correctly signed for.' Then he put the pad down again and lined it up carefully with its neighbour.

I said, 'Whoever he was, that man was not Martin Berry.'

The official's eyes widened with alarm. 'Not Martin Berry? This is most irregular!'

'Did you ask for identification?'

'He showed me his payslip from Southaven council. Martin Oliver Berry, I remember now. Nice name, Oliver. The wife's brother's name, as a matter of fact. Well, this is a shocking state of affairs. I'm extremely sorry, Mr Berry, I never imagined – I mean, you'd just telephoned, then someone turns up here a few minutes later, what was I to think?' He looked around him, trying to draw comfort from the orderly surroundings which he'd created.

I said, 'Please, don't get upset, it's not the end of the world.' I glanced sideways at Matt, who silently mouthed the words, '*Yes it is.*' He was right, of course, but it wasn't helping. I turned to the official again. 'What did he look like, this chap?'

The lost property man tried to pull himself together. 'Let me think, now, let me think. Not a big man, about my height probably, but fond of his food I should say. Glasses, the old-fashioned sort. Smart suit. And he sweated a lot. He was grumbling about the heat, though it's always cool enough in here.'

I pretended to be relieved. 'But that's Mr Cudleigh! One of my colleagues at the town hall. I was telling him about the briefcase yesterday, complaining I couldn't find the time to get here and pick it up. Good old Colin! Must have found himself in Liverpool this afternoon and decided to do me a favour.' It would be too much to say that the official now began to smile, but my words had begun to chip away at his anxiety. I said, 'Just like Colin to claim to be me. Always play-acting!'

'So you'll be able to get the briefcase back from this gentleman? Normally I'd have to draw up an incident report, there's been a breach of regulations.'

'There's no need for anything like that. Consider the matter closed.'

'Well, if you're sure.' The man still looked doubtful. His eye strayed to the counter again, and he had another go at removing the ghost of my palm prints.

I said, 'Thank you, you've been very helpful,' and I turned to go, with Matt alongside me.

But behind us a sad voice said, 'You wouldn't care to take an umbrella, would you?' And as I turned back, the lost property man opened one of the cupboards and a dozen umbrellas fell out, leaving untold numbers behind them pressing forward for release. He picked one up off the floor and examined it. 'How about this one? Years of use left in it, I should imagine.' He held it out to me. 'Please take it. I'm fighting a losing battle here.' With his free hand he opened the next cupboard, and more umbrellas joined their fellows on the floor. 'It never ends. Every day they come in, sometimes two, sometimes three, sometimes twenty. Day after day after day.' His hand moved to open the next cupboard, but I held up my own hand to stop him.

'We'll take it.'

'Oh, thank you, sir, thank you. At least that's one I'll never have to see again.' He reached the umbrella towards me gratefully and I accepted it with a nod. 'Can't have you going away empty-handed. If you could just sign for it – ' So I signed for the umbrella, or at least Martin did, then leaving the lost property man to pick up its fallen comrades we rejoined the less orderly world outside.

When the door had closed firmly, I turned to the wall, banged my head twice against the enamel plate, and groaned.

Matt said, 'All right, there's no need to milk it.'

I said, 'Please kill me now.'

He said, 'Don't be such a drama queen. It's a setback, that's all.'

'Hah! Not two minutes ago you were telling me it was the end of the world!'

'I've bounced back.'

I peered into his dark, relentlessly positive eyes. 'You know you can be extremely irritating.'

He nodded. 'People have said. But I have my uses.'

'Name one.'

He thought about this. 'Carry the umbrella for you?' So Matt took charge of the umbrella while we retraced our steps and caught the next train back towards Southaven. Once on the train, he fiddled with the umbrella constantly, until I began to fantasise about wrapping it round his neck.

I said, 'If you were Colin Cudleigh, what would you do next?'

Matt scratched his back with the umbrella handle. 'I'd destroy the briefcase, chuck it somewhere it could never be found. Then I'd burn the documents. Always assuming these documents aren't just a figment of your imagination.'

'If they are, why did he bother to retrieve the briefcase? I agree with you, that briefcase is history. It was our best lead, and it's gone.' Then I fell silent, at least outwardly, though in my head the familiar voice cursed me for an incompetent fool. Why had I never realized where the briefcase must be? It was small comfort that it seemed to have taken Colin Cudleigh several days to crack the problem too. Now he'd beaten me to the prize and I was left with nothing.

At Shoreside, the station between Otterdale and Welldale, Matt suddenly stopped playing with the umbrella. He'd been provided with a fresh source of entertainment. Scores of girls from Shoreside High School boarded the train, noisily taking up all the remaining seats and the standing room as well. The end of term beckoned, and they were in high spirits. Two older girls sat next to us, sixth-formers probably. I say girls, but really they were young women now. It was obvious what Matt was thinking, he couldn't keep his eyes off them. He seemed disappointed when we had to leave the train two minutes later.

Slowly we ambled back to the Cortina. There was nothing to

hurry for now. But then I began to think of the two bottles of Riesling in the fridge, of sharing them with Matt pressed against my shoulder on the narrow settee, of modestly acknowledging his praise of the magnificent fish pie, of curling my arm around his warm shoulder. Perhaps it might still be possible to salvage something from the ruins of the day. As he settled down in the passenger seat I said, 'What happened to the umbrella?'

He screwed up his face in self-reproach. 'Damn! I must have left it on the train.'

I said, 'These things happen,' and we drove back to Leigh Terrace.

*

At the top of the stairs I was just fumbling in my coat pocket for the keys when I heard the telephone bell begin to ring inside the flat. Experience led me to expect that by the time I'd found the key, turned it in the lock, negotiated the hallway and dug the phone out from its hiding place under the books and magazines which covered the living room floor like leaf-mould in the forest, the caller would have abandoned hope and the bell would fall silent. Today, someone of above average persistence was apparently trying to contact me, since despite the fact that I'd taken a little extra time to trip over a copy of the Collins *Field Guide to the Birds of Britain and Europe* and fall full length between the table and the settee, when I finally did pick up the receiver and say 'Hello?' I was answered by a human voice.

What with the disorientation which results if you suddenly find yourself at ground level when you hadn't expected to be, the front of my mind had lost focus, and was less curious as to the caller's identity than it was amazed to see the living room floor already returned to its natural state of disorder less than forty-eight hours after Martin Berry's killer had tidied it up. So when I half heard a young woman's voice saying, 'Could I speak to Matt Standish please?' it took a couple of moments before I realized that I wasn't Matt Standish and would have to go and fetch him. I put down the receiver and, after a detour to hang my jacket in the hallway, went through into the kitchen, where Matt was just lifting the kettle off the hob.

I said, 'I'll do that. It's for you.'

Somewhat surprised, Matt left me. I filled the kettle, lit the gas, then crossed towards the door to eavesdrop. I heard, with some gaps between: 'No, what a shame! Yes, it does. The thing is, though, I was supposed to be – Well, yes, if you like. No, honestly, it's just that – But you might get bored with me. If you say so. Of course I'm not, I was just a bit worried about – Yes. Yes. OK then. All right. See you then. Bye.'

Abandoning my post, I moved to the sink to rinse out a couple of mugs, so Matt was addressing my back when he returned to the kitchen and said, 'I gave your number to my mother in case she needed to find me. You don't mind, do you?'

I rubbed at a tea stain with my thumb. 'But that wasn't your mother.'

'No. She gave it to Eileen.'

'Everything all right?'

'Yeah, fine.'

I reached for the tea towel but, as Matt had pointed out the previous day, it had become the favoured habitat of several humble life-forms and it seemed cruel to disturb them. So I placed the wet mugs on the drop-leaf of the cabinet, threw a tea-bag in each one, then added a single spoon of sugar to the first mug and half turned towards Matt with a question in my eyes. He said, 'I usually take three,' then while I spooned sugar into the second mug he said, 'You know this evening?'

'I do.'

'This other nurse, the one who's leaving, she's gone down with appendicitis.'

'Nasty.'

'Big emergency, rushed into theatre.'

'So she won't be leaving after all.'

'No, hah hah, very good. Anyway, Eileen was wondering – '

I took the milk out of the fridge. I knew perfectly well what Eileen was wondering but it's rude to finish other people's sentences. My self-restraint went for nothing, though, because Matt then abandoned that sentence and started a different one.

'Obviously she's free now this evening so she thought she could meet me instead. It's not as if you've started cooking or anything. You don't mind, do you?'

'Why would I mind?'

'And I'm no use here, I mean, for work or anything. Without the briefcase there's nothing we can do. We could eat tomorrow evening instead.'

'I don't know what time I'll be back from Manchester.'

'But – I'll be coming with you.'

All at once it seemed terribly important to reorganize the jars and tins in the cupboard. I began to remove them one at a time and slam them down on the counter. I said, 'I'm going to Manchester on my own.'

'What? You can't do that!'

'You'd get in the way. If I turn up to meet Leah Armstrong with someone she's never even heard of, I think she's the type to freak out. Then there's the money, the fares and all the meals. Besides – ' And out of the corner of my eye I could see, still pegged up on the line, the monochrome photograph of Gerry Gibbs lounging indolently against the Jaguar, the peak of his cap pulled down over his eyes. 'I was thinking of going out on the town when I'm finished talking to people, and I don't want you cramping my style.' Then I reached into the bowels of the cabinet and pulled out a tin of ham so old that it might have gone with Scott to the Antarctic.

Matt said, 'Why are you being like this?'

'I'm not being like this.'

'If you'd rather I didn't see Eileen tonight, just say so.'

Now he expected me to beg him to stay. He must be loving this. 'Of course I want you to see Eileen. An ideal companion. If you break your other arm she'll know exactly what to do.' There was a silence. I carried on playing with the tins. I didn't look at Matt but it's a fair bet he was chewing his lip. Then after a few seconds I weakened. 'You could come over on Sunday if you want, I could tell you how I got on in the big city. If you're not going to Mass.'

'Sunday's band practice. Eileen said she'd drop in, it'll be the first time she's heard us.'

Somehow I'd managed to forget about the Sand Lizards and their regular Sunday session. 'That'll be a treat for her.'

Matt didn't like my tone. 'I suppose you think we're just a load of spotty, talentless kids with delusions.'

'Certainly not. If you had spots I'd never have hired you.'

The kettle was getting noisily excited now. After a pause, Matt raised his voice to say, 'Listen, forget about the tea, all right? I think I'm going to go.'

'Whatever you like.'

'I can't deal with you in this mood. I'll call you Monday morning.' He left the room, and shortly afterwards I heard the flat door close behind him. The kettle shrieked and I turned off the gas.

When I'd made the tea I went into the bedroom to hunt through the pockets of the trousers I'd worn on Tuesday. Then in the living room I put the mug on the low table, settled back into the settee with the phone on my lap, and dialled a number. After two or three rings, Gerry Gibbs answered curtly with his name and nothing more.

I said, 'It's Sam. We met on Tuesday. Outside Mrs Berry's house. You gave me your number.'

'Oh! Sam the window cleaner, I remember. How are you? Sorry if I sounded a bit short when I answered, most times it's the boss so I try to be businesslike. Done cleaning windows for the day, have we?'

'Yeah, I'm shagged out. Gets too hot for window-cleaning in this weather.'

'Roasting, isn't it? I'm cooking in my own juices up here. Don't get me wrong, it's a fabulous little place, but I'm right under the roof, no insulation.'

'Over the garage, didn't you say?'

'I can be out of here and start up the Jag in thirty seconds flat.'

The conversation dipped for a moment. Then I said, 'And have you done driving for today as well?'

'No such luck. They're going out for an early meal, then on to a show in town. You might not think it to look at her, but Angela enjoys a bit of a song and dance. I've still got half an hour though.'

'Just resting?'

'Something like that. I tell you what, it's hot, isn't it? I'm sitting here in my underpants. What about you?'

Well I knew what he meant but I said, 'Me?'

'Yeah. What are you wearing?' Despite the shift to more personal material, Gerry hadn't modified his tone. He might still have been talking about the Jaguar.

'Oh – same as you. Not much of anything, really.' Which was true enough if you discounted the shirt, the trousers and the shoes. 'This place is up in the roof too. You boil in summer – '

' – and freeze in winter, you don't have to tell me. Anyway, Sam – are you going to honour us with a visit?'

'That's why I'm ringing. Thought I might nip over to Manchester tomorrow, do a bit of shopping, stuff like that. I wondered if you'd like to meet up for a drink, early evening? If you don't have to work.'

'No, no, my night off, Saturday, unless there's something special happening.' Then his speech was interrupted by a yawn. 'Oh – I'm sorry. I think it's the heat. Gets to you, doesn't it? And everywhere you touch yourself you break out in a sweat.'

In a more practical frame of mind I'd have suggested that in that case he should stop touching himself, but after a few minutes talking to Gerry Gibbs it wasn't practical considerations which were dominating my thoughts. I said, 'So, are we going to meet?'

He said, 'Do you know the Rembrandt?'

I did. His choice of venue neatly confirmed that we'd been reading each other correctly. I said, 'Sixish?'

He said, 'Do you have to get back to Southaven afterwards?'

I said, 'Maybe. We'll see.'

He didn't push the point. 'Till tomorrow, then. Wear something nice.' And he rang off.

Perhaps I thought it a bit strange that Gerry had never once mentioned Martin's death. Probably from his point of view it was just some misfortune which had struck his boss's family, but really no concern of his. What definitely did jar with me was the Wetherleys' unconventional approach to mourning. Clearly they weren't going to let a little thing like the murder of their son-in-law interfere with life's pleasures, and I wondered whether Monica knew how they'd chosen to spend the evening. I could imagine her objecting, and her mother responding in that quiet, starchy voice, 'But Monica, dear, we'd already paid for the tickets.'

I took a sip of the tea. The day had gone badly from the very beginning, but at least now I'd lined up a date for the following evening. I couldn't have Matt thinking I'd come straight back from Manchester for cocoa and an early night.

Meanwhile, I still had to get through the rest of Friday somehow. It was nearly six o'clock now, so as soon as I'd rescued my cigarettes from the Cortina I repeated my performance with the TV aerial and sat down to watch the local news. There was no nonsense this time about sponsored knits, Danny Craven got top billing. I suppose when a place the size of Otterdale manages to produce two murders in three days, even *Look North* can't help realizing that it's a story. The police were refusing to comment on whether these two events were linked, but what they were prepared to say was that a man had been taken in for questioning in connection with Danny's death. Perhaps Friday wasn't turning out to be a great day for Joe Braithwaite either.

4

Knowing that the police were interviewing the wrong man over Danny Craven's murder did nothing to lighten my mood. Admittedly, when the truth came out Hargreaves would look an idiot, a development not to be sniffed at. But what if the truth never did come out? With Hargreaves so desperate to nail Joe Braithwaite, corners might be cut, evidence be overlooked. Though once I could never have imagined such a thing, now I even wondered if the DI might be capable of fitting Braithwaite up, less concerned about justice for a dead man than about weeding a known villain from his patch. If I'd had the briefcase I could have put a stop to all that. The contents would almost certainly have proved that someone was playing dirty over the Empire redevelopment, with the borough surveyor currently the leading contender for the role. Cudleigh was Martin's boss; Danny had written Cudleigh's number on the front of yesterday's paper. Now Danny and Martin were dead, and if the police didn't think the connection worth investigating then they simply weren't doing their job. So perhaps it was time I shared a little more of what I knew with my old chums on the force, and got them to pile the pressure on Colin Cudleigh.

On the other hand, this was *my* case, and I wasn't about to let Hargreaves steal it from under my nose. If he was too stupid to link these murders, then that was his look-out, and I had no intention of saving him from the consequences of his own folly. Matt had been right, losing the briefcase was no more than a setback. I could still go it alone, solve the crime, and show up Southaven's finest for the hapless numskulls that they were.

My first thought was to rush over to Cudleigh's house and pile on a little pressure of my own. I checked the phone book, but either he lived outside its range, which seemed unlikely, or his number was ex-directory. I had a contact in the GPO who could have got me the address, but I could only reach him during office hours. By the time I got hold of him it would be Monday morning, and the borough surveyor would be back at his desk in the town hall.

In any case, what was the point? The only evidence I had was the torn-off number. Even a hair-trigger type like Cudleigh was unlikely to be worried by that. For now, I would have to drop that aspect of the investigation and try something else. Perhaps my trip to Manchester would throw up new leads. I needed to find out where Monica had really been on Monday night, and I was determined to crack her alibi.

In the meantime, how to survive Friday evening? The fridge was stuffed with fish pie ingredients, but the idea of fish pie for one lacked appeal. Besides, I felt too agitated to stay in the flat. Instead, I walked over to Crowburn House, had a brief word with Aunt Winnie and Uncle Fred, then climbed the stairs to my office, meaning to type up my notes.

But when I started to reflect how much had happened in the past two days, the task defeated me. So, lifting the typewriter to one side, I took a few sheets of paper and began to make lists and diagrams, not concentrating too hard but letting the back of my mind organize the material as far as possible. There was a list of everyone I'd spoken to so far. There was a constellation showing Martin and Danny at the centre with a network of relationships all around them. There were clusters of material in boxes – the killer's three messages, a group of Lies I Have Been Told, a box for the Empire, and a box of People I Have Suspicions About, though that ended up bursting out of its borders and becoming identical to the list of everyone I'd spoken to.

All this produced no concrete results, but I felt calmer now and more in control. For several minutes I sat with the papers in front of me, re-ordering them from time to time, adding afterthoughts. All sense of frustration and failure left me. Yes, bad things had happened and at present I could do nothing to put that right, but it was pleasant sitting here at my desk while beside me the evening sun threw dancing sycamore leaf shadows on the wall. And then I found myself writing THIS IS HOW THE KILLER FEELS TOO. If I was going to make a habit of slashing people's throats or splintering their skulls with rocks, I'd need to be able to sit back afterwards, forget about all that, and enjoy the simple things life offers. I could hear those leaves rustling now, I wanted to be outside with them in the summer breeze. I locked up and left the building.

It was past eight o'clock and I was hungry, but I was thirsty too. On Friday nights a rowdy and less wholesome crowd replaced the usual weekday drinkers in the Railway Tavern, so it was towards the Velvet Bar that I turned my steps. For a moment I heard an echo of the old excitement. There would be strangers, I might meet someone, who could tell how the night would end? Matt was welcome to the stale familiarity of the steady girlfriend, I preferred to keep my options open. And perhaps in order to savour the anticipation for a few more minutes, I found myself going a longer way round, strolling some distance along the Promenade, where the familiar buildings stood transformed in the late sunlight.

The Velvet Bar was already doing brisk trade. I could see none of my occasional cronies but there were several new faces and no doubt others would arrive in time. Generally I enjoy the Velvet Bar much more in the company of Bernie Foster, and I might have phoned her to ask if she fancied joining me but for the fact that I'd just seen her the night before. I didn't want her to think I was depressed and needy. Besides, without Bernie I would be free to strike up new acquaintances. I settled my backside onto a bar stool and paid Leslie Lush for the bottle which he'd already opened and begun to pour. As he flicked the change from the till into his palm, he said, 'Look at this! Just look at my till! I've got shillings, five pees, ten pees, florins, ten bob notes, sixpences, pennies, fifty pee pieces – is it any wonder I've got no idea whether I'm coming or going? I say roll on February and let's get rid of all this old stuff once and for all. I mean, two hundred and forty pennies to a pound – whose bright idea was that?'

I said, 'I expect it was the Romans, like a lot of things.'

'I dare say, but once they'd been overrun by those Visigoths you'd think we'd have seen sense. I could understand it if we had twelve fingers – Yes, love, what can I get you?'

And Leslie turned to serve the mauve youth, who'd suddenly appeared at the other end of the bar, apparently undeterred by his experience of the previous night. While trying not to catch his eye, I caught it, and it spoke loudly of ill will.

I suppose that must have been the turning point. Though the mauve youth wisely kept out of my way, my mood had definitely begun to slump. None of the new faces looked interesting. I'd walked into the place with more than a touch of the old swagger, now I began to dread anyone approaching me, to dread the inevitable question, 'And what do you do?' to which I'd be forced to reply, 'I'm a bungling, half-witted, ruinously obtuse private detective, how about you?' When the juke box treated us to *The Carnival Is Over*, slashing my wrists began to seem like the only rational way forward.

Instead I drank up, stubbed out my cigarette, said goodnight to a rather surprised Leslie, who'd clearly expected me to be in for the long haul, and went home via the chip shop where, recognizing the importance of nutrition in maintaining optimum mental performance, I asked for fish as well as chips. Both had just emerged sizzling hot from the fryer, so I left the folded newspaper unopened until I'd let myself into the flat, undressed, rediscovered my dressing gown in the wardrobe where the killer had hidden it, and put it on. Only then did I transfer the food to a plate (a bourgeois habit I'd picked up from Aunt Winnie), douse the whole lot in tomato sauce, and finally take my place on the settee in front of a repeat episode of *The Liver Birds*.

For as long as it took me to consume the fish and chips, smoke one cigarette and extinguish it amongst the left-over sauce, I could be counted with the happier members of the human race. Afterwards, a decline set in. Once again my mind was reviewing the week's grim events and pouring scorn on my own ineffectual part in them. To make matters worse, my fish pie grievance kept surging up into my gullet like acid reflux, sourer and less digestible now than when I'd first tried to swallow it several hours before. My eye kept straying to the empty seat beside me. Obviously this nonsense couldn't be allowed to continue, so I marched through into the kitchen, opened one of the bottles of Riesling, poured out a generous glass, drank some, topped it up again, and replaced the bottle in the fridge. In the living room I turned down the sound and lifted the phone onto my knee. What did it matter that Bernie might pass comment? If you can't talk to a friend when you spot your edges fraying, what price friends?

It took some time for her to answer, and I began to wonder whether she'd gone out on the town. But then a quiet, sleepy voice said, 'Hello?'

I said, 'Hi, it's me.'

'What's wrong?'

'Nothing – nothing. I'm just calling.'

'For God's sake, Sam, did you have to? I told you I'm on an early tomorrow, I've only just got off to sleep.'

And now I did remember, but it was too late. 'Sorry, I forgot.'

'Honestly, you're that full of yourself sometimes – '

'I'll call you another time, it doesn't matter. You just go back to sleep.'

The door buzzer buzzed.

'I bet I won't be able to get off again now.'

I put down my glass and took the phone to the window. 'Yes

you will. I'm really sorry. Look, I've got to go, someone at the door.'

'Oh, brilliant – !' But I replaced the receiver without waiting to hear any more, then leaned out of the open window and looked down. Mark Howell was on the front steps, looking up.

I said, 'Business or pleasure?'

Rather tetchily, Mark said, 'Just pass me the keys and stop messing around.'

I said, 'Nice to see you too,' then fetched the keys and dropped them down to him. When I'd fastened the dressing gown more securely, I opened the flat door and stepped out onto the top landing to greet my visitor. Even in the dim light, the grime of ages festered all too visibly around the skirting boards. It was time I went into attack mode with the scrubbing brush, but that had been true for months and I still hadn't got round to it.

I could hear Mark's footsteps on the uncarpeted stairs long before I caught sight of the man himself. In welcoming him to my home over the years, I've used a sliding scale of physical means from chaste affection to osculation-with-intent, but when I saw the expression on his face I ditched the whole idea. Even before reaching the top of the stairs he said, 'I've got a bone to pick with you.' It wasn't hard to guess what this must be about. I knew from long experience that my usual patter tended to wind Mark up, so the prudent course now would have been to say nothing, and for once I took it, standing with lips clamped tight while Mark walked past me into the flat. Not meeting my eye, he pressed the keys roughly into my hand as he went. I followed him and shut the door.

Mark came to a halt in the living room and turned, clearly spoiling for a fight. He was still wearing the same shit-brown suit and mustard tie which I'd first seen on Tuesday evening. I said, 'Take a seat. Glass of wine? Tea?'

He ignored this and said, 'Hargreaves called me in this afternoon. Said he wanted to get something absolutely clear. He said there could be no place on the Southaven force for anyone who didn't toe the line. He said if there was anything I wanted to get off my chest, now was the time to do it.'

We stood facing one another about four feet apart. I could see Pauline Collins emoting silently behind Mark's left elbow. 'So what did you do?'

His anger rose a little. 'What could I do? Cilla had told me you'd dumped me in it this morning so I wasn't surprised, but what was I supposed to say? I sat there, and there was one of those silences where you can hear your own blood rushing about. This is your fault, Sam! Hargreaves had forgotten all about this, then you have to go and dig it up again!'

'I don't understand. Why didn't you just say, "No, sir, there's nothing I need to talk about, thanks all the same." You'd have been off the hook, simple as that.'

Mark's tone softened. 'Because – because part of me wanted to tell him the truth.'

I said, 'Blimey, Mark,' and sat down on the arm of the settee.

'I know. Normally I'd have done exactly what you just said, and been out of that office in seconds. I don't know what got into me.'

'So now you're angry with me because you can't trust yourself to keep on lying.'

No one likes being told why they're angry, and it made Mark angry again. 'No, it's because you never stop pushing at me to come clean or quit the job! Why can't you let me handle this *my* way?'

'For Christ's sake, Mark, you're engaged to Cilla Donnelly! How is that a success?'

'You've got a nerve, lecturing me like this. You were on the force nine years, and you passed for straight the whole time!'

'It wasn't legal then.'

'Oh, come on, Sam! The law may have changed but you know as well as I do it's business as usual on the force. In fact, it's worse than before. I'm looking over my shoulder every minute of the day.'

'Then leave the job.'

'Your answer to everything. Why should I have to quit? It isn't fair!'

I shrugged my shoulders. 'You can't change the world on your own.' But he didn't respond. I could see he'd begun to think something through.

The fact is, I'm a beer drinker, and I really don't know much about wine. But I do know when my glass is empty, so now I picked it up and said to Mark, 'One for you as well?' Still thinking, he shook his head. But in the kitchen I searched out another cleanish glass, then I brought both glasses and the bottle back with me. When I'd poured my own drink I said, 'Sure?'

Mark was at the shelves reading book spines, the way Martin had done on Monday evening. Distractedly he said, 'Yeah, OK,' and I filled his glass. He turned, and I could see that he'd loosened the knot of the mustard tie. It was another airless evening and the room was stifling. He said, 'I've had an idea.'

I passed him his drink. 'Go on.'

Mark held the glass the same way Monica Berry had held her cigarette. Months had probably passed since he'd drunk anything stronger than instant coffee. He said, 'Me and Cilla.'

'Yes?'

Mark now put the wine on the low table, took off his jacket, and lowered himself onto the beanbag with an easy movement. He said, 'The way it's going, we'll have to get married sooner or later.' I grimaced and he said, 'Yeah, I know, bad idea.' Leaning forward to retrieve the glass from the table, he drank about half of it as though it was water. I don't think he really understood alcohol. Then he said, 'But what if one of us had an affair?' And he looked at me triumphantly, eyes bright with invention.

I said, 'Sorry, you're going to have to explain.'

'It would have to be me, it's not fair on Cilla. Suppose we let it be known that I'd been getting a bit on the side, and she'd found out?'

'But then you'd be at square one again.'

Mark warmed to his theme. 'No we wouldn't, that's the beauty of it. I could make out it had all been a stupid mistake and I was begging her to take me back, and she could act like she was torn between pride and forgiveness. Couples can keep that sort of routine going for donkey's years! So we wouldn't be going out with each other any more, but we wouldn't need to pretend we were going out with anyone else either. It's perfect!'

I stared at the diminutive officer in his corduroy bower. I'd known him seven years without once seeing his methodical nature illuminated by such a vivid flash of creativity. Really I'd have liked to celebrate this, but was it wise? 'Isn't that all a bit *Peyton Place*, Mark? I mean, it's asking an awful lot of you and Cilla. You'd need weekly script meetings and rehearsals for all your big scenes.'

He attacked the Riesling again. 'Don't exaggerate. A few dark looks and awkward silences and we'd be home and dry. I need the toilet.' He then demonstrated to us lesser beings that it was perfectly possible to rise from the beanbag with untroubled fluency, and there was a sharp crackle while the terylene trousers and the Bri-nylon carpet sorted out their differences.

In Mark's absence I switched off the TV and lit myself a cigarette. I might have put on music, too, but music is another thing which winds Mark up. Then I heard him come back into the room behind me, and a moment later felt his fingers in my hair.

This was nice until he said, 'You know you're going bald?'

'I am not going bald!'

'You can't buck the evidence.' He walked round to resume his place on the beanbag, peeling off the mustard tie as he went and dropping it on top of his jacket.

'I'll accept that I may possibly be thinning. Very slightly.'

'How long have you had that dressing gown?'

This was typical of Mark. Without warning he would suddenly shove you under the microscope and ruthlessly examine every thread of your being until you screamed for mercy. 'There's nothing wrong with this dressing gown. It matches your vile suit.' I clutched the lapels protectively.

Mark was shaking his head. 'It's an antique. And your tassels are unravelling. Anyway, what do you think of my idea?'

'Idea?'

'About me and Cilla.'

I took refuge in the wine for a moment. Then I read Mark's expression, pleading, serious. I said, 'Frankly, it stinks. But – if that's the way you want to play it, Mark, then yes, it would probably buy you some more time. I think you're mad, but I suppose you're not going to change now.' He was smiling, and I remembered how it used to be when we first met, the way he looked for my approval, the smile whenever he won it. And that made me say, 'By the way – congratulations.'

He didn't understand. 'Why?'

'I'm just guessing, but I imagine the reason Hargreaves put you through the mangle today is that they're intending to promote you.'

His face was deadly serious again. 'You reckon?'

'I reckon. Could be soon. You deserve it.' I picked up the bottle. 'More wine?'

He covered the glass with his hand, meaning to refuse, then changed his mind. 'Oh, why not? Don't suppose it'll kill me.'

I poured, topped up my own glass and raised it to him. 'Here's to you, Mark. Every success.'

He smiled again, clinked his glass against mine and said, 'You've been a good friend to me, Sam.'

'No I haven't. I'm horrible to you because I got thrown off the force.'

'That wasn't my fault.'

'That's what I'm saying. I ought to be piling the whole blame on them, but I snipe at you instead. Really rubs it in when I see how well you're getting on.'

'You're not doing too badly.'

I laughed. Then I stopped laughing before it got out of hand. 'My bank account's running on empty, I haven't a clue where the next job's coming from. And my tassels are unravelling.'

'The braiding too.' He leaned across and lifted the hem to show me. 'Needs stitching.' Then he let it go.

'I'll get the staff onto it in the morning.' There was a silence. I couldn't tell what Mark was thinking, but I was wondering why we'd ever broken up in the first place and whether there would always be this distance between us. So he wouldn't hear what was on my mind, I said, 'You pulled Braithwaite in, then?'

He looked surprised at the change of tack. 'Yeah. We got a warrant, found blood-stained shoes in his dustbin. Soles match the prints at the scene.'

I may have looked surprised myself. If the killer wanted to frame Braithwaite for Danny's murder, he or she was being more thorough than I'd expected. 'But let me guess – Braithwaite says they're not his, and they're not his size.'

'Only half right. He says they're not his, but they're size ten and so's he.'

'And so am I, for that matter. Perhaps I should organize myself an alibi before the DI decides to fit me up for this instead.'

'That's another thing, Braithwaite has no alibi. His wife was at her mother's.'

'What time did Danny Craven die?'

'Two a.m., give or take. We've gone door to door, no witnesses. But Hargreaves is determined to make this one stick.' He sipped on the wine. He seemed to have found a rhythm now.

'This morning he had some crazy notion Braithwaite could have killed Martin Berry as well.'

Mark raised a couple of startled eyebrows. 'He said nothing about that to me. No, in the Berry case it's all about the red Mini.'

'What red Mini? No, hang on, I remember you telling me. Seen parked in Vaughan Close the evening of the murder.'

'That's right. The witness said it looked out of place in the street.'

'What does that mean? Too grubby for a smart neighbourhood?'

Mark shrugged. 'Possibly. But the DI's had us track down every last red Mini in Southaven. We've been calling the owners in for questioning, it's been like *The Italian Job* in the car park. Nothing come of it so far.'

I hesitated. It was pleasant to be getting on so easily with Mark for a change, I didn't want to spoil it. I lit another cigarette and straightened the dressing gown over my knees. The torn-off scrap of newspaper was looking up at me from the table, daring me to speak. I picked it up and handed it to Mark. There would be no going back now.

Mark said, 'What's this?'

'You'll have found a copy of yesterday's Gazette on Danny Craven's kitchen table, with a corner of the front page missing. I called in on him yesterday morning and borrowed this when his back was turned. Thought it might be interesting to know who he'd been phoning.'

Mark suppressed any desire he may have had to do a Hargreaves and complain about me meddling. He just said, 'And whose number was it?'

'The borough surveyor.'

This went over quite big, and I was pleased. If anyone on the Southaven force was sharp enough to spot the significance, it was Mark Howell. Now more than ever I expected recriminations, and I hurriedly said, 'I've not been withholding this, we only found out this afternoon.' Well, it had been lunchtime, but that didn't sound so good.

Mark said, 'We?'

I don't know why, but I hadn't meant to tell him about Matt. I said, 'Did I say "we"?'

'You said "we". Meaning, you and person or persons unknown.'

Perhaps I was just in the mood to come clean. 'Oh, yes. I have a sort of assistant. A trainee.'

'Since when?'

'Since two days ago. Very bright kid. Highly promising.'

Mark's head tilted, the way it tended to do when he was feeling satirical. 'Pleasant-looking young chap, I suppose?'

I frowned. 'No, no. Ugly. Fat. Terrible acne. Mind like a razor though, that's what counts in this game. Anyway, there's more.' And I told Mark the whole history of the briefcase and the Empire redevelopment. What point could there be in keeping it to myself any longer? Besides, I wanted to give Mark something, and despite the fact we were getting on well and the night was sultry and the wine was flowing, I had a feeling that was the only kind of something which he'd be likely to accept.

Of course, Mark was only human, so when I'd brought the saga to a close he did finally say, 'Why on earth haven't you told us this before?'

'There never seemed to be a good moment. And sometimes I'm not quite sure we're on the same side.'

To my surprise, that explanation seemed to satisfy him, because now he dropped the subject, whistled, and said, 'Colin Cudleigh! That's a bit awkward. The Super isn't going to like it.'

Sometimes my intuition runs much too far ahead and makes a fool of itself. Perhaps it was doing that now. It was saying, What could possibly link Colin Cudleigh, the Superintendent, and the strange tone of voice which Mark was employing? Then I said to Mark, 'You've joined the Masons, haven't you?'

He wasn't pleased, and the tetchy note returned. 'What makes you say that?'

'Because if Cudleigh and the Super aren't signed up I know nothing about how this town works – which I do, as it happens. And because you're an ambitious but still insignificant young DC who just said "the Super" as if he was your mate.'

Mark glowered.

I said, 'Sorry, didn't mean to stick my nose in. Can't help having good radar.'

'I wish you'd switch it off sometimes.'

'Don't look so grumpy. I'm sure it's a sound career move, you have my total support.' As a matter of fact it gave me a sinking feeling, as if I was losing Mark to regions where I could never follow him, but this was no time to go blabbing the truth. 'In that case, I assume there's not much chance of you pursuing the borough surveyor with the full rigour of the law?'

'We'd need damn good evidence first.'

'What about this phone number? And the fact that someone fitting Cudleigh's description collected the briefcase from Exchange station?'

Mark made a face. 'Hardly a smoking gun, is it? If we had those documents you seem to think Martin Berry had got his hands on – '

'Why is everyone so sceptical about the documents? They exist, or at least they did until late this afternoon.'

'I'm sorry, Sam. I don't think there's much we can do.'

I sat back, revolving the wine glass in my hands and casting a practised eye over the slim and pleasing form of my ex-comrade. Despite my disappointment that he hadn't picked up the Empire angle and run with it, other matters seemed to be forcing themselves on my attention. For example, I couldn't help thinking that those little round ears appeared in urgent need of nibbling. Of course, it was only an opinion, but I held it strongly. I said, 'Are you comfortable on that thing?'

'Yeah, I'm fine.'

'You're sure you don't want to come and sit here?'

'What, so you can interfere with my clothing?'

'Would that be so terrible?'

But Mark looked at his watch. 'I should be going. I'm on again at seven, I've barely slept this past few nights.' He raised his shirt collar, reached for the mustard tie and began to fix it neatly in place.

I said, 'You haven't finished your wine.'

'Probably just as well. Enjoyed it, though, made a nice change.' He grabbed the jacket, rose smoothly to his feet and put it on. Then he pocketed the number Matt had torn from Danny's newspaper. I wondered if this precious evidence would ever see the light of day again.

I said, 'You never told me what happened in the end between you and Hargreaves.'

'Oh – nothing, really. I pulled myself together and said I didn't understand what he meant. He said, was there anything in my personal life inconsistent with me being a loyal officer.'

'Put you right on the spot.'

Mark gave me a pitying look, as if I was a particularly dense pupil. 'No, Sam, not at all. Because there isn't, is there? So I looked him in the eye and said no, and that took the wind right out of his sails. End of interview.'

I followed Mark out into the hallway and then onto the top landing, where he turned and looked into my face. He said, 'We should do this more often. I never seem to find the time.' Then he hugged me. He wasn't a natural hugger, but this was one of his better efforts. Perhaps the wine had loosened him up a bit.

With his head still against my shoulder, I said, 'Stay tonight.'

He detached himself, but kept his hands on my arms. Though so much shorter than me, he could do a neat trick involving a special smile and wrinkling around the eyes which would always leave me feeling thoroughly talked down to. He deployed it now while he said, 'Don't you think we're past all that?' Then he shook me affectionately and turned to go. From the half-landing he called out, 'Sleep well, slaphead.'

His light steps echoed round the stairwell. I waited to hear the street door slam shut behind him.

Saturday

1

'You'll have seen the Gazette?' At seven thirty in the morning, Sandy Smythe was making a pretty rich assumption. 'I didn't want to call you too early, I do realize not everyone gets up with the lark. It's a disgrace, though, isn't it? And not a single letter!'

I rubbed one eye with my free hand. It had been a rough night. Amazingly, I'd resisted a strong urge to open the second bottle of Riesling after Mark had left, and instead had gone to bed around midnight, expecting my virtue to be rewarded by eight hours of uninterrupted sleep. But at two o'clock the hippies through the wall had started playing Crosby, Stills, Nash and Young at full throttle, followed in due course by an hour or so of Hendrix. Eventually, just when I was wondering why no-one ever blasted out Nina and Frederick in the middle of the night, silence fell. I think there comes a point where my neighbours are too stoned to get up and change the record. After that the heat took over from the noise. It seemed the most unrelieved of all the humid nights we'd recently suffered, and when finally I did doze off again my dreams at first were bloody, drawing inspiration from a couple of road accidents I'd attended as a rookie cop and been trying to forget ever since. But the dream which Sandy Smythe's call had disturbed found me once more in the phone box at Otterdale, calmly watching passengers file out of the railway station as I drew on the finest cigarette I'd ever tasted. Something of this improbable heaven still hung about me despite the best attempts of Smythe's fierce baritone to scare it off.

I explained that the house no longer enjoyed the services of a paper boy since the last one we had was captured by the psycho in the basement flat and held hostage for four hours in a dispute over an unpaid bill, and that I'd been too busy so far to get out to the newsagents. 'Oh, I see. Well, you'll not believe it, Mr Rigby, but there isn't one single letter in today's paper about the Empire. I know for a fact that several of the SOE people wrote in, damn good letters too if you'll pardon my French, and there's bound to have been others as well – everyone I've spoken to is up in arms about it!'

'You think Morgan Williams has lost interest?'

'He was only too keen to run the story on Thursday. I'd even say there was a twinkle in his eye, and he's not a man much given to twinkling. Something's happened to change his mind.'

'What sort of something?'

Sandy Smythe discharged an impressive snort at the other end of the line. 'It's obvious, isn't it? He's been got at. The local Mafia have leaned on him. So instead of our letters, what do we get? A hideous artist's impression of the proposed Addison's store, right on page three where you can't miss it! I'm that mad I could spit feathers.'

Sandy Smythe was probably right, except that there's no single local Mafia running Southaven. So who exactly had been having a quiet word with the editor of the Gazette? I couldn't see Colin Cudleigh making matters worse by sticking his neck out, and according to Norman Breeze the actual developers, Bayley Consortium, were from out of town and would be unlikely to have influence over an independent spirit like Morgan Williams. There was nothing to be gained by telling Smythe that I now shared his suspicions about the borough surveyor, so once I'd tut-tutted a little about the Gazette's disappointing performance I changed the subject and said, 'Is there anything in the paper about this latest Otterdale murder?'

'I haven't noticed, to be honest, my mind was on other things. Yes – here it is on the front page.'

I said, 'Danny Craven is the man you saw Martin Berry with on the train last Monday.' There was a silence. Eventually I said, 'Hello?'

'I'm still here. I just can't believe it. They looked so happy.'

'Have you talked to the police yet?'

'No, I – I keep putting it off.'

'Just do it. Ask to speak to DC Howell.'

'I will, I promise.'

'And you still say there was no-one with Martin Berry when you saw him pass your house later that night?'

One, two, three. 'You've slipped up, Mr Rigby. I told you, I never saw him again after they got off the train.'

'Oh yes, of course, I'm sorry.' And after reminding him to ring

Mark Howell as soon as possible, I ended the conversation.

The chief problem caused by Sandy Smythe's early call was not that it cost me half an hour's much-needed sleep but rather that it allowed me extra time to dither over what I should wear for my excursion. While it's true that I'm a provincial hick devoid of fashion sense, I hoped to conceal this fact from the good citizens of Manchester. Consequently, when I'd bathed and shaved off my two days' stubble I spent long minutes digging around in the hinterland of the wardrobe for forgotten clothes which might enhance my credibility, and longer still torn between the few practical options which presented themselves. In the end I chose a quite new green shirt with long lapels and a lozenge pattern, which I'd worn once for a party and then abandoned. There were forgotten pairs of trousers too, but since I couldn't get into any of them the trusty brown cords would have to do. Fortified by tea and toast, my bag packed, the leather jacket stuffed with vital phone numbers, I tumbled out onto Preston Road round about nine thirty, bright with anticipation of the day's adventures.

Because I'd chosen to walk along Fleetwood Street, where cars greatly outnumbered pedestrians, it wasn't until I came closer to the station that I began to suspect my appearance was attracting unwanted interest. I soon understood why. Among the unusually large crowds pouring out of the station, the colour orange predominated. I'd forgotten that this was the day of the annual Orangemen's parade. Thursday's Gazette had reverberated with the loud complaints of local tradesmen angry that the event had been scheduled on a Saturday for the second year running. It was hardly the ideal time to be wearing green.

Self-conscious now, I pressed on for the ticket office, temporarily housed in a pre-fab building at the edge of the concourse, then picked up a copy of the Gazette. Another Liverpool train had just come in, and to reach my platform I had to swim against a tide of brightly-dressed revellers, the younger ones already exercising their orange plastic kazoos. I wondered whether Matt would make a point of keeping out of town on such a day, or whether the absence of distinguishing marks would be protection enough against his more volatile anti-religionists. The Battle of the Bogside had ramped up feeling on both sides and in Matt's shoes I'd have been inclined to steer clear. But then, I was the one wearing a green shirt.

I boarded the train without incident and grabbed a window

seat. I'd had time only to settle myself and study the brief report of Danny's murder before the doors closed and we were on our way.

The small diesel trains serving the Southaven to Manchester line were less than ten years old, but as a result of some peculiar genius in their design had already achieved rust-bucket status. Older passengers who remembered the steam express service which had polished off the journey in a cheerful fifty minutes could only reflect sadly on the paradox of progress as the train lurched and rattled over the long succession of points at the start of its ninety minute odyssey. Once clear of the town, the line struck inland past low-lying fields of young green corn. Even through scratched and dirt-flecked windows it was a fine sight, and a country-lover such as Mark Howell might now have pressed his nose against the glass. Preferring to hide mine in the Gazette, I turned to page three in search of the picture which had apparently spoiled Sandy Smythe's morning.

If the image the developers had supplied was accurate, then the proposed Addison's store, or 'stone' as the Gazette had it, would be unlikely to confer architectural distinction on the Boulevard. Though faced in brick and less brutal than the stark new concrete fountain in front of the town hall, a topic on which Morgan Williams had allowed many local Pevsners to fulminate, the façade was no match for the Palladian elegance of the Empire. At that moment quills were doubtless being sharpened all over Southaven, but would Williams suppress these efforts too? Smythe had been right, the letters page featured not a hint of any objection that the scene of Marie Lloyd's triumph was to be brought low.

At Wigan I had to budge up a bit to avoid being sat on by small children. In doing this I made the mistake of running one hand beneath the seat, which is when I discovered the wrinkled ball of chewing gum, like a tiny brain, which some passenger had stuck there long ago. At Wigan too came the first brick mills and warehouses, impressive enough in themselves but the mere overture to the oratorio awaiting us further up the line. With one arm constrained by the fidgeting elbows of a six-year-old boy, whose idea of entertainment was to kick the seat repeatedly with his heels, I managed somehow to grapple my way to that reliable highlight of the Saturday Gazette, the double page of funeral reports. I wanted to know just who had attended the farewell shindig of Alderman Stanley White. As Norman Breeze had told me, the turnout was gratifying, and his own name appeared amongst the usual suspects, the Town Clerks, Baybridges and Spaldings of our narrow world, about a third of the way down a very long list indeed. But it was for a different name that my eye was scanning the small print, and near the bottom I found it: *Mrs C. Cudleigh, also representing Mr C. Cudleigh.* Only something of considerable importance could have kept the borough surveyor away from Alderman White's funeral, and I was pretty sure I knew now what that had been. In his cups, Martin must have told Danny Craven all about his plan to blow the whistle on Cudleigh's doctored survey. With Martin dead, Danny had set up a meeting with Colin Cudleigh and tried to turn that information into cash, a meeting which took place while Stanley White was being eulogized. No wonder I'd had the sense that Danny was holding something back from me. Then, hours later, Danny's sleep had been extended indefinitely by a cool, calculating hand. Yet the borough surveyor himself had shown that coolness played little part in his nature. Some other intelligence must lie behind all this.

When next I looked up from these musings, the city had reached out to embrace us, dwarfing the noisy train with its noisy passengers. And everywhere there was brick, as the millions upon millions of individual bricks making up the superstructure of Manchester's industrial glory blended together to form one vast cathedral of brick, blackened here and there by two centuries of soot but still overwhelmingly warm and red in the sunlight. Everywhere chimneys punctuated the skyline, a few of them making their own contribution to the late morning haze.

Though the age of steam was past, no-one had thought to tell Manchester Victoria station, whose grime-encrusted bricks offered a poor welcome after the colourful promise of the city's approaches. As more passengers had joined, the train had become hot and claustrophobic, and I'd found myself hoping that the rank smell of sweat had its source in armpits other than my own. To step off onto the platform should have been a relief, but now I remembered that Manchester was never noted for the sweetness of its air, and that the thousands who made this journey in the opposite direction every year were just as eager for the chance to breathe as they were to stuff sand between their toes.

I made my way out onto Corporation Street and took the map from my canvas bag. The heat was oppressive, but Mancunians, undeterred, thronged the pavements as far as the eye could see, showing off their bright summer clothes. For the first time I felt my usual city panic. Even without bonus Orangemen, Southaven too could boast huge crowds on a hot summer Saturday, but here, miles inland and crammed on narrow footways between tall buildings, they hummed with a taut expectancy not far from violence. Perhaps the café Leah Armstrong had appointed for our meeting might offer a refuge.

The sensible course would have been to join New Brown Street at its northern end and walk down, but in dividing my attention between the map and some of the more eye-catching passers-by I missed the turning onto Withy Grove which would have taken me there, and turned instead onto Cannon Street, which cut across New Brown Street at about the mid-point. Not knowing on which section the café would be found, I now had to decide whether to go left or right. On the left, matching redbrick buildings flanked the entrance to the street like sentry towers, but I could see no evidence of shops or shoppers. So instead I turned right, where a rough car park at street level replaced bombed-out buildings. Though Manchester is still a young city as cities go, there was nothing new about New Brown Street. Keeping a lookout for the boutique Leah had mentioned, I wondered how long Brown Street could have been in existence before this ingénue came piggy-backing into the world on its august name. As there's never a local historian handy when you need one, I was still wondering this when I spotted the words EIGHT DAYS A WEEK in plain lettering above a gaudy window display on the other side of the street. Though I was ten minutes early, I crossed and went inside.

The trippy sounds which greeted me were so different from anything to be heard in the lounge bar of the Feathers Hotel that it might be misleading to call them muzak. A quick glance around me suggested that this was no place for S. Rigby. Even the green shirt would have been scorned here, though it represented my boldest attempt in recent times to bring my wardrobe up to date. Seeing a staircase at the back, I struck out for it, and from the top I could see at once the café area which Leah had told me to expect. In large bowls on the counter, a display of foodstuffs I couldn't immediately name awaited the lunchtime rush. When I'd strolled across and nervously presented myself, one of the young women behind the counter asked what I would like. It was too early to eat and in any case the heat had sapped my appetite. The woman's hair intrigued me, some of it braided, some plaited, and some left to roam free, a liberty of which it was taking full advantage. We didn't get much of this kind of thing in Southaven. I said, 'Coffee?' just like that, as though I hadn't a clue what I wanted but hoped that she might enlighten me.

She said, 'Is that the bean or the acorn and chicory?'

My city panic reared up again, waving its arms around and begging me to go home now while there was still hope. It had been bad enough drinking ersatz coffee because of the war without it reappearing years later in the name of health. In the present context I couldn't be sure what type of bean the woman might be referring to, so I said, 'Perhaps tea?' She began to list the teas on offer. I closed my eyes and imagined myself sitting up at the bar in the Railway Tavern with a pint and a cigarette. When she'd finished I said, 'Do you have just tea?' She scowled, prepared the drink, then took my money.

At the one free table, I was just lighting up when my neighbour coughed dramatically and pointed to the No Smoking sign above the counter, so I was forced to kill time by tackling the Gazette's quick crossword. After about ten minutes I looked up to see a rather short young woman in a pale lemon crop top and a large felt hat arriving at the top of the stairs. Lifting her head so that she could peer from beneath the brim, she rapidly assessed the occupants of all the tables and then crossed to the counter, her flared trousers dragging a little on the floor. I thought it probable that this was none other than Leah Armstrong, even though she'd apparently not realized that I was the man she'd come here to meet. Scraping back my chair, I went over to join her. She didn't look like the sort of woman you call Miss Armstrong, so I said, 'Leah?'

She turned sharply and looked up into my face, an act which required her to tilt her head back a very long way. Unless she took the hat off, we were going to find communication difficult. She said, 'Yes?'

I held out my hand and said, 'Sam Rigby.'

Leah took the hand limply and then let it go, after the fashion of Angela Wetherley. Then with a guarded smile she said, 'I don't know why, I thought you'd look quite different.'

The wild-haired woman now chipped in and said to Leah, 'Can I get you anything?'

I said, 'Let me get this.'

Leah said, 'No, it's all right. Apple juice, please. Some ice would be good, if you've got it.' Something about the way she'd turned down my offer suggested a history. Perhaps I wouldn't demand anything in return, but she wasn't going to take the chance.

I said, 'Not eating?'

'Not hungry. It's very good here, though. I come in my dinner break sometimes.'

Leah paid and picked up her drink, and we sat down. She took the hat off and stuffed it into her shoulder bag, which seemed to be made from bits of old carpet and had a large pair of sunglasses peeping out of the top. Altogether she seemed well equipped for this outing and very much at home. To minimize distraction I folded the newspaper away in my own bag. 'I'm sorry to make you come out like this when you've not been well.'

And now that I could see her face properly, she did look washed out, with a yellowish tinge to her skin. With her straight brown hair, careful make-up and hooped earrings, she appeared stylish rather than good-looking. Alongside Monica, she would suffer in the comparison. She said, 'It doesn't matter. And I was tired of rattling around at home.'

I said, 'So you work near here?'

She nodded. 'Round the corner. It's a left-wing bookshop, not quite my thing really but I like it there.'

'Your housemate said it was lovely.'

Leah smiled again. 'That was Sylvie. We're not really housemates, we have our own rooms.'

'Like a bed-sit.'

She stopped smiling. 'I suppose so.' And she took a long drink of the juice.

'Aren't you worried your boss could see you out and about?'

'He wouldn't mind. Tries really hard not to exploit the workers. Grace got me the job, as a matter of fact.'

'Grace Berry?'

'I couldn't settle to anything after I left uni. And employers weren't exactly falling over themselves to have me – I never did get the degree. I'd thought psychology would be more interesting but it was all rats and B.F.Skinner.'

I said, 'The rats don't seem to bother Grace.'

'She loves them, calls them her babies. She just likes looking after things.'

'And people?'

For a brief moment Leah caught my eye before looking down again. 'Grace is a very kind person. People get her wrong because she speaks up for herself, but you always know where you are with her. I've learned a lot from Grace.'

'So have you settled to the book trade now?'

Leah made some sort of face, but like the woman herself it was hard to read. 'I don't know. I like the other staff, but – ' She shrugged her shoulders. 'Anyway, the boss hasn't found a place to move to yet.'

'I don't understand.'

My ignorance evidently appalled her. 'You mean, you don't know?'

'Know what?'

She made a gesture with her arms, expansive by her standards. 'All this is coming down! It's been in all the papers for months, years even.'

It hadn't been in the Gazette, but I didn't point that out. 'Redevelopment?'

'Huge new shopping centre. It's a shame, I really love this part of the city. I know it's a bit run down, but you've got all these interesting little businesses springing up, like this place for example. It's like a cross between Carnaby Street and those tight little alleys off Charing Cross Road. Do you know London, Mr Rigby?'

'Call me Sam.'

'I'd love to live in London, but I don't see how I'll ever manage it.'

Perhaps I was meeting Leah on a bad day, but I got the impression that even in Manchester she was already lost and rootless, and I couldn't imagine her doing any better in the capital. Sidestepping the issue, I said, 'Still, everything goes eventually, doesn't it?'

Leah's face became unexpectedly stern. 'It doesn't have to. Grace says it's capitalism. She says capitalism needs constant change to fuel demand, so we're always having to lose things, things with life in them still, things we love. She says that's why people have this sense of loss all the time.'

'I'd never looked at it like that.'

'She says the only people who'll benefit from this new shopping centre are the developers and their pals on the council.'

There was a silence, and I can't pretend I minded. I'd heard quite enough of what Grace Berry had to say, and I wondered why I didn't just declare an end to the softening-up phase of the interview and blunder in with my killer question. Perhaps I hadn't expected Leah to be quite so fragile, if in fact she really was fragile and it wasn't all a performance. One way or another I needed to take control. I said, 'Are you very fond of Monica?'

The change of subject didn't surprise her. She must have been reading my mind. 'I've known her for ever. Since I was this high.' One hand demonstrated.

She hadn't given me a proper answer, but I pushed on to the main event. 'Because there's something that puzzles me. Apparently you told Martin that Monica was still sleeping with Rupert Heysham. How is that the action of a loyal friend?'

Some colour now invaded Leah's cheeks. When you've spent time and effort crafting a killer question, that's just the sort of reaction you're hoping for. Seconds passed while she searched for a killer answer, but she didn't have one. I tried to help out. 'It must have been difficult for you, feeling the way you did about Martin.'

She said, 'Excuse me,' rose quickly, made for the stairs and disappeared. If she hadn't left her bag I might have supposed that was the last I would see of her, but now too I noticed a sign for the toilets, pointing the way she'd gone. I waited, but not patiently. The longer Leah's absence, the more prepared her answers would be when she returned. I drank off the last of my cold tea. I drummed my fingers on the table, at least until my smoke-averse neighbour treated me to a homicidal glare. I picked a bit of black fluff off my shirt. I wondered what it would be like at such times to have Inner Resources to fall back on. Then finally Leah's small figure came in sight again, her face looking yellower than before. She resumed her seat and said, 'Been the same all week. Dicky tummy.'

I said, 'You should probably be at home.'

'I'll head off in a minute, if you don't mind. I'm sorry, I know you've come a long way.'

'Yes, and I'll tell you why.' If I wasn't going to have the luxury of more time with Leah, I needed to get everything said. 'Monica insists she spent Monday night with you. The police believe her. I don't.'

Leah looked away from me a little, fixing her attention on the wall behind my shoulder. 'Why not? Of course she was with me. We had a couple of drinks at the pub down the road. Then I put up the spare bed and she stayed at mine so she wouldn't have to drive straight off, but when I woke up in the morning she'd already gone.'

'Did you talk to people in the pub?'

'I can't remember. Sometimes we see people we know.'

This was a fuller version of the story than I'd heard from Monica, but that didn't mean I found it any more convincing. I said, 'You know what I think, Leah? I think you're suffering from a belated attack of conscience. I think you genuinely were Monica's loyal friend until Martin came on the scene, but the minute she married him you couldn't stop thinking it should have been you. You've been trying to undermine the relationship ever since, despite the fact Martin clearly wasn't interested, but the whole time your conscience has been nagging at you. Then Martin dies, the game's over, and suddenly Monica comes on the phone asking you to say she spent the night at your place. So now you're playing the loyal friend with all the stops out, trying to make amends for going behind Monica's back.'

'It's not true! She was with me, I swear it.'

'Don't you care that whoever killed Martin is out there laughing at us? He's killed again since – he has, or she has – and who's to say there won't be more deaths before it's over? Yet you're sitting here lying to me as if it all meant nothing.'

As I'd spoken, Leah's eyes had been turned everywhere except on me. Finally they'd come to rest on the empty glass in front of her, which she was turning slowly between her hands. When I'd finished she said nothing for a while. Music still drifted up to us from the shop below, and a group of excitable customers were ranged near the counter, arguing about what to order, so that when Leah did speak at last, in a quieter voice than before, I had to lean forward to hear her. 'What does any of it matter? You can't bring him back, can you?' She looked up at me now. One eye overflowed and a tear set off down her cheek. 'If you think me or Monica had anything to do with Martin's death, you're insane. Why can't you just leave us alone?'

Almost as swiftly as before, Leah rose, collected the shoulder bag from the back of her chair, and headed for the stairs and freedom.

2

Though my talk with Leah had not provided much in the way of answers, it did vindicate my long-held opinion that telephone interviews are a waste of time. If I'd merely spoken with Leah on the phone I would still be assigning her a very minor role in the investigation. For reasons yet unknown, Monica was lying about her activities on Monday night, and loyal Leah was simply covering up for her. But sitting across the table from Leah, bells rang and whistles blew. Apparently she had reasons of her own for supporting Monica's story, and a half-formed explanation kept pushing forward in my mind then slipping away again when I tried to see it clearly. For now all I could do was hope that I'd fare better with Rupert Heysham.

I wasn't due at the new lab until one o'clock, so there was still time to enjoy a hot dog on a bench in Piccadilly Gardens and watch the buses come and go. Municipal flowers and weary shoppers wilted in the heat. What we all needed was rain. Perhaps even my mind needed rain. Something should have been happening up there, but it wasn't. I flicked onion off my trousers, consulted the map, and started walking.

I found the Renold building without difficulty, mainly because it was exactly where Rupert Heysham had said it would be, tucked in behind the main UMIST building at the corner of Sackville Street. If I hadn't seen the latter before, I would have felt compelled to stop and gawp at it. It was the sort of giant structure which the brain struggles to grasp either whole or steadily, but after previous fruitless attempts I'd realized that the best plan was simply to file it under 'very big thing made of bricks' and move on. By way of contrast, the Renold building was all concrete and glass, and mercifully it knew when to stop. I climbed the steps and went in.

To my left, a reception lodge or lair was the home of a rubicund man in a uniform. No doubt he would be able to direct me further on my way, but aware that I was now, for the first time in my life, on university property, I began to worry that the mode of speech which served when buying sausages in Southaven might not pass muster here. All I would risk was, 'Wetherley laboratory?'

The porter made a thoughtful face, said, 'That's new, isn't it?' then reached beneath the counter for a clip-board and began leafing through the attached sheets. 'Here it is, G32. I'd take the lift if I were you or you'll have no breath left when you get there.' I thanked him and moved on along the broad corridor, which soon opened out into a bright atrium with the lifts to one side. Beyond, a board directing me to the Bowling Green Tavern confirmed my prejudice about the centrality of alcohol in academic life. With most students departed for the summer, someone had been waxing the floor here, and the smell lingered pleasantly in my nostrils as I entered the lift and pressed G. The ascent was slow and easy. As far as I could recall, none of my teachers had ever so much as uttered the word 'university', but in spite of that my mind had somehow collected a variety of images of university life involving drink, gowns, punting and, more recently, damage to Paris property. Now I could add this effortless ride in a gleaming elevator. It must be nice to have things done for you all the time. Presumably getting a degree did require a little work, but with smiling staff constantly waxing your floors work must take on the character of a hobby, an amusement to pass the time between sessions in the Bowling Green. Now the lift slowed, the doors slid smoothly open. I stepped out into the silent upper realms.

A man of about my own age, with very long curly hair and heavy glasses, was waiting to go down. For a split second I considered asking him the way to the lab, but he looked far less approachable than the ruddy porter and far cleverer, and in any case a moment later he'd disappeared into the lift and the doors had closed. Wall signs indicated which rooms lay in which direction, but seemed to lose interest after G30. Displaying the cool rationality for which I'm celebrated throughout Southaven, I set off towards G30, hoping either that the porter had misread the number or that G32 could be found some little way beyond it. But when after a lengthy hike I drew up there, a glass panel in the door revealed a small room with a couple of desks and a marked absence of bubbling retorts. What's more, G30 stood at the furthest limit of its corridor, as I did of my plans for running down the Wetherley lab. At that point others might have admitted defeat, returned to the lodge and thrown themselves on the porter's mercy, but fearful that I'd made some mistake and he might think I was stupid I roamed aimlessly about floor G for the next ten minutes, feeling more excluded with every step I took. At last, when I'd begun to consider ripping a fire extinguisher from the wall and hurling it through one of the windows to relieve my mounting hysteria, I noticed that between rooms G12 and G13 stood two adjacent doors, apparently unmarked. But leaning closer I could just make out the faint pencil tracings which announced G32 on the first of them, and WETHERLEY LABORATORY on the second. I took a moment to breathe deeply and unruffle the feathers which had been ruffled by my recent experience, then rapped loudly on this second door. A voice said, 'Come in!' so I did.

I was met by the smell of paint, perhaps a few days old now. Two men stood over by the windows in the large and cluttered room. They must have been looking out when I knocked, over the railway viaduct towards the rear façade of the UMIST building, and reflected light from its countless sunlit bricks softened the utilitarian atmosphere in the north-facing laboratory. Perhaps, though, it was too soon yet to call this a laboratory. A few items of what I took to be computing equipment stood isolated on work-benches, but far more remained to be unpacked from the dozens of boxes stacked on the floor. The younger of the men, short and bald, with a spotted bow-tie and wire-framed glasses, could well be the unlucky psychology tutor Monica had rejected in favour of Martin Berry, but I couldn't guess the identity of the big man in the finely-tailored suit. Skirting the boxes, I made towards the younger man with hand outstretched. 'Sam Rigby. Sorry I'm a bit late.'

Rupert Heysham shook my hand confidently enough, and without confirming his name said, 'Did you find us all right?'

'Yes, thanks, no problem at all. Excellent directions.' Of course, if Heysham had been more practical and less of an egg-head he could have told me what to look out for and spared me ten minutes of private hell, but I let that go.

He said, 'And this is Walter Wetherley.'

I was surprised, and it irked me that I was surprised. Why shouldn't Wetherley turn up in the lab which bore his name, if only in pencil? Wetherley's powerful hand now gripped mine, and in a strong voice he said, 'Very glad to know you, Mr Rigby. My daughter's told me all about you. And Rupert here said you'd be dropping in, so I thought I could kill two birds with one stone, make myself known to you and have a quick look at progress in the lab while I was about it. Any news of your investigation? Any breakthroughs? I like to be kept informed, Mr Rigby. Rupert will tell you that, won't you Rupert?' Wetherley detached the powerful hand from mine, and used it to squeeze the other man's narrow shoulder.

Rupert Heysham smiled, gamely enough, and said, 'Always hell to pay if you don't get your regular reports.'

'And quite right too. I'm putting a lot of cash into this project, I want to know where it's all going.' He looked around the room with proprietorial satisfaction. Though there wasn't much to see yet, he still said, 'Marvellous, isn't it? The face of the future, Mr Rigby, you mark my words. Or so Rupert tells me.'

'Only because it's true! But Mr Rigby doesn't need convincing. He's already a big enthusiast for AI, we were discussing it the other day.'

Walter Wetherley reacted with interest to this. 'Are you really?' With a modest gesture I waved away the implied recognition of my superior insight. Wetherley continued. 'To be honest, before last Christmas I'd never heard of it. Then Rupert and I were enjoying a particularly fine glass of port on Christmas Eve when he began to introduce me to ideas I'd never imagined. I say ideas – I should say, *opportunities*.' Wetherley's broad, vigorous face became if possible more animated. 'Such opportunities! Do you know anything about business, Mr Rigby?' I opened my mouth to speak despite having nothing to say, but fortunately Walter Wetherley swept on without waiting. 'No, well, I suppose you wouldn't, with coming from Southaven. I've always regarded Southaven as the jester to the court of Manchester: we do all the serious work while you provide the entertainment. You can tell a town's not up to much when the Germans don't even bother to bomb it. Still, I suppose life can't all be making and doing.' His expression let it be known that he regretted this. 'But if you knew anything about business you'd realize that the one thing you must never do is *stand still*. The minute you stand still, you're finished. I don't mind telling you that I've made a substantial amount of money out of property. You ask me how I've done it. Well, there's no magic to it, no secret formula. The fact is, where others hesitate I seize the day. *Carpe diem*, Mr Rigby, *carpe diem!* Isn't that right, Rupert?'

Heysham smiled again but made no attempt at a verbal response.

'But do you see me resting on my laurels? Do you see me for one moment standing still? Of course not. And do you want to know why? I'll tell you. Because everywhere I look there are younger men – it could be you' – pointing at Heysham – 'or you' – pointing with less confidence at me – ' – ambitious young men who'd stop at nothing to take every last penny off me. There's only one thing for it – you *have* to *stay* a*head* of the *game*.' For emphasis he repeatedly jabbed one finger into the smaller man's shoulder, whose only protection was a fawn v-neck sweater, but Heysham showed no sign of complaining. 'Today, property's doing well. We're riding the back of the biggest consumer boom in history. But what about tomorrow, eh? Eh?' Walter Wetherley seemed to expect a reply, but the moment I opened my mouth he said, 'If you knew the answer to that, you'd be a millionaire, like me. But personally, I think property could be on the way out, and if you're looking for a safe haven there's no better choice than manufacturing. There'll always be manufacturing, won't there? I'm a Mancunian born and bred, and what we do in Manchester is, we make stuff. I know I don't look it but I'm getting a bit long in the tooth now, and I've a hankering to make stuff myself, while there's still time. But not the old stuff, not steel or textiles or motor cars. I want to make the stuff of the future. Rupert here has shown me the door to a whole new world, a world of intelligent machines. And *I'm going to make them*. In ten years' time everyone on the planet will be using Wetherley Machines. That's the future, Mr Rigby. Grand, isn't it?'

The last question was definitely rhetorical, and after it a blessed silence fell. Wetherley beamed complacently, and Rupert Heysham removed himself one step to the right, taking his shoulder beyond range of further attack. So far I'd spoken not a word to Walter Wetherley, and if he once got started on another monologue this could turn out to have been my last opportunity. So I chose my ground carefully and said, 'To a successful man such as yourself, I dare say Martin Berry must have seemed like small beer.'

Wetherley hesitated for a moment, then gave me a condescending look which seemed to include Martin in its scope. 'Have you met his parents at all, Mr Rigby? Have you been to that shop?' I thought I detected some effort to keep the disgust from showing through. 'Stink bombs. Party hats. How the devil do they expect to make money out of *party hats*?'

'But Martin had a good job on the council.'

'That's true enough. Brought in a living wage, and you can't fault council work for security. Hardest job in the world to get yourself sacked from, though he'd never have landed it in the first place without a helping hand. But was Martin going anywhere, that's the question?'

Through these exchanges, Wetherley's tone had moderated somewhat, as if in deference to the departed. I pushed my point a little further. 'You must have been very disappointed when Monica decided to marry him.'

Wetherley stole a glance at Rupert Heysham, who had begun to look uneasy now that his benefactor was the subject of forensic questioning from an acknowledged master. It was plain from the look on Heysham's face that questioning Walter Wetherley was simply not done. Wetherley said, 'I've always indulged my little girl, Mr Rigby. Too much, some would say. She had her heart set on marrying Martin Berry and I did everything in my power to make sure she'd be happy and comfortable. I realize she's none too thrilled at losing him, but given time she'll come to see that it was for the best. There was no future in it, Mr Rigby. That may sound harsh, but I speak as I find.' Wetherley now checked his watch. 'Is that the time? I'm due on the first tee in half an hour. Tedious, of course, but business is business. In any case, you two don't want me butting in on your conversation, do you?' He shook hands with both of us, and when it came to my turn he said, 'Glad to have met you finally, Mr Rigby, and I wish you all the best for the investigation. We can't have killers on the loose in a place like Southaven. It doesn't seem right, does it?' He moved to the door, where he turned. 'Oh, and Rupert? Keep me informed.' With a half smile and a nod, he left the room.

The space seemed to expand around us. Heysham gave a sigh, as if he'd been holding his breath while Wetherley was present, and exercised his new freedom by walking away from me and running one hand over some of the boxes. Stuck for an opening, I said, 'You must be very proud.'

'Of all this? Yes, I can hardly believe it. Still a long way to go, though, a bit daunting really. My colleague Clem Brewster was here this morning helping me unpack.'

I said, 'Hair? Glasses?'

'You saw him leaving, did you? Brilliant young man, absolutely brilliant, teaches in the department of Computation here at UMIST. I must say they've welcomed me here with open arms, despite me belonging to the Uni proper, technically speaking. Mind you, Walter's cash must have sugared the pill.'

Years ago, a bloke in a bar had tried to explain to me the precise relationship between the University of Manchester Institute of Science and Technology and the University of Manchester, but I lost heart at an early stage and begged him to stop. It pained me not to know, but it was paining me far more finding out. Of course,

I drank Newcastle Brown in those days and that may have had something to do with it.

I said, 'You're lucky to have an influential figure like Wetherley behind you.'

'Don't I know it. This could be the opportunity of a lifetime, incredibly prestigious!' Heysham's round face darkened a little. 'It's a long road, though. Years of research.'

'Was he right? Are machines going to be doing all our thinking for us in ten years' time?'

Rupert Heysham smiled. He had a pleasant smile, and though he might not have been your first choice to model swimwear there was something fresh and wholesome about him which I could imagine appealing to a young woman like Monica. It was hard to tell his age exactly, but I'd have thought he was still a few years shy of forty. Marriages with wider age gaps have been known to work well enough. He said, 'It's more a case of them thinking for themselves. Walter's always inclined to be a little over-optimistic, but I do think we'll be seeing extraordinary advances. Clem's been consulting with this chap Winograd at MIT, brilliant young man, absolutely brilliant, not published yet but got a great future ahead of him. We're working on our own British variant of the same ideas. Of course, Turing worked here at Manchester, as you probably know, so it seems fitting that we should be the people to take his ideas forward.'

Once again I was fearful of looking stupid, but I didn't often find myself in a world like this, talking to a man like Rupert Heysham. I took a chance and said, 'Forgive me – I mean, it might be obvious – but I don't quite see the use of a psychologist in a project that's all about machines.'

Heysham glowed, and hauled himself up to sit on one of the work-benches, the better to instruct me. 'That's exactly where we have the edge!' He took off the wire-framed spectacles and polished them on his jumper while he spoke. 'It's all about how you view intelligence. The computation men are struggling with it, they're trying to model something they don't really understand. But psychologists have done the research, we can tell you now what intelligence is.'

This was the kind of discussion you might enjoy during a lock-in at the Railway, only to discover that it made no sense in the morning. I said, 'Well, what is it then?'

Heysham slipped the glasses on again and said, 'Behaviour.' He seemed terribly pleased about this.

'Behaviour?'

'Yes, behaviour. *Learned* behaviour. Oh, some small part might be innate, there's an almighty scrap going on about that, just how much if any, how that could work, and so on. But mostly it's learned behaviour. Stimulus, response, stimulus, response. And if we can learn in that sort of structured way, then so can a machine.'

I took another risk. 'So you're saying that the term Artificial Intelligence is tautologous.'

Heysham's brow wrinkled. 'Am I?'

I dug deeper. 'Yes. Because it's *all* artificial, in a way. Even in humans.'

The brow smoothed again. 'I see what you mean, and you're right. There's no mystery about it. Intelligence is just the label we give, after the event, to behaviour that we've constructed one block at a time. As a matter of interest, what was your own subject?'

'My subject?'

He smiled again, his bald head gleaming in the light from the window behind him. I would have liked to show that head to Mark Howell and contrast its notable lack of hair with my own well-stocked crown. 'I'm assuming there's an environment of structured learning behind those intelligent points you raise.'

'Environment of structured – ? Oh, you mean a – ' But I found I couldn't say the word. I was beginning to feel very hot in the unfamiliar room.

'I take it you did go to university?'

Now Heysham had said it for me. Unfortunately the only environment of structured learning I'd attended was the secondary modern, where my education had been largely confined to the playground. I said, 'Not as such, no.'

'You surprise me. It's never too late, you know. And a bit of life experience can work in your favour.'

I said, 'You don't need a degree to get on in life.'

'No, of course not. I wasn't suggesting – '

'Does Wetherley have a degree?' Heysham didn't reply, but his face said no. 'Yet it's Wetherley's money that's making all this possible.' Now it was my turn to walk around fingering the boxes. I said, 'Be a terrible blow if you had to back out for any reason.'

'Back out? What are you talking about?'

I turned towards him and tried for an expression of sympathetic understanding. 'Have you heard from the police yet?'

His eyes widened with alarm. 'The police? No, should I have done?'

I'd more or less convinced myself that Rupert Heysham was harmless, and it seemed a shame to put the wind up him like this. But then, you have to take your pleasures where you can. 'The thing is, Mr Heysham – '

'It's Doctor, actually. Dr Heysham.'

'Oh, beg pardon. Credit where it's due, and all that. The thing is, while I haven't always seen eye to eye with the police during this investigation, there's one area where our thoughts are so close you couldn't get a cigarette paper between us. We both agree that neither you nor the Wetherleys have ever accepted Monica's marriage to Martin Berry. We know that you've continued to see her, even though she was a married woman. I don't say that anything improper has occurred, but I do say that you've been putting pressure on her, plying her with gifts, constantly reminding her what she's missing by having chosen your rival instead of you. Now Martin's dead and Monica's free again. Naturally the police have been asking themselves who stands to gain most from Martin's death. Now they realize it's you.'

'Me!'

'Yes, you, Professor Heysham.'

'Actually, I'm not a – '

'So they've been rooting around, compiling a case, and I'm afraid it's not looking very good for you at the moment. Your hairy colleague may have to carry on without you. Because unless universities are more tolerant than other institutions, I should imagine that the scandal of an arrest for murder – '

'But I didn't do anything!' Heysham's agitation was pitiful. The approach which had so signally failed when I'd first met Danny Craven was working a treat with Monica's other suitor.

'I'm afraid it's inevitable now. Perhaps tonight, perhaps first thing in the morning when you're just dipping toast in your egg, that knock on the door is bound to come.'

'This is terrible!' Sweat had broken out on Heysham's brow. The Wetherley was witnessing its very first experiment, with Heysham providing a textbook response to my stimuli. Grace Berry's rats would have paid good money to see this.

'So you'd be well advised to have your story water-tight. Where exactly were you on Monday evening?'

'I was – ' He hesitated. It was heart-warming to see that even with so much at stake he couldn't bring himself to cast doubt on a friend's reputation without at least some inner struggle. 'I was at home. On my own.'

I oohed and tut-tutted. 'That's a shame, isn't it? Because it doesn't matter how strong your motive for wanting Martin out of the way, if you'd just had company on Monday night then you'd be in the clear. Are you *sure* you were on your own?'

'Yes, I told you.'

'Absolutely positive? I know how easy it can be to overlook the presence of a guest, especially if they're small and don't make much noise. Think harder, Mr Heysham. Your whole future could depend on this. Didn't you perhaps have just a *tiny* bit of company?'

'No. No! I was on my own, for Christ's sake. Now stop this!'

It was possible that I'd never been lied to so often in the space of a single week. I might not have minded so much but I was trying to catch Martin's killer, and it was as if none of these people gave a damn about him as long as they could protect their own petty secrets. If I'd had patience in the first place it would have worn away to nothing by now. A train making towards Oxford Road was passing on the viaduct beneath us. The passengers would have been much too far away to witness me thrashing the truth out of Rupert Heysham, twisting apart those annoying little glasses and smashing his boiled-egg skull against the work-bench. But would that be the proper way to behave on academic turf? Yes, it was tempting, yes, it would be fun, but might I not feel afterwards that I'd let myself down?

By now I'd moved some eight feet away from Heysham, but I closed the gap quickly enough. Startled, he tried to sidle away from me along the work-bench but in a second I'd grabbed him by the equally annoying bow-tie and was dragging him towards me, squealing like a rat as he came. I heaved his face up to the level of mine, gently removed the glasses with my free hand and placed them on the bench beside him. I said, 'I'm going to give you one last chance, Rupert, OK? And remember, all you have to do is say yes, and there'll be no embarrassing visit from the boys in blue and you can carry on building your little empire here as if all this had never happened. So – was Monica Berry with you on Monday night?'

Heysham had turned his head to one side. It might have been fear, or it might just have been my onion breath. In a quiet voice he said, 'Yes.' I let him drop back onto the work-bench, released my grip and moved away from him a little. He immediately picked up the glasses and put them back on.

'There! That wasn't so difficult, was it?' To be honest, I was disappointed that he'd given in so easily, but you can't have everything.

'She came round for dinner. She stayed the night.'

'In your bed?'

'No! No, we haven't slept together since she met Martin. But we kept on seeing each other. She said she didn't want to lose my friendship.'

'And you always hoped that some day she'd see the light and come back to you.'

Rupert Heysham tried to straighten the bow-tie. I thought it was probably beyond straightening but I didn't say so. 'I don't know. I think mostly I'd given up. But she still wanted to see me, and Monica isn't the sort of person you say no to. Besides, her father liked me to keep an eye on her.'

'And he was paying for all this.' I indicated our surroundings.

Heysham ignored the remark. 'In any case, she needed a friend. There was something wrong. I don't know what, exactly, she never told me, but she said I cheered her up so now and again I would invite her over.'

Since our little talk the previous morning, I knew well enough what had been troubling Monica, but I kept that to myself. 'You realize she used to tell Martin she was with Leah Armstrong?'

'I didn't like that, it felt grubby. But she said Martin was terribly jealous.'

I turned my back on Heysham to search for the canvas bag, which I'd dropped near the door as I came in. I was thinking that it didn't take Marj Proops to see how all this would play out. Monica would grieve for a few months in the lonely house in Otterdale. Heysham would be there for her whenever she needed a shoulder. Gradually she would spend more and more time in Manchester. Then one day Heysham would pop the question, she would say yes, and Wetherley would have a high-flying son-in-law in the family business, just like he'd always wanted. I found my notebook and pen and turned back. 'That'll be all for now, Dr Heysham. I'm glad you saw reason in the end, and I'm sure you'll feel the benefit when you think it over. Could I have your number at home, in case of loose ends? Though I think you've told me all I need to know.' He gave me the number, and I said, 'By the way, I shouldn't worry about the police. I may have slightly exaggerated their interest in you. But at least if they do call you've got a nice little alibi.'

It was clear from Heysham's face that this was the moment he realized I'd been playing him. He coloured slightly, and I thought he might show spirit then and call me a bastard, or whatever might be the fashion in insults among psychologists. In fact I generously left a brief silence for him to do just that, reasoning that in retrospect he'd feel happier about our encounter if he'd hurled abuse at me while he had the chance. But when nothing came I said, 'Good luck with the lab,' and left him to lick his wounds.

The thing about alibis is, they cut both ways. It made no difference to Monica that her alibi was now to be provided by her ex-lover rather than her friend. But what about Leah? At last it dawned on me why she'd so super-loyally persisted in lying about Monday evening. It wasn't Monica's alibi that bothered her, it was her own. As I stepped from the lift into the glare of the atrium, light seemed to flood my consciousness too. It was just a hunch, but it fitted all the facts. If I was right, in the past few weeks Leah had had good reason to feel nothing less than murderous rage towards Martin Berry. And now Leah had no alibi.

3

I got off the bus on Alexandra Road then turned up past the convent in search of the address which Grace Berry had given me. I remembered the protective note in her voice when she spoke of Leah Armstrong, the warning that I shouldn't bully her, but I had a job to do. It wasn't my fault that Leah had been bending the truth. The tree-lined road dozed in the afternoon heat. To either side, handsome brick-built villas testified to the former wealth of Whalley Range, but their current state of neglect told a new story of student house-shares and sub-letting. I was hot and thirsty now, and really I should have taken a refreshment break after my interview with Rupert Heysham. But that would have meant delay, and after the frustrations of the past few days movement came as balm to the soul.

Leah's house, when eventually I reached it, turned out to be one of the most unloved in the long street. Double-fronted, built in yellow brick with courses of red, its flaking paint and drooping gutters cried out for attention. The wide front garden had not been improved by the addition of an area of hard standing on which two equally dilapidated cars were currently parked. The ancient Humber wouldn't have been out of place in a motor museum, but I was more interested in the second vehicle. It was a red Mini.

Though Harry Hargreaves would have counselled against jumping to conclusions, stock in the Hargreaves Method stood pretty low at present, and I saw no particular reason not to jump immediately to the attractive conclusion that this was the red Mini seen on Monday evening by one of Monica's neighbours.

There was no doorbell so I used the lion's-head knocker. After a while I used it again. Finally the door opened very slowly and a tall, emaciated girl with a mass of brown curls stood impassive beyond it. Somewhere in the house, Pink Floyd were setting the controls for the heart of the sun. I said, 'Is Leah Armstrong here?'

Her expression unchanged, the girl said, in a monotone, 'What a shame. You've missed her. Gone half an hour.' The voice seemed familiar, and I guessed that this must be the famous Sylvie I'd spoken to on the phone.

'Do you know when she'll be back?'

'She didn't say. Might be ages. I dunno.'

Apparently the week's frustrations weren't over yet. I said, 'Never mind, thanks,' and turned to go, but then turned back again and pointed to the Mini. 'Is that Leah's car?'

'Yeah. But she's not taken it, she's only gone up the park.'

'Well why didn't you say so?' I was beginning to think the gods had thrown Sylvie in my path on purpose, to liven up a slow afternoon. 'Which park?'

'There's only one park. That way. Alex Park. Lovely. She sits by the lake.'

I walked back the way I'd come, feeling hotter now and thirstier. But at least there was still a chance of talking to Leah. At the main road I crossed over and continued down to the park entrance on the corner. At first I didn't see Leah. Beyond the lake the grass had been seared yellow in the long spell of hot weather, and an informal game of football was making a further contribution to the damage. But the tall, closely-planted trees hadn't suffered in the same way, and as a humid breeze disturbed them and the leaves showed light and dark along their nodding branches I began to think that Sylvie hadn't been far wrong, and that if Alexandra Park wasn't exactly lovely it was still the loveliest place I'd seen in the city that day. The haze was thickening now beneath high cloud, but the light was intense enough, and I put a hand to my forehead against the glare as I searched for Leah Armstrong.

In the shade of a sprawling willow, Leah sat alone on a bench at the lakeside, watching the swans through the large oval sunglasses I'd seen in her bag earlier. The bag itself, and the felt hat, were nowhere to be seen. She must have spotted me before I noticed her, because when I came up to sit next to her she stayed quite still, eyes fixed ahead of her, as if resigned to the fact that the importunate man she'd shaken off at lunchtime had now turned up in her retreat. I said, 'Pleasant spot, this,' but she exercised her right to remain silent. The thwock of tennis balls drifted across to us from the nearby courts. For most people, this was just another lazy Saturday afternoon.

I said, 'You're pregnant, aren't you?'

Leah nodded.

'Martin's?'

At first she made no response to this, and I could only imagine the conflict that must be raging in her head. Finally she nodded again, then heaved a deep sigh. I was probably the first person she'd told.

A young woman holding a very small boy by the hand walked past us along the footpath. Twenty yards away they stopped and began feeding the ducks with the remains of a bag of sliced bread.

I said, 'Southaven police are searching high and low for a red Mini seen in Vaughan Close on Monday evening.'

Now Leah's head inclined towards me a little. 'Are you going to tell them it was mine?'

'That depends, doesn't it.'

Leah turned back towards the lake. The breeze picked up again, setting the dry leaves in motion, and for the first time I thought I could smell rain. Earnestly, the young boy threw bread towards the squabbling ducks.

Leah said, 'Not as old as it looks, that car. But no-one's ever really cared for it.'

I said, 'Tell me about Martin.'

'What's to tell? Girl meets boy, falls in love, boy marries girl's best friend.'

'That must have hurt.'

Leah was silent for a moment, then said, 'Ever since we were in school together, Monica's always had everything I wanted. My dad was a greengrocer, just a simple shopkeeper like Martin's. We never had any money. The business did badly, I don't know why, God knows he worked hard enough. Then when I was sixteen he went bust. He couldn't face it, he killed himself. My mother married again, they moved away, I don't see her now.' The voice was calm, quiet, but Leah held one fist in a tight ball. 'Monica's never had to deal with anything like that. She's lived like a princess her whole life, she only ever had to flick her fingers and people came running.'

'Why be friends with her if you felt like that?'

Leah smiled, a half smile with no joy in it. 'I came running too. You feel you don't have a choice.'

'And Martin?'

'I'm not sure. I used to think she'd got him wound around her little finger like the rest of us. Now I think perhaps he knew what he was doing.'

I needed to be certain what Leah meant. 'You're saying it was about money?'

Leah looked away up the path, where the boy was giggling as a wide throw from his mother sent the ducks paddling frantically across the water. 'Grace said it was history repeating itself. Monica's mother had been this posh barrister's daughter, then she goes and marries Walter, long before he had all that property he keeps bragging about. He'd wriggled out of war service somehow, he was just a rent collector for some big landlord or other. My dad told me that so I'd realize old Walter was no better than anyone else, as a little girl it was easy to be in awe of him. Then, years later, it all happens again – Monica gets hitched to Martin, a complete nobody as far as her parents are concerned.'

I said, 'If he'd married for money, why was Martin so upset when he thought Monica might be having an affair?'

Leah said, 'You don't know much about marriage, do you? Besides, he probably did think he loved her. When you do something for all the wrong reasons, you lie to yourself, don't you? I'm not even sure he fancied her that much.'

I said, 'And do you think he fancied you?'

'When our gang went out together he always spent far more time with me than Monica. I let myself think that meant something. I let myself think he was making a sort of marriage of convenience, that behind the façade Monica would carry on seeing Rupert while Martin got together with me. I had everything worked out, but then he wouldn't sleep with me. I couldn't understand it. So I told him about Rupert and Monica.'

'But their relationship was over, they were just meeting as friends.'

'That's not how it looked to me.'

'They both say so and I believe them. Perhaps you saw what you wanted to see.'

Leah pursed her lips like a spoiled child. She said, 'It's done now, anyway. Martin was furious, but he didn't dare to confront Monica. We were at a party when all this happened. He never used to drink much, but that night he was drinking, like he was trying to swill down his anger. Then he took me upstairs. It was one of those really chaotic parties, you could easily get away without being noticed. I'd longed for that moment. I thought it was going to be the beginning of my real life. But – we were in that room ten minutes and he never touched me again. That was three months ago.'

The woman and child had gone now. A swan came gliding by, cool and faintly sinister on the dark water, and two moorhens dived out of its path like yachts avoiding a liner. I said, 'Did Martin know? I mean, about the – ?'

Leah's fist unclenched and she rested the hand on her belly. 'That's why I went to see him. After that night at the party he kept out of my way. When I found out I was pregnant I tried to catch him on his own but he made it difficult. Then last Monday I knew Monica would be here in Manchester with Rupert. Apparently it was just a last-minute thing, Rupert had telephoned and seemed really keen to see her, so she left a message for Martin at work and then rang me. I was supposed to be her cover story if Martin asked questions. Anyway, I saw my chance and drove over to Southaven, but when I rang the bell there was no answer. I waited for hours in that stupid road.'

'And then what did you do?'

'What do you think? I went home, about ten, ten thirty perhaps.'

'So you never saw Martin the whole evening?'

Leah shook her head. 'And he never knew he was going to be a father.' Suddenly Leah shivered, though the heat remained stifling.

'I don't know what I'm going to do now. I thought Martin would leave Monica, we'd bring the child up together.' She took off the sunglasses and turned towards me. 'Are you going to tell the police?'

I said, 'No. But eventually they'll realize they need to spread the net a little further than Southaven. It'll look better if you go and find them before they find you.' Beyond the trees a mass of cloud was building, trapping the heavy air beneath. I said, 'Are you going home now?'

'I think I'll just stay here a bit longer. Not much to go home for, really.'

I said, 'I'm sorry about Martin.'

She smiled a thin smile and looked down at the hands folded in her lap. 'He'd never have left her though, would he? Just a fairy story.'

I wondered whether to pat her hands but decided against. In my mind I rehearsed various consoling exit lines, then decided against those too. I picked up the bag and walked away.

*

It was a little after three thirty and my business in Manchester was done. But for my wounded pride, I would now be about to catch the train back to Southaven to spend an evening with Matt and a delicious fish pie. Of course, it wasn't too late; I could ring Matt and ask if he was still free. I would first have to make up for past shortcomings by feigning interest in the details of his night out with Eileen, then casually mention that fish pie remained on the menu if he felt in a fish pie mood. But then I remembered how easily Eileen had persuaded him to cut me out of his Friday night plans, and suddenly I was damned if I was going to back down. Although at this point there flashed on my consciousness a will-sapping picture of domestic bliss, involving mood lighting, Charlie Parker, inexpensive hock, and the touch of Matt's shoulder against my own, with a little effort I was able to blank this out, more than ever determined to have nothing to do with the man until necessity and Monday morning brought him back into my life.

For now, there was always the consolation of my date with Gerry Gibbs, even if that did mean having to pretend to be a window cleaner. More than once in the past days I'd given his photograph an appreciative glance, where he leaned back with easy assurance against the Jaguar, eyes hidden from view by the lowered peak of his cap. In truth I was tired, maybe exhausted, and even without Matt the image of the settee, the music and the wine might have lured me back to Victoria and the ultimate prize of home soil, but for the fact that I'd have been left wondering for ever how my evening with Wetherley's chauffeur might have worked out. Like his boss said, you've got to seize the day.

I took the bus back into the centre, smoking my last cigarette on the upper deck. The conductor, a West Indian boy with a lucky gap between his front teeth, seemed to find me amusing. As he handed over my ticket he studied me as if I was a caged specimen then said, 'Where you from?' I told him and he said, 'Southaven? Never heard of it. They all like you in Southaven?'

I said, 'Pretty much, yes.'

He whistled in disbelief. 'How far away is it?'

I pointed and said, 'That way, about forty years.'

'Not as dumb as you look, are you?' And he walked off smiling, his backside sticking out behind the too-short jacket.

The rain held off still, but when I got down from the bus near Piccadilly Gardens the sky was darkening and the breeze carried the promise of rain more surely than before. With a new pack of cigarettes in my pocket and a spare in my bag for Sunday, I strode up to Kendals department store, bought white underpants with none of the drama which had scuppered my earlier attempt in Butterworths, then changed into one of the new pairs in the toilets. Feeling ready for anything which might come, I ate a burger and beans in a Wimpy bar, washed down by soapy coffee. The meal was cheap, but the important thing was to line my stomach in case it turned out to be another of those nights when the beers seem to order themselves. I was still hungry when I'd finished, but there had to be somewhere to put the beer.

I came out on Deansgate into a liminal world between afternoon and evening. Most of the shoppers had gone now, leaving the streets half empty. In homes around the city, people were tucking into their cheese sandwiches in front of *Voyage to the Bottom of the Sea*, before tarting themselves up in the bathroom ready for the week's big night out. Even the weather seemed suspended between two worlds. Bright summer was forgotten and the wind of change blew strong over the day's rubbish where it gathered in the doorways, but still the rain would not come. I set off for Sackville Street again. It was already six o'clock, but I meant to be fashionably late.

The Rembrandt stood on the corner of Canal Street. It was the sort of area people describe as run down, but I doubt whether it had ever been run up in the first place. I liked it. Cities can't all be glitz and glamour or there'd be nowhere to pick your nose. When I'd originally known the Rembrandt, it was called the Ogden Arms and catered to an entirely different clientele. As a spotty youth I'd had a romantic weekend in Manchester with an older bloke who painted the sets at the Pier Pavilion, and on a chance visit to the Ogden Arms we'd been thrown out for the hanging offence of looking a bit different. By the time of my last visit, a year or so back, the new regime had long been in power and there was fresh paint on the walls and an actual towel in the toilets. Reflecting that perhaps civilisation is making some sort of progress after all, I swung in through the door from Sackville Street and peeled my eyes for Gerry Gibbs.

The place was almost empty. As if Sinatra hadn't been bad enough, Dorothy Squires was now doing it her way on the juke box. At this rate it would be Tiny Tim's turn next. At the far end of the long bar, a middle-aged transvestite kitted out for a WI meeting was in conversation with the barman, a dark, foreign-looking boy in his mid-twenties wearing a black t-shirt moulded tightly to his olive skin. In the middle of the room, two older queens in full leather looked up from their drinks as I walked in, examined my credentials, then looked away again. And Gerry Gibbs sat alone at a table under one of the dimpled Canal Street windows, with a glass of something orange in front of him and a roll-up in his hand.

I walked over to the table. Gerry said, 'It's rude to keep a girl waiting.'

I said, 'Do you want another gin in that?'

He looked from me to the drink and back again. 'It's orange juice. But I'm fine, thanks. Say hi to Bruno for me.'

Anticipating my move, the barman had abandoned his chat with the transvestite and stood now at my end of the bar, waiting with rather un-English enthusiasm to serve me. There was a strong possibility that the bitter would be undrinkable here so I ordered stout, bottled, since they didn't have it on draught. When the barman brought it I said, 'Gerry says hi.' He smiled across at Gerry, Gerry smiled back. I handed over a pound note, and at the till the barman frowned, took out change uncertainly, then put some of it back again. I said, 'Still not got to grips with the currency?'

He turned to me and smiled again. The dark face and white teeth reminded me of Matt. 'Got to grips? I haven't heard that before, I like it!'

I said, 'Where are you from?'

'Lisboa. You say Lisbon. I'm here at school for the summer to improve my English.'

'Sounds pretty good already.'

'I try to get to grips with it. You should check the change. The little sixpences make me nervous.'

I took the bottle and glass over to the table, put my bag on the floor, then removed the leather jacket and hung it over the back of the chair next to Gerry's, which already carried a similar burden. My own jacket had probably seen a couple more years' active service, but otherwise there was little to distinguish between them. Gerry said, 'I like the shirt.' While the stout settled I told him about the Orangemen's parade, and he laughed. 'You'd better watch yourself on the way back, there's bound to be a few who've had a skinful.'

'Thanks for the tip. Do you always abstain or is this a special occasion?'

He said, 'I've seen the damage it can do. No offence.'

'None taken. Probably depends how you were brought up. My aunt claims my mother's milk was mostly brandy.'

I could tell Gerry didn't want to run with this subject, so I topped up my glass and waited for him to take the lead. Eventually he said, 'I don't see much shopping.'

'What? Oh – yeah, my shopping expedition. Disaster. Nothing in my size. Anyway, I just fancied the day out really.'

'Make a change from cleaning all those windows. Besides, I should think you've got enough shops in Southaven.'

'Do you know the place?'

'Just day trips when I was a kid.' He stubbed out the roll-up now, and I took out my own cigarettes and offered him one. He said, 'No, ta, I never could get on with those things. But I thought you were trying to cut down.'

I said, 'First one I've had today. I can't seem to drink without smoking.'

At this point, Bruno came out from behind the bar with a metal dish and a cloth, and as he crossed to our table I could see that it wasn't just the t-shirt which was moulded to his body. He tipped the solitary roll-up butt into the dish, wiped out the ashtray, and replaced it on the table. Again he smiled at Gerry, Gerry smiled back. Bruno returned to his post.

I said, 'Do you two only talk through intermediaries?'

Gerry was watching Bruno's back as he walked away. 'Body like that, why talk?'

I said, 'He seems to like you.'

'People do.' And I imagined they probably did. Gerry wore the plain white shirt and blue jeans without affectation, and his long body spoke of ease and openness. Perhaps the expensive-looking wristwatch seemed out of place, but would you have had him sully that perfect wrist with something cheap off a market barrow?

A group of kids in their late teens came in, chattering excitedly. There was a strong smell of after-shave as they wafted past us. I said to Gerry, 'Do you come here often?'

He smiled and said, 'I go everywhere. It's my city.'

'Must give you a hectic schedule.'

'Nothing I can't handle. I've been roaring around the place since I was a lot younger than them.' He indicated the boys at the bar who, watched patiently by Bruno, apparently had no idea what they wanted to drink or who was going to pay for it.

I said, 'Did your folks not take a view on this precocious roaring?'

Gerry said, 'I was spared all that nonsense, thank God. Children's home. They said I'd been left in a basket on the church steps, but that's probably bollocks. They liked to give us a past.'

'Can't have been much fun.'

He shrugged. 'I enjoyed the challenge. Serial absconder. You didn't really mind being brought back because it gave you another chance to break out. Broke out for good eventually, went where I couldn't be found.' His hand reached for the cigarette papers. 'What about you? You got family?'

I told him the basic facts while he rolled his cigarette. Then he borrowed my cigarette to light his own from it, as if we'd been friends for years. He blew out smoke and said, 'Funny thing, I never wanted parents. Some of the other kids did, or they'd had them once and missed them, but I couldn't see what kind of a gap they'd be filling. I'm starting to understand now, because of the Wetherleys. I don't get on great with Angela, she's a starchy old bird as you could probably tell, but the thing is, she's there, every day, reliable. But old Walter's different. Always done right by me, has Walter.'

'You said you'd been with him a while.' I stubbed out my cigarette, half hoping this might bring Bruno out from behind the bar again, but though he'd finished serving the boys now he showed no sign of interest.

'Yeah, I was doing a job for one of his employees, he took a shine to me, brought me into the fold. I was always a bit wild before that, to be honest. You've got to live somehow, haven't you? No use relying on charity. If you've got assets, you've got to maximize your return.'

I wondered if Gerry had picked this language up from Wetherley. I said, 'What sort of assets?'

He said, 'Oh, you know,' and put the roll-up to his lips again. The downy moustache was neatly trimmed, the fingernails were cut close. Perhaps after all some effort went into the casual image he presented. Now that I looked again, I could see that the cool white shirt had been freshly ironed.

I said, 'And do the Wetherleys realize you like blokes?'

'None of their business, is it? I do what I want in that flat, they don't come near.' He downed what was left of the orange juice with every indication of pleasure, and said, 'Have you always cleaned windows?'

Some people walking into this situation would have prepared their story. I'd had twenty-four hours to do just that, and I felt a sudden rush of resentment that the part of my brain which was supposed to smooth my path through life so rarely turned up for work. With the sense of jumping off a tall building I opened my mouth and heard myself say, 'Man and boy. As soon as ever I could stand I was up that ladder with a damp cloth.'

A shadow passed across Gerry's features. He said, 'I was hoping this was the point where you'd tell me the truth.'

I said, 'What do you mean? Back home they all call me George Washington.'

'Oh, come on. If there was an award for World's Worst Impersonation of a Window Cleaner, you'd have won it hands down. You're some sort of detective. You were working for Martin Berry, I heard the Wetherleys talking about it.'

I said, 'This is depressing. I put a lot of effort into that performance.'

'You were shit. I liked the vest, though.' And he grinned. His teeth were a bit crooked but I suppose there couldn't have been much time for orthodontics when you were continually running away from home. He said, 'Did you find out what you wanted to know?' Then he stubbed out the roll-up.

'Martin Berry hired me to look into – into a particular matter. I came here today to complete that investigation.'

Now Bruno emerged from behind the bar again, cloth in hand. More customers had arrived, but in the last couple of minutes he'd been joined by the landlord, who served drinks while Bruno attended to the seemingly crucial business of the dirty ashtray at our table. The butts went into the dish, the ashtray was wiped clean. Bruno smiled at Gerry, Gerry smiled back, Bruno returned to his other duties.

Gerry said, 'So it's case closed then, is it?' I should just have said yes but I hesitated, and he said, 'What, so you're still investigating?'

'Possibly.'

'Don't tell me you're trying to find out who killed him? I thought we had police for that kind of thing.'

I said, 'Do you want another drink?'

'Not just now. You haven't answered my question.'

I wasn't sure how much information I wanted to share with Gerry Gibbs. I said, 'I met your boss today.'

'Really?' It was hard to tell whether the surprise was genuine or not. I'd assumed that Gerry and the Jag must have been waiting for Wetherley somewhere by the Renold building, but if so perhaps Wetherley had not kept his chauffeur informed of what went on inside.

I said, 'Quite a character. You've landed on your feet working for a man like that.'

Gerry slipped a lucky hand inside his shirt and gently scratched his chest. 'He's changed my life, has Walter. He says you can be anything you want to be. You don't aim high, you get nowhere.'

'I take it that means you won't be driving the Wetherleys around for ever.'

'Just a stepping-stone, isn't it? I've got plans.'

'Anything specific?'

Gerry gave me a suspicious look. I saw that look on everyone's face eventually. 'What's this? Are you investigating me now?'

I said, 'Sorry, force of habit.'

'Oh, I don't mind. Quite nice, as a matter of fact.' And he gave me a different sort of look, one which I saw less frequently. Then he said, 'Do you want another bottle of that?'

My glass was nearly empty. 'I was going to get one for you.'

'Don't worry, I'm loaded, got paid yesterday.' He unwound his long form from the chair and picked up my empty bottle. 'The same?' I nodded and he loped over to the bar. While I lit myself a cigarette, I watched as the landlord flipped the lid off a bottle for me and poured orange juice and lemonade for Gerry. Some banter went on between them in the meantime, but the place was filling up quite rapidly now and I couldn't make out what they were saying. Bruno was busy further down the bar, but found a moment to smile at Gerry, who smiled back. You'd have thought they'd be fed up of that game by now but apparently not.

At the table again, Gerry said, 'Been doing it long, investigating?'

I thanked him for the drink and began to pour it. 'A few years now. I was a cop before that.'

'Can't pretend I'm surprised.' He set about making himself another roll-up. 'Why did you leave? Nice secure job, the rozzers.'

I told him about the incident in the changing room and the subsequent chat with the Super. He said, 'This other bloke's still on the force, the one you snogged?' I nodded. Gerry said, 'People like that just want to be respectable, but he's wasting his time. The thing is, we're beyond the law, aren't we? Doesn't matter how many Acts of Parliament they pass, we're always going to be on the outside looking in. They're coming down on us worse than ever, you can't even take a piss in a cottage now without having your collar felt.' Again he lit his roll-up from my cigarette.

Something had occurred to me while Gerry talked. I said, 'Did you know Martin Berry was adopted?'

He turned away from me a little as he blew out smoke. I thought the change of subject had surprised him. He didn't answer straight away. Then he said, 'Yeah, I did. We had a little conversation this one time.'

'At the wedding?' He looked quizzical. I said, 'The other day you mentioned talking to Martin at the wedding.'

'It was at the reception. I suppose Monica must have told him about my background. He came over to me and said we had something in common. He looked so happy that day, he was just having the best day ever, I think he wanted everyone else to be happy too. And of course I was just staff really, I was supposed to hang around at the side and keep my mouth shut, it was like he had to cross a line to talk to me. I thought that was big of him, he didn't have to do that.'

Another leather-clad customer pushed his way in through the Sackville Street door, and behind him I could see that at last the rain had begun to fall, though not yet heavily. Something was happening in the back of my mind too. I said, 'Do you think Martin liked you?'

'How do you mean?'

'Well – Bruno likes you, I can see the landlord likes you.' I left a short pause for effect. 'I like you. What about Martin?'

Gerry smiled, but something had taken the edge off his composure. He said, 'He'd just got married to Monica, for goodness' sake. I mean, he probably did like me in his own way, but – Is this how you are when you're interrogating people?'

It was my turn to smile. 'This is just the warm-up. You should see me when I really get a sweat on.'

Gerry raised an eyebrow and flicked ash off the cigarette. Then he looked at me more directly and said, 'How about coming back to the flat and giving me a thorough going-over?'

There didn't seem much point in pretending I'd misunderstood. I said, 'This is all very sudden.'

'Why else do you suppose I gave you my number?'

'I thought you might want your windows doing.'

He said, 'I bet you're a bit dangerous on the quiet, aren't you? If I'd had a mother, you're exactly the sort of bloke she'd have warned me about. Anyway, I like older men.'

'Who's older? I'm barely out of kindergarten.'

He was reading my body language. 'You're holding back, what's the matter? You said you liked me.'

'I thought you were lining Bruno up for tonight. He's watching you now, he's not going to be pleased.'

'Sod Bruno, all right? I want to be with you.' He leaned in closer. 'You know you'll regret it if you don't.'

Well, I hadn't exactly got anything else to do. Matt was with Eileen, Mark didn't want to know, and Martin was dead. I said, 'There's no risk of me seeing the Wetherleys?'

Gerry leaned back again, more confident now. 'They're at some posh dinner. And I can run you to the station in the morning before they're even up.'

'What, in the Jag?'

'Don't be daft, I've got my own wheels. Are we on?'

The fact was, I'd fancied Gerry Gibbs since the moment I saw him getting out of the car on Tuesday morning. Nor had it done his case any harm when he'd peeled off the tight leather gloves and leaned back against the Jag as if he owned half of Southaven. If in recent years I'd grown more used to being the pursuer than the pursued, surely I could make an exception in such a good cause? I stubbed out my cigarette and began to drink up. Correctly reading the signs, Gerry said, 'Good man,' stubbed out the roll-up, gulped down what remained in his glass, swept one of the beer mats from the table into his jacket pocket, then rose to his feet.

I'd stood up myself and was just lifting my own coat from the back of my chair when, as if magically attracted by the fresh butts in the ashtray, Bruno once more came out from behind the bar to deal with them. Feeling a little awkward, I said, 'Thanks, Bruno. Hope you have a good summer.' And Gerry smiled at him as before, but this time there was no answering smile from Bruno. I felt his eyes on our backs as Gerry led us out of the Sackville Street door into the evening drizzle.

Gerry said, 'Looks like we might get a bit damp.' I followed him round the corner onto Canal Street, where he stopped by a big Norton parked up on its stand. 'No crash helmets, hope you don't mind. Don't believe in them.'

I said, 'Look – Gerry, I'm sorry. I can't do this.'

'What?' He looked thunderstruck, as if I'd just told him that he was the secret love child of the Queen and Bernard Breslaw. Actually, I was quite surprised myself. 'I don't understand.'

'It's not you, honest. You're a really sexy man and I must be insane.'

'What's the problem?' He brought one hand up to my cheek, playful, maybe affectionate. 'I thought you wanted to investigate me?'

'I just need to get home. It's been a pig of a week.'

He smiled ruefully. 'You realize you've screwed up my chances with Bruno now as well?'

I said, 'You could grovel. Always works for me.'

Suddenly he drew me towards him and kissed me, and when I didn't argue he got more serious about it until we were enjoying the kind of session that can get you drummed out of the Southaven constabulary. Though you might risk a peck on the cheek after dark, it just wasn't done to kiss a man on the street like this in broad daylight. Yet somehow with Gerry's tongue tickling your tonsils you couldn't quite think why that should ever have been a problem. I don't know how he did it, but there it was. Perhaps the landlord had slipped something into his lemonade.

We separated, and Gerry said, 'See what you're missing?' Then he lowered the bike down from its stand, and swung his leg over the saddle. 'Safe journey home.' With a couple of deft kicks, he brought the bike to life.

I said, 'No hard feelings, I hope.'

'We'll have to see, won't we?' Then the bike cruised slowly off up the street, turned left, and was gone.

I went straight to the Union Hotel and had another drink, keeping a sharp eye on the door in case Gerry decided to do the same. Our encounter had left me shaken. I wasn't in the habit of turning down offers from attractive men, and given that three hours ago I would have considered getting off with Gerry Gibbs to be a fitting and desirable conclusion to my Manchester trip, I couldn't help wondering what had happened to change my so-called mind. What was the point of buying new pants if I was just going to cry off when the going got interesting? Neither the drink nor the cigarettes I smoked seemed able to help me with this puzzle. When I glanced round at my fellow-drinkers they appeared ugly and vicious to a man, like members of some alien species. No question about it, it was time to be heading home.

The rain had redoubled its efforts now, and I half walked, half ran to Victoria station, where as luck would have it I jumped on a Southaven train just as the guard's whistle was blowing. This minor triumph in my battle against adverse deities temporarily repaired my mood, and I took the Gazette from my bag and tried to squeeze a little more juice out of it. But then we were stuck for twenty minutes outside Appley Bridge, and as I watched the gloom gathering on the sodden fields the full darkness of the week's dark happenings came down with it too. By the time we were once again lurching over the points at the approach to Southaven, gloom had swallowed everything. Manchester had been my last best hope of a breakthrough, and I'd come back empty-handed. I hadn't the faintest notion what to do next.

The three men hanging around near the ticket office and passing a bottle from one to another didn't concern me much at first. It's true that the largest of them wore a silver majorette's hat topped by orange crepe, and I did think I heard him mutter 'Fenian bastard' as I walked by, but you can't go flaring up at every little threat. I still felt relaxed enough as I came out into the pouring rain on Station Road, heard Wilf call 'Last orders!' through the open door of the Railway, and continued round onto Fleetwood Street with measured and untroubled steps. But then the angle of a toyshop window a few yards further along confirmed what my intuition had begun to whisper. The men were following me.

Even so, I didn't rush to judge their motives. Perhaps they only meant to enquire after the address of my tailor, in which case an extra turn of speed on my part should be enough to deter them. It wasn't. Another window, an estate agent's this time, showed that if anything they were closing the gap. As far as I'd been able to see in the dim light by the ticket office, they were a tough-looking trio, all under forty probably, and it was doubtful whether any of them spent much time in front of the bathroom mirror. I allowed myself a burst of anxiety, just enough to fuel the framing of a plan.

Like a bird with a chick in the nest, at the first opportunity I drew them away from the direction of the flat, away too from the handful of Saturday night drinkers hurrying to catch that all-important final round. I turned up Bolton Street, towards the site of the old engine sheds, long demolished, and once on Bolton Street I ran, the bag clutched to my side to stop it swinging. Breeze in my face, rain streaming off me, the dark mood of the train journey was forgotten. I risked glancing back. As I'd hoped, my pursuers occupied a sliding scale of fitness, and the biggest of them was now lagging some yards behind. Rain after the long dry spell had brought out snails in their hundreds, which crunched underfoot as I ran. With every step, steel cords pulled tighter in my chest, but it was too late to give up smoking now.

I was making for the open, brick-strewn ground where the sheds had once stood. It was nearly dark, and if I could get far enough ahead of the men I might be able to lose them amongst the piles of rubble. Now I heard a shout of 'Fuck!' and when I looked round again the lumbering giant at the back, his silver hat now lost in the general rush, was limping on what I took to be a twisted ankle. One down, two to go. But the youngest and fittest of the men had pulled well forward of his mate now and ran almost on my heels, so that we arrived on the rough surface of gravel and cinders at the same moment. I felt his hand on my shoulder, then his foot reached forward of my ankles and struck down, and suddenly I was on the ground, the bag rammed painfully into my side.

But in falling myself, I'd brought down my assailant too. I couldn't risk being on the ground still when the second man reached us. Scrambling up out of the mud, I hurled the bag away from me. I'd have to search for it later among the scattered debris, but just now it was restricting my movement and it had to go. As I came up, so too did the young man, but before he had time to get his balance I threw a neat punch to his jaw which sent him down again. A moment later, something with the force of a truck thudded into me from the side, and when I hit the dirt it came right down on top of me. It was the second man, arriving late but in fine style. Either the fall had winded him or he'd not anticipated such spectacular success, because he now lay quite still on top of me for a couple of seconds like an exhausted lover, during which time I became aware of an unpleasant stinging sensation in the ear which had broken my fall. Then the first man, now on his feet again, started kicking my exposed flank with what felt like lead-capped boots. This seemed to inspire his companion, who managed to lift himself off my chest with one arm and slam a granite fist into my face, twice.

It didn't help much, but just then my mind pointed out that if I hadn't been so skittish I could at that very moment have been making passionate love in Didsbury instead of lying flat on my back being beaten to a pulp by thugs in torrential rain. It also occurred to me to worry that my good brown cords must be getting dirty, and I wondered who I could present the bill to if they needed specialist cleaning. But when the boot kept coming and the fist came down for the third time, these thoughts gave way to rage. He didn't realize it yet, but the man lying along my body had made a stupid mistake. When he raised his arm the fourth time I was ready, I spun the two of us over, and kneeling on his chest I lifted his soft round head with both hands and slammed it down onto the surface beneath. Unluckily for him, I'd rolled us onto an area of flagstones with little in the way of damp earth to absorb the blow. The man with the lead boot hadn't seen this coming, and for a while he left me to do as I pleased, which was, to pick up the head repeatedly and smash it down again. Looking into the bloated, piggy face below me I seemed to see the shape of all the week's frustrations, and I became determined now to go on smacking the head against the flags until it burst open and released its nasty, vindictive spirit. The kicking man now tried to pull me away by the shoulders, but I was having far too good a time to let him succeed. Down went the head, and down, smash, smash. Its owner was beyond speech now, but in the half dark his wide, white eyes pleaded with me to stop, only I couldn't stop because I was going to kill him, and the head smashed down again and again. But suddenly, just when I had a nice rhythm going, a huge mass like a medicine ball swung into the side of my skull, I fell sideways, and from the ground I saw that the limping giant had finally joined us and put an end to my fun.

My victim groaned, the young man went to his aid. But Fatty Arbuckle had reached into his trouser pocket for something. I heard a click, then he was bearing down on me, a blade in his outstretched hand.

The young man shouted, 'Leave it! Ozzie's hurt,' and the big man duly left it, folded away the blade, and put it back in his pocket. Together they lifted their dazed comrade to his feet and looped his arm over the young man's neck. I thought they were finished with me now, but as the other two made their first slow steps towards the street the big man turned, crossed over to me where I lay propped up on my elbows, and kicked me in the jaw. Then he rejoined his mates, and he and the young man carried their wounded from the field.

*

Just how long Braithwaite's goons had been shadowing me, waiting for their chance to strike, it was impossible to say. I thought it safe to assume that, despite the Orange fancy dress and the Fenian jibe, the three Adonises whose finesse I'd recently experienced could be none other than the hired muscle of our old pal Slasher Braithwaite, perhaps tipped off in his custody cell that it was Sam Rigby who'd first implicated him over Martin's death, and keen to send me the message of thanks by nuncio which he wasn't at liberty to give me himself. I just hoped to God he didn't know where I lived.

Sitting up in bed an hour or so after the event, with my kidneys aching, my head pounding, my gashed ear fizzing beneath a sticking plaster, and my jaw threatening to split in two and drop into my lap, I was forced to congratulate the boys on a job all too well done. It was a few minutes past twelve, and the night should yet have been young. Standing naked in the kitchen earlier on, my body still damp with sweat after the bliss of a hot bath, I'd looked long and hard at the Riesling in the fridge, then shaken my head sadly and closed the door. In the hallway I'd searched my coat pockets for the cigarettes – the leather jacket, indestructible, had survived my ordeal with nothing worse than a few scuffs which could only add to its charm, while the unlucky green shirt had somehow managed to get ripped beyond repair – then taken a cigarette out of the crumpled pack, put it straight back in again, and cast the pack aside. The depressing truth was that I didn't want alcohol, or nicotine. I didn't even want sex. What I really wanted was a nice early night.

If word of this got out my reputation would be ruined, but there's only so much a man can take, and this week I'd taken it. Perhaps this was how it felt to be old and out of the race, like Grandad Eli in the home at Marshfield. Though a copy of *Teach Yourself Astronomy* lay on the quilt in front of me, I couldn't even face the prospect of reading. I was finished, washed up, dead in the water.

Dead in the water, like Martin. He and Monica looked back at me from the photo resting against the bedside lamp, Martin's smile fixed for ever now in a final verdict on the life he'd left behind. It was a very handsome face. Small wonder that when it had appeared in the Railway Tavern I'd seen what I wanted to see and spun for myself the honest, wholesome Martin who'd since been slowly unravelling. Despite his bitter accusations, it wasn't Monica but Martin who'd played away, and it was clear enough now that the homely carrot-grower and mainstay of the Otterdale B team could calculate and manipulate like anyone else. Disenchanted, I had to admit that I no longer knew who Martin was. He seemed different through the eyes of everyone who spoke about him, Monica, her parents, Grace, Danny, Leah, and now Gerry Gibbs. I clung to this last certainty: disgusted by his boss's lies over the Empire survey, Martin had intended to risk his job exposing the fraud. Perhaps the world had seen bolder heroes, but none of them had ever sat hip to hip with me on the narrow settee drinking my Scotch.

Rain gusted against the windows. Whenever it eased, I could hear further off the steady drip, drip, as water leaking through the roof found its way into the bucket on the outside landing. I took the photograph in my hands to look again at the impossibly contented ghost of Martin Berry. And the more I looked, the more Monica, shoulders hunched tight against some imagined gale, seemed out of place, as if she were a stranger who'd wandered into this happy scene by accident.

I swung out my legs, murmured an oath at the unexpected pain, took the bride and groom through to the kitchen in search of scissors, cut Monica out of the picture, and then brought Martin back to bed.

Sunday

It was still raining heavily when I woke up the following morning at around half past nine. Half past nine! Due to some oversight on the part of the gods, the team of aunts, Smythes, anxious neighbours and over-eager young assistants who'd been conspiring all week to rob me of my sleep had for once been allowed to shirk their task. Nor had I been disturbed by dreams of any kind, at least none that I could remember in the rain-soaked light of day. I'd actually slept well.

Perhaps that explained why I could now detect a faint glimmer of optimism relieving the previous night's Stygian mindscape. I wouldn't go so far as to say I felt cheerful, but as I moved and stretched in the bed and the long litany of my painful injuries made themselves known, I experienced them more as trophies than marks of divine disfavour. The new day might be just as frustrating as its predecessors, but Sam Rigby could take it.

Past catastrophes had taught me that the first thing I needed to do was empty the bucket on the landing. By now it was almost full, so full in fact that when I carried it back through the hallway I managed to spill water over my shoes, but they were still damp from the previous night so that hardly mattered. With the bucket emptied down the sink and set in position again, I took a moment to give myself due credit for this display of domestic efficiency.

It then occurred to me that I had no other useful activities planned for the day, or indeed for the rest of my life.

The temperature must have dropped during the night because a significant gale was now blowing through the flat. I went round shutting windows. That done, I had a cigarette, dressed, then toasted the sole surviving crust from the loaf which Matt had bought on Thursday, and washed it down with tea. Remembering belatedly that there were now eggs in the cupboard, I boiled two of them and ate them, wishing there was more toast. I smoked another cigarette. And when I'd done that, I sat at the kitchen table wondering how I could possibly survive the rest of the day.

On Sundays there's a noticeable falling off of activity in Southaven, and since nothing much happens here on the other six days anyway this can result in a Sabbath black hole of eventlessness into which your hopes and dreams and eventually sanity itself are inexorably sucked. All attempts to fight back are doomed. The only sensible course is to consider Sunday a battle lost before the first shot has even been fired.

So perhaps it's surprising that eleven o'clock found me at my desk in Crowburn House, reviewing the lists and diagrams I'd made on Friday evening, and adding fresh squiggles where appropriate.

Aunt Winnie and Uncle Fred would long since have left for church in Marshfield, and I had the building to myself. With its peculiar antique smell, you could easily imagine that the place had stood for far longer than a single century and would stand, square and decent, for centuries yet. Perhaps this made it the best possible container for my shifting thoughts, as they flashed into being like sub-atomic particles, left brief traces of their erratic motion on the surface of my mind, then danced off as suddenly as they'd come to play some unknown role in other universes.

Yesterday evening I'd felt that I was returning from Manchester with nothing. But was that strictly true? Although I could be sure now that Monica, Leah and Rupert had played no direct part in Martin's death, intuition still nagged at me. Some false note kept spoiling the account of Monica's harmonious evening with her ex-lover. Leah had said it was a last-minute arrangement: why had Rupert been so keen to see Monica at such short notice? And why did I feel now that in coming back from Manchester I'd somehow left the real scene of the crime behind?

There were questions in Southaven too. Did Norman Breeze have the least idea that the colleague whose integrity he'd made so much of on Thursday had spent Friday afternoon running round after a dead man's briefcase which contained incriminating evidence? Was it perhaps Norman Breeze himself who'd leaned on the editor of the Gazette to withhold letters critical of the Empire redevelopment? And why would Sandy Smythe not admit that he'd seen Martin again late on Monday night after Martin's scrap with Danny Craven?

Then there was the whole baffling issue of Joseph 'Slasher' Braithwaite, who kept turning up on the fringes of the investigation despite apparently having nothing whatever to do with Martin Berry, and who was currently cooling his heels at the taxpayer's expense.

I could see no solution to any of this. At first I'd assumed that I'd be able to track down Martin's killer in a matter of hours, now I doubted whether the job could ever be done at all.

Outside the rain lashed down. Minutes passed and turned to hours.

Eventually I closed up the office and went downstairs hoping for a chat with Fred and Winnie, but there was no sign of them. Sometimes they stayed out for lunch after church, or went for a drive in the Anglia, not that it was the best day for driving. I left a note, and splashed my way home through the rain.

It was after two by now and I was hungry. I wondered whether to eat more eggs, or to get radical and finally cook the fish pie, but the thought of eating alone put me off. The Sand Lizards would at that moment be busy practising in a garage somewhere, to be joined eventually by Eileen. You had to feel sorry for the poor woman, but it was her own fault for going out with a man who dabbled in neighbourhood rock.

I took the Saturday Gazette from my bag, turned to the TV listings, and had just decided to admit defeat and settle back on the settee with a glass of wine and the International Eisteddfodd from Llangollen when someone buzzed at the door.

Since the Coach and Horses at Merechurch closed at two on Sundays, I had a pretty shrewd idea who this might be. I opened the window and looked down. Though all I could see was the crown of a bright pink umbrella which must once have belonged to a little girl, and though the only living form visible outside its circumference was the squat brown hindquarters of an unfamiliar dog, the very unexpectedness of the image confirmed my suspicions. There would be no point in dropping down the keys, as I would be unlikely ever to see them again; my visitor had form on this issue. I padded down the stairs on stockinged feet and opened the front door.

My mother said, 'Nice weather for ducks. Not interrupting, am I?' I held the door wider, and she lowered the umbrella and stepped inside. The dog followed her meekly and shook rainwater onto my jeans. 'This is Bowzer. He's no bother, really. Are you, pet?' My mother leaned down to detach the lead, and the dog wagged its fat stump and gave a single, surprisingly high-pitched bark. It was a curious, improbable animal, perhaps the product of a bull terrier playing fast and loose with some more decorative dog.

I closed the door and led the way upstairs. At the top, my mother leaned the umbrella against one wall, while Bowzer stopped to lap water from the bucket. We moved on into the living room, where the dog crossed the floor, cocked his leg over a pile of books, and pissed liberally. My mother said, 'For heaven's sake, Bowzer, you've had half an hour to do that outside.' I fetched a cloth and mopped up, though in fact the dog had confined its attentions to a three-volume set of *Lord of the Rings* so there was no harm done.

I said, 'Cup of tea?'

The dog had curled up on the bean bag, eyes closed, chin resting on its paws. My mother meanwhile had lowered herself slowly onto the settee, to the accompaniment of dramatic groans. Whenever she remembered, she suffered from arthritis. 'That would be nice. Unless – ' Now her tone became more confidential. 'You wouldn't happen to have a little drinkies, would you, Sammy love?'

'Had they run out at the Coach?'

'Surely you don't begrudge your own mother a drink?'

I knew she wouldn't be particularly bothered what form the alcohol took, so by way of reply I returned the cloth to the kitchen, opened the remaining bottle of Riesling, poured out an ungenerous glass, and carried it through to place it in my mother's hand. She said, 'Aren't you having one yourself?' She had a sharing temperament.

I said, 'Perhaps later,' and watched her enjoy the first approving sip. At the same time, I began to take in the details of her outfit, a tiger-stripe jacket worn over leopard-skin leggings. The legs themselves were painfully thin, as was the rest of her. I said, 'What on earth are you wearing? Have you started breaking into zoos now?'

'I'm not taking fashion tips from you. Besides, this is a classic look, it'll never go out.'

'Only because it's never come in. And you're wearing odd shoes.'

'I keep on getting home without one. I do wish you'd stop finding fault, you're as bad as Winnie.' She put the glass down and checked her jacket pockets. 'Drat, I must have left my ciggies on the bar.' Then she gave me a look requiring no interpretation, so I fetched my own cigarettes and lit one for her. She blew out smoke, indicated my face and said, 'What happened to you?'

I put a hand up to touch the impressive bruise on my jaw. 'Line of duty. You should see the other fellow.'

My mother smiled. 'Are you sure you won't have a drink with me, Sammy love?'

I looked again at the rail-thin legs, the bony, rounded

shoulders. 'Would you like something to eat?'

'I had a bit of a snack at the Coach.'

'A packet of crisps, if I know you. Go on, I was going to cook anyway.' So the fish pie did finally get made. While I prepared it, my mother smoked and drank at the kitchen table, and once it was in the oven we took the bottle through into the living room. I had a glass of wine myself then, wedged in beside my mother on the settee. I said, 'Whose is the dog?'

Though he was apparently asleep, Bowzer's ears now angled themselves more favourably for eavesdropping on the conversation. 'Ivor's.'

'Your new man?'

She nodded. 'He's down south at his sister's this week so I'm holding the baby.'

'What does Ivor do?' Though I should have learned better by now, I still felt pathetically compelled to vet my mother's boyfriends.

'Nothing, these days. He used to work for the CIA but he took early retirement with his kidneys.'

I let the brain grapple with this. 'I suppose you mean C&A?'

'He's always hard up, which is a bit of a nuisance. But he does have his good points, if you know what I mean.' She nudged me, and I spilled wine on my jeans. 'His name's Prentice but I always say it ought to be Biggun. Ivor Biggun!' She cackled wheezily.

'For God's sake, Mum, you'll play havoc with my Oedipus complex.'

'It's high time you grew out of all that.' She appealed to the dog for support. 'Isn't it, Towzer?' The animal opened one eye.

'Towzer? You said his name was Bowzer.'

'Really, Sammy, do you think I don't know what the dog's called? I hope you're not going deaf on top of everything else.'

'What do you mean, everything else?'

My mother wriggled in the seat. Wherever she sat she was never comfortable for long, except possibly on bar stools. 'I was telling the doctor about you. He says you're going through a phase.'

'I'm thirty-four.'

'Are you seeing anyone?'

Off the top of my head, I couldn't exactly remember. 'Might be.'

'You should be settling down at your age, I don't care if it's a man or a woman or what it is. You need to bite the bull by the nettle, it's no good being on your own. I can tell you that from bitter experience.'

'No you can't, you're never on your own more than five minutes. You should hear Aunt Winnie on the subject.'

'Take no notice of Winnie, she's never been the same since that prolapse.' Then she topped up her glass and said, 'I hope this isn't the only bottle.'

'Well it is, so take it easy. I'll go and check on the food.'

In the kitchen, I took the opportunity to breathe deeply, after which I let the pie brown a little while I cooked peas, then served up and took the plates through with a fork for each of us. We sat side by side in silence and made a start, the windows rattling in the gusty rain. Bowzer, or possibly Towzer, heaved a deep sigh. After a while my mother put her fork down, turned a little towards me and said, 'This is nice, isn't it?'

'We aim to please.'

'I don't mean the food, Sammy love. I mean – ' With a gesture she took in the meal, the two of us, the room, and the rain-soaked town outside.

I said, 'Yes, I suppose it is.' And I suppose it was.

Satisfied, my mother picked up the fork and continued eating. But it wasn't long before she stopped again and pushed the plate away from her on the low table. 'That was very good, thanks Sammy.'

'You've barely had half of it.'

'You know I'm not a big eater, you shouldn't give me so much to start with.'

'Try and eat some more. There's no pudding. Unless you want an orange.'

But her hands had already moved to the cigarette packet. When she'd lit herself one, I said, 'By the way, Harry Hargreaves sends his regards.'

My mother then started coughing, and didn't stop until I'd put my plate down and patted her on the back. She said, 'Why were you talking to him? Not angling for your old job back, are you?'

'What, and give up a thriving business? We were discussing a case, that's all.'

'Nice of him to remember me after all this time.'

'Well you shouldn't flatter yourself. You know he only got you off that charge because you were related to a serving officer and it would have reflected badly on the force.'

'If you say so, Sammy. Is he keeping well?'

'Same as always.'

'I was sorry you two never got on better.'

'Not my fault, he just doesn't like me. No taste, some people.'

'He struck me as the sort who didn't like to show his true feelings.'

'What, you worked that out during ten minutes in the interview room? No, he shows his feelings all right, ask anyone down at the station.' At that point I remembered Cilla Donnelly's left-field remarks. Given my serious misreading of Martin Berry, how could I be sure I was doing any better with Hargreaves? But – no. That sneer, those yellowed teeth: his meaning was clear enough and always had been. I said, 'As a matter of fact, this case is all about the Empire cinema.'

My mother looked blank.

I said, 'You know – the Empire. You worked there almost a year when I was a kid.'

She shook her head. 'No, love, you've got it wrong. That was the Roxy. Don't you remember? Phoebe Bannerman got me the job.'

Not for the first time in my mother's presence, I sensed the ground dissolving beneath me. 'The Roxy? You're joking. It was the Empire, I used to sit in the café with a lemon barley water late afternoons, waiting for you to come off shift.'

'Your mind's playing tricks. I've never worked at the Empire.'

'The Roxy didn't even have a café.'

'Of course it did. Jessie Cunliffe ran it, Fred used to do odd jobs for her husband Bill before the war.'

'But that was the Empire!'

'You've got it all muddled up. Honestly, Sammy love, how you ever manage to do your job with a mind like that is a complete mystery to me.' She checked her watch. 'I said I'd drop by at Ken Whitaker's later on and listen to his new stereo. And he's got colour TV now, he came into some money.'

'You wouldn't be lining him up as a replacement, by any chance?'

My mother leaned far enough back to give my shoulder a reproachful shove. 'What a dreadful thing to say. Ken's lonely since Edie passed away, it's the least I can do.' Then she was silent a moment while she reassembled her expression. When she'd picked one she felt happy with, she said, 'You couldn't lend me ten pounds, could you, Sammy love?'

Now at least I knew why my mother had called round. It's true that occasionally she would turn up without actually wanting anything, but that only made both of us nervous so she tried not to do it too often. I said, 'I'm a bit strapped.'

'I could pay you back when my dole money comes through. Please, Sammy, I'm really stuck and I need to put something by for the rent.'

Well, I couldn't have her out on the street. 'I can manage a fiver, but that's all you're getting. Last time I saw you, you said you were going to look for a job.'

'I did try, Sammy love, but they don't want people my age. And I'm only a year or two short of retirement, it hardly seems worth the bother.'

'It's not a year or two, it's five years.'

I got up then, perhaps purposefully, because my mother looked anxious and said, 'What are you doing?'

'Clearing the plates.' She looked relieved. 'And then I'm going to dig out Thursday's Gazette and we're going to look through all the jobs until we find you something.' With that, I removed the plates, dumped them in the sink, put the kettle on, then left the newspaper in my mother's lap so she could get started while I brewed tea. But when I took the drinks through, the Gazette had slipped to the floor and my mother was lighting another cigarette. I said, 'Come on, play fair. You know you'll feel better if you can land a nice little job. You hardly knew yourself when you were in the canteen at Brockhursts.'

'There were some lovely boys worked there. Took ten years off me.'

'Well then.' So I spread the paper across our knees and we went slowly down the columns. The experience was discouraging. I began to think my mother might have a point. 'What about this? Inspectress Packers at Mallards in Braemar Drive – that's not far from you, you could walk it in ten minutes.'

My mother frowned dismissively. 'More like twenty, with my legs. In any case, they want young girls. It says twelve pound five shillings rising to fourteen pound nine and eleven for over 21's. I don't want to be surrounded by a lot of squawking teenagers.'

And things went on in similar vein. Eventually I gave up and laid the paper aside. 'You've not touched your tea.'

My mother said, 'I'm all right with this,' indicating the wine glass, but when she leaned forward to top it up again she discovered that the bottle was empty. There was a moment's uncertainty. Then she checked her watch and said, 'Is that the time? We ought to be moving on, Ken's stereo won't listen to itself.' Recognizing the change of tone, Bowzer lifted his head from the bean bag, leaving behind a dark patch of dog-drool on the fabric. When she rose, grumbling, to her feet, the dog rose too, wagged its stump again, and tilted its oddly small head enquiringly.

I said, 'You don't have to go, I'm not busy.'

My mother said, 'I'd offer to help with the washing up but I know you like to do things your own way.' She lit another cigarette.

I said, 'Take the pack, if you want.'

'That's kind of you, love.' She pocketed the cigarettes, and the dog and I followed her into the hallway. Then she said, 'You haven't forgotten that fiver?'

The money was still in the pocket of my brown cords, now several extra shades of brown after their waste-ground adventure. I fetched it and placed it in my mother's hand. She made a girlish face and said, 'You're sure you couldn't just stretch to the other five?'

I don't know why, but suddenly I saw red. 'For God's sake, do you think I'm made of money? Get yourself a job, or squeeze some out of this Ken person or whatever his name is. I never see you from one month's end to the next, then when you do show up it's all about money.'

There was a heavy silence. The hallway was poorly lit, but not so poorly that I couldn't see the wounded expression on my mother's powdered face. Eventually, not meeting my eyes, she said, 'I suppose it's no more than I should expect. Obviously I've been a terrible mother. I thought you might have forgiven me but I see that's asking too much.'

'Mum – '

'Come along, Bonzo. We know when we're not wanted.' She let herself out onto the top landing, picked up the umbrella, and started down the stairs, the dog skittering behind her. Rainwater still dripped into the bucket. There wouldn't have been much point in calling after her so I spared myself the effort, closed the door, turned into the kitchen, then scraped what remained of the fish pie into the bin.

*

It was nearly midnight when the buzzer buzzed again.

The intervening hours had not passed well, but they'd passed, which is the main thing. I'd spent the evening exhibiting my wounds in the Railway, where I drank all the alcohol which I'd failed to drink the previous night. By the time I left the pub at ten thirty it had stopped raining, the first positive development of the entire day. I'd expected the drink to ease the pain of my injuries, but every step of the walk home seemed to unveil fresh agonies, the only consolation being that I'd probably feel even worse next morning.

How many times my visitor had had to press the buzzer before the noise finally woke me, I've no idea. I heaved myself out of bed, stumbled through to raise the front window, and looked down to find Matt looking up at me. However, this wasn't the ebullient, annoyingly cheerful Matt of recent visits, but some sort of reduced version I'd never seen before, as if someone had been letting the air out. I said, 'Have you got no home to go to?' He didn't answer, so I fetched the keys and dropped them down to him. After Mark Howell's attack on my once much-loved dressing gown, I would now have felt embarrassed to be seen wearing it. All I could think of instead was to pull on a pair of the new underpants which I'd bought in Manchester. This left a considerable acreage of bruised and battered flesh on display, but if I'd imagined that Matt's first action on seeing me would be to express interest in these badges of my recent heroism, I was a good way wide of the mark. Instead, when I met him in the hallway he trailed miserably towards me and tried to fold himself into my chest, and I found myself embracing him rather gingerly so as not to crush his broken arm. I could tell that he'd been crying, though he was now doing his best to hold back the tears. I said, 'What on earth's the matter?'

From somewhere near my right nipple, he said, 'Eileen.'

'She's not dead?'

Now Matt pulled back a little, so that he could look into my face. 'Don't be daft. She's dumped me.' And he resumed his previous position.

It would have been insensitive to say, 'Oh, is that all,' and I managed to resist. Cautiously, I held Matt a little tighter. Though my ribs had started to complain, I could think of worse things to do in the uninspiring hallway of my flat than embrace attractive men with broken arms. But the trouble was that I regarded the hallway as a place of transit, and I was finding it difficult to settle to the task. I said, 'Do you want tea?'

I could feel the warmth of his breath on my skin. He said, 'Not now. Bed.'

'Bed?' And I loosened my grip involuntarily.

Matt looked up at me again. 'I'm really tired. I was trying to sleep but I just kept going over and over it all in my head. I just wanted to be with someone. Is that all right?'

'When you say "with" – '

'Just someone there with me, so I can sleep.'

I lowered my arms. 'You realize you'll probably be the only one of us who does sleep?'

But Matt said, 'Christ, Sam! What happened?' He'd finally noticed my wounds.

Gratified, I said, 'A little run-in with Slasher Braithwaite's pals.'

'Jesus! How many?'

'I'll tell you all about it when you've given me the low-down on Eileen. The woman must be insane. Do you need the bathroom or anything?'

Matt lifted his nose and said, 'I can smell wet dog. And cigarettes.'

'Oh, that. My mother was here this afternoon.' Matt looked confused. 'With a dog, obviously. She smokes like a chimney.' In a way it was a stroke of luck that she'd taken my cigarettes. Rather than buy more in the pub, I'd simply cadged a few.

Matt said, 'Lead on, Macduff,' so I led the way into the bedroom. He said, 'Can I take the far side of the bed? So you don't roll onto my arm.' The bed stood pushed up against the wall.

'Whatever you want.'

He pulled off his shoes. 'I see you keep your curtains on the floor. Nice touch.' He ducked out of the sling and draped it over the hook on the back of the door.

'If you're going to pass comment I might have to ask you to leave. Do you want help with that?' Matt was making heavy weather of unbuttoning his shirt with one hand.

'If you don't mind.' I didn't. I unbuttoned the shirt and he shrugged out of it. Then I lifted the white vest carefully above his head and over the cast on his injured arm.

I said, 'It might be better if you do the trousers yourself.'

'But they're the hardest part.'

'I dare say.' I left him to it and went into the bathroom to take a leak. The fourth pint had just worked its way through. Then I brushed my teeth for a second time and took a look at myself in the mirror. I had the appearance of a man who'd been brawling and come off worst. The sticking plaster on my ear had started to work loose so I yanked it off, but this did nothing to improve the general impression.

When I rejoined him, Matt was sitting up on the far side of the bed, the quilt pulled up to his chest, and looking a lot less miserable than before. His clothes were stacked on a chair, underpants topping the pile. He said, 'What's with the photograph of Martin Berry?'

I couldn't think of a sensible reply, so I just slipped the picture onto the shelf of the bedside table and said, 'Before I get in, let's be clear about this. You do know I fancy the arse off you?'

He said, 'Only natural.'

'And despite the fact you're lying there in all your glory you seriously expect me not to interfere with you in the middle of the night?'

'Absolutely.'

'I think I hate you.'

'You'll get over it.' He patted the bed with his good hand. 'Hop in.' So I hopped in and sat up beside him. He said, 'Put the light out,' and when I'd done as I was told I felt him shift closer to me and his right arm curved around my shoulders. 'Tell me about Braithwaite. And Manchester. How did you get on with Leah Armstrong?'

'No, you first. I can't have you upset like this, it might affect your work.'

Matt's hand idly stroked my upper arm. 'You know I said Eileen was coming to listen to the band?'

'Yes?'

'She hated it. And I mean hated. She said that if we weren't the worst band she'd ever heard, that was only because she'd once sat on the panel for a talent contest at Pontin's.'

I whistled. 'Fighting talk. But I don't understand. Why did she have to be so honest? Why couldn't she just smile in all the right places and say "extraordinary" or something like that? Has she never heard of lying?'

'While I was with the band she was quite complimentary. But then we were having a drink afterwards and she happened to say my voice tended to go flat in the upper register.'

I could now guess where this was leading. 'Go on.'

'So I was a bit peeved, and I said there was nothing wrong with my voice and what did she know about it anyway? And she said as a matter of fact before she was a nurse she'd had lessons with one of the finest singing teachers in the county. So I said I didn't care who she'd had lessons with, she obviously had cloth ears. Well, that put her back up, and she said she wished she did have cloth ears because then she might not have suffered so much when she listened to the band. And it went downhill from there.'

I sought out Matt's thigh and massaged it consolingly through the quilt. 'So now you've parted, citing musical differences.'

'She said some terrible things.' There was a dangerous quiver in Matt's voice now. 'I'm not really that irritating, am I?'

'Well – '

'I thought she really liked me. I thought we'd be together for ever.'

If I didn't do something, there would be more tears. I quit massaging, put my left arm around his shoulder and drew him closer. At the risk of bending the truth myself, I said, 'Now stop this. You've had a tiff, that's all. In a day or so – perhaps two, you've got to make allowances for pride – she'll be round your house begging you to take her back.'

'Do you really think so?'

Privately, I had my doubts. What if Eileen had noticed him looking at men the way I'd seen him look at Danny Craven? I said, 'Yes, I know so. The two of you are going to look back on all this and laugh.'

Matt was silent. I couldn't tell whether he'd been convinced by what I'd said or not. He resumed stroking my arm. Then he said, 'Your turn.'

'What? Oh, yes, Manchester.' So I gave him a short account of my trip. I'd meant to say very little about Gerry Gibbs, just that we'd had a drink together, but the mood was so companionable and in the darkness there was so much arm-stroking from both parties that I found myself revealing all.

Matt said, 'What came over you? Sex on a plate and you turned it down.'

'I have world-class willpower.'

'Yes, but why? Something must have put you off, unconsciously.' Then after a moment he said, 'You were funny on Wednesday night.'

'Was I?'

'Of course I'd heard of Sigmund Freud, you dummy.'

'Then why – ?'

'Just because I knew my way round a building site, you seemed to imagine I must be thick as shit.'

'I thought you had a natural, unspoiled intelligence.'

'Same difference. So I played up to it.'

I let my stroking hand stray across Matt's chest. 'That was very naughty, taking advantage of an old man. I may have to punish you.'

Matt said, 'I've gone stiff.' But he only uncurled his arm from my shoulder to rest it on the quilt. 'Shall we get some sleep?'

'If you want. Do you need to be up early?'

'I was planning to come round and see you, but I'm here already.' He slipped down from beneath my arm to lay his head on the pillow. 'I hope you don't snore.'

'Trust me, that's the least of your worries.' I settled down beside him. We were both lying on our backs, and after a few seconds Matt's hand found mine and squeezed it.

'Thanks for letting me stay.' Then he withdrew the hand, and gradually his breathing became more even, and within a couple of minutes he seemed to be asleep. I was beginning to drift off myself, so I was startled when a very dozy voice said, 'I wonder if it was Sandy Smythe.'

'If what was Sandy Smythe?'

'That Eileen had the lessons with.' Then following a pause, 'I'm sure I've seen that Gibbs bloke somewhere before.' After which I heard no more from him.

Most people would consider it little short of sadistic to forbid a child from eating sweets, then lock them in a sweetshop overnight. As predicted, I now lay awake. With nothing better to do, or at least nothing that was permitted, I tried to turn my mind to the quest for Martin's killer, but it kept veering back again to thoughts of the living body which lay inches from me in the bed. I began to think that, as tough experiences go, being beaten up by Braithwaite's thugs had something to recommend it, since at least they were good, honest thugs and you knew where you stood.

But eventually I did sleep. One thing I hadn't been able to fathom about *The Interpretation of Dreams* was why it contained so many reports of dreams simply bristling with phallic symbols ripe for Dr Freud's unmasking, but not a single one about actually having sex. I now made up for this omission. Apparently I'd decided that the only way to discover the identity of the murderer was to sleep with everyone even remotely involved in the case, reasoning that when eventually I came to the culprit the intimacy of the moment would lay bare the darkness of their soul. And so it turned out. Now the killer lay full-length along my body, their head resting against my own. In a few seconds I would know the answer, I would draw back to look at the face. But then a voice said, 'When you've seen my face, I'll kill you.' I wanted so much to find the truth, not knowing had become a physical pain smarting inside me. But I didn't want to die. Martin and Danny were dead, they'd gone where they could never be found. I wanted to go on living. And so I lay absolutely still, my head so close to the killer's that we seemed to merge into one. And as I lay there, someone shook my shoulder.

It was Matt. He was saying, in an urgent whisper, 'Sam, wake up! I've thought of something!'

A dull twilight painted every object in the room the same dull grey. 'Can't it wait until the morning?' I wasn't even sure whether I was still dreaming.

'I might forget.'

I rolled onto my left side. Matt's face was very close. 'This had better be good.'

'It is. You remember how it puzzled me that Martin had left the briefcase on the train?'

'Oh, God, not the briefcase again.'

'If the contents were really that important, surely there's no way he'd ever have forgotten it?'

'You think the documents were never in the briefcase at all?'

'Yes, they were. But he must have known the bad guys would try and get hold of them. What if he'd made another copy just in case, and left it somewhere really safe that they'd never think to look?'

Even in the half light there was no mistaking the wide-eyed inspiration animating Matt's features. He clearly believed he was on to something.

And so did I.

I knew immediately that Matt must be right, and I knew too where Martin would have hidden the copy. It was all so obvious now. This would change everything. Confronted with proof of his deception, Colin Cudleigh would be bound to crack and tell us what he knew. But if he himself hadn't killed Martin, how likely was it that he knew who had?

You might think this was a curious time to find myself

especially captivated by those full lips, slightly parted, which had so often caught my attention in recent days. But then, I'd never been this close to them before. So when I'd said, 'A bit of a marvel on the quiet, aren't you?' it seemed only natural to incline my head an inch or two closer and lightly brush those lips with my own.

I could tell Matt wasn't surprised. He didn't draw back, but for a couple of seconds I thought he would just let it go, accept this token of my regard and leave it at that. But then he inclined his head an inch or two towards mine, and I felt my lips brushed lightly in return. A period of indecision followed. It seemed as if all thought had stopped, just like my breathing. Then, in unison, the two heads inclined themselves one inch and came together in the middle, and this time when the lips met they stayed met. I let my body move closer until I could feel the plaster cast against my chest, and my hand reached over to settle on Matt's back, drawing him towards me. The lips explored. My hand slid down towards Matt's hip.

But then he pulled away. 'No.' He lay on his back again.

I said, 'What's the matter?'

'I'm with Eileen.'

'She just dumped you, remember?'

'It was a tiff, you said so yourself. I'm going to get her back.'

'What if she doesn't want you back?'

'Why shouldn't she?'

I ploughed on without thinking. 'What if this thing about the band was just an excuse? What if she's realized that the only reason you're with her is that you're too scared to admit that what you really want is a man?'

'Is that what you think?'

'That's what I think.'

There was a moment of nothing. Then Matt threw back his side of the quilt and snaked his way down to the foot of the bed.

I said, 'What are you doing?'

'Guess.' He got out of bed, crossed to the chair and picked up his underpants.

'Matt – don't go.'

'You're an idiot. You don't know what you're talking about.' He hopped from foot to foot, pulled up the pants and grabbed his trousers.

I said, 'Let me help you,' and swung my legs out of the bed.

'Don't bother, I'm fine.'

'Give me the trousers.' So he leaned against the wardrobe and I helped him into the trousers one leg at a time. I slipped the vest over his head and arms, held the shirt while he angled himself into it, then fixed the sling neatly in place. Matt was silent. If he'd been hoping to make a dramatic exit, my faithful dresser routine had fatally undermined it.

He sat on the bed to pull on his socks and shoes. I watched for a while then said, 'Matt – '

'I'm not listening to you.'

'Yes you are. I think we like each other. There's no need to get in a flap about it.'

He stood up, came close, and glared into my face. 'You know what? Stuff your stupid job.'

When he left the room I didn't follow. Soon I heard the flat door close behind him.

I looked at the alarm clock: quarter past five. There was absolutely no hope of sleeping again now, but on the other hand, what would I do if I got up? I climbed back into bed, straightened out the quilt and sat with my knees drawn up to my chest. After a while this seemed ridiculous so I let the legs stretch out again. Then I could feel a dull ache in my kidneys where they'd been harassed by a heavy boot, so I settled down under the quilt and curled up to try and get more comfortable. And then I slept.

Once more, for the last time as it turned out, I was enjoying a cigarette in the phone box at Otterdale. Behind me, the blue-coated woman rapped on the glass. I stubbed out the cigarette, carefully placed the butt alongside all the others neatly lined up on the metal shelf, turned, and pushed open the door. The woman's eyes were huge behind thick lenses. She said, 'You again!'

I must have been asleep for an hour or so, the daylight was much stronger. My brain logged messages of pain from every corner of my body, but I didn't care.

At long last the back of my mind had succeeded in making itself heard up at the front.

I knew who'd killed Martin Berry.

Monday morning

At the other end of the line, Aunt Winnie's voice said, 'Do you realize what time it is? Fred's barely got the breakfast going.'

I said, 'Marvellous. You complain if I don't get up, you complain if I do get up. A suspicious person might think you just enjoy complaining.'

'When you've finished being rude, I've got things to do.'

'Listen – do you have a phone number for Derek?'

'Of course. He's office manager, if there's a problem overnight he's the one we've to call.'

'Well can I have it?'

'Derek's not likely to appreciate being rung at this hour for nothing.'

'It's not nothing, Aunt Winnie. I've realized he holds the key to these murders out at Otterdale.' And I meant that literally, as near as damn it. 'Now will you give me the number, or not?' After which, she obliged.

I'd waited days for this breakthrough, so it was hardly surprising if a certain twitchiness was now disturbing my famous sang-froid. Still, when a very sleepy Derek came on the line I did my best to lay the situation out for him as calmly as I could, and, sleepy or not, Derek had no difficulty grasping what needed to be done. Promising to be at Crowburn House within half an hour, he rang off.

That left me plenty of time to make another call.

When the cheerful voice answered, I said, 'Morning, Rupert! Sounds like you're up bright and early. Sam Rigby here.'

'Oh.'

'Got time for a quick word, have you?'

'I thought we'd said everything on Saturday.'

'So did I, Rupert, so did I. But you know how things can get overlooked. I was talking to Leah Armstrong after I left you. She happened to mention that your evening with Monica last Monday was something of a last-minute arrangement.'

'Yes, I suppose it was.'

'And why was that, Rupert? You don't mind me calling you Rupert, I hope? The thing is, I expect if you wanted to invite Monica over you'd normally plan ahead. You're a busy man, aren't you, and then she would need time to get her story straight so she could feed Martin some lie or other – '

'They weren't lies.'

'Of course they were lies, Rupert. I may not have gone to the world's best environment of structured learning but I know a lie when I see one. So I'm asking myself, what was different on Monday? Why the unseemly haste?'

Heysham was rattled, I could tell. 'It was just a spur of the moment thing. I thought it would be nice to see her.'

'I'm very sorry, Rupert, but I think that's a lie as well. Perhaps you've got into a habit without realizing.'

'I'm telling you the truth!'

I tut-tutted. 'I must say I'm disappointed in your behaviour. This was not the response I'd been hoping for. Perhaps I'm giving you the wrong stimulus, is that it? Would it help if I came over?'

'No!'

'Are you sure? I could be with you in no time. We could finish what we started on Saturday. That would be nice, wouldn't it?'

There was a brief silence, then Heysham said, 'All right! I'll tell you.'

I wasn't proud of myself. It was taking a sledge-hammer to crack a nut, but sometimes you have to stoop, don't you?

As soon as I'd heard Rupert Heysham's story, I dressed and drove over to Crowburn House. There was still no sign of Derek. Knowing that I was expected, Uncle Fred had cooked breakfast for me, and finding myself suddenly ravenous I bolted down eggs, bacon, tomatoes and toast as if I was eating my first meal for a week, or my last on this earth. Eventually the yard door swung open and Derek Lethbridge and the Moulton appeared. Fred was pouring tea for Derek, but without letting the man stop to drink it I steered him quickly through the green baize door and along the corridor to the front office of Crowburn Estates. I could see that in his hurry this morning he'd cut himself shaving, but I had no sympathy. What kind of person would shave at a time like this?

Perhaps my condition was infectious, because Derek seemed nervous, and it took him longer than usual to get the strongroom door open. I'd been in there several times as a child and marvelled at the stacks of files and boxes, the venerable ledgers ranged in neat rows on the mahogany shelves, all lit by a single naked bulb. Derek knew what he was doing, so I waited for him beside the counter. It wasn't long before he emerged, the file clutched under his arm. He crossed the room and set it down in front of me.

The Empire cinema file occupied an ancient folder in buff card with linen gussets at the side. Age had begun to blacken it, and it was tied with a dirty pink ribbon threaded through a metal eyelet. Now that it lay in front of me, I felt a moment's hesitation, a shyness. Seeing this, Derek said, 'It'll all be in there, Mister Sam.'

I said, 'How likely is it that someone else would need to look at this file?'

Derek shook his head. 'Since the council bought out Lady Tufnell, it was a dead letter as far as we were concerned. We might never have opened it again. Mr Berry would understand that, he'd have been quite safe to leave something in the file if he wanted to keep it out of harm's way.'

'You realize if I'd not been in such a hurry to meet Norman Breeze, you'd have got this out for me on Thursday?' I didn't say it, but I was also thinking that Danny Craven would still be alive.

'Strange how things happen, isn't it? But there's no help for it now.'

With Derek at my shoulder, I unfastened the knot which Martin himself must have tied, and opened the folder. It was fat enough, and I'd been worrying that we might have to go through every single document, right back to the deeds of the grand house which had first occupied the Empire site. But right at the front stood a brand new foolscap envelope. Derek said, 'That doesn't belong.' I lifted it from the folder. It was unsealed. I slipped the contents out onto the counter.

Two sets of photocopied pages were each held together by a staple in the top left-hand corner. I said, 'Do you want to interpret? Not quite my scene.'

Derek patiently studied the documents. The wall clock ticked noisily. In the distance I could hear Aunt Winnie hoovering the rug in the Old Man's room. Finally Derek laid the two sets of papers down side by side. 'What we've got here is two entirely different surveys of the same building.' His hand rested on the papers to the left. 'This one here finds a few minor problems which need attention, but otherwise gives the Empire a clean bill of health.' The hand moved across. 'Whereas this one rings the building's death knell. Damp, subsidence – everything they said in the Gazette and more besides. And the important thing is, Colin Cudleigh has signed both documents on the very same day.'

'Which was when?'

'Two weeks ago.'

'But Derek, it doesn't make sense. If Cudleigh was being paid to provide a false survey, why draw up an accurate one as well? And Sandy Smythe told me the SOE people had been waiting weeks for him to get round to the job, even though it was clearly so important.'

Conflicting emotions fought in Derek's expression. He hadn't chosen to spend his whole working life in the ordered sanctuary of the Crowburn Estate Office with a view to embroiling himself in fraud and murder. On the other hand, he had the sharpest of sharp minds, and there was no denying that present circumstances gave him the chance to exercise it to the full. He was enjoying himself, and trying not to. He said, 'I think I know what happened.'

'You do?' This was almost too good. I wondered whether to offer Derek the post of investigator's assistant which had unexpectedly fallen vacant at half past five this morning.

'Yes, I was thinking about it while I cycled over. I was thinking, why has all this blown up now, seemingly out of nowhere? And yet the developers are obviously well down the line with their plans and their artist's impressions.'

'You saw that in the Gazette?'

Derek frowned. 'Not pretty, was it? Anyway, the scheme was well advanced, like I say, but still they hesitated to press forward. So I thought, what's changed in the last couple of weeks?'

While I had to admire Derek's Socratic method, I wished he'd get a move on. 'Well, what has?'

'Alderman White died. Stanley White was chair of the planning committee. He had a nose for dodgy dealing, he'd have taken one look at the borough surveyor's report, the false one I mean, and never stopped asking questions until he got to the bottom of the whole rotten affair.'

Something had occurred to me. 'You don't think they had him killed?'

'Heavens, no. Really, Mister Sam, you can't go round seeing mayhem everywhere, it'll turn your mind. Stanley's heart had been bad for years, it's a wonder he lasted as long as he did.'

I returned the documents to the envelope and put it back in the folder. 'Do you mind keeping this in the strongroom for the time being?'

'Aren't you going to the police with it?' Derek eyed the folder anxiously, as if it might burst into flames at any moment.

'Of course, of course. But – not just now. There are things I have to do first.' In view of what Mark had told me on Friday evening, if I was going to approach the police about Colin Cudleigh I needed as strong a case as possible or I'd simply be shown the door.

Ten minutes later I was once more out on the coast road, speeding towards Otterdale. I say speeding, but actually I was stuck in a queue behind a Riley Elf, proceeding at a stately thirty-two miles an hour. In my head, I went over the implications of Derek's theory. Knowing they would have to get their bid past Alderman White, the developers had hesitated for so long that finally Colin Cudleigh had decided to present the accurate survey report, leaving the field clear for SOE to launch their project. But then, at the last minute, Stanley White had died. You could imagine the fluttering in the hen coops, the sudden change of plan. With the one remaining obstacle removed, Cudleigh now handed the borough engineer his fictitious and damning verdict on the Empire. What choice did Norman Breeze then have but to invite Bayley Consortium to resubmit the proposals which he'd previously rejected?

And somehow, Martin Berry had found out what was going on. It wouldn't have taken much – a telephone conversation overheard, a document left visible on Colin Cudleigh's desk. He'd assembled the evidence he needed and then, probably last Monday morning, he'd confronted his boss and given him a chance to redeem himself by withdrawing the false report. No doubt Cudleigh played for time, promised to think it over. But instead he set in motion the chain of events which led to Martin's death.

As I slowed to turn off at the Otterdale roundabout, a rumbling sound from somewhere beyond my left foot told me that the clutch problem I'd first noticed on Friday had failed to rectify itself during the weekend. I'd always known that the Cortina disliked me, but if it meant to throw a tantrum it had picked a really bad time. I patted the dashboard and said, 'Please – not now, OK?' And this conciliatory approach must have worked, because, rumbling apart, we completed the journey to Traherne Close without trouble.

It took Sandy Smythe some time to answer the door. When finally he did, he was wearing trousers but no shoes, socks or shirt. Thick grey hair thatched his shoulders and tumbled down over his barrel chest. Though he wore no glasses either, he must have recognized me easily enough, because he now said, 'Oh, it's you.'

'Sorry, did I get you out of bed? I thought you were an early bird.'

'I've not been sleeping right. You'd better come inside.' He led me down to the same comfortable room where we'd had our interview on Thursday, then left me for a moment and returned buttoning his shirt. He sat down opposite me, in the upright chair.

I said, 'Have you talked to the police yet?'

He nodded. 'Went down to the station on Saturday, asked for that detective you mentioned, DC Howell. He couldn't have been friendlier, made it all very easy for me.'

'Not too easy, I hope?'

In his present state, even this simple remark was enough to unsettle Sandy Smythe. 'What do you mean?' Though he wore the glasses now, they hadn't managed to restore the image of the robust, energetic man I'd met just a few days before. His face was a bad colour, and his hands moved incessantly. Some inner turmoil had been weakening the big man's sturdy constitution.

I said, 'I'm not surprised you can't sleep. Conscience is a hard taskmaster.'

'I've done nothing wrong!' The tone was almost a child's.

'It's not what you've done though, is it? It's what you haven't done.' He was silent, the hands still working together nervously, twisting, kneading, the knuckles very white. I said, 'Martin Berry was going to be a father, did you know that? No, I suppose you couldn't have. Thanks to the person you're so keen to protect, a child's going to grow up without a dad.'

'I might have made a mistake. It was dark!'

I shook my head. 'You'd have known him anywhere. That aura – unmistakeable, isn't it? But I suppose he shrank back into the shadows when he saw you. You spotted them both coming up the road, you called out to Martin Berry, the other man hung back when Martin moved towards you. What did Martin say?'

Sandy Smythe sighed deeply. He was a simple man, a man of action. Suppressing a dark secret day after day had cost him dear, but perhaps he could release it now. He said, 'I think he'd been drinking, he wasn't really very nice. I introduced myself, asked if he knew anything about the borough surveyor's report, told him we intended to challenge it. He said we were wasting our time, we could kiss goodbye to our precious cinema. Then he carried on up the road.'

'With his companion. The man who was going to kill him.'

'I didn't know, did I?'

'But you do now. It's time to tell the truth.'

Smythe bent forward, his head in his hands. After a while he said, 'What about my reputation? And they could arrest me, couldn't they? It's not exactly legal, what we do up there.'

'Come on, Sandy. Out with it.' And at last Sandy Smythe told me the story.

When he'd finished, he said, 'This other man who got killed – if I'd spoken up sooner – '

'Danny Craven put his own hand in the fire. It wasn't your fault.' It was, obviously, but I wasn't in the mood to rub Smythe's nose in it.

There was a faraway look in his eyes now. 'You're right, I'd have known him anywhere. He was always my favourite, even though I didn't really know the first thing about him. I suppose – well, I suppose I'd loved him, once upon a time. How could I turn him in?'

I left Sandy Smythe with his memories, let myself out of the house and fired up the Cortina. One thing still puzzled me. I couldn't understand why Martin had been so unsympathetic towards Sandy Smythe, since Martin himself was trying to expose the false survey and clear the path for SOE to take over the building. But I'd have to sort that out later. For now, I had my first witness who could put the killer in Otterdale on the night of the crime. And if my hunch was right, Smythe hadn't been the only person to see him.

I parked up on Station Parade, bought cigarettes, and lit one out in the street. The relief was instant. How I'd come this far today without nicotine, I couldn't imagine. Whatever else I might think about Matt going out of my life, at least now I could enjoy a good fag when I wanted one. I smoked it all the way down to the bottom, flicked the butt into the gutter, then walked along to the laundrette and stepped inside.

It hadn't required genius to deduce that of all the businesses on the parade, the laundrette was the one most likely to hand out blue work coats to its employees, so I was pleased but hardly surprised to find my dream-woman bending to scoop damp clothes from one of the machines. There was no-one else in the place. With her broad back towards me, I didn't think she'd noticed me come in, and if I'd stood behind her now and said 'Boo!' there could well have been a nasty incident. I waited while she straightened up, transferred the clothes to a dryer, then fed it with tokens to set it working. Then I said, 'Excuse me?'

She turned. The lenses were not as thick as the grotesque objects of my dreams, but they were thick enough just the same. She said, 'You again!' again.

I moved a little closer and said, 'No, it isn't. At least, it was me you saw on Wednesday morning, but not on Monday night.'

The woman now subjected me to careful examination. 'Well, I'll be blowed – you're right! You're not him at all. I'm that short-sighted I must have given up looking at things properly.'

'And then when I opened the door of the phone box and there was all that cigarette smoke – '

'I just assumed it must be the same person. But how did you know? Who are you?'

'Sam Rigby, private investigator. Pleased to meet you.'

She shook my hand and said, 'I'm Eunice. Any time you need a service wash, I'm your man.'

'You don't happen to do curtains, do you?'

'If they're not too big. Or we have a dry-cleaning machine, up the end there.'

'I might come back. But about Monday night – '

'Are you investigating that man in the phone box?'

'The murder last Monday, up at the Lake View.'

'It wasn't him that died?' She read my expression. 'The murderer!' She sat down rather suddenly on a bench at the side.

I sat down too, a little distance away. 'Can you tell me what happened?'

'On Monday night?' She gathered her thoughts. 'Well – it's my daughter, you see. She married a fisherman in Aberdeen.'

'Congratulations.'

Eunice frowned, not welcoming this interruption. 'It's two years ago now. But the thing is, she was expecting. Monday teatime I got a telegram saying she'd gone into labour, three weeks early. Dougal was away at sea, several days out. We're not on the phone at home, I keep badgering Victor but he says it would bankrupt us, I'd never be off the damn thing. So I had to come out to the phone box to call the hospital for news – we live just round the corner.'

'And every time you wanted to ring the hospital – '

'That same blasted man was in there with his blasted cigarettes, rabbiting away and watching the trains come in.'

'You could see that's what he was doing?'

'I'm not blind, you know.'

'What time did all this happen?'

A stubby finger went to Eunice's chin. 'It would have been towards six the first time I turned up. I came back roughly once an hour until half past ten. Little Kirstie was born just after ten o'clock. I didn't call again until next morning.'

'So you saw this man – ?'

'Three, perhaps four times. He made me wait. It was funny, I noticed he'd left his cigarette butts all in a neat line. I thought there was something odd about that at the time.'

'The classic mark of a killer.'

Her eyes were wide. 'Really? And to think, I was this close to him. Have they caught him yet?'

'It won't be long now. Could you pick him out in a line-up?'

'I'd do my damnedest. And I'd know his voice anywhere, I got sick of the sound of it.'

I stood up. 'You've been really helpful. When the police get in touch, just tell them what you've told me.'

Eunice followed me to the door. 'Wait till Victor hears about this!' And as I set off towards the Cortina, a ringing voice added, 'Don't forget those curtains!'

I started back towards town. After my experience with the Riley Elf I decided to opt for the inland route. But traffic was heavy, it was a fine, cool, blustery morning and the shoppers and day trippers were streaming in from Liverpool and the dormitory towns between. Everything was coming together now, I was impatient to make further progress. By lunchtime I should be ready to face Colin Cudleigh with what I knew, but first I thought it could do no harm to drop in on Sandra Snelgrove at the bar of the Feathers Hotel. I should really have talked to her sooner, but I was asking her to risk her job and she owed me no favours that I could think of. Surely, though, even Sandra's tight-lipped loyalty must have its limits, and if murder couldn't get her talking then I didn't know what could.

I let my thoughts run ahead to the moment of triumph. I could imagine Harry Hargreaves' expression when he realized that I'd cracked the case single-handed. He and the Southaven force were going to look pretty stupid.

But then, just as I was approaching the roundabout at the top of Lancaster Road, I floored the clutch to change down and nothing happened. I wrestled with the stick but it was no use, the box had jammed in top gear. Travelling at thirty still, I hit the roundabout. My emergency brain swung into action. If I'd braked there was a good chance I'd stall in the middle of the traffic, so my autopilot must have decided that in the short term the safest thing to do was keep going. I pushed in ahead of a very startled driver in a blue Mini Clubman, then pressed on around the roundabout. After a couple of complete revolutions I began to think that, although there was a certain fairground thrill to be had from all of this, an exit strategy might be useful. It took one more circuit to refine the plan, then I drove up onto the central island, braked sharply, cut the engine, and came to rest in the middle of a floral display celebrating fifty years of Southaven Rotary Club.

It was only then that I noticed the panda car lurking in Harbour Road, just short of the roundabout. I'd sat there myself in times gone by, waiting to pounce on unlucky motorists. Inevitably, one door of the panda car now opened, and a stout, grey-haired officer stepped out, straightened his cap, crossed with some difficulty to the island, and leaned down to address me through the open window. He said, 'We don't very often see that done, sir.'

I said, 'Morning, Cal. How's life?' For the gods had sent Cal Shaunessy to deal with this situation.

Cal said, 'Well – Sam Rigby, as I live and breathe! Still sleuthing, are we?'

I said, 'You couldn't do me a little favour? Could you radio in and get someone to call Paul Sidebottom's garage? The clutch has gone, this is going to need towing.'

'A favour? I don't know about that. There must be a phone box somewhere near here.'

I pushed open the door and got out, forcing Shaunessy to step back. Passing motorists drove erratically as they gaped at us, and although I'd managed to avoid causing an accident while still at the wheel, bets were not yet off. 'Yes, Cal, a favour. You know, those things you do for a person when your big fat mouth has cost them their job.'

'I've told you before, it was your own fault. You should have been more careful where you put your tongue.'

'Will you do it, or not? And I'm going to need one of you to wait with the vehicle. I'm on a case, I've got to get into town.'

Cal shook his head gravely. 'No can do, I'm afraid. We're due off shift in twenty minutes, we were just about to leave.'

'But it's an emergency!'

Cal raised his eyes skyward. 'Why does everyone have to be in such a tearing rush these days? Really, Sam, you need to learn to slow down, you'll give yourself an ulcer. I'll sort out the garage for you, but you'll have to wait here yourself.'

'Please, Cal – '

I laid a hand on his arm. He looked down at the hand, then he looked at me. I removed it. He said, 'Enjoy the wait. If you see anyone speeding, take the registration. We're down on our quota this month.' Then he dodged traffic to return to the panda car, and in a couple of minutes it set off towards town.

If I'd intended to make the local gendarmerie look stupid, getting myself marooned on a traffic island three miles from HQ wasn't exactly the best way to go about it. Yet again I'd given Cal Shaunessy a juicy slice of gossip, and by lunchtime the news would no doubt have travelled round the entire station. I smoked a bitter cigarette, and waited.

It took Paul half an hour to arrive with the tow-truck, but at least he did arrive, and in his usual good spirits. Getting the Cortina off the island proved more difficult than getting her on there in the first place, but eventually we succeeded in hitching her up and began the slow journey back to the garage. By now I was grinding my teeth with frustration. I left the car with Paul, thanked him, made a reckless promise to pay him at some point, then set off for the Feathers. In such conditions, with the sun coming and going between white clouds and a fresh breeze off the sea, this should have been a very pleasant fifteen-minute walk, but instead I poisoned it with paranoid imaginings. Earlier today I'd been getting above myself, and now I was to be punished for it. My spectacular floral breakdown was just the beginning, I could sense it. There was worse to come up ahead.

The first question I wanted to put to Sandra Sidebottom née Snelgrove was whether she'd overheard anything at all about the mysterious Bayley Consortium. Alan Baybridge was one of her regulars, frequently to be seen in conversation at the bar with the Feathers' owner Jack Spalding, just as Martin and I had seen him the previous Monday. If he didn't turn out to be the Bay in Bayley then my intuition was letting me down. No wonder Baybridge had looked so cheerful that night – the decision to go ahead with the Addison's project had been taken, and he could look forward to building yet another profitable landmark in the town.

But as soon as I emerged from the revolving door into the hotel foyer, I was met with a piece of good luck so outstanding that I considered handing my paranoia a modest allowance there and then, and retiring it to a bungalow at Cleveleys. On a tall easel beside the reception desk, the usual board announced today's occupants of the various function rooms. According to this board, a meeting had started, twenty minutes earlier, in the Derby Room. The hosts were Bayley Consortium.

An inner voice prompted me to stop and think, but I threatened it with Cleveleys and it shut up. Following the signs, I took the stairs to the first floor by twos, strode along the corridor and came to a halt outside the Derby Room. Again, it might have been a good idea to pause at this stage and plan out what I meant to say. But I was desperate to learn who I would find on the other side of that door, and besides, words usually come by themselves, even if half the time they're the wrong ones. I took a deep breath and went in.

Large windows onto the Boulevard filled the room with light. Smoke hung over a long table running from left to right, and among the more humdrum cigarettes the piquant tones of a cigar reached my nostrils. A dozen people were seated at the table, which was scattered liberally with papers. Most of these people were strangers to me. No doubt some represented Addison's, and such a project must require the involvement of accountants and legal experts too. The only woman in the room, a secretary, appeared to be taking the minutes. Like everyone else, she looked towards me as I came in.

But three people in the room I did know. Alan Baybridge and Jack Spalding sat side by side on the far side of the table. And in the chairman's seat at its head sat the man responsible for the cigar smoke, the '-ley' in Bayley, Walter Wetherley himself.

If my abrupt entrance had surprised Wetherley, he gave not the least indication. He said, 'Mr Rigby! Good of you to drop in. Is there something we can do for you or is this more of a social call?'

Though I had novelty on my side, if I'd now moved closer to Walter Wetherley the evident authority he enjoyed among these people would place me at a disadvantage. Instead I crossed to the foot of the table. I felt like a ferret about to worry at the trouser-leg of power.

To Wetherley I said, 'Bad news, I'm afraid.'

He said, 'Dear, dear. Whatever's the matter?' When he spoke, all heads turned from me to look at him.

Now I addressed the company in general. 'This project's finished.' The heads turned back to me again. 'There's a perfectly viable scheme for the Empire to continue as an entertainment venue. I suggest you all pack up and go home.'

Wetherley smiled scornfully. 'Ah, the usual Southaven problem. You've not kept yourself informed, Mr Rigby. The building's been condemned.'

'By the borough surveyor.'

'That's right.'

I paused to savour the moment. Or perhaps I was just milking it. 'There's nothing the matter with that building. Someone – someone in this room' – and I looked at Wetherley without naming him – 'has paid the borough surveyor to prepare a false report.'

There was now a rather satisfying murmur of astonishment. I couldn't be sure how many people at the table knew about the fraud, but it was quite possible that there was only one, Walter Wetherley. The fewer people involved, the less chance of discovery. Wetherley now said, 'You're talking tripe. We've all seen the survey, it's a model of thoroughness.'

'Yes, isn't it? And so's the other one.'

'What on earth are you talking about?'

'The borough surveyor signed off an alternative survey on the very same day. An accurate one. The building passed with flying colours.'

'Have you been drinking, Mr Rigby?'

'I have photocopies of both reports in my possession. Other copies were in the possession of a member of the borough surveyor's staff, a man named Martin Berry.' I addressed Wetherley again. 'The name might be familiar to you, Mr Wetherley, because he happened to be your son-in-law.' I turned to the room again. 'A week ago Martin Berry announced his intention of going public if the false survey wasn't withdrawn. By the end of the day, he was dead.'

More murmuring broke out. Most of those at the table were clearly unprepared for such revelations, and they looked anxiously towards the project's prime movers for rescue from their disquiet. Alan Baybridge said, 'Surely you're not accusing anyone here – '

But Wetherley interrupted him, his tone newly genial. 'I think I see what's happened. Colin did mention to me that some weeks ago a junior member of his team had drawn up a preliminary survey which gave the Empire a clean bill of health. But Colin wasn't satisfied with it and decided to go over the place himself.'

'Then why put his signature to both surveys?'

'This is all a misunderstanding. I tell you what, Mr Rigby – why don't I try and get hold of Colin and have him show you round the building, so you can see the problems with your own eyes?' He pushed back his seat and stood up. There was palpable relief around the table as Wetherley seized the initiative. 'Alan – could you take the chair for five minutes while I see to this gentleman?' Baybridge assented, and Wetherley shepherded me out into the corridor, one large hand on my back.

When the door had closed behind us, I said, 'I thought the future was meant to be Wetherley Machines, not supermarkets in Southaven.'

'It's far too early in the day to give up my property interests. Besides, I'd never even heard of Artificial Intelligence when this scheme was first proposed.'

'Yes, I should imagine it's a while now since Colin Cudleigh first smelled an opportunity and decided to keep you informed. Martin told me you had a friend on the council here – you knew Colin before, didn't you, when he worked for the council in Manchester? Must have been handy for a property man like you to have someone on the inside. I presume it was Cudleigh who got Martin his job?'

'I'm sure he was the best applicant for the position.'

We waited for the lift now. We were only one flight up, but you can't expect a man like Wetherley to walk when he can ride. I said, 'Rupert Heysham told me what happened on Monday. You rang him out of the blue at lunchtime, pressing him to invite Monica over that evening. Presumably Cudleigh had just phoned you with the news of Martin's ultimatum.'

'My wife said Monica had been feeling a bit out of sorts, I thought Rupert might cheer her up.'

'So it had nothing to do with wanting Monica out of the way?'

Wetherley raised bushy eyebrows. 'I think you're in the wrong profession, Mr Rigby. You seem to have a brilliant imagination but scant regard for facts.'

The lift arrived, empty, and we stepped in. Neither of us spoke while it descended. Though a metal plate claimed the lift could accommodate ten people, alongside Wetherley I felt crowded, suffocated, and when the doors opened I stepped out immediately into the cool foyer, leaving Wetherley to follow in his own time. Soon the hand was on my back again, steering me towards the bar. 'Why not have a drink while I call Colin? There's not much choice here, but in Southaven you have to be grateful for what you can get. I'll come and find you in a minute.' Then he pressed a pound note into my hand and walked away.

It was now just past eleven thirty and the bar was open for business, but I found Sandra Snelgrove alone in her domain. She said, 'Sam! Twice in as many weeks. What's the big attraction?'

I said, 'You, obviously. I'm nursing a secret passion.'

'That'll be the day. Drink?'

'Yeah, I'll have a Scotch.' While Sandra organized the drink I folded the pound note very small and shoved it into the charity lifeboat on the bar. With my own cash I paid for the Scotch. I was just explaining to Sandra how her worthy spouse had recently become my knight in shining armour when, sooner than I'd expected, Wetherley summoned me from the doorway. I crossed to speak to him.

'Very fortunately, Colin's not too busy. He says he'll be more than happy to see you and set your mind at rest. Just give him fifteen minutes to get over there and open up the building. Do you know the stage door, down the passage on the right?' I said I did. 'Then I'll leave you in Colin's capable hands.' He patted me on the shoulder and turned to go.

I said, 'Just one more thing.' Wetherley faced me again, displeased. 'Did Martin even realize that you were involved in all this? His own father-in-law.'

Wetherley was silent for a moment. Then he said, 'I must get back to my meeting. Good day, Mr Rigby.'

Nobody says 'good day' any more, and when Wetherley had left me those two words lingered in his wake, strangely threatening for all their surface affability. I put through a call of my own from the booth beyond the reception desk, and then rejoined Sandra. To my relief, it would no longer be necessary to ask her any awkward questions. I now knew far more about Bayley Consortium and Wetherley's part in it than I could ever have expected to learn from Sandra, even though her boss Jack Spalding had contrived to get his snout in the trough along with everyone else. Instead, we stuck to the more entertaining subject of her brother Malcolm's amours, while I braced myself alcoholically for the interview which lay ahead. Ten minutes later, I was out on the Boulevard again.

I crossed the road and walked steadily up towards the Empire. Perhaps Cal Shaunessy was right, perhaps I needed to pace myself better. There was no point in rushing ahead to meet the danger which I knew must be waiting. I'd covered about a hundred unusually sedate yards when a voice behind me called out, 'Sam!'

I stopped. Matt came running towards me, cutting in and out

amongst elderly pedestrians, an anxious half-smile on his face. When he drew level he said, 'I've been looking for you everywhere. I tried the flat, I've just been in Crowburn House – '

'Did Derek tell you about the documents?'

'Derek?'

'Office manager, bald as a coot.'

'He seemed a bit wary. Said he'd seen you earlier, but that's all.'

'The thing is, you were right. Martin left copies of the two surveys in the strongroom at Crowburn Estates.'

If Matt now looked annoyingly pleased with himself, I suppose he'd earned it. He said, 'What did I tell you? And I've worked out something else, too. I figured out where I must have seen Gerry Gibbs before.'

'On the dunes a few years back, with Sandy Smythe. Turning himself a little hard cash. Can we keep walking? I have a date.'

Matt walked beside me. 'That's not fair. How did you know about him and Smythe?'

'It was partly something Gerry let slip about his assets.'

'What assets?'

'Then when you were half asleep you mentioned him and Sandy Smythe almost in the same breath, like your brain was trying to fit them together. I've been out to Smythe's place this morning, he says Gerry was with Martin that night.'

Matt said, 'Where are we going now?'

'We?'

'Is it all right if I tag along?'

'And why would you want to do that? I'm an idiot, remember?'

'Sam – '

'Apparently I don't know what I'm talking about. You told me to stuff my stupid job.' I could feel the blood rushing to my cheeks.

Matt grabbed my arm to stop me walking, and we turned to face one another under the trees. The stream of pedestrians divided to flow around us. From above, an intoxicating scent of lime-flowers reached down to me. Matt said, 'It was a tiff, that's all. We've had our first tiff.'

There's a great deal of room for confusion in human affairs, and it's always best to try and get things clear. I experimented with opening my mouth a couple of times, then managed to say, 'Do you mean – do you want us to be – ?'

Matt turned away, chewing his lip. Then came another half-smile, apologetic. 'It's a bit of a step. I might need time.' He looked up into my face. 'Is that OK?'

Matt was right, it would be a step, perhaps a hard one. It wasn't the sort of thing you could keep quiet in a town like this. People filed past us still, but I saw only Matt's face, the question in his eyes. I said, 'Come on, we've got work to do,' and started walking.

Alongside, Matt said, 'What's this about you having a date?'

'I'm supposedly meeting the borough surveyor in the Empire.' And I brought Matt up to speed with recent developments.

'Why do you say supposedly?'

We'd now reached the alleyway running down to the stage door. I said, 'How reckless are you feeling this morning?'

'How can you ask such a question? I'm a Standish.'

'Just take your cue from me and you'll be fine. And whatever you do, don't let him get under your skin.'

The stage door stood open. A dim bulb lit the dusty corridor. To one side, the reception office lay in darkness. I knew the way, I'd spent hours exploring every inch of this place when my mother had worked here. Unless, of course, it had been the Roxy. At any rate, I led Matt further in, the corridor turned, there were steps, and then we were standing in the black-draped wings.

I put a finger to my lips for silence, and crept on past the prompter's box to the edge of the proscenium arch, from where I could look into the auditorium without being seen. Very little light was reaching us here, and behind me Matt stubbed his toe and swore under his breath. The fire curtain and the cinema screen had both been hauled up into the flies. There was an overpowering smell of history, rich and dark, as if Little Tich, Marie Lloyd, and the whole crazy exotic gang of them had just this moment left the stage to brush past us towards the dressing rooms.

I peered out cautiously with one eye. Now I could see why so little light penetrated backstage. The whole area of the stalls was in shadow, unlit, with the only light coming from the deco wall fittings of the circle above. And on the centre aisle of the circle, round about row C, Gerry Gibbs, in uniform again but hatless, sat very still, waiting with the kind of patience I've never had.

I guided Matt down into the corridor and told him what I'd seen. I could find no light switch at the bottom of the narrow dressing room stairs, and had to press my cigarette lighter into service. If it occurred to Matt to ask why I needed it now that I'd quit, he kept the question to himself. Three flights up, a connecting door opened onto the public areas, and here daylight found its way through again. Matt followed me down a long corridor with its fading carpet, until finally we reached the open area which years ago had been the Empire café. Windows gave a view onto the Boulevard and across the tree-tops to the irregular roofline of the shops beyond. This was the place where I'd sat so often with my lemon barley water, waiting for my mother. At least, it was either here or the Roxy. From this level, three pairs of doors opened directly onto the back of the circle, but all the doors were hooked back now, the entrances covered by what appeared to be the same thick velvet curtains I recalled from twenty-five years before.

My voice low, I said to Matt, 'If I dry up, keep him talking.' Then I made for the centre doorway and drew the curtains apart, and we walked through into the auditorium.

Further down along the aisle, Gerry looked round, calm, unhurried. He uncurled himself from his seat and moved to lean back against the balcony rail, the pale ghost of the distant stage framing his long figure. Unless of course it had been at the Roxy, this was the exact spot where my mother had stood so often with the refreshment tray slung from her shoulders. Gerry said, 'I don't like to be tight-fisted but the invitation was just for one.'

I said, 'Last-minute change of plan. You'll have to improvise.' I led the way down to row E, at the level of two further curtained doorways giving access to the side aisles. Matt and I sat across from one another, the central gangway in between.

Gerry said, 'Who is this anyway, your girlfriend? Or did you just pick her up on the way over?'

Matt shifted uncomfortably. I said, 'Your luck's run out, Gerry. We have a witness who saw you with Martin on Monday night, heading for the Lake View.'

'Go on then, surprise me.'

'Sandy Smythe.' Gerry looked blank. 'A man you used to meet on the dunes while maximising the return on your assets.'

'That old gargoyle? He's half blind.'

'And you were seen repeatedly in the phone box by the station, waiting for Martin's train. You'd expected him around six, but he was late, five hours late as it happened. And naturally you had to keep Wetherley informed.'

'Likes regular updates, does Walter. Takes an interest in the detail.'

Our voices seemed lost in the empty space. 'Then when Martin did show up, he was with Danny Craven, and they set off in the wrong direction. Ruined your plan completely. That is, if you ever had a plan.'

Gerry bridled at this slur. 'Of course I had a plan. I was going to let him invite me in, make it look like a burglary gone wrong. I'd been told to get the briefcase off him.'

Matt said, 'But wouldn't he have been surprised at you turning up out of the blue? To him you were just his father-in-law's driver.'

'She speaks! I'm impressed. But you're only half right, you've missed some of the earlier episodes. The point is, Martin liked me. I'd had a few cosy chats with him.'

I said, 'You told me you'd only spoken once.'

Gerry found this amusing. 'I told you all sorts of things. Anyway, you could say I'd piqued his interest.'

'You had him gagging for it.'

'Well, all right, if you're going to be crude. All he needed was the opportunity. And it was a shame I couldn't oblige really, but you've got to keep control. When I saw that he didn't have the briefcase with him, I realized there was no need to go back to Vaughan Close. By the time he left that other bloke's house the streets were deserted. I got the idea of walking him up to the lake, less risk of leaving any evidence.'

'I presume you'd come over on the Norton?'

'Left it in the station car park. No particular reason anyone should notice it there. I thought of driving Martin up to the Lake View, but it's the kind of thing people remember, the noise of a big machine like that after midnight.'

Matt said, 'So were you right? Was he pleased to see you?'

Gerry turned to me and said, 'Nosey, isn't she? I don't know how you put up with her. But yes, he was pleased. Very pleased, as a matter of fact. I just went right up to him in the street, said I'd been waiting for him, made it plain enough why I was there. He'd had some kind of a barney with his chum, apparently, but when he thought he was about to get his leg over he soon forgot all that. I said, let's go up to the lake first, have a dip, cool off.'

'But Sandy Smythe saw you on the way.'

'I can't believe he recognized me. Must be three years since. And he's *that* close to needing a dog and a white stick. Still, me and Martin got up to the lake eventually. It was a perfect night, moon, hardly a breath. He was drunk, talking a lot. He was telling me about his mother – his birth mother.' Gerry's lip curled, he shook his head. 'I think he was *ashamed* of what he'd come from. Why be ashamed? I mean, here you are, and that's it. But that wasn't enough for him.' Gerry's voice was quieter, he seemed to be reliving the moment. 'Anyway, I was getting sick of that particular topic, I asked if he'd like me to undress him. He was nervous, laughing, I don't think he'd done anything with a bloke before. I knew the type from my time on the streets. Then I told him to close his eyes, I'd got a surprise for him.'

'And you smacked him over the head with the nearest blunt object.'

'Amazing how easy he went down. It was a shame, like I said. Still, business is business.'

'And all because he'd threatened to blow the whistle on your boss's grubby little scheme.'

Gerry looked at me with pity. 'Blow the whistle?' And he gave a short, unpleasant laugh. 'You poor, sad man. You really don't understand how the world works, do you? Martin was never going to blow the whistle. He *wanted in*. Told Cudleigh that if there was cake going, he was having some. A nobody like Martin Berry – old Walter couldn't allow that, now could he?'

There was a silence then. I'd lost my appetite for talking. Eventually Gerry sighed. If he'd been expecting a quiet morning, it wasn't turning out that way. He said, 'What am I supposed to do with you two now? I had in mind a nice little accident for Sam here, but two of you – '

'Just give up, Gerry. You're finished.'

He shook his head. 'You realize I can't let you leave the building?'

Matt said, 'Leave? Why would we want to leave? This is the best show I've ever seen here.' And he had a point. In the spotlight, Gerry came doubly alive.

I said, 'I understand why Danny Craven had to die, he made the mistake of trying to blackmail Colin Cudleigh. But why all that nonsense with the note on the mirror and the bloody shoes?'

Gerry shook his head. 'That was a shame, too. I try to be single-minded when I'm working, if you don't focus you can slip up. But I'm only human. The body on that man! It was hot in the bedroom, he'd thrown back the covers, he was sleeping like a child. I found myself just standing over him, sort of drinking him in.' He shrugged his shoulders. 'Snapped out of it eventually, got the job done.' And as if this had reminded him of a pressing task, Gerry pulled something from his pocket, flicked open the blade, and began cleaning under his finger-nails with the tip.

I prompted. 'But what about the shoes?'

Gerry's eyes remained on his work. 'Oh, that. You know I told you I've got plans? Joe Braithwaite used to be Wetherley's collector back in Manchester, I worked for Joe. Walter took a shine to me, like I said, but he cut Joe loose after a while, Joe was doing too much business on his own account. Then Joe moved here to Southaven, started again.'

'And while he's doing time for Danny's murder, guess who's going to step in and take over?'

Gerry looked up. 'Ten out of ten. I've got Joe's boys onside already, they'd do anything for me.'

'Like beating up some unfortunate bloke who didn't want to sleep with you.'

'Only took one phone call. I see they made quite an impression.' And he grinned.

I said, 'Vanity, isn't it? You just can't bear it when people don't worship at the shrine.'

'I couldn't understand your problem. What did you want, green stamps?'

'There was something wrong, I could smell it. Your jacket – the phone box woman actually mistook me for you because it's so similar to mine. Then when we were leaving the bar you picked up a little souvenir, only a beer-mat but you had to have something. That's vanity too, isn't it? Wherever you go you like to leave some trace of yourself, like those notes you left for me at the office and my flat. Then there was the motorbike. You'd wheeled it under the yard wall at Crowburn House when you broke in. The back of my mind was telling me not to go anywhere near you.' I began to wonder if I'd had a lucky escape. 'If I'd gone back with you, what would have happened?'

Gerry raised an eyebrow. 'What, you think I was going to kill you? Those others had to go, they posed a threat. But you – ' He laughed, for rather longer than I thought necessary. 'I'd seen you in action, remember? That window-cleaner stunt has to be one of the most embarrassing things I've seen in my entire life. I told Wetherley there was more chance of Barbara Windsor becoming prime minister than of you ever finding out what was going on.'

I said, 'Sorry to have proved you wrong. Turns out you do make mistakes sometimes.'

'You've got nothing on me. Apart from you and Raquel here, no-one knows the first thing about it.'

'But they will. In an hour or two the borough surveyor's going to be pulled in for questioning. He's always been the weak link, with so much evidence against him he'll crack and implicate your boss. And if you think there's any hope of Wetherley protecting you, I'm afraid you really haven't understood how the world works.'

That riled him. 'Walter would never let me swing! He looks out for me, always has.'

I said, 'You really believe you're like a son to him, don't you? Wake up, Gerry. You're one of the servants, that's all. Now give yourself up, it's your only chance.'

Gerry was silent. He'd stopped cleaning his nails now but the knife remained gripped in his hand. Though he'd made mistakes he wasn't stupid, and he knew this was the endgame. He stood at bay, alert, somehow magnificent in the sharp-cut uniform, face and body in the light, the darkness of the unlit space behind him.

Finally he indicated Matt and said to me, 'A good shag, is she?' Again Matt shifted in his seat. It was the kind of talk he hated, that had so repulsed him when he heard it in the Velvet Bar. Gerry said, 'She's a pretty thing. Something of a look of Bernadette Devlin on steroids.'

Across the gangway, I could sense Matt holding himself back. Under my breath I said, 'Matt – '

Then recognition sparked in Gerry's eyes. 'Wait a minute – I've seen you before, haven't I? You're taller, you've filled out a bit, but it is you, that sweet face, those lips – up on the dunes all the time, weren't you, always on your knees, couldn't get enough. They used to call you Lighthouse Lil.'

Matt glanced towards me briefly, and away. Gerry went on. 'Well, I'm honoured – Lighthouse Lil come to pay her respects.' He turned to me now. 'The things she used to get up to, you'd not believe it. She was anybody's, absolutely anybody's, always up there showing herself off. I reckon she's got to be the filthiest bitch – '

'Bastard!' Matt was out of the seat and hurling himself down the slope to get his one good hand round Gerry's throat. I got up too but it was useless, Gerry grabbed him and swung him round, held him in a lock, the knife at his ribs behind.

'Bastard, am I?' Gerry turned to me now. 'We don't like that kind of talk, do we Sam?' And then the knife plunged in, suddenly Matt's eyes were wide, pleading with me not to let it end like this. Gerry drew back the knife, I heard Matt exhale, the light died in his eyes. Stepping aside, Gerry turned, gently pushed Matt back, Matt dropped over the rail into the dark. From below came a sound I didn't like, then no sound at all.

I rushed at Gerry, he flashed the knife at me, we stood close, half crouching. Gerry said, 'One down.'

I called out, 'Mark! Mark! Now would be a good time!'

Briefly worried, Gerry checked this way and that around him. Nothing happened. He smiled. 'Expecting the cavalry, were we?'

Then through the curtains to the left of me, two fresh-faced police cadets filed uncertainly into the auditorium. They looked about eleven years old. A long row of seats still separated them from the man with the knife. Gerry laughed. 'Is that the best you can do?' But the curtains on the other side parted too. A burly officer I vaguely recognized came in, followed by Cilla Donnelly.

I said, 'For Christ's sake, somebody call an ambulance. There's a man overboard.' Cilla understood, and went out.

Behind me, Mark Howell said, 'Sorry about the delay.' I could hear his steps as he walked down the centre aisle towards us.

'What the hell took you so long?'

'Hargreaves refused to release the manpower. He said you were an imbecile.'

Gerry said, 'You see, I told you. It's not just me.' But he wasn't looking quite so sure of himself now.

I said to Mark, 'Did you hear any of that?'

'Any of what?'

'We got a full confession out of him, you were supposed to be listening.'

'I've just this second arrived.'

I rolled my eyes and straightened up. Gerry was still pointing the knife, but I could see his confidence was fading. I said, 'Put the knife down, you're making a fool of yourself.'

'That's rich, coming from you.'

'It's over, Gerry.'

'You've got nothing on me, not a scrap.' But he didn't believe what he was saying.

'Trust me, your boss is going to throw you to the wolves. There are witnesses now as well.' I said to Mark, 'And when you get a team over to his flat, you'll find a nice collection of mementos from the crime scenes. Maybe even Martin Berry's pants.'

At last, Gerry lowered the knife. He'd passed some kind of tipping point, there'd be no more protests now, no more denials.

He said, 'His pants? You won't find them there.' He unzipped his fly and tugged out white cotton.

Mark said, 'Jesus Christ.'

I said, 'Come on, Gerry, this is boring. These people want to get back to the canteen for their break. Why don't you just come along quietly like a good boy?'

'What, and spend the rest of my life cooped up in one of them places? You must think I'm daft.' Then, from nowhere, a smile spread wide on his face, warm, confident. He was pleased with life and with himself. He said, 'Serial absconder, me. Go where I can't be found.'

The movement was quick, I couldn't have stopped him. The knife slashed across his throat, he staggered back against the rail, and then he was gone, following Matt into the darkness.

Afterwards

I expect you'll be anxious about the Cortina.

If I'd felt any attachment at all for that car, it had gone up in smoke while I waited amongst the Rotary Club bedding plants for Paul Sidebottom and the tow-truck. When Paul said it would need a new clutch, and started talking figures, it was the final nail in the coffin. I contacted a dodgy dealer I know in Welldale, and in exchange for what was left of the Cortina and the sum of £90 he was prepared to let me have a B reg. Hillman Minx with red upholstery, no questions asked. When I looked underneath I couldn't help noticing a lot of recent welding, but since nobody wants to hire a private investigator without a car I didn't feel I had much choice.

Another bonus was that Jonesy was happy to allow me a few months to pay off the ninety quid, though heaven only knew what favour he would try to exact from me some day in return. But as it happened, from mid-July the work started pouring in. In particular there was a nice run of missing persons cases, which I always love right up to the point where I winkle them out of their hidey-hole and it turns out they don't want to be found. So for a while I've been quids-in, and the work's now piled so high that I could do with a helping hand.

Though Harry Hargreaves set woundingly little store by my own testimony, he faced the more serious problem that no court in the land was likely to convict Joe Braithwaite for Danny Craven's murder on the basis of such flimsy evidence. Finally, through gritted teeth, he released the man to continue his charitable work among Southaven's less affluent citizens.

But Hargreaves had better luck with Colin Cudleigh. As I've said, Harry was never one to be impressed by a rolled-up trouser-leg, and it's probable that the chance to discredit one of the Super's cronies lent an extra relish to his interviews with the borough surveyor. Cudleigh cracked wide open about the Empire fraud, how he and Wetherley had worked it out together. The lost property man from Exchange station picked Cudleigh out of a line-up as the man who'd collected Martin Berry's briefcase, though the briefcase and its contents have never come to light. But while for the most part the borough surveyor sang like a canary, on the matter of the two killings it was a different story. He knew nothing about any killings. All he would say was, that when Martin had tried to muscle in on the Empire deal, and again when Danny Craven had demanded money to keep the whole thing quiet, his first action had been to call his old pal Walter Wetherley and dump the crisis neatly in his lap.

I'd have paid handsomely to eavesdrop on Hargreaves's little chats with Walter Wetherley. Apparently Wetherley had engaged a hot-shot young solicitor wearing the most expensive suit Mark Howell had ever seen, who repeatedly advised his client that silence would be the best defence. But Wetherley was a man born expressly to give the world his full and frank opinions on every subject, and for him silence would have been a worse punishment than prison. Volubly and at length, he denied every accusation made against him. But when Manchester police raided his office, they found an eloquent paper trail linking him to Cudleigh and the Empire fraud, which no amount of bluster could talk out of existence.

Though Hargreaves now accepted that Gerry Gibbs had been responsible for both the Otterdale murders, his attempts to prove that Gerry had acted as the executive arm of Walter Wetherley were frustrated both by Wetherley's denials and a complete lack of hard evidence. With Gerry dead, it was easy enough for Wetherley to claim that his driver had acted alone for motives which had been carried with him to his grave. I offered to take the stand against Wetherley in court, but Hargreaves was right about this: even a barely competent barrister would have torn my testimony to shreds in minutes.

It'll be some time next year before we find out whether the fraud charge against Wetherley and the borough surveyor actually sticks, but the case looks strong and the smart money says it will. Even so, Mark says the most they're likely to serve is five years, and there's every possibility that in as little as eighteen months we could be welcoming them back into our midst again, to work their own special magic.

With the accurate building survey substituted for its fictitious rival, the council once more turned to Sandy Smythe and his colleagues to breathe new life into the Empire. Champagne flowed at the next SOE meeting, and the group adopted me, Sam Rigby, as their unofficial hero, the man who'd saved the Empire for posterity. They were planning a fresh drive to recruit volunteers. They were planning a rolling programme of improvements to the building.

They were planning a grand gala launch in the spring.

But that was before the fire.

The story went that two small boys had somehow got into the building and started playing with matches. It was a matter of record that these boys existed, they'd had to be rescued by the fire brigade, but sceptics might wonder just what, or who, had put it into their heads to turn Junior Pyromaniac in the first place. Whatever the answer to that, it was certainly a wonderful blaze, and half the town came out to watch. Old-timers declared it the finest conflagration on the Boulevard since the Opera House went up in 1929. By the time it was over, there wasn't a great deal of the Empire left.

So Addison's are back in business. Wetherley was obliged to step down from the team, but otherwise the plan goes on as before.

I blamed myself for what had happened to Matt. Although, to be honest, I partly blamed the lime-flowers too. Before that moment under the lime trees, I'd had not the least intention of letting him anywhere near Gerry Gibbs, but when things between us had shifted onto a new basis it suddenly seemed unthinkable to send him away. If there was danger, we'd face it side by side. Hargreaves was right, I was an imbecile.

So it was fortunate that Matt was a fully paid-up, card-carrying Standish, who practised falling from great heights before breakfast every morning just to keep his hand in, and laughed mere stabbings to scorn. Nevertheless, his life hung in the balance for twenty-four hours, and there were wild scenes at the Infirmary as the Standish clan foregathered. That's when I discovered that I wasn't the only person who blamed Sam Rigby for Matt's condition. When she found out who I was, Matt's mother flew at me with fists flailing, and I was forced to beat a retreat. Even when Matt rallied, there was still some risk that he might lose one kidney, but after a couple more days that danger too was past and he was on the slow path to full recovery.

Inconveniently, the fall had broken Matt's other arm, and weeks went by before he was able to do much for himself. So it was lucky that the Infirmary employed one nurse who regarded gratifying Matt's smallest whim as something akin to a religious duty. Eileen took back what she'd said about the Sand Lizards – or most of it, anyway, the woman did have some integrity – and bent herself to the task of shovelling food into Matt's hungry maw and regularly sponging down every inch of the sacred body. Not that I'm bitter, but the fact was that Matt was allowed no more than two visitors at each session, and since I wasn't family, and since one of the two visitors was invariably his mother, I was effectively excluded from seeing him, thus leaving Eileen free to weave her seductive spell.

After a month or so he was sent home, but when I rang to speak to him he seemed distant. I couldn't tell whether his mother was listening, or whether he was simply trying to freeze me out because he was back with Eileen. I didn't phone again.

I tucked the photograph of Martin Berry into his file at my office, wrote up the case, and locked it all away. If there were lessons to be learned, I was in no mood to learn them. I shoved the whole thing to the back of my mind.

And there it stayed until yesterday evening, when I had one of my nights in the Velvet Bar with Bernie Foster, who had of course been the source of my information about Eileen. She brought news. Apparently Leah Armstrong had moved in with Grace Berry, and when the baby arrived they were going to bring it up together. I thought that would probably be one very lucky child. For the first time in weeks I got home with a smile on my face.

And this morning, I phoned Matt. As I said, the work's been piling up, and when I'd enquired how he was and heard his cagey replies about the novelty of possessing functional arms again, I asked if he'd like to consider having his old job back. He said, possibly. I said, did he want to meet me in the Railway this evening and talk it over. He said, OK.

Though Matt's tone had been non-committal, when I got out onto the Boulevard after our inconclusive conversation I found a world subtly transformed. It was late September now, the first leaves were turning from green to gold. We'd had rain in the night, the whole town felt washed clean, ready for anything. When I came up to the blackened remnants of the Empire, set back behind the formal garden with its benches and its mermaid fountain, I noticed that two bulldozers had begun the long work of clearing the site, and I stopped to watch. After a minute, a voice beside me said, 'Mr Rigby?'

It was the borough engineer. He wore a somewhat lighter suit than when we'd met before, but even without the funeral attire Norman Breeze looked like a man poised to perform obsequies for the dead. He could change the suit, but not the skull-like head that topped it. I said, 'Mr Breeze. Good morning to you.'

He said, 'I believe I owe you an apology. You were right about Colin Cudleigh, I was wrong. If I said unpleasant things, I'm very sorry.'

'In your shoes, I expect I'd have done the same. Don't worry about it.'

He nodded acknowledgement. 'That's very generous of you. The truth is, I was fooled by appearances, and I should have known better. But I shall be able to repent at leisure now.'

'Why's that?'

'I've decided to retire, hand on the baton. To be honest, I've got no stomach for the fight any more.' His eye strayed to the building site with its mass of twisted girders. 'This thing with Colin, it's quite taken the stuffing out of me. I would never have believed it possible.'

The pain was evident in his voice. I said, 'Perhaps he thought he was acting for the good of the town.'

The borough engineer gave a rueful smile. 'I'm afraid we both know that's not true.' Then his expression hardened. 'What's become of Southaven, Mr Rigby? What's become of people?'

I guessed he wasn't in the market for answers, so I didn't try selling. I doubted whether people, or Southaven, had changed that much at all, but perhaps I might see things differently if I ever reached Norman Breeze's age.

He watched now, reflective, as the dust from a toppled wall rose in eddies and blew across to land on the grass in front of us. 'Many's the film Betty and I saw in there when we were courting. Fine films they were too, classics, not the sort of thing you get nowadays.' He shook his head sadly. 'We don't go any more, but I'll miss the place just the same. A building like that, you think it'll be there for ever.' Then he appeared to rouse himself from private thoughts. 'Well, I mustn't keep you, no doubt you've got things to do.' He shook my hand. 'I'm glad we've had this little talk.'

I watched him walk away then until his long, bony form merged into the trees of the Boulevard and he became one with the town he loved.

But he'd been wrong, of course. Fire, bomb, dry rot, wrecker's ball, it makes no difference. By one means or another the old place was bound to go eventually, swept away on the tide like everything else. Who can resist when that current comes surging round?

In the meantime, I had lost souls to track down. I turned to face the sun and walked on.